DRAGONS
in the
DUNGEON

DRAGONS
in the
DUNGEON

Adventures in Lachspeur of Yore

The Campaign that Ended all Campaigns

(Or did it begin them?)

Diane McGyver

Quarter Castle Publishing
where imagination is magic
New Scotland, Canada

ABOUT THE AUTHOR

Lady Diane McGyver fell in love with the fantasy genre when at the age of 13, an awesome Dungeon Master introduced her to Dungeons & Dragons. From there, she landed in the world created by Terry Brooks and then the ones by Mercedes Lackey. By the age of 16, she was truly lost to other realms and dreamt of one day living in one or two.

Her future goals are to write fantasy stories in a peel tower near the Atlantic Ocean where she'll raise chickens, vegetables and Trouble.

Text Copyright ©2023 Quarter Castle Publishing

Hardcover with Jacket ISBN: 978-1-927625-88-0
Hardcover ISBN: 978-1-927625-87-3
Paperback – Standard Print ISBN: 978-1-927625-86-6
eBook ISBN: 978-1-927625-89-7

Cover Design: Diana Tibert
Interior Design: Diana Tibert
Editor: J. Leonard Horton
Published March 23, 2023

Quarter Castle Publishing
Nova Scotia B0N 1Y0 CANADA
quartercastlepublishing.com

0123QCP032

Quarter Castle Publishing bore the complete cost of publishing this book and received no financial assistance from outside sources.

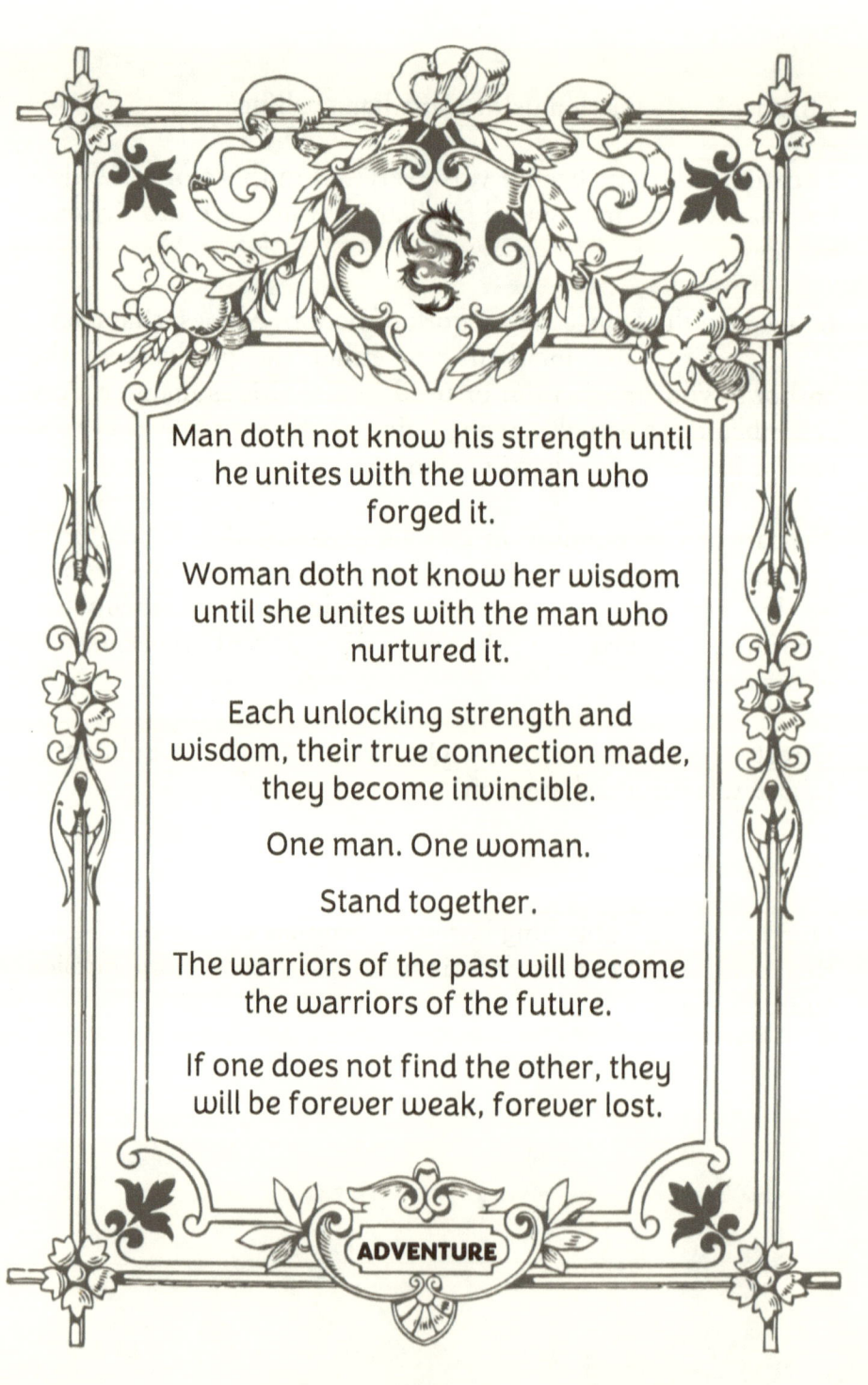

Man doth not know his strength until
he unites with the woman who
forged it.

Woman doth not know her wisdom
until she unites with the man who
nurtured it.

Each unlocking strength and
wisdom, their true connection made,
they become invincible.

One man. One woman.

Stand together.

The warriors of the past will become
the warriors of the future.

If one does not find the other, they
will be forever weak, forever lost.

ADVENTURE

Table of Contents

Author's Note

For those unfamiliar with life in the 1980s, parts of this story might sound fantastic. For me and the majority who lived and loved that decade as teens and young adults, we believe it was the best years to be alive. We had freedom and prosperity. Not to mention the great music, TV shows and movies, of which some are mentioned in this novel.

Setting this story in the 80s gave me the freedom to focus on the best things, the simple things. Simple. It's one way to describe the 80s. Basic and down to Earth are two more. It was a time when families were strong and were the heart of their communities. Dads worked close to home and Moms performed the most important 'job': raising the next generation. Everyone sat down together for supper, they spent as much time outdoors as they did indoors and screen time was unheard of unless weather was foul. We were the generation of no seat belts or bike helmets, staying out 'til sunset and beyond, and riding in the back of open trucks.

We played Cops and Robbers, Cowboys and Indians, British Bulldog and Red Rover. Most of our toys had no batteries. They were skipping ropes, lawn darts and Rubik's Cubes.

We were ignorant to the world outside our neighbourhoods unless it was huge news, such as a spaceship exploding upon launch. Limited outside news was perfect. Our focus was on the important stuff in life – family, friends, adventures – and we weren't needlessly distracted by the rest of the world. We worked hard, played harder and dreamt large.

This is everything I want in a fantasy world.

To my American readers: This story is written using the Canadian spelling I learned in grade school. This means I'm sceptical instead of skeptical. I sail in harbours, not harbors, and I paint the landscape with colour, not color. I realise (realize) I may appear illiterate to Americans unfamiliar with Canadian spelling, but I will not apologize for retaining my culture, one I'm proud of.

Diane

Dedication

To the players of the game.

To the adventure we seek with each roll of the die.

Forward

...In the time of King Thodrin peace came to Lachspeur of Yore. The four races of intelligent souls worked alongside to restore that which was lost in The Great Tonn Mara. The catastrophe claimed many lives. Those who survived were changed as too was the land they inhabited. The forces unleashed tore a hole in the fabric, creating a threshold for intelligent life from other worlds.

Them souls who venture to-and-fro neither grow old nor maintain youth as one world snatches seasons while the other ignores them except for a few vital seconds.

Those adventuring from other worlds beyond have shaped Lachspeur in subtle ways, bringing their notions, trinkets and beliefs. In cases, the foreign has inhabited for so long, no one knows its origin, here or there.

The dance between worlds is magical, graceful and at times chaotic. The few who traverse more than one are blessed and cursed in one breath.

Those who remain ignorant to wisdom are destined to remain captive of Lachspeur of Yore. Only through voyages on high seas will they discover the true meaning of journeying between worlds. Share it, it could be by the wielder of this quill, but where be the adventurous spirit in such impartings?

No, only through adventure, risk and magic will true knowledge and wisdom be gained.

Page 134, The Untold History of Lachspeur of Yore
Captain E. W. Tyde,
the last of the druids of Eldridge Mountain

Below are individuals who assisted when I searched for a tavern, inn or town name. These are their Twitter handles. If you're interested in roleplaying games, particularly Dungeons & Dragons, visit their page and follow them.

CalStaff @CalstaffTheGold
Nowhere Inn at Hermit's Hollow and The Three-legged Mare at Westdun

Captain Graybeard US @CaptGraybeard13
The Three Barrels Tavern and Hostel at Blue Sea Village and Badgers Waren, the tavern where Rosalind played Mediaeval Dungeon Adventures

Noelle.Morte @NoelleMorte
Lizzy's Liquid Lizards and Billiards at Moore Thyme

Raven Wulfgar @Ulfhedrengr
Hermit's Hollow from his suggestion of Hermit's Haven

T-Shirted Historian @thetshirtedone
The Lady of Shades Hostelry, Sapphire Lane at Moore Thyme from the suggestion of The Lady of Shades Inn

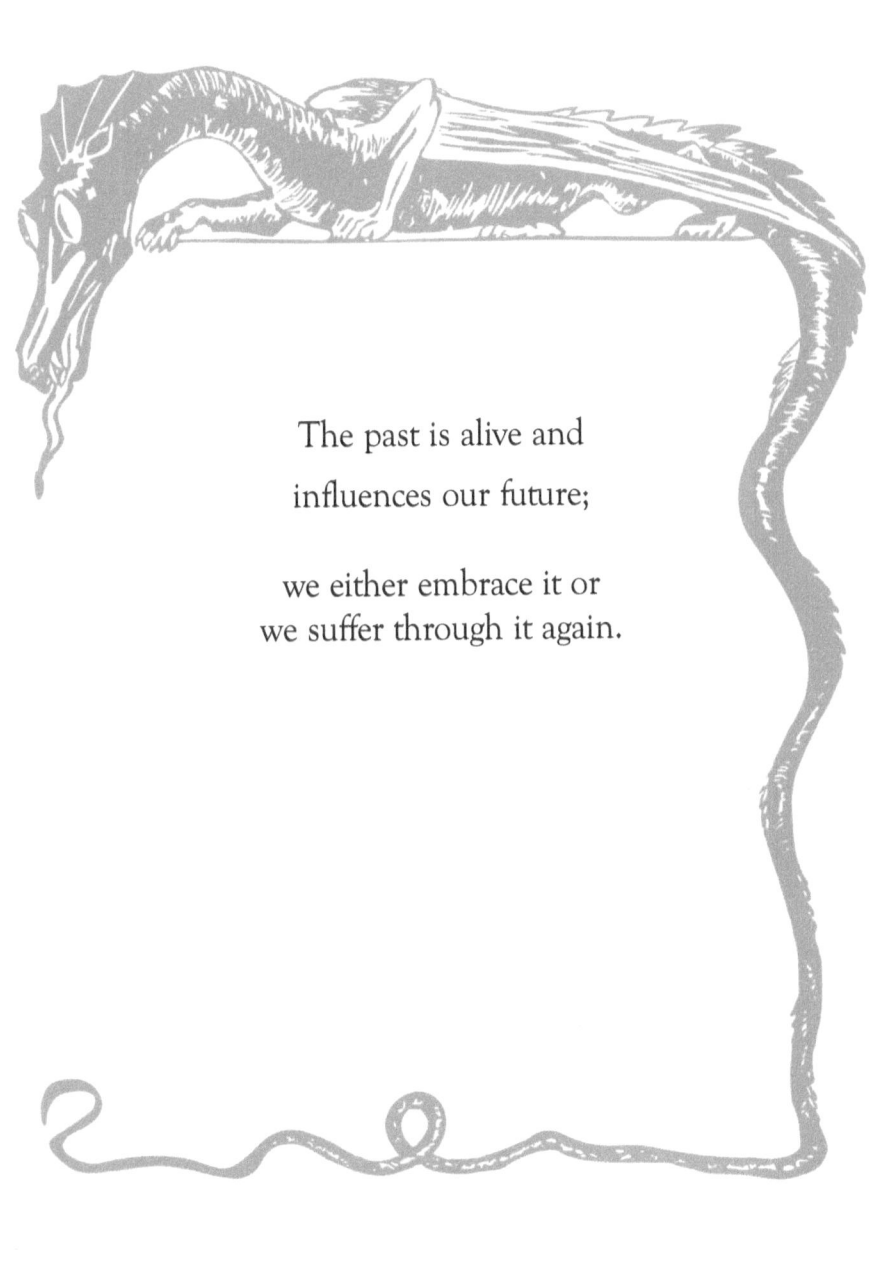

The past is alive and
influences our future;

we either embrace it or
we suffer through it again.

1

Short Drawbridges

NIMBLE DIDN'T BOTHER to lift her head when the thick wooden door opened, but she felt the slight breeze that circulated the tangy odour of men who hadn't bathed in days. The door opened only to throw in another prisoner, one who would slam into the cold, stone floor, groan in pain and curse the guards who put him here. She'd done it. The ones before her probably had. The two since she arrived today had done it. So, when the smack on the stone resulted in a heavy groan, she knew what followed.

"Damn you! I curse your mother for your birth."

"That gains no favours in my eye," snapped the guard.

"Take a long walk on a short drawbridge."

Nimble's thoughts rattled around. The accent sounded strangely familiar. She hadn't heard it before, yet... Off a short drawbridge? It, too, sounded familiar yet foreign. She did not know this man, but...

The door slammed shut, and the new prisoner hurdled more insults at the guards, whose laughter faded down the hallway.

She cast a curious gaze at the stranger. He struggled to get into a comfortable position, wiggling his hips until he got his weight centred. Like her and the other prisoners, his hands were secured with cord behind his back. His clothing was like most others except he had more layers. Beneath an evergreen jerkin made from heavy cloth was a long-sleeve, forest green shirt with an open neck that revealed a brown shirt beneath. His brown trousers were patched at the knees, and winingas of slightly darker brown protected the lower part of them. His brown boots went as high as his ankles and were similar in style to most she'd seen. His unkempt hair, shoulder length, was the same colour as his winingas.

In general, he was like the rest of the prisoners, only his accent, minor clothing accessories and his advice to the guard made him different. He would fade into the background of the gloomy prison as soon as he realised there was no escape, and she could return to staring at the floor, wishing she was anywhere but here. His words replayed in her mind. She thought about the familiar and the foreign.

"Pier," she said.

He glared at her, the fire of the fight still blazing in his grey-green eyes. Discoloured skin around one of his eyes and a bright red cheek indicated he'd been in some sort of scuffle. Giving her the once over, the fire dwindled. "What?"

"Isn't it pier? Long walk on a short *pier*?"

His expression grew curious. "Yeah. But..." He considered her for longer than she'd have liked him to, then spoke in a calm voice. "Where'd you hear that?"

"In my head."

"I mean the expression. Have you heard it before?"

"Somewhere. Long ago." That must have been it. She didn't remember where or when, so it must have been long ago.

"Do you use it?"

She shook her head. "I've never heard anyone use it."

"So where did you learn it?" He leant closer, scrutinizing her clothes and hair.

"It was in my head when you said it."

"Interesting." He scanned the large room, the space the other prisoners referred to as the dungeon. It could easily hold 50 prisoners but today contained only about a dozen. Some were asleep. Others leant against the wall watching the new man in their presence take in his surroundings. When the man made eye contact with her, he appeared more interested in her than the others. "Do you know Lady Luck?"

"Is she a prisoner?"

He half grinned. "She's your guardian angel."

"I've never met her."

"She's as elusive as John Wayne."

"I don't..." That name was as familiar as it was foreign. "Is that your name?"

"No. Do you know him?" He appeared to hold his breath, waiting for her answer.

"I don't think so, but I can't be sure."

"Does he sound familiar?"

"He does, but I do not know him."

His subtle nod transformed his expression. He knew something she didn't. "How long have you been here?"

"Since this morning."

A prisoner nearby, a man in his mid-30s who called himself Carl, chuckled. "She says that every day. She was here when I arrived."

The new prisoner looked his way. "When was that?"

"Three days ago."

"She's lying?"

He grunted. "Hard to say. Nimble doesn't talk much."

"Nimble?" He turned back to her. "Have you figured out how to escape yet?"

"No one escapes," she said. "Anyone who tries, dies."

"You've witnessed it?"

"They told me this morning."

Again, Carl chuckled. "The guards tell us every morning so's we don't forget. If we get caught escaping, it's the blade."

"Harsh." The new prisoner scanned the room, taking in the walls, door and ceiling 25 feet above. His eyes rested on the lone window near the ceiling. It was the only light source, and the setting sun shot its bright rays in to illuminate the space. Wooden shutters were tied open to either side, leaving air to circulate. Birds flew in and out at will and when it rained, like it had earlier in the day, the wind blew it inside. "I've got an idea."

"Success or failure, either way, you'll never see the inside of this dungeon again." Carl rested his head against the wall, finding peace in his decision to accept fate.

"I don't plan to rot here." He twisted and got his knees beneath him, then rose to his feet. Gazing up at the window, his eyes sparkled.

"Ain't tall enough to reach it," said Carl.

"Alone."

"I ain't helping, and sure ain't no one here willing to risk life to help you."

"No one?" The stranger eyed Nimble. "Not even you? I know you can do it. We get up there, the rest is easy." Several prisoners laughed, but that didn't deter him. "Are you going to wait to be sold off as a slave for the mine, or will you choose your own destiny? You gonna roll the die or let the Adventure Master do it for you?"

Again, his words sounded familiar yet foreign. It was like he spoke a different language, one she'd heard but never learned.

He fell to his knees before her and stared into her eyes. A scar on his forehead looked dark. Painful. "You know you can. You're hauflin, right? It's why they call you Nimble. Why you're barefoot. Shorter than the average woman. Together, we can do this."

Hauflin? Was she? Her thoughts tumbled over each other. She had been called that long ago. And yesterday. Gazing up at the window, she couldn't imagine reaching it. She was not that tall. And what was on the other side? She glanced at the prisoners, waiting to see what they'd say. Knowing what they'd do made her hesitate.

"You and me," he whispered. "We're cut from the same cloth." His grey eyes with flecks of green enticed her. "We got this." He forced himself to his feet, then moved behind her, where he lowered himself against her back. "Sit still."

His shoulders were a few inches higher than hers and when they pressed against her, she turned to see what he was doing. Movement on her wrists pushed her hands against her lower back. What was he doing?

"Hold them still," he whispered. "A little bit more. Almost there."

The steady rhythm jostled her until she felt her hands break free. He had cut the leather binding them. "Why did you do that? If they find me like this, they will kill me."

"They won't find you. Now cut mine." In his bent fingers, he held a twisted piece of metal.

She stared at the metal. At this point, she could call a guard and tell on him, but they might kill her anyways. Grabbing the blade, she quickly cut through his straps, then stared at Carl. "Belchap, right? Carl." She looked at other prisoners. "Haword. Milton. I will find your families. They will know your fate. If it is what you say, they will rescue you." She glanced at the other prisoners. "All from Belchap?" Many of them nodded, their expressions eager. Exactly what she wanted to see. "A rescue for one will be a rescue for all. How long will it take me to reach your home village?"

"Four days on foot," said Carl, his eyes ablaze with hope.

"Then look for rescue in eight." She turned to the man who guaranteed her escape. "What do you want me to do?"

He stood beneath the window. The setting sun shone its last breaths of light sharply on the wall opposite it. "Simple. I throw you up. You tie together the ropes bracing the shutters, then tie that to something secure and I climb up."

She squished up her nose. "You're going to throw me up there?"

"I rolled an 18 for strength." He grinned. "I'm guessing you might be a hauflin thief, so you—"

"I've stolen nothing," she snapped.

He grimaced. "I didn't say you did but your attributes will ensure you're capable of doing what I ask."

"Hauflin? What is that?"

"Your race." He bent low and intertwined his fingers. "One foot on and while you spring, I'll throw."

Second thoughts bombarded her. She'd never done anything like this before. If she missed, she'd crash into the stone floor, or... She considered the man before her: he'd break her fall.

"No second thoughts. Keep your mind clear." He grinned. "Like a rocket. Five. Four. Three. Two. One."

She leapt onto his hands and while she sprang up, he shoved with all his might. Startled by the sudden thrust upwards, she almost forgot to find secure footing. She grasped the top of the shutter and swung over to the window ledge, latching onto the side to ensure she didn't fall through. Looking down to what awaited her made her stomach lurch. It was more than 100 feet into waves crashing against the stone castle wall. Looking left and then right, there was nowhere for them to go.

Several seagulls flew past at eye level, screeching to alert guards of her escape. The birds circled, then soared along the shore for a short distance, then dove towards the water, skimming the surface as if on a wild ride.

She leant out to look up, but a soft whistle caught her attention. The man who had thrown her up was motioning for her to get the rope. What good would it do them? It was only about 30 feet long, far short of the water, which she had no intentions of entering.

His arm movements became quick, aggressive. She had to obey. If she returned to the prison, he might kill her, or the guards would. Her only hope for freedom lay outside on the darkening landscape, but she'd need help from the man who had claimed she could escape. She unfastened the rope and pulled it from its holding hooks, then she took the rope from the other shutter, tied the two lengths together, secured it around the thick hinge and threw the end down to him.

Before it hit the floor, he grabbed it and climbed up. "Good job. Next time, don't hesitate. We afforded it this time but next time, we might go indebt."

Weird. The way he spoke. Not like anyone she'd met.

He fed the rope over the windowsill towards the water. As predicted, it dangled far above the surface. "Can you swim?"

"No," she said, not leaving room for doubt.

"Hold on tight then." He turned his back towards her. "Arms around the neck. Feet around my waist."

"Seriously?" A violent tremor shook her.

"Unless you want to learn to swim on the way down."

She swallowed hard. Drowning had to be less painful than death by the blade. There was no turning back now.

"Not so tight." He wriggled his shoulders. "I need to breathe."

She loosened her grip and wrapped her legs around his waist. When he hoisted himself over the side, her heart leapt into her throat. She closed her eyes. Hearing and feeling what was happening was enough. He paused at the end of the rope, and she waited for the free fall, but after several long seconds, it didn't come. Instead, they moved sideways. What was he up to?

She opened her eyes. He was walking across the stone, his boots gripping the jagged sides of the wall. Nothing lay ahead of them but more wall. Was he looking for a better spot to plunge into the cold ocean water? She glanced down. Nope. It all looked the same from here, 70 feet above it. He stopped and before she drew another breath, he launched himself off the wall. They sailed above the water, passed beneath the prison window, then he flung himself forward. Clamping her eyes closed, she waited for the dreadful crash.

A solid thud, jolt and a gasp of excitement forced her eyes open. They landed on a narrow balcony. Several clay pots with plants growing inside decorated the space. The door leading into the castle flung open, and a woman dressed in a pretty gown stared out at them. A second later, she screamed and slammed the door.

"Curse that luck." He pushed her from his back, ran to the opposite end of the balcony and looked over. "Not good."

Once again, the door opened, and a man stepped out brandishing a sword.

"No better." He picked up a clay pot and threw it at the man's chest. It sent him flying backwards into the castle, where another scream erupted. Frantically, he peered over one side of the balcony, then the other. No options and frustration taking over, he grabbed Nimble and jumped onto the rail.

"I'd prefer to fight," she said. "Not die on rocks."

"Trust me."

Before she drew another breath, she was airborne and quickly descending into dark waters. When she struck the surface, she wanted to scream but instead sealed her mouth shut and covered her nose with her hand. The frigid waters sent a shock wave through her body. In the turbulent current, she lost her grip on him and within seconds, he was gone. Tumbling and fighting to find her way to the surface without even a slither of moon to guide her, she kicked and swatted the water. The pressure in her lungs grew and fear set in. Her muscles strained, and she grasped handfuls of water to pull her upward, all the while the current pushed her sideways. Releasing a bit of air through her mouth, she battled on, wishing with every stroke, her hand would find air. When it finally did, she shot out of the water only to be jerked backwards by an unknown force. Thrashing about, she tried to free herself.

"It's me! Get a grip."

She clung to his arm. Hot from the rush to survive, she quickly cooled with the chilly wind whipping against her wet skin.

"This way." He held onto her hand, swimming with only one arm, and dragged her through the waves to the base of the castle wall. The waves slapped them against it, but he held on, fighting the relentless tide. "Over there." He pointed to the river running beneath the castle. An expansive archway allowed water to pass under. "The tide is coming in. It will help us."

"Do what?"

"Escape." He yanked her from the wall and dragged her through the waves.

Gulping saltwater, she sputtered and spit. Several times the waves shoved her against the stone wall and banged her knees and feet. Her dress swam around her armpits, leaving her lower half covered in only panties. Not that anyone could see with her submerged in the ocean with hardly enough light to illuminate their way. She was going more by feel and the shimmer of starlight off the water's surface.

They slipped inside the archway and disappeared from the sight of anyone searching for them from the balcony. If an alarm to alert others of their escape had sounded, she didn't hear it. The roar of the sea and its echo within the archway drowned out everything.

The tunnel was long, and she could barely see the end that was faintly illuminated. Between here and there was pitch black.

"Hold on tight," he whispered. His voice sounded loud within the tunnel. "I'll never find you if we separate."

She held on to him with one hand, pushed forward with the other and kicked her feet. By the time she reached the open air, her muscles ached, but he didn't stop. He warned her not to speak, and he swam silently away from the arch and along the field towards the forest. A pair of ducks quietly paddled past, giving them lots of room, and spring peepers added music to their movement. Bugs swarmed overhead and mosquitoes buzzed in her ears. The man kept swimming. It felt like he'd never stop. Her body grew numb from exertion and freezing water. By the time he dragged her onto the shore, she was dead weight. She lay against a mound of dirt, breathing heavily and shivering.

He collapsed to the ground next to her and heaved great breaths. But he didn't remain still for long. Sitting up, he searched the river towards the castle, then swung his head to view what lay upstream. "We can't stay," he said, still out of breath. "Get on your feet. We'll follow the river, get out of the village and head west." He rose and shook his body.

Water sprayed her, and she looked away. "Is that where Belchap is located?" She rose to her knees and wrapped her arms across her stomach to generate heat.

"Why?"

"We have to go there. Tell the families of these men where they are so they can be rescued." Her teeth chattered on the last word.

"You were being sincere?"

"We owe it to them. We would never have escaped if I didn't tell them that."

"They had nothing to do with our escape."

"Sure they did." She stood, straightened her water-laden dress, wrung out sections along the hem, then rubbed her arms. "Earlier today, Carl was talking to another man. He was hoping someone would try to escape. He'd call the guards and try to buy his freedom by telling on them."

"Seriously?"

"As soon as we reached that window, he'd have made an awful racket to alert the guards."

"Damn," he said under his breath.

"They're desperate. They know what awaits in the mines."

"Come on." He grasped her arm. "They'll be looking for us."

He led her into the forest. Once she got started, he released her. Weaving around bushes and trees, they found a footpath, and he increased his speed. She hurried to keep up, struck her foot on a rock and tumbled to the ground. Pain shot up her leg. If not for freezing to death, she'd have lay there. He helped her to rise, and they continued.

Several minutes later, he slowed his pace. A noise sounded up ahead. "Shhh." He crouched low and slipped through the underbrush, stopping near a clearing with a small cottage lit up from the inside. A woman dressed in revealing clothing stood on the porch, beckoning to the man who secured his horse at the hitching post.

"You're late," she said, not a hint of anger in her voice.

"Taking care of business before I indulge in pleasure." He wrapped his arm around her waist and pulled her near. "Pleasure is what I seek tonight." He kissed her firmly.

"Come. Night passes, and morning will come soon enough." She dragged him inside and closed the door.

"Four days by foot?" He stared at the horse.

"Four."

"Two by horse. Let's go." He leapt up, approached the horse cautiously and patted its nose before untying the reins from the post.

She'd never stolen a horse before, and she doubted she wanted to steal this one. Horse thieves hanged. Glancing between the door and the horse, she followed it onto the narrow lane. After travelling a few hundred feet, her rescuer climbed into the saddle.

"Up." He held his hand out for her.

The night was cold and would only get colder riding a horse and wearing wet clothes. She dug into the saddlebags and was rewarded with a black cloak. After putting it on, she slid the bottom corners over the opposite shoulders to create a snug wrap. Her body relaxed and generated heat. She had forgotten what it felt like to be warm. Taking a strip of twine from another pocket, she tied it around her waist to secure the cloak.

"Hurry. Fashion won't save you if someone sees us."

"It was not I who threw me into the icy ocean."

"I saved you."

"Almost drowned me, and now you want me to freeze to death. It is not like I wear trousers and several layers of clothing. You even have boots to warm your feet."

He frowned. "Fine. But you can fix the cloak after we get away from here. What you've got will keep you warm."

"I am drenched and freezing. And I will be sitting against a waterlogged rat whose wet hair will whip my face." She finished securing the cloak and reached for his hand. It was cold and sent a shiver down her arm. Settling into the saddle, she tried not to press too hard against his back. He still dripped water. Feeling him shiver, she wondered if the saddlebags held another cloak. Or did he not feel the cold?

"What is your name?" she asked.

"I don't have one."

"Certainly, you do."

He thought for a long moment while he brought the horse to a walk. "Call me Cormac."

"Is that your name?"

Dark shadows hid his expression, but he didn't sound impressed. "Does it matter?" He focussed on the horse, and soon they were jogging at a steady pace, quickly putting distance between them and the castle guards who searched for them.

2

Memories in the Wind

RUSTLING LEAVES STIRRED Cormac from a deep sleep. His senses awakening reminded him of the beating he'd taken from the guards when he had been captured yesterday. They had ambushed him in the market while he had tried to buy a loaf of bread. Four men pounded his back and gut until he dropped. They stripped him of the few coins he carried and his only weapon: a knife found a few months earlier.

He opened his eyes and stared at the woman he had discovered in the dungeon. The beating and the risk to his life was worth it when he realised who she was. For years, he had searched the land looking for her, or someone like her, and had given up. But now, his hope renewed, he had a way to escape this hell. She'd escape it, too, but not in the same manner.

At this angle, she appeared to be sleeping peacefully, but he couldn't see her entire face. Wrapped in the cloak, her fine attributes were hidden. When he'd first seen her, his anger had turned to curiosity, then admiration. Sitting on the floor, hands tied behind her back, she had stared at him through a veil of tangled brown hair. The thin, sleeveless grey dress she wore covered the vital parts and exposed the rest of her skin. No doubt, she'd been cold, sitting on the stone floor with not even shoes to retain heat. Now, wrapped in the cloak, colour returned to her face, and her body ceased to shake. He thought it had been fear that made her tremble but evidently, it was the cold.

He wanted to be blunt, ask her how she got to this world and where she came from, but she wouldn't remember, and he risked losing her. If she suspected what he wanted, she'd run... for a day, then she'd forget about him. From what the prisoners had said, he guessed she had no talisman to ground her, making her memories fleeting. Each night, they'd evaporate into the wind, and she'd start the morning anew. He'd know if this was true soon enough.

Nimble, which probably wasn't her real name, stirred, stretched and opened her eyes. For a long moment, she stared into the sky, perhaps watching birds fly between trees. Or maybe wondering where she was and who she was. A pleasant expression spread across her face but when she saw him, it tightened.

"Sleep well?" he asked.

"Fair enough." She dragged her tongue across the roof of her mouth to gather spit. "You?"

"The same." He stretched, then rose to his full height. Human status didn't provide him with extra height because all humans in this land were short, shorter than the ones where he came from. That meant the dwarfs, hauflins and elves were not that much shorter. Stories he had heard while growing up were wrong. Sort of. They had judged the other races shorter than humans without knowing humans were also short. The tallest man he'd seen probably didn't measure more than 5 1/2 feet. Most were like him, five feet.

"Do we have food?" she asked.

"No. We'll sell or trade something at the next village." He went to the horse, threw on the saddle and secured it. They had travelled for several hours the previous night and were well off the main road, but he didn't want to take any chances of being found with a stolen horse, so they'd continue to travel west as the crow flew.

Once in the saddle, he helped her climb up behind him. She was light and nimble, as her name suggested. No doubt, she was a hauflin thief, which would come in handy on his journey. Given his location, it'd take three weeks to reach Harmon of the Wood on horseback.

Six hours later, they entered Village Doorock. He had passed through here a few times over the years. It was a quiet place where people went about their daily business as if they had lost hope of anything changing. It was horrible desperation, something he could never get used to. Little did he know when he arrived in this land that it was not the exciting, action-packed, magical place he had dreamt it to be. Instead, it was a stagnent, dangerous place that lacked the magic of imagination. His fantasies of being a great fighter with friends to share adventures with were only that: fantasies. He couldn't afford a sword, let alone make friends with people who appeared soulless. The lessons in fencing he had taken before he came to this land had been a waste of time and money. In the years he had roamed this realm, searching for the spark he believed existed, he spent most of his time looking for items he needed to survive: food, clothing, shelter. There was no time to seek quests or search for treasure.

He steered the horse to the small village market. When they had stopped for the night, he'd gone through the saddlebags and found a few interesting items to barter with. It'd get them food, the only commodity besides clothes that mattered.

Before entering the market, he motioned for Nimble to dismount, and he did the same. Here, guards didn't patrol. Only villagers travelled the streets. He saw a stand selling bread and walked towards it. They also had a green, spikey food called asparagus, which ripened early in the season. It tasted like broccoli stalks. He'd tried it cooked and raw; he preferred raw. While it might exist in his world, his mother had never bought it.

He glanced at Nimble. She took in the scene, her eyes large and curious, her steps light. "Have you been here before?"

She shook her head. "I'd remember if I had. So many colours, happy things. Music."

He looked back at the market. Unlike most places he'd visited, it did have some colour. Now. It hadn't before. Though most of the colour was in the produce and goods that lay on the tables more so than in the people's clothing and stall decorations. Although some people wore clothes in colours other than grey, most wore black and white. Music? Mixed in with the many voices, he heard a stringed instrument playing in the distance. Strange. He hadn't noticed that before.

Stopping at the stand, he gazed upon the bread, and his stomach begged him to grab it. The bright green asparagus also caught his eye.

"Not you again," said the vendor.

"Yes, me again," he said.

"Not you. Her." He pointed at Nimble. "Do you know where Loggie is now?" He leant towards her, a frown upon his face. "Belchap. Because of you."

"What did she do?" asked Cormac.

"Filled his head with silly dreams. Taught him to dance. Encouraged him to sing. Now he thinks he's fine enough to perform for the king. My boy left because of her. I have lost my only son."

Damn. These circumstances were not good for bartering. "We are going to Belchap. We shall fetch your son and send home."

The man's eyes widened. "You'd do that for me?" He turned to Nimble. "Will you convince him to come home to Popa?"

Her blank stare told him she didn't remember this man nor his son. "We will, won't we, Nimble? We will find him at Belchap and tell him he needs to come home."

Her eyes darted between him and the stall keeper. "Yes."

"Good. A happy day when my boy returns." The keeper turned back to Cormac. "Find him. He is young. Too young to be gadding about like a seasoned man who has earned his footwear for wandering."

"We will. Loggie, you say?" The man nodded. "Working for the king, you believe. He shall have coins to share."

The keeper huffed and raised an eyebrow. "He's not that good. He'll be a street minstrel by now. Singing for food scraps, he will."

"We shall find him just the same." He slowly withdrew the two beeswax candles wrapped in thick brown paper. "I have no need for these, kind sir, and I wonder what you have to trade for them."

The keeper's eyes widened. "Beeswax. A fine coin indeed." He peered closer. "The finest of quality."

"I need no coin, only food for our journey to Belchap."

"Certainly." He scanned the table. "While I wish to offer more, I can give only what I know I can get from the people of Village Doorock. Not many can afford such luxuries but those who can, would buy two loaves of bread and ten stalks of asparagus."

"I could get more in Belchap, but I will be hungry long before then, so I accept the trade." He placed the candles gently in the hands of the keeper, who stared at the sticks as if treasure.

The keeper wrapped the candles in the paper and tucked them out of sight. Then he laid out the bread and asparagus. "I wish you safe journey. Speedy journey. Successful journey. Send my offshoot home to Popa."

"Thank you. Consider it done." Cormac tucked the food into a cloth sack he'd found in the saddlebags and bid the man good day.

Walking away, he glanced at Nimble keeping pace. "Do you remember this Loggie? Will you recognise him if we see him?"

She stared at the dirt lane ahead. After a long moment, she said, "I have not met him."

Great. This memory loss served him in one way but presently, it was causing problems.

3

Setting Out on a Quest

THE UNUSUAL TASTE of the green spikes bought at the market made Nimble's lips quiver. They were juicy and crunchy. She'd never tasted anything like it. In one way, it was familiar but in all others, it was as foreign as the man who sat near her by the riverbank. When she'd awakened this morning, she'd found him sleeping beneath a tree. Fearing him dead, she'd shaken him, and he'd awakened with a start. After he came to his senses and calmed down, he offered her half a loaf of bread and this green vegetable. She ate in silence, enjoying the scenery, the birds singing and the bees buzzing from one pretty flower to the next. The rippling water added to the lovely morning as did the shy fairy hiding amongst the reeds on the opposite shore.

"We will reach Belchap today," said the stranger. "Have you been there?"

She considered the question, then wandered onto another question. "Why are we going to Belchap?"

"We're on a quest."

She sat up straighter and gave him her full attention. "Really? I want to learn more."

"First, we must find the families of Carl, Haword and Milton. These men are prisoners, and we need to alert their loved ones so they can be rescued."

"That is truly noble. Have you seen these men?"

"Yes, they helped us escape."

She searched her memory for details. "I was a prisoner?"

"The guard knocked you out. You are better now."

She felt her forehead. There wasn't even a bump, but she had bruises on her arms and legs. "We shall find their families. What is the second?"

"A man has lost his son named Loggie. He believes he is in Belchap, and you must convince him to go home."

"Me? Why?"

"Loggie will listen only to you. His popa says your lovely spirit will convince him to come home."

She stared at the water, thinking about what she'd say to convince him. "It will be done." She stood. "I am ready for the challenge." Surprise ripened on the stranger's face. "But first, I must know your name."

"Cormac, as it was yesterday."

"Good." She waited until he mounted, then leapt into the saddle. "It is a good day for adventure."

"How do you know that?"

"The fairy told me."

He stared at her over his shoulder. "Where did you see the fairy?"

"Can't say. She's shy."

He didn't believe her and turned towards the front. The horse picked up speed, and she held onto the man's waist.

Several hours later, the first houses surrounding Belchap came into view. They were small farmhouses surrounded by sprawling fields. Crops grew in large swathes and sheep grazed in pastures. A wagon pulled by two horses passed, and the man at the reins nodded and bid them a good day.

"Where shall we look for these families?" asked Nimble.

"Perhaps the market. Everyone goes there."

"Good idea."

Riding past the farmhouses, more buildings appeared. Some were small, some were long and some were tall. Many people were out and about, working the fields, tending to chores and walking from one point to another. Occasionally, someone would see her and wave with a big smile. She returned the wave. The people in Belchap were a happy, friendly bunch.

They rode down one street, then another until they reached the impressive town market. There were many stalls and even more people. Brightly coloured flags, signs and banners decorated stalls, and their keepers displayed their merchandise in a well-organised fashion to catch the eye of buyers. In the distance, someone played a flute and was accompanied by a stringed instrument. A voice. Someone was singing. It was more like a carnival than a market. She tapped her hand on her knee to the rhythm of the music. This generated a glance from Cormac. His silly expression made her giggle.

"We should dismount," he said. "We will better be able to talk to people."

She slipped off the horse and landed gently on the ground, hardly stirring dust, unlike when Cormac hit the ground. It was like he wanted to make a solid thud and a brown cloud.

"Who shall we ask first?" she said. "That man over there?" She pointed to a man selling cloth. "Or that woman over there?" She pointed to an older woman spooning out hot liquid. "Women know where their men should be. Let's ask her." Without another word, she trotted over to the woman. "Excuse me, ma'am. I've a question to bother you with."

The woman stared at her. "You like soup?"

"Maybe later. We," she pointed to herself and Cormac, who appeared shocked by something she didn't notice, "are looking for someone who knows Carl. Do you know him?"

"Never heard of him. Is he from Belchap?"

"Yes. Do you know Haword?"

She shook her head. "Are they brothers?"

She thought about this and didn't have an answer. "Do you know Milton?"

The woman's eyes grew wide. "He is my son. He was to return days ago, yet he has not arrived." She leant forward. "Do you know him?"

Nimble ushered Cormac closer. "This man has seen him. He's a prisoner. He needs rescuing. We were sent here to tell you."

"Prisoner!" she squealed, drawing the attention of those nearby. "Where? Is he alive?"

"Alive. He is..." She turned to Cormac. "Who holds him prisoner?"

It was his turn to speak, and he took his time doing it, so much so the woman grew impatient.

"Speak, boy!"

"Dunvain Downs. They are being held by the king."

"How do you know this?"

"We were also prisoners. We escaped."

"You left my son to die?"

"No. He was unable to make the climb or the..." He thought for a moment. "He would not have survived the ocean waters."

"And you did?"

"I am an excellent swimmer." He pointed to Nimble. "She would have drowned if not for me."

Nimble stared at him. "You did not tell me this." She wrapped her arms around him, pinning his arms to his sides. "Thank you."

He grew warm and when he spoke, his voice trembled. "You're welcome? It was what you would have done for me."

"But I cannot swim like you. We would have drowned."

"But we didn't. More importantly, we survived to bring this message to Milton's family. He, Carl, Haword and about ten other men from Belchap are being held in the prison awaiting their transfer to the mines."

The old woman's hands flew to her mouth, but they couldn't conceal the shock on her face.

"We must do something!" said a man nearby. "King Stowell must be told. He will rescue them." The growing crowd echoed the sentiment.

"Did you say one of the men was Carl?" A woman in her early 20s stepped forward.

"Yes," said Cormac. "Do you know him?"

"He's my husband. He and Haword went to Dunvain Downs to trade our candles. Beeswax. The finest kind."

"Both were well when we last saw them," said Cormac. "They asked us to come here. Tell you of their fate. They hope your king will rescue them."

"It must be done," said a voice in the crowd.

"To the kingdom!" said Carl's wife. "You must come, too. Tell King Stowell what you have seen and heard."

"Well, we do have other business, and—"

"That can wait. You will come with us."

"We will," said Nimble. "We will tell the king. It is the quest we were sent on, and we will do it." She marched alongside Carl's wife, smiling at others as they joined in.

Before they reached the kingdom, they were 100 strong. Loud voices filled with hope and determination erupted from the crowd. When guards stepped out to block the procession, Carl's wife came face-to-face with them. Nimble stood by her side, but Cormac remained a few steps behind.

"Let us pass," said Carl's wife.

"For what reason?" one guard asked.

"To see the king. Men of Belchap are being held prisoner at Dunvain Downs." She went on to give details and before she completed her tale, the guards were escorting her and her followers over the drawbridge to the castle.

A young guard fell into step with Nimble. "It is good to see you."

"Good to see you, too," she said. "I am on a quest."

"Another one?"

"I have many. What is your quest?"

He chuckled. "The same as last time. To protect the king."

"That is a noble quest. Is the king alive?"

"As alive as he was before."

"You are doing an excellent job. Are you coming with us to see him?"

"I will take you to him. He will be happy to see you."

"Me. I am no one special."

"He thinks so."

"He is too kind," she said.

They crossed the drawbridge and entered the courtyard. Someone up ahead hollered, then someone from behind replied. Guards joined in on the march and before long, they were entering the king's Great Room. When everyone who could fit in, fit in, a man in brown clothes stood in front of the crowd and tooted a long horn. It was so long, the end rested on the floor. The crowd fell silent, and the man spoke.

"King Stowell of Belchap will meet you."

"How exciting," she said to Cormac, who stood behind her right shoulder. "I've never met a king." She stretched her neck for a view.

A man no taller than Cormac came from a side door and stood by the horn blower. He was dressed in a fine outfit of dark blue material trimmed with white. His knee-length, long sleeve tunic was held snug around the waist by a leather belt, double looped. The belt held an intricately-designed scabbard with a sword with a decorated hilt. His matching blue pants billowed at the knees and were tucked into thick white woollen socks. He bowed slightly, then sat in the large ornate seat on a short rise. Milton's mother fell to her knees before him.

"Please! King Stowell, I beseech you. My son and many others from Belchap have been imprisoned." She told the king her story, then said, "This man," she pointed at Cormac, "brought the news."

King Stowell stared at Cormac, then ushered him forward. "You have seen these men?"

Cormac hesitated but slowly stepped before the king and fell to his knees beside Milton's mother. His voice, when he finally spoke, was low and lacked its usual confidence. "Yes, your majesty."

"You do not sound convinced. You have seen them in prison?"

"Yes. I did."

Nimble tilted her head. His shaky voice was not what she expected. Stepping forward, she stood beside him. "Your Majesty, we escaped the prison in which these men are held. They asked us to come here and tell you their story."

He raised an eyebrow and smirked. "You certainly are popular. Were you seized for entering forbidden places?"

She searched her memory. "I cannot say."

"Said with such innocence, I am at your mercy to believe you." A shallow grin briefly brightened his features, then he pushed it aside. "How many men?"

"A dozen," said Nimble. "Perhaps more by now."

"Can you tell me exactly where they are held?"

She looked to Cormac, who nodded.

"Come with me." The king stood. "The rest of you, return to your daily chores. We will rescue these men and return them home."

Milton's mother and many in the crowd thanked the king, then everyone shuffled slowly from the room.

Nimble fell into step beside the king and followed him through the exit door and down a long hallway. Cormac followed closely behind her. After several turns, she entered a room with a long, thick table and several bookshelves. Light poured in through two tall windows, highlighting the large map on the wall. Dispersed around the room were weapons for battle: swords, daggers, crossbows and spears. She drank in the sight, fantasizing about the adventures that had started here.

"I trust you know not to touch anything."

She stared at the king. His expression left no room for doubt. "If I am not permitted, I will touch nothing."

"You are not permitted."

"Is anyone else?"

"Me and my men only."

"Not even a feel?"

"Not even a feel."

"It's like you've had others who took advantage of that."

"Indeed." He frowned, then turned to the others. "Bring me the diagram for Castle Dunvain Downs."

A uniformed man went to a bookshelf, thumbed through a section with large, thin books, then pulled one from the shelf. He took it to the table and opened it. Then he opened it again and again until the one book was a map that measured six feet by eight.

Nimble had never seen a book like this, and she leant over it to see how it came apart and how it would fold up to return to a book small enough for a child to read. The colours and images on the page caught her attention. The details leapt out at her, and she imagined herself walking through the courtyard and into the castle.

"No." The king grasped her hand before it reached the book. "Hands off."

She tucked her hand to her side, gave him half a glance, then returned her attention to the map.

"Where are the men held?" asked King Stowell.

Cormac studied the map, walked along the table's edge, stopped and studied it further. He lifted his hand to touch the map, but quickly drew it back, giving the king a cautious glance.

"You may indicate their location," said the king. "This sprite, however, is banned from touching anything in here."

Cormac looked between the two but didn't say anything. He pointed to a tower near the water. "This window here. They are in this room."

"Are you certain?"

"Yes. We climbed out this window and landed on this balcony. This tower here," he pointed to the only other tower on the shoreline, "doesn't have a balcony. We swam to the arch, beneath it and upstream to escape."

The king studied the map in silence for several minutes. Nimble studied it as well, taking in the exits, the rooms and surrounding support buildings. It was vast. Feeling an odd movement at her legs like a snake weaving around them, she looked down. A grey and black cat with a large fluffy tail rubbed against her calves. Soon, it was purring loudly. She no sooner picked it up when the king spoke.

"Put it down."

She hugged the cat and spoke with her eyes as well as her tongue. "But it's a friendly cat; it's not—"

"Down."

She slowly lowered the cat to the floor, patting it after it was out of her arms. "It likes me."

"Oh, I know. But nothing good comes from it."

"You don't know that."

"Yes, I do."

Her mouth froze open. He could see the future? She closed her mouth, released the cat and stood straight, wondering what he saw for her future.

"You say these men are destined for the mines?" asked the king.

"Yes," said Cormac. "While they dragged me to the prison, they told me I'd be taken there, too. They didn't say which mine, only the slave mine."

"Interesting." The king stood straight. "Are there any other details you'd like to impart?"

"No, that's it."

"Thank you for keeping your promise. I will inform the prisoners when we free them. I'm sure they wonder if you followed through. It will renew their hope in good people." He motioned to a guard near the door. "See they each receive a small sack of food for their troubles and loyalty to the people of Belchap. And surely keep an eye on the sprite. Don't let her wander nor touch anything." He frowned at her. "Hands in pockets."

She slowly slipped them inside.

"Ensure they remain there."

"While I believe you are a benevolent man, you have a weirdness about you I cannot explain."

"Think hard. You'll find your explanation."

"This way," said the guard.

She placed her palm on her belly and bowed slightly. "Good king, I bid you farewell. Until next time."

"Next time." He rolled his eyes. "I'll be watching for you."

She smiled and followed Cormac and the guard from the room and down a hallway. When she looked down, she saw the cat following.

"What did you do to make the king so suspicious of you?" asked Cormac.

"I don't know. I think he's paranoid."

The guard leading the way chuckled. "This way. To the kitchen."

4

Beneath the Dragon's Noggin'

CORMAC GUIDED THE horse away from the castle. He glanced back several times and imagined the preparations the guards were making to advance on Dunvain Downs to rescue the prisoners. The king made no mention of him accompanying them, and that suited him fine. He enjoyed daring adventures, but he wasn't interested in attacking a castle or going to war. It was too violent and would certainly end his life sooner than expected. No, he wanted to survive this world and escape with all limbs intact.

He caught sight of Nimble. Now that he had the key to unlock the doorway to home, the last thing he wanted was to be dragged into unnecessary violence. He considered the woman. She was pretty in an odd, wild way, but he didn't want to think too much about her. That would make him hesitate, and he couldn't afford that if he wanted to get home. With her memory erased each night, the value of her life was minimal. His fingers went to the opening of his jerkin below his neck and felt the solid object beneath his shirt. He could fix her memory but again, if he did that, he'd hesitate to sacrifice her, and that was not an option unless he wanted to surrender to this unforgiving land.

"Are we on to our next quest?" Her large brown eyes sparkled in the sunshine as they took in the activity near the castle and across the drawbridge.

"Yes, though we will not be generously rewarded like we just were."

She caught his gaze. "The food was unexpected. Those are the best rewards. His name is Loggie, you say?"

"Yes. If he's like his father, he's slightly shorter than me, taller than you, large in foot, barefoot, brown hair, larger than normal nose. You know, dwarf-like."

"I've heard of dwarfs. They are strong."

"Supposedly. They're usually not that jolly but apparently this young man is quite jolly. He sings and dances."

"How wonderful! I will look for someone full of happiness." She set her eyes on her surroundings and scanned the people before her.

An hour later, on the outskirts of the market, Cormac spotted a sad little man sitting on a block of wood holding a small stringed instrument and staring at the ground. He had brown hair and thick bare feet. He was dwarf, but was he the dwarf he sought?

"What do you think of him?" He pointed to the down-hearted man.

Nimble stared at him, an eyebrow raising the longer she held her gaze. "Possibly. Probably. But he looks like a sad sack, not a happy camper."

That expression. He hadn't heard it in a long time. It was from his homeland.

"Only one way to find out." She jumped off the horse and rushed over to him. The moment he spotted her, his face lit up and he rose to meet her.

"Rosalind! My eyes ached to see you." He pulled her into his arms and gave her a long hug.

Cormac dismounted but hesitated to approach the two. They appeared as long-lost friends, perhaps lovers. What was their relationship in Village Doorock? Had they fallen in love, and had Nimble wandered off one morning after not remembering what had happened? Odd feelings stirred in his chest. If they were in a relationship, it wasn't right to take her away from it.

"This is my friend. Cormac." Nimble ushered Loggie forward, and he obeyed. "He is a great man. He saved my life. He is a noble man. He keeps his promises."

Loggie stuck out his hand. "Any friend of Rosalind's is a friend of mine."

"Rosalind? You know her real name?" Cormac shook his hand.

"No!" He laughed. "She would not tell me. A trickster, she is. But a beautiful, happy one that will bring no harm."

"So you gave her the name Rosalind?"

"I drew her to my side while playing *Rosalind, That Girl I Love.* What do you call her?"

"Nimble. When I met her, that's what they called her."

"Nimble Rosalind," he exclaimed. "The perfect name."

"Loggie, we have a message for you," said Nimble. "Your Popa begs for your return. He misses you and wants you home."

"Home." The happiness faded. "If successful, I'd want to stay in Belchap. Failing, I am ashamed to go home. I am stuck." He hung his head low, and the small stringed instrument dangled at his side. "I cannot go home and tell Popa I failed. The king does not want to hear my song."

"Did you see the king?" asked Nimble, slinging a comforting arm across his back.

"At a distance. I played, and the scullery maids pushed me out the door. They do not like my songs."

"Hmph." She squared her jaw and stared at the ground. "That's not fair. If the king were not so busy at this moment, I'd take you to him."

"You know the king?"

"We do. We just left him. He has a quest of his own and will be preoccupied in the coming days. No time for music. Maybe when he completes his quest. We shall return, and I will convince him to listen."

"What do I do until then?"

"Come with us."

"What?" Cormac's face twisted. "I can't stay here. I need to — I have someone I have to meet."

"Who?" Nimble stared up at him.

"It's an old friend. A man I haven't seen for a long time."

"What's his name?"

He hesitated, then realised no one knew the man, so it didn't matter if he said his name, and Nimble would forget by morning. "Harmon of the Wood."

"Sounds interesting," she said. "We shall visit with Harmon of the Wood, then return to see King Stowell. Come, Loggie."

"Wait. He can't come." That would ruin everything.

"Why? He is our friend."

"You don't know him."

"Yes, she does," said Loggie.

Cormac's mouth hung open. While Loggie remembered her, she didn't remember him. He stared, searching for a reasonable answer to why he couldn't come. Then he remembered the message he was to deliver to Loggie from his popa but before he spoke, the man's face turned from quizzical to surprise and finally deep concern.

"I need to go," said Loggie, tucking his stringed instrument into his shoulder sack. "Quickly."

Cormac looked over his shoulder. There was nothing unusual in the crowd behind him... Except two men were questioning merchants and bystanders.

"Come with us," said Nimble. "Get on the horse."

Rough fingers dug into Cormac's ribs, and he found her pushing him towards the horse. "Why?"

"They do not look friendly. Up."

He no sooner mounted and she jumped up behind him. Without missing a beat, she grabbed Loggie's hand and helped him to sit on the rump of the horse behind the saddle. This looked awkward, and it felt odd. While the horse was a good size, three people was a lot even if one was hauflin and one was dwarf.

"Go. Hurry."

"There he is!" shouted one of the men, who rushed forward.

Not wanting to wait around to see why the men wanted Loggie, Cormac steered the horse away from the crowd and trotted towards the edge of town. Once out of view of the men, he shot his voice over his shoulder. "Why are they looking for you?"

Loggie sheepishly grinned. "A hungry belly makes for slippery hands."

"You stole food?"

"It was only a loaf of bread. Carrots. A cucumber. Nothing more. Except three potatoes. And an onion."

Cormac frowned and steered the horse down a lane that would take them north, away from Belchap and closer to Starlight Ridge where Harmon of the Wood lived. It would take almost three weeks to find the wise wizard. In that time, he'd lose this trickster or convince him to go home.

"We have plenty of food," said Nimble. "We will share."

"Thank you," said Loggie. "That is mighty generous."

Cormac thought so, too, particularly since she had said *we*, not *I*, which meant she expected him to share his food, too. There were few days in this land when he had enough food to feed him for several days, and now he was expected to give it away to a stranger.

They travelled for two hours through lush forest. In some places, trees overhung the dirt roadway, creating patches of shade. Nimble was thankful she had a cloak to keep out the chill. This morning, she had wrapped it in a fashion to make it appear as a dress, one that kept in the heat and allowed free movement of her arms and legs. With a piece of thick leather, she secured it around her waist. The horse beneath her stopped, and she looked ahead to see what made Cormac halt.

"Dismount. We'll wear out the horse if we continue all day at this pace with us on its back." Once they got off, he did, then flipped the reins over the horse's head and led it along at a walking pace.

"Where does Harmon of the Wood live?" asked Nimble.

He shot her a quick glance, then returned his attention to the road. After a long moment, she asked again, and still he hesitated.

"Do you know?" she asked.

"Vaguely."

"That sounds like no," said Loggie.

"I know where in general. It's past Fields of Blue and through the Forest of Wild Lilies."

"Never heard of them."

"You've never been out of Village Doorock before now, so I'm not surprised."

"I read!"

"Congratulations. Do you read maps?"

Loggie fell silent except for a low grumble. Kicking a stone to the side of the dirt road, he shoved his hands into his large pockets.

"Do you read maps?" Nimble asked Cormac.

After stumbling over what looked like doubt, he spoke. "I've been to these places. I'm an explorer."

"Do you have a map?"

"I don't need one."

"So, no, you don't. Where is this Forest of Wild Lilies?"

"We must pass below The Dragon's Noggin' and cross The River of Great Turmoil and Fields of Blue, and then we'll enter the forest. Harmon is on the opposite edge."

"These names sound made up. Are they real?"

"Of course, they are."

She stared at him, trying to read his eyes. He looked away, took in a great breath and straightened his spine. The longer she stared, the pinker his neck became and the higher the colour rose into his cheeks. Why did he lie to her?

They walked in silence for more than an hour. Nimble was going to suggest riding again so they'd reach the next settlement before dark, which was only a few hours away, but a strange sound reached her ears, and she scanned the road ahead, looking for the animal that made it.

The trees and bushes grew closer to the road here, and the bend blocked her view of what lie ahead. A cautious whisper on the wind forced her ear up, and she listened for more from the forest fairy. Before another word was spoken, a shadow flashed from the bushes, and a thick club smashed against Cormac's chest and dropped him to his knees.

She leapt back, but a strong arm wrapped around her neck and picked her off the ground. Beating the arm with her fists and kicking her feet against the solid wall behind her didn't set her free. She struggled to gather breath and through watery eyes watched two large men beat Cormac with clubs. One leapt on top of him and secured his hands in front with cord. Loggie was secured in the same fashion, then the men looked at her.

"Grab her arms," ordered the bearded man, who looked vaguely familiar.

The man holding her tightened his grip, and another tied her hands together. Once secured, he threw her to the ground. She landed on her elbows in a cloud of dust. Choking on dirt, she gasped for breath.

"I'll teach you not to steal." The bearded man struck Cormac. Not hearing what he wanted, he hit him again and kicked him over to his back. Then he ripped off his boots and straddled him. He glared down at him and shoved his black leather bracer with steel studs under his chin and forced his head upward. "I'd kill you here, but I want to see you suffer in the Black Mines of Shep." He punched him, and Cormac spit in his face, which resulted in another punch. The man half stood, unbuckled Cormac's belt and ripped it from the pant loops. "If I tire of you before the mines, I'll hang you with this!"

Cormac's eyes bulged, and he lunged for the belt, but the bearded man kicked him to the ground. "Please! Please, don't take my belt! Anything. Not the belt."

The man laughed so hard, spit flew from his mouth. "A keepsake? From a lover? Something of value? Like my horse you stole?"

Cormac rose and dived for the belt dangling from the man's hands, but the man stepped aside, and he smashed into the ground. He rose and charged the man again, hitting him in the midsection and grasping the belt. Holding tightly to it, he didn't let go until the other three men beat him off.

Nimble watched curiously. The belt meant a lot to Cormac, or he wouldn't risk his life to retrieve it. The defeated expression on his face tugged at nerves in her chest. She'd never seen anyone fight for something as simple as a belt. Nor had she heard anyone beg and plead for such an item. It was as if they stole his child, his left leg, the last morsel of food that would sustain life.

The bearded man glared down at her, surveying her body as if it repulsed him. Lashing out, he grabbed the end of the leather securing her cloak and ripped it from her body. Then he yanked the cloak off her shoulders. When he recognised the long shirt she wore beneath it, he tried to wrench that from her body, too, but her hands were tied together. He shoved her to the ground, leaving her with only the shirt and short, sleeveless dress that left the lower half of her legs and feet exposed. "Dirty hauflin. This needs sanitizing to rid it of your germs."

In short order, her hands were secured to a long rope. Loggie, who cowered before the men, quietly allowed them to do the same to him. Defeated and laying on the ground in an awkward position, Cormac's hands were fastened to the end of the rope.

"From here, you march," said the bearded man. He secured the rope to the saddle of the horse Cormac owned, or had stolen, then mounted a second horse while holding the reins. "To the mines."

The man led the horse away, and Nimble lurched forward. She glanced back to see Cormac. He was dragged for several feet before he got his legs beneath him and staggered along blindly, stumbling here and there, being dragged again, then getting to his feet.

She turned forward to study the men. They were cruel. Hardened soldiers who gave no thought to their prisoners. This meant she didn't have to give them second thoughts either. The four men were much larger than her, even larger than Cormac. They were strong, wore a sword and dagger each, and carried leather pouches on their belts. Compared to the average person, they appeared to have everything they needed, including the confidence to capture three individuals and deliver them to their doom.

But everyone had a weakness. She just had to find theirs and exploit them. For the next three hours, she toddled along and focussed her attention on her captors. The bearded man's name was Clive. He was the leader, the one who gave the orders. So far, he had looked back at her only once. Instead, he watched the trail ahead and spoke to the men with him only when they spoke. Every few minutes, he adjusted his position in the saddle as if he had an injury he accommodated.

The man who rode beside him was Sandford. Smaller than Clive and clean-shaven, he looked over his shoulder every five minutes. Sometimes he stared at her, but mostly his eyes settled on Cormac. Of the four, he was the most talkative.

The two men leading the procession wore thinner beards than Clive. The blond one was Ralph. He had a wife who was to give birth soon, and he was anxious to return home. From his comments, he didn't want to be here but was forced to come by Clive.

The dark-haired man had yet to be named. He was full of curse words and a fondness for saying, "Get yourself into it, then get your own self out of it." He glanced at the prisoners a few times and when he did, the smirk on his face told Nimble he enjoyed what he saw.

By the time the sun was low in the sky and they stopped in a small clearing for the night, Nimble had decided she didn't like these men and would take measures into her own hands to part ways with them. It was a simple, obvious decision, but once made, it made the doing what had to be done easier.

A soft thud behind her made her turn. Cormac, exhausted from walking, injured from the beating and the multiple draggings at the end of the rope, had collapsed into the weeds. He stared forward, his eyes wide and glossy. Dried blood splattered his face and large wear marks grew from the edges of the rope around his wrists. If ever she'd seen a man ready to give up, it was him.

A thought from earlier in the day entered her mind. They had entered Belchap on a quest. Two quests. During the conversations, she'd learned he had saved her life. Her gratefulness for this act had been pushed to the back of her mind but now it stood brightly in the fading sun. Returning the favour was a must.

With the rope slack, she walked over and knelt next to his head. "We'll be okay," she whispered.

He stared up, his cracked and bleeding lips remained still.

She leant closer. "Don't lose hope."

He closed his eyes and pressed his cheek into the weeds.

She threw a glare at Clive, who secured the end of the rope around the thick trunk of a tree. For several long moments, he paid her no attention, but she continued to stare, sending anger in his direction. Then, as if feeling an itch he couldn't scratch, his eyes were drawn to her. He smirked and went to his horse. His indifference fuelled her anger, and she sat next to Cormac and schemed, all the while twisting her wrists in slow, short movements and fingering the loops of the rope securing her hands.

Loggie staggered over and plopped down beside her. "Do you know these men?" he whispered.

"No. You?"

"Never saw them before." He glanced at Cormac and not seeing a response, continued. "We've turned towards Village Doorock, so they are not from Belchap."

"In other words, you did not steal from them."

He nodded. "But from what they've said, you did, and him." He jerked his thumb in Cormac's direction.

"I don't know them."

"Shut up!" shouted Clive. "Basil, take this." He tossed a length of rope to the other man. "Secure their legs for the night."

Nimble sat up silently and allowed them to secure her legs at the ankles, watching the rope loop around, taking note of its weakness. In her mind, she retraced the route with the end of the rope.

Cormac kicked at them, and they fought to tie his feet together. Seeing the strength they put into it made her cringe. It was tied as tightly as they could get it, which meant the knot would be challenging to undo.

Loggie, on the other hand, sat quietly and let them complete the task without a word. His knot was tied as loosely as hers was.

Clive and his companions set up camp, ate without offering her food, then bedded down for the night. She lay down as if to sleep, but she didn't close her eyes. In the dim light, she waited. Clive took the first watch. Three hours later, he woke Ralph. Perfect.

Her hands already free, she tucked her knees into her chest and worked to loosen knots around her ankles. Ralph rested against a tree trunk, watching the dirt road in the direction they travelled. Occasionally, he glanced to where they had come, cast a lazy eye on the prisoners, then returned his gaze to some point in the distance. His head slowly relaxed against the trunk, and she saw his eyelids sag into sleep position.

"A moment more," whispered a sweet voice in Nimble's ear.

She smiled, sensing the forest fairy nearby. The cord and rope removed from her limbs, she poised her muscles for movement and chartered her route visually. She glanced over her shoulder at Cormac, who stared ahead, his expression blank, his body still. Loggie rested a few feet away, asleep.

When the whisper came, she slowly turned, put her finger to her lips and hushed Cormac. His eyes widened and he went to sit up, but she stopped him. "Don't move," she whispered so low, she feared he didn't hear it.

Then she was up, moving slowly, silently, deliberately. Creeping around the sleeping men, she chose her targets, taking their boots they had removed to air dry, a sharp knife and Cormac's belt. He wouldn't leave without it, and she wasn't risking his clumsy body waking them. She glided to the horses, who still wore their saddles. She tightened the cinches, replaced the bridles with reins, then secured the boots to two of the horses. While tying them, she felt an unusual bulge in one of the boots. Reaching inside, she found a slim pocket. Inside was a strange key. She slipped it into her pocket and returned to Cormac and Loggie.

Cormac reached for the belt and once in his hands, he held it to his chest. In the low light of the rising crescent moon, she thought she saw tears. How an object as plain as that well-worn belt could invoke these emotions was a mystery to her.

Working silently, she cut the cord securing his wrists, then worked on the thicker rope binding his feet. Once done, she put her hand over Loggie's mouth and woke him as gently as she could. He still woke with a start, making more noise than she hoped and when he opened his mouth to speak, she silenced him by putting her finger to her lips.

"Hurry," whispered the wind.

Crouching low, she led them to the horses. As soon as they guided the mounts away from the hitching post, one neighed. Another nickered. Casting a quick glance at Ralph, she found him still, but movement around the firepit that had long burnt out of fuel caught her eye. She climbed into the saddle and held tightly to a horse with no rider. Loggie also led an empty horse with boots tied to the saddle, leaving the dreadful men from Dunvain Downs without transportation and footwear.

"Get up!" shouted Basil. He leapt to his feet and drew his sword.

This stirred the other men, who followed his order and charged at her with hatred in their eyes.

She kicked the horse beneath her and trotted onto the road. Once on an even surface, she encouraged the horse to run faster. Between the many sounds of hoofbeats pounding the dirt, she heard curse words and threats shouted at her. The voices faded into the night, and she focussed on putting distance between her and those horrible men. Glancing over her shoulder, she saw Cormac and Loggie keeping pace. She did not know where she was going. It didn't matter. It never had. Wherever the wind, her feet and the fairies took her was where she was meant to be.

The cool wind whipping her skin chilled her bones, and she recalled the familiar feeling. More than an hour later, Cormac shouted to halt, and when she brought the horse to a stop, she dug into one of the saddlebags, found the cloak and pulled it on. Its warmth wrapped around her like loving arms, calming her nerves as well as the goosebumps.

Cormac leapt into the bushes, then emerged carrying his boots. After slipping them on, he removed the henchmen's boots and threw them into the bushes, where they disappeared from sight.

"Do you know this area?" asked Nimble.

"Vaguely," said Cormac.

"Do you know where we go from here?"

"Yes."

"Lead." She guided her horse to the side and let him pass.

Loggie came alongside her. "Not expected," he said, out of breath. "I cannot go home. They will find me. Hang me."

"I won't let that happen," she said.

"You cannot stop them."

"As long as you're with me, I can." She forced a smile but even in the dim light, she saw the worry on his face. "We'll fix this, one way or another." She turned and followed Cormac into the night. She didn't know how, but she'd remove the threat to Loggie's life. He was supposed to be a happy soul, playing music for the king, not a fugitive on the run on a stolen horse.

5

Rosalind, That Girl I Love

THE NEW DAY'S sunshine spilling over the horizon blinded Cormac with its brilliance. His tired eyes burnt from lack of sleep and high emotions. Feeling the weariness reach deep into his bones, he searched for a place to rest. The desperation that had drained his energy yesterday had disappeared in the escape but now, his body craved sleep. To cover their trail, they had passed silently through a small village and had travelled two hours more before he even considered stopping. While they had left the men from Dunvain Downs with no means of quick travel, his mind imagined every possibility that would put them on their trail and have them overrun them before dawn. It didn't matter how farfetched, in his mind, they were only five minutes behind him.

"There." Nimble pointed to a narrow trail that ran alongside a river. "Let's follow it a half mile, then rest. They won't look for us there."

He crossed the narrow bridge and steered his horse onto the trail, dragging the riderless horse behind him. In other circumstances, he'd have released the horse, gave it to someone or sold it, but he didn't want to leave behind a trail for the men to follow. Since finding his boots, he'd taken a right at a fork in the road, then continued past a turn-off to the left, and took the road to the right a mile later. Only when he got on this road did his heart stop pounding in his ears. It would take another day of travel before his hands stopped shaking and that irritating urgency in his throat that made him jump at every unusual sound to dissipate. The incessive urge to look over his shoulder would last much longer.

The winding path took them away from the river and through dark shadows beneath evergreen trees. He glanced back, saw Nimble and Loggie and no one following, then turned ahead to scan the trail from one side to the other, looking for movement, listening for sounds that belonged to humans hiding in bushes ready to ambush him. His nerves vibrated, and his heart once again boomed in his ears. Sweaty hands gripped the reins, and he clenched them into fists, preparing to fight.

Several hundred feet later, the path returned to the river, and the glare off the water made him look away and close one eye for relief. A little farther, and he'd stop. He wouldn't sleep, but he'd stop. What was he thinking? He had to sleep. Could sleep. Last night, he feared sleep more than the mines the men threatened to deliver him to. He felt the comfort of the belt around his waist and touched it with his open hand. It secured his pants but more importantly, it secured his memories. Without it, he'd be like Nimble, waking each morning to start anew.

"Here."

He turned to Nimble's voice. "A little farther. Up at that bend."

She stretched her neck to see around him. "Okay. No farther."

They traversed the remaining 600 hundred feet, and he stopped in a small, grassy clearing that provided an excellent view of the path they had travelled to reach it. He released the reins, put his weight in the stirrup and swung his leg over the rump of the horse. When he hit the ground, pain shot through his body, bringing him to his knees. He gasped for breath and absorbed the aches surging through him. Riding had numbed the injuries but now, they were wide awake and reminding him of the beatings he'd taken and the falls while being dragged behind the horse.

"Let me help." Nimble grasped his arm. "Lay down over here."

He rose on shaky legs and let her lead him to a grassy bank. Easing himself onto the ground, the bruises screamed for attention, and he groaned with tears welling in his eyes.

"I'll see if there's a blanket." Nimble searched the saddlebags and came up with a woollen blanket, which she spread over him. Then she took a thick shirt she'd found, folded it and tucked it beneath his head. "It won't take away the pain, but you'll be more comfortable."

"Whatever drove those men, they indeed didn't like you," said Loggie, settling next to him. "You'd think they'd be happy to have recovered their horse unharmed."

Cormac half chuckled. "I'm surprised they went through all this trouble to find it."

"Maybe it's special to him, like your belt is to you." Nimble cut a thick slice of bread and handed it to him.

"Maybe." He bit into the bread, then took a drink of water. "We'll sleep here until a few hours before sunset, then start out again."

"Where will we go?" asked Loggie, taking a bite of bread.

"Starlight Ridge. This road will lead us there. It will take three weeks."

"That's away from Dunvain Downs and those men, right?" asked Nimble.

"In the opposite direction of that town."

"Good. I don't ever want to go back there."

"Neither do I." He finished the bread, took another drink of water, then lay back. He closed his eyes to ease the sting, and his mind fell into the back of his head and darkness overtook him.

Waking with a start, he stared at the sun glistening on the gently flowing water. A blue heron waded along the opposite shore, its long legs easily keeping its body above the water. A small swarm of insects followed it. Beside him, Nimble slept in a ball, curled up in the cloak Clive had earlier ripped from her body. She slumbered as if she had not a care in the world. A gentle smile caressed her lips, suggesting she was dreaming a wonderful dream.

Loggie slept on the other side of her. Sprawled on his back, his arms out to the side, he looked like he had collapsed and fallen fast asleep upon landing.

The horses grazed nearby, one drinking water from the stream. A bird in a tree sang a sweet song, and he listened. Not many birds sang in this world, so this one stood out. Something zipped by quickly, and he sat up, looking to where it went. He stared at the bushes and listened for several minutes. Whatever it was didn't reappear before Nimble unfurled and stretched her limbs. When she opened her eyes and saw him, her blank stare revealed another new day in her life had begun.

"I'd say good morning, Nimble, but it's late afternoon." He wiped sleep from his eyes and cringed from hitting the cut on his brow. The rest of his injuries cried out for attention, and he settled his nerves to reduce it to a dull roar.

"Where are we?" She sat up and gazed upon the water.

"I'd say we're near Maisa Ridge." He thought about the route they'd taken. Escaping and putting as much distance between him and the men from Dunvain Downs had been the objective, not running to a certain location.

"Is that a village?"

"Small town. We won't be staying. Only passing through."

She looked him up and down with a curious eye. "Did you... Who did this to you?" She glanced at Loggie, who stirred.

"A couple of bad guys. I'll be okay." He rose slowly and groaned from the pain in his midsection. The clubs had done a good job at making bruises deep inside. He imaged a few ribs got bruised, hopefully not broken. Staggering to the water's edge, he fell to his knees and splashed water on his face. The coolness awakened his senses further, and he plunged he face into the stream. Coming up, he swept back his hair and shivered. All he wanted to do was lay back, rest, heal, but he had to keep moving. With luck, he'd be home in three weeks.

Home. It had been a place he'd longed to escape from. Now, he only wanted to feel the safety a civilized society could offer. Thoughts about what he might return to flooded his mind for the millionth time since he realised years ago he couldn't go home the same way he had departed. Would he arrive in his world at the same spot, the same time he had left? Would he see his parents and they not know he'd been gone for more than five years? Or would they have searched for him, wondering all this time if he had run away or was killed, his body dumped in a place no one found? Would Clarice still look like she had on the night of graduation, her blonde hair pulled up in a bun, ringlets framing her face and that blue satin dress highlighting her amazing body, or would she have mourned his mysterious disappearance, moved on, married and have children?

It seemed impossible for him to have missed the past five years with his family and friends. If he had, it would be... He thought of the year he'd left. It felt like a century ago. If time had passed equally there as it had here, it would be early winter 1992. Maybe even January of 1993. He wondered if people were still dancing to *Eye of the Tiger* and watching *MacGyver*.

The magic paper. He had forgotten about it. Harmon had given him a piece the size of a playing card and told him when another from his world was found to send him a message using it. The spell to return him to his world took time to prepare, and Harmon wanted to have it ready for when he arrived. Harmon asked for only a few details: the person's name, their race and how long it would be until they arrived at Starlight Ridge. Cormac could record the message with any small stick and send it by burning it.

Loggie knelt at the stream, startling him from his thoughts. He dunked his face into the water, shook it, then turned to him. "Are we going to ride all night?"

"Just 'til midnight. Sleep for a few hours and get on the road at dawn."

"That's a sound plan. Those men won't find us. We've come too far, taken too many turns."

"I like your thinking. But just to make sure, we won't leave an obvious trail." He glanced at the horses. It was annoying to drag them along, but he'd keep them close until he was several days away from here.

After eating from what was found in the saddlebags, they mounted and retraced the path to the road. Cormac surveyed the road in both directions to guarantee it was empty of travellers, then emerged. He set a quick pace to ensure anyone travelling behind him wouldn't overrun him. The pain in his side and lower back begged him to go slower and after an hour of steady riding, he submitted. By this time, the subtle aches had turned into throbbing agony, and he paced himself.

When the first dwellings of Maisa Ridge came into view 30 minutes later, his body felt like it was on fire. He tried to sit still, absorb the pain and keep his thoughts straight, but all his attention was on fighting to stay in the saddle. Reaching the middle of town, he heard Nimble speak but couldn't make out the words. She rode in front of him and forced his horse to stop.

"I've been here before," she said. "And I think there's an inn a short distance down that lane."

"So." He gritted his teeth.

"We're spending the night there."

He stiffened and pain shot through his back. "We can't," he gasped.

"You're lucky you made it this far. Another hour, and you'll be on the ground. We must stop."

He wanted to argue that fact, but she was right.

"Lead the way," said Loggie, who was guiding the second riderless horse.

"Try to stay in the saddle until we get there." Nimble took over the lead and directed them down a lane that bustled with early evening activity.

Maisa Ridge was a medium size town. Maybe 5,000 people lived here. There was no castle, and the governing forces lived in the centre of town in a fort similar to what he'd seen in old western films. From his few visits, the town folk and the constables who kept law and order were a friendly bunch.

Nimble took the second side street and directed them to a building with a large sign: *Glumock's Tavern and Inn.* He remembered seeing the business while passing through. Recalling the many campaigns he'd played with his friends, he wondered what the inside looked like. Probably smoky with a roaring fireplace and shadowy areas where mysterious strangers hung out. This was a point in the game when they were usually sent on all-night adventures where they'd find gold coins, a magical item or clues to search for treasure. He wasn't up for any of that, so he'd avoid the tavern, lock his window and door, and sleep well.

"Over here." Nimble directed them towards stable doors. "You got room for horses?" she asked the man scooping up horse droppings from the front entrance.

"Indeed," he said with a thick accent. Sparkle danced in his eyes while watching her. "Won't last, Missy. Fills up quickly as darkness 'proaches." He scratched his short beard with rough hands.

"Great." She dismounted and led the two horses inside.

"Whatcha needin' two fo' this time?"

Nimble hesitated, glanced at Cormac, then spoke before he had a chance. "You see, our two friends..." She bowed her head and spoke in a sad voice. "They didn't make it. We're returning their horses to their families."

The man grunted and raked his eyes over Cormac. "Should travel with better company," he mumbled, then shuffled into the stable. "Got the perfect spot for 'em. Keep safe, I will."

"Thank you, kind sir." She tossed a shallow smirk at Cormac and followed the man inside.

Cormac hesitated to dismount. He feared he was too weak to stand. "Loggie." He motioned for him to come close. "Give me a hand, will you?"

Loggie held the reins of both his horses in one hand and reached out to support Cormac's arm. He snatched him quickly and tried to hold onto him but with only one hand, his attempt failed and Cormac collapsed. He swayed on his knees, trying to regain his balance. This was the worst beating he'd taken in his life. It'd take weeks to heal.

"Boy, take this hoss," said the stable keeper, who returned with a boy no older than 14 and directed him to take Cormac's horse. "Give me you arm." He drew Cormac's arm over his shoulder and heaved him up.

Cormac groaned from the sudden jolt of pain and took short breaths to absorb it. "Thank you."

"Just lookin' out for like-minded folk." He directed him to a bench inside the stable. "Sit here, and you friends will get you inside when they ready."

"Thanks again." He rested against the wall and relaxed his muscles. A good night's sleep on a soft bed would do wonders for his body. He closed his eyes and listened to the activity in the stable: the squeak of leather straps unfastening, the jingle of moving saddles, the crispness of brushes stroking horses and the soft thud of hooves hitting the floor after cleaning. If he was horizontal, he'd be asleep, but he kept his senses about him, waiting for Nimble and Loggie to return. Right now, he didn't care if he ate. He only wanted sleep. His head tilted to the side, and he felt the weight of life drag him into darkness. His eyes rolled back into his head and...

Nimble handed the server a shiny coin. Loggie called it a copper piece. She'd found it and a small collection of others in a pouch in one of the saddlebags. These coins, which Loggie helped her sort out the value, paid for their room, the stable keep of the horses and her and Loggie's meal at the tavern. Cormac was sleeping in their room, having been carried there in a half-awake state by Loggie and Matthew, the stable hand. While his condition played on her mind, she'd seen men in worse condition recover. Who and where those men were, she didn't know. The important fact was, they lived to run again.

"How long have you known Cormac?" Loggie sat on the opposite side of the thick wooden table, relaxing on the bench like he was on tour of a spectacular city. The two candles in thick pottery holders lighting their space illuminated his pale blue eyes and sharp cheek bones.

She shrugged. "I suppose as long as I've known you."

He hmphed. "I should have guessed. Do you trust him?"

This question bounced around inside her brain for a moment. Did she? Her memory didn't offer any answers, so she dug deeper, into her gut where most of her decisions were made. "Yes."

"He said he met you in the prison of Dunvain Downs. Do you remember being there?"

She shook her head. "What was I doing there?"

"I don't know." He sat up, leant across the table and became serious. "I think someone has put a spell on you."

She baulked. "What kind?"

"One that steals your memory."

She searched the surface of the table, looking for clues. The dark wood held many marks from past patrons, some more harsh than others on its surface. Near the wall, on the edge of the candles' glow, someone had carved *AJ* and *Peg*, separated with a heart. Another carving stated *Jenna was here*. "Who would do such a thing?"

"Someone who doesn't like you?"

She grimaced. "But why? What good would it do them?"

"It might bring them pleasure, thinking you can't take joy in what you've done or cherish the people important to you."

"It is odd I do not remember yesterday. Nor the day before." She thought hard. "I think I do this often. Sometimes I remember things. Smells. Faces. But then the memory evaporates. Or I can't see it clearly. Sometimes all that is left are feelings felt in the memory."

"We must find a paladin."

"What is that?"

"A great healer. They have sworn an oath to heal those in need. While they can turn away those who do evil, they cannot refuse a fair soul like you. If you are under a spell, they can remove it. Set you free."

She straightened her spine and leant closer to him. "Where do I find one?"

"That's the problem. They seldom stay in one spot. They're always on noble quests."

"In general, where are they? A castle? A village?"

"Anywhere."

"In this tavern?" She scanned the many faces in the dimly-lit room and tried to imagine what a paladin looked like. Were they old? Young? Did they wear a uniform? A sword? Specific armour?

"Doesn't look like one is here," said Loggie. "Though some wear disguises to blend in."

She frowned. "How will we find one then? Put up a sign: Paladin Wanted?"

"We ask around discreetly."

The server came to their table with plates of food. After setting them on the table, she asked, "Anything else?"

"Yes," whispered Nimble. "Do you know a paladin?"

Surprise ripened on the servant's face. "They generally don't want to be known. And I'm happy to oblige."

She leant forward and whispered, "I'd be happy to keep their identity secret."

"That which is unknown is easy to keep secret." She turned and walked away.

"That wasn't helpful at all." She stabbed a carrot with her fork. As she chewed, she double-checked the people in the tavern. If a paladin was here, what would he look like? Through the thin veil of smoke floating in the air from the lit pipes and the roaring fireplace, she spotted a man sitting alone in the corner, off to the right of the hearth. The mysterious man wore a short cloak, dark clothing and no hat. From beneath the edge of the cloak, a short sword poked out. "What about him? Does he look like a..." she leant close and whispered, "a paladin?"

Loggie cast his gaze in the man's direction. "No. He looks like a criminal."

Nimble sat back and continued to eat. The warm food tasted so good that for several moments, she forgot about what they were talking about and concentrated on eating. The slice of beef was juicy and easily cut. If she had tasted better meat, she didn't remember when. The perfect mixture of salt, pepper and some sort of green spice was delicious on the cubed potatoes that tasted like they had been fried, not boiled. Poking the last green pea and putting it into her mouth, she put down the fork and relaxed. That was the best meal ever. She lifted the mug of wine to her lips. Even that tasted amazing.

"The crowd is growing," said Loggie. "The stable hand wasn't wrong. If half these people are spending the night and came on horseback, the stable will be overflowing." He pushed his empty plate aside, took a long drink of ale and smacked his lips. "This gives me an idea." He pulled his cloth shoulder sack towards him, untied the string holding it closed and withdrew a three-stringed instrument.

"What's that?" asked Nimble, taking another drink of wine. It was fruity. The one she had before the meal tasted sweet, but this one was smooth.

"A rebec." He smiled. "You play? Oh, let me guess." He put up his finger. "You do, but not well."

"How do you know?"

"I've heard you play."

It felt weird that he knew more about her than she did. If a spell had been cast upon her, she needed it gone. She looked back to the corner where the mysterious man sat. He was still there, nursing a drink after his meal. On the table open in front of him was a small book. This held his attention even when a group of young men in the centre of the room got rowdy.

Loggie balanced the instrument on his shoulder and held it there with his chin. He dragged the stick with the string on it across the three strings of the instrument and a lovely sound filled the air. He dragged the stick back and forth, creating a rhythm. He adjusted one string, then repeated the rhythm. Satisfied with the sound, he whispered, "Let's see how generous this crowd is."

He downed his ale in one gulp, went to a small platform near the fireplace and placed the empty mug before him. It was only about two feet square and a foot high, but it gave him enough room to stand and be seen by patrons. Without a word, he played a lively tune. Several of the rowdy men stomped their feet and clapped their hands. The barkeep grinned and put a bounce in his step while he served the next customer.

Nimble looked towards the mysterious man in the corner. His attention had been stolen from his book, and he stared at Loggie, brow bent as if he tried to figure out what he was doing. Casting a quick gaze around the tavern, she thought he was looking for someone until his eyes locked with hers. Shock, or was it curiosity, washed over him, then he drew his attention back to his book.

She stared until the song ended, but he kept his attention on the pages. Given the dim light, if he surveyed the room through peripheral vision, she couldn't tell.

Three of the rowdy men jumped up and dropped coins into the empty ale mug and encouraged Loggie to play another. He did, and for the next 30 minutes, he played, sang and danced on his tiny stage. When he played *Rosalind, That Girl I Love*, an odd feeling stirred in her gut. Whether it was hearing the name he called her or the familiarity of the rhythm that drew her to it, she didn't know. Several patrons dropped coins into his mug. Nimble had lost count around 12. All the while, the mysterious man kept his eyes on the book.

"Thank you, kind gentlemen and ladies." Loggie bowed and came up with the mug. "I shall drink to you this night."

The crowd cheered, stomped their feet and clapped. Loggie left the stage, grinning and bowing a few more times. "Thank you. You are too kind." He plopped onto the bench, and the server who had been at their table earlier arrived with a mug of ale.

"On the house," she said. "For the lovely entertainment."

"Thank you. It will quench my thirst." She walked away, and he turned to Nimble. "This is better than street performing. I am awarded coins, not sassy remarks." He poured the coins onto the table and counted them. "Twenty-three coppers. I hope there is a tavern at the next town we visit."

"At this rate, you'll be rich in no time."

He laughed. "I've no desire to be rich in money. Love is what I desire."

"Who do you expect to love?"

"I've not yet found the girl, but I will. I know it is not you."

Her eyes widened. "Me? I... Have I said something?"

"More of what you didn't say. We are friends."

"Good friends."

"Yes. The best." He took a long drink of ale and smacked his lips. "Yesterday, I feared for my life. Today, I rejoice in it."

"Remind me of this evening tomorrow. It is a good memory."

"Done." He emptied his mug. "We should return to our room. Cormac has a four-hour head start. He'll rise and find us in dreamland

and smelling of alcohol. He'll think we have been spirited away." He secured the rebec in the sack and tied the string.

Nimble emptied her mug, set it on the table and prepared to rise. That's when she noticed the mysterious man gone. She scanned the tavern. He wasn't here. Darn! She wanted to see where he went, and now the opportunity to learn if he was a paladin was gone.

She followed Loggie from the tavern and into the hall. They ascended a flight of stairs and began down a long hallway lit with lanterns at both ends. Between the two beacons of light was thick shadow. Hearing footsteps behind her, she didn't know what was happening until Loggie crashed into the wall and collapsed onto the floor. A dark figure rushed by her. It leapt out the window at the end of the hall.

"Cursed!" Loggie pushed himself up and chased after him. "He's got my coins!"

Nimble raced to keep up. Outside the window, the thief had jumped onto a narrow landing with steps leading to the ground. Loggie was already halfway down, so she leapt onto the platform and flew down the stairs. For several minutes, they weaved through one alley after another, dashing from one shadow to the next.

She heard voices up ahead and rounding a corner, she saw an odd sight. The thief they were chasing fell when he crashed into two men who stood close together. One of those men was the mysterious character from the tavern. He was still on his feet, but the one with him had fallen with the thief.

Loggie came to an abrupt stop. "He's got my—"

The thief grabbed the pouch he'd dropped in the fall, jumped to his feet and sped off. Loggie pursued him. The fallen man grabbed the other sack on the ground, gave the mysterious man a haunted face, then scrambled to his feet. His sack sounded like it contained coins.

The mysterious man growled, revealing a thin scar on his cheek. He and his friend set out after Loggie and the thief. Nimble followed but didn't get too close to the strangers. Not knowing their intentions caused concern for her and Loggie's well-being. The thief deserved what he got, but they were innocent bystanders wanting only to regain what had been taken from them.

Many turns later, Loggie tackled the thief and shoved him into a wall. They scuffled until the mysterious man tapped the thief on the shoulder with his sword.

"Get up!" he commanded.

Loggie scooted aside, away from the sword and put up his hands. "I want only my coins. He stole them."

"They're here." The other man tossed the sack, and Loggie caught it awkwardly. "Now get. We'll deal with this rogue."

"As you ask." Loggie got to his feet and stumbled towards Nimble. "I say we leave him to his fate."

"Are you going to kill him?" she asked.

The mysterious man scowled at her. "Not unless he doesn't cooperate."

"Come on," whispered Loggie, pulling her with him. "This isn't our fight."

"Give me the sack," the man held the sword up to the thief in a threatening manner.

"Oh, this?" He chuckled uneasily. "Didn't know it was yours." He tossed the sack to him. "Sorries all around. My mistake. An off night."

"Off?" said Loggie. "In general, you succeed in stealing?"

The thief chuckled again and inched his body away from the group. Once he felt secure, he slowly rose. "I'm just a poor boy, looking for food. So hungry." He put his hand over his stomach.

"You don't look under fed," said Nimble. "You're just a lying, no good thief. An incompetent one at that."

The mysterious man shot her a glance, a smirk developing on his face. He turned back to the thief. "Go home. Thank the stars you did not wrestle with someone out for blood."

"This could have been different if you were dealing with killers," shot Nimble. "But we're good folk."

Again, the mysterious man shot her a look.

The thief scurried into the shadows and disappeared, leaving her and Loggie with two armed strangers. "That's our cue to leave, too," she said, stepping back and letting Loggie pull her away. "But before we go." She slowed her feet. "By any chance, are you a paladin?"

The mysterious man chuckled. "Is that what you seek?"

"Yes. Are you one?"

"No. Why do you need one?"

"Don't answer that," whispered Loggie.

"I've a problem I need solving," she said.

"Then you need an assassin, not a paladin."

"Killing someone is not going to remove the spell cast upon me."

"Sure, it will. When the spell caster dies, all his spells go with him."

"Really?" She turned to Loggie. "Did you know that?" He shook his head, and she continued. "But there are other ways to remove a spell, right?"

"What spell has been cast?" When he didn't get an immediate answer, he said, "Obviously, not a hag spell. Perhaps a spell that makes you cold."

She glanced at the layers of clothing she wore. At the moment, she felt warm, but that was only because of the dress, long shirt and cloak, and the fact she'd been running. "Possibly. Do you know of a paladin who could help?"

The mysterious man looked to his younger friend, a young man no older than Cormac, one who had shoulder length, light-coloured hair. He was thin for human. Maybe he wasn't human.

"Do you know of a paladin travelling the area?" he asked while tucking the sack he'd taken from the thief inside his cloak.

"Several, but they've no time for a tavern wench."

"I am not a tavern wench no more than you are a great wizard." She crossed her arms and fought the tug on her sleeve by Loggie, who tried to get her to walk away.

"I do not strive to be a great wizard." He mimicked her and crossed his arms. "I saw you in the tavern. Enjoying wine and music."

"You have low expectations for a tavern wench."

"Seen one, seen them all."

"I think the same of fools."

The mysterious man chuckled. "While I enjoy watching you take down young men with your wit, I've business to complete this night. If I meet a paladin, I'll alert him to your cause. Now go."

"I agree," said Loggie, pulling harder on her arm. "We bid you good evening and fair transactions."

"We'll meet again." She was unsure of why she said that, but something in her gut told her she would.

"That's what you always say." The man sheathed his sword and directed the man he was with down an adjacent alley.

Loggie pulled her with him. "You've met him before?" he whispered.

"Apparently." She followed him down the alley and onto the street. Turning right, she didn't recognise any of the shops. They'd run a fair distance, in and off streets, in and out of alleyways. Searching for familiarity, she found herself lost.

"This way," said Loggie, turning down an adjacent street.

"Are you sure?"

"No, but we'll see where it takes us."

A half hour later, she was still searching for *Glumock's Tavern and Inn* and wondering if she should ask the two men leaning against the wall near a shoe shop that had closed hours ago.

"No," said Loggie.

"I didn't say anything."

"I saw it in your eyes. I'm sure we're getting closer."

"Hey," she shouted to the two men. "Is this the way to Glumock's Tavern?"

"That street." One of the men pointed to a street that went in the opposite direction.

"Thanks." She walked towards it. "See. Most people can be trusted. They're not all bad."

"You have a lot to learn."

"I learn it. I forget it," she mumbled. "I'm tired of not knowing my name."

"It's Rosalind."

She frowned at him. "Why do you say that?"

"I see it in your eyes when I say it. Our names are ingrained deep in our brains at a young age. When we hear it, it triggers a response."

"I suppose. It does attract me."

"All I know is your name isn't Nimble." He pulled her along and marched towards the tavern.

6

Elvesnes

BRIGHT RAYS OF light shone through the windows of Glumock's Tavern illuminating the spacious room. The modest fire in the fireplace worked to remove the chill of early morning, but Cormac felt the cold and buttoned his thick vest. Scanning the room, he took note of the faces. They were mostly middle-aged men. Travellers, who stopped for the night. A few sat with women, but the majority of the 20 or so patrons sat alone.

The server brought his meal and set it in front of him. She also delivered Nimble's and Loggie's breakfast. Nimble gave the server three copper coins and thanked her for the delivery.

Steam from the hot meal filled his senses. Hot meals were rare and something to savour. Most of his food consisted of tough bread and cold fruits, vegetables and berries. No meat. With no means to build a fire nor a pan to heat food, the only time he ate a hot meal was when he had something valuable to trade or a few coins to buy it at a market, which didn't happen that often.

The hot aromas made him hungrier. Just before falling asleep in the stable yesterday, his stomach had sent a message to eat, but he hadn't acknowledged it. After his long sleep, food consumed his thoughts, and he dug in. The tavern occupants, Nimble and Loggie were quiet this morning. He imaged it was a different scene last night but since his travelling companions appeared well, there was no overnight campa— He looked closer at Loggie across the table. A green and blue bruise below his eye that hadn't been there yesterday coloured his skin.

"Anything happen last night?" he asked.

"Nothing," said Nimble, who had sandwiched egg and bacon between two slices of thick toast and prepared to take a bite.

"Loggie?"

He shrugged. "Nothing unusual."

He didn't believe him. It didn't matter. They were safe, no major injuries resulted in whatever happened, and they'd leave Maisa Ridge as soon as they ate and saddled the horses. He enjoyed his breakfast in peace with the sounds of silverware clanking against pottery and quiet chatter, then they gathered their gear and walked to the stable. Along the way, a man bumped into Nimble, and both fell to the ground and scrambled to rise.

"Sorry. So sorry. Half asleep," the young man mumbled, head down with his hood pulled half over his face. "Late night. Too much ale." He shuffled off and disappeared around the building.

Nimble brushed off the dirt and picked up the saddlebag and sack she'd dropped in the collision.

When Cormac turned to continue to the stable, he caught sight of Loggie. The man's face twisted in confusion, and he stared after the stranger as if trying to solve a mystery. Loggie glanced at Nimble, then back to the spot where the man had disappeared.

"Know him?" asked Cormac.

Loggie pulled his attention from the spot and stared at him for a moment before answering. "No." He didn't sound confident.

They continued to the stable and within the hour were riding out of Maisa Ridge and heading north, where they'd encounter a crossroad ten miles from town that led west towards Starlight Ridge. Cormac's body felt better today, but the bruises reminded him not to do anything too physical or move in certain positions, or pain would be his reward. Switching his mind from the town, he scanned the area ahead for travellers and looked over his shoulder for them. Specifically, he searched for the four men who hunted him.

Between him and the crossroads, he passed more than a dozen people. Some on horseback, two on a wagon and the rest on foot. They were the usual travellers he'd seen a thousand times while he journeyed this fantasy land. He seldom spoke to them and if he did, it was a simple, "Good day," or "Hey." Their faces went by without registering. He forgot them as quickly as they travelled out of sight. When he'd first arrived in this realm, he made an effort to befriend people, but it didn't last. Now, he wasn't interested in knowing anyone. He only wanted to go home.

Nimble was another matter. She'd let the first lone rider pass without a word, but when the couple on the wagon said good morning, she broke into a full conversation. She asked where they were coming from, where they were going and the conditions of the road ahead. When she started telling them from where she travelled, he intervened.

"Is that rain?" he said, cutting her off mid-sentence. "Those clouds are turning dark." He looked at the man at the reins. "Did you encounter rain?"

"A spell late yestermorn," the man said. "None since, and I hope not 'til we reach Maisa Ridge and find cover."

"We'll delay you no further then in case they're rain clouds. Safe travels." He directed his horse to a trot and once the wagon was out of ear shot, he spoke to Nimble. "Don't talk to people. They'll remember you and where you're going."

"So."

"So?" He glared at her. "What if they meet Clive and his men. They'll tell him where they saw us."

"And Clive is?"

"Dangerous."

"He's not wrong, Rosalind," said Loggie. "Let's smile and wave and keep going next time we see someone."

"Good idea," said Cormac. Every traveller they met after that was greeted in that manner: a smile, wave and *a good day.*

At the crossroads, he steered his horse west, and Nimble and Loggie followed in silence. They were told the route before leaving Maisa Ridge. Nothing more needed to be said. If memory served him, they wouldn't reach the next village until overmorrow, which meant camping in the woods for two nights. Now that they had coins and he had experienced the safety of an inn and the hot meal to break the fast, he unwillingly looked forward to sleeping in a bed beneath a solid roof. His brain told him to forget the idea, but his body said otherwise.

He didn't know the exact route to Starlight Ridge and Harmon of the Wood, but he knew the general area. He'd been there only once and that was more than four years ago.

The days and nights passed quietly, and he rode past the sign to Romarin in mid-morning. The usual light grey clouds had turned darker and while he considered stopping in case they opened up, he'd ride on and put up with the rain. By the time they entered the core of the village, it was drizzling. Nimble wore the only cloak and given her attire, she needed it more than he did. This left him with nothing to keep him dry.

"An inn," suggested Loggie. "With a tavern."

"Why a tavern?" he asked.

"Profitable."

"Dangerous. We won't be stopping."

"But the rain."

"We ain't made of sugar."

"What's the hurry," asked Nimble. "I agree with Loggie. Better to be under a roof than sleeping in a puddle tonight."

He was about to speak when lightning lit up the sky. It wasn't safe to ride in a thunder storm.

"That settles it," said Loggie. "Rosalind and I are getting a room. If you want to continue, do so. We'll catch up tomorrow. Or maybe we'll take our own path. I have no interest in seeing this Harmon of the Wood. He's your friend, not mine."

He cursed under this breath. He couldn't make them come with him. The only thing binding him and Loggie was Nimble, and she had the freedom to go wherever she wanted. Telling Loggie to mess off and kidnapping Nimble was not in his plans. In his mind, he imagined her coming with him without fuss, yet he had to get rid of Loggie to do that.

"Excuse me, sir," said Nimble to a man passing by. "Is there an inn with a tavern in the village?"

"Three."

"Can you direct me to the mid-range priced one?"

He grinned. "That would be Blue Dragon Keep." He pointed ahead on the road. "Up there. Past two lanes. Take a right; it's opposite Norn Sanctuary."

"Interesting," she said. "A tavern and sanctuary together. One can rely on the other for business."

He chuckled. "It is what we believe."

Cormac steered his horse along the street and took the third lane on the right. It was lined with two-storey shops. The standard for most of this land. Businesses on the bottom; living quarters on the top. It was all so typical. The structures were the same just like the new subdivisions being built where he came from. Every house had the same design. So what if they were different colours. Walk in one, he walked in them all. There was nothing architecturally interesting about any of them. Nothing magical. Nothing special. That monotony was repeated here.

"A music shop," said Nimble. "Let's visit it later."

"Yes," said Loggie. "I would love to."

"A magic wand shop?" Her voice rose. "Incredible. Lucinda's Enchanted Wands. Let's go there, too! We'll see what they have besides wands."

Cormac stared at the shop. He'd never seen a magic wand shop. He hadn't even seen a magic shop. A wooden sign with an image of a caldron, a cat and stars swayed in the breeze above the door. The edges of the large picture window had been painted with lines swirling around the moon, the sun and stars. Beneath the darkening sky and through the drizzle, the deep greens, browns and purple gave a magical feel to the place. He wondered if they really sold magical wands or they were like the witches' shops at home, a place of high expectations and no return. They sold trinkets to decorate a room but held no real magic.

"Now that's a sanctuary."

He turned to Loggie's voice and followed his line of sight. The impressive stone structure was a mini castle complete with a turret for a bell tower. The three-storey structure was only about 75 feet wide, and the elaborate entranceway took up half of it. Carved stone statues of knights stood guard on either side of the doorway. The wooden doors leading into the sanctuary were each six feet wide and 14 feet tall. Wide black iron hinges secured the doors, and a ring as large as a basketball hung on one of the doors and encircled a dragon's head with its mouth open wide. No one stood outside or sat on the stone bench resting near the doorway. It looked vacant, abandoned, but the single light flickering in the round blue window above the entrance indicated otherwise. Below it, carved into the stone, read NORN SANCTUARY. He'd never seen anything like it in this realm nor his home realm.

"We need to go there, too," whispered Nimble.

"We don't need sanctuary," he said.

"Yet we'll go anyways. It calls to those it wishes to see. And I hear it whispering to me."

He swung around. Her expression was one of awe, as if she'd seen the most magnificent sight in her life, and that what she most desired rested behind those doors. Granted, the sanctuary was a great looking building, but it didn't entice him to enter. "We should stay out of sight."

She frowned. "Do you fear living?"

"Dying."

"If that is where you focus your energy, you will never live. In essence, you've already died inside."

He turned back around. What did she know? Every morning, she was reborn; her history, all of it, good and bad, erased from her memory. She saw this world with new eyes daily. She felt the same every day as he had when he first arrived: inspired, hopeful, fascinated. Reduced to hunting and grovelling for survival forced him to see how silly he had been to believe in an enchanted fantasy world. If there was a hell on Earth, this was it.

Grumbling under his breath, he searched for the stable. Most inns had them nearby, often adjacent to the inn, sometimes across the lane. Lightning shot through the sky and was quickly followed by a clap of thunder. The drizzle turned to rain and as if someone turned the tap of his misery further, the downpour grew heavy by the time he approached the sign over an alleyway that read Blue Dragon Stable. The narrow lane was wide enough for a small cart and horse but would not accommodate a larger wagon pulled by two horses. It took him to the back of the inn and tavern to a large, thick-timber barn. A man was shutting one of the large doors leading into it but stopped when he saw him approach. The man waved him forward.

"Not fit for rats nar ducks ou' there." The middle-aged man wore a grey flat cap. The long-sleeve shirt beneath black suspenders was similar in colour. His outfit was topped off with well-worn black trousers and ankle-high black boots.

"Ducks love this weather," said Nimble after entering the shelter.

"Ay, but not the thunder," said the man. "Terrifies them silly."

"I thought ducks were naturally silly." She dismounted and gave her cloak a shake to shed water faster.

"Ay, but thunder creates a different type of dingbat."

She giggled. "You're well versed in duck."

"It's my business to be knowledgeable in many things." He stuck out his hand. "Marty Matig, ma'am. You'll be staying the nigh' I foretell and be needing a place to bed down your horses and selves."

"You are exceptionally wise, Mr. Matig."

He rolled his eyes. "Call me Marty. A friend if you need."

"Thank you, Marty. I am Rosalind. This is Loggie and Cormac."

Cormac cringed. He never gave a name he used often at a place like this, particularly under these circumstances.

"Grea' to mee' you folk," said Marty. "Travelling with the fines' kind you are."

"The best," said Loggie. "I assume this is a fine establishment."

"Tiz tha'. None better in Romarin."

"Excellent. I'm looking forward to a warm dry sleep and a hot meal."

"We've both, bu' firs' we ge' the animals stalled. Then me boys will tend to chores of grooming and feeding." He turned. "This way."

Cormac followed, glancing from side-to-side, looking for people who might know him. While sleeping outdoors would have been uncomfortable, he'd have feel safer. Too often, things went down inside inns with taverns, and he wanted no part in it. Given the time of day, he'd have ridden for at least another eight hours, putting more distance between Clive and him, and decreasing the distance between him and Harmon.

Thunder boomed overhead, and rain beat on the roof. Maybe staying put for the night was the best option. Surely if Clive was on his trail, he'd also seek refuge.

An hour later, his gear tucked away in the room, his clothes dry from sitting at the hearth in the tavern and enjoying a hot drink of coffee, he scanned the room and took in the many faces of those who also sought shelter from the weather. It was a mixed crowd. Some were young, some middle-aged and a few were old. Most were men. Elven men. Second in number were humans, then dwarfs. Of the 50 people, he saw only two hauflins, not including Nimble. Or Rosalind, as she was calling herself today. It was middle of the day. Lunch time in his homeland. In populations that followed the elven culture, they called it elvesnes. It consisted of a hot drink and bread, either toasted or not, with either butter or fruit jam. In his case, he had butter only on toast.

Hearing a twang of strings, he found Loggie sitting on the opposite side of the hearth with the rebec on his shoulder. Beside him sat Rosalind, looking up at him as if she was ogling a famous musician like

Charlie Daniels and he was set to play *The Devil Went Down to Georgia*. He'd never heard Loggie play but he doubted he was any good. If the king's servants turned him away and he couldn't make money on the street, he probably sucked.

Loggie adjusted the strings on the rebec, struck the bow against them, liked the sound, then played several notes. Then he played a slow song, speeding it up to a moderate beat within a minute. Rosalind clapped her hands to the beat, grinning broadly.

Cormac had to admit, Loggie wasn't all that bad. Not perfect, but not bad. He scanned the crowd. They watched with pleasure, pausing their conversations to listen. When the song ended, they clapped and one cheered. "Another!"

Loggie struck the strings again and played a sweet melody. Then he played another. After nine or ten songs, he stood and bowed. A few people flipped coins to him, and one woman handed him a coin. Hmph. Now he understood why Loggie thought taverns were profitable.

A short time later, the storm let up, and while he wanted to return to his room, Rosalind said no.

"Go if you want," she said. "You look pretty sore. You might need the rest. I don't. Loggie and I are going to explore the village."

While he was sore and didn't want to venture too far and aggravate his bruised stomach muscles, he didn't want them to get into trouble or expose themselves too much. Glancing around the tavern, hearing the customers talk about how good Loggie played made him think it was already too late.

"I'll come. I've never been to a wand shop."

"We're also going to the music shop," said Loggie.

"Fine. I'll come."

"Probably other places, too," said Rosalind.

"I get it. I'm coming." He followed them out the door. The sky was still dark, and thunder rumbled in the distance but at the moment, it wasn't raining. A few others took advantage of the break in the rain and were out, too. Walking along the street, he watched his step to avoid horses and wagons and kept an eye open to see if Clive had made it to Romarin. Certainly, he couldn't have. It was many days away from where he had left him. Clive would have been granted a miracle if he had been able to trail them here. Still, he—

"The music shop first," said Loggie. He grinned at Rosalind. "Less trouble to be found there."

"We could make our own," she said, falling into step with him.

"Let's not," said Cormac.

"Party-pooper," she quipped.

While the intentions of the remark was like a clip to the head, inwardly he smiled. He hadn't heard it since he'd arrived. Once in the small shop, he walked along the outer wall, gazing at the many unusual instruments. Some resembled those from his homeland. Others, like the...he leant forward to read the name...zanfona was nothing like he'd ever seen. It was a type of stringed instrument, but he had no idea how it was played. Farther on, he spotted a hurdy gurdy. He remembered the name from a movie, but that was all. It was boxy, and he wondered if it sat on a table or the knee to be played. The keys, arranged like on a piano, looked like the push buttons on a car radio. He wondered if they were pulled out, programed and pushed back in.

He moved on, took note of where Rosalind and Loggie had gone, then gazed around the shop. The place smelt of freshly-sawn wood, linseed oil and leather, and reminded him of the woodworking shop in high school except there were no machines here, only finished products.

"This is a fine example of a hurdy gurdy," came a voice a few feet away. The shop keeper directed a young woman to the instrument. "It arrived only last week. It's been admired by many. It won't last."

"May I sample its sound?" asked the woman, whose voice was as smooth and as sweet as honey. Her long, straight hair of the palest gold framed her face and covered her back.

"Of course, maiden. Please, have a seat." He directed her to a cushioned chair. Once she was seated with her feet squarely resting on a short block to create a level surface, he placed the instrument on her lap.

She opened the lid, revealing strings and other gadgets, adjusted a few buttons, then closed it. A minor position adjustment, and she turned the crank on the side and pressed a key. She continued and played a short melody.

Cormac stared in amazement. It sounded like she played a bagpipe, not a stringed instrument. She played another short tune, a livelier one, then a slow one. Her fingers flew over the keys while her other hand kept turning the crank.

When she finished, the keeper clapped. "You're a natural. This was made for you."

They dickered about price, and Cormac walked deeper into the shop and met Rosalind and Loggie fiddling with flutes.

"I'm not sure," said Rosalind.

"I am. You have no music ability," said Loggie.

"Such harsh criticism."

"The truth may hurt, but it will save you from false hope and my ears from irritation."

"If I do not try, I cannot fail nor succeed."

"If you must try, buy the cheapest, then sell or trade it when you remember you've no talent."

"That doesn't sound supportive."

He shrugged. "I'm practical."

She picked up a small flute, put it to her mouth and blew. It was loud and sharp.

"Softer," ordered the shop keeper. "If you are untrained, do not try. Allow others who are."

She looked at Loggie. He took the flute and played softly. "It is a fair enough flute for you."

"Pocket bamboo piccolo flute," corrected the keeper. "Piccolo for short."

"It is a reasonable price," said Loggie. "And it's small enough to fit in your pocket." He looked her over. "If you had a pocket."

"We don't need it," said Cormac. "Money is better spent on food."

"You'd rather a full belly and an empty soul?" said Loggie. He turned to her. "Get it and a good laugh will be had."

She frowned at him and walked to the counter, where another keeper, a younger version of the man helping the woman with the hurdy gurdy, gave her a cloth sleeve to carry the piccolo in and told her the price. Loggie picked out the correct change from her coin bag, which she had found, not Cormac, who begrudgingly allowed her to keep it. And now she was wasting money better spent on food and lodging. The things she was gathering, like the leather wristband that appeared out of nowhere yestermorn, were unnecessary to survival. While she may not remember where she bought it, he'll remember she has it when the money runs out and they're sleeping on the cold, hard ground and scavenging for food. Many times since she had found the coin pouch, he considered stealing it during the night. He would then control the coins, and she wouldn't remember having owned it. The only thing stopping him was Loggie, who would remember.

"Thank you, music man," she said to the keeper. "I will play this often. I will play it loudly."

He grinned. "Everywhere. But here."

She sauntered out the door, gripping the instrument in her hand.

Cormac followed and drizzle greeted him. Glancing around the street, he looked for Clive. Shopping during a time like this was insane. He should be hiding, waiting out the storm away from prying eyes. Instead, when Rosalind walked towards Lucinda's Enchanted Wands, he followed silently. She opened the door, and chimes signalled her arrival. Loggie went in next, holding the thick wooden door decorated with stars, the moon and the sun, open for him. Stepping over the threshold, an odd aroma assaulted him. It was... He searched his memory but couldn't remember where he'd smelt that smell before. It was long ago. Far away. It was a mixture of seaweed and wildflowers. Or...evergreen. No. Thoughts rambled inside his head, as he struggled to identify the odour. It was raw. Woodsy. Fruity. Tart.

"Dried sea apples."

He turned to the voice and saw a woman the same size as Rosalind standing near a collection of windchimes. Or charms. Or...

"Gwynt charms," she said. "To ward off negative energy and to increase life energy." She reminded him of an older version of Stevie Nicks in the *Stop Dragging My Heart Around* music video. It was one of his favourites, and he remembered it well. This woman even had the raspy voice. Her dark green eyes were outlined in black mascara, and her lips were painted vibrant red, which contrasted sharply against her slim, deep purple dress with puffy elbow-length sleeves. The headgear keeping her long, thick, burgundy hair in place was more mesh than material and had a spray of purple feathers surrounding a red jewel on the side.

"Dried sea apples? Are they edible?" he asked.

She smiled slyly. "It depends. Care for a nibble?"

"No. I just ate." He had no intentions of tasting anything this woman had to offer.

"Pity. It would improve your...style."

He cautiously moved forward, scanning the shop and discretely glancing at the shop keeper to see what she was up to. "I don't think we need anything here," he said to Loggie in a low voice. "We should leave."

"And miss all this wonder?" His eyes sparkled while he took in the many strange objects on the tables and shelves and hanging from the ceiling in the dimly-lit room illuminated with candles and lanterns placed in locations to accent the goods. There were so many items, it reminded Cormac of the gaming stalls at the fair by Banook Lake on Dartmouth Natal Day. Every conceivable space was occupied with something as if thousands of customers would arrive and buy it all. Along the outer walls were huge displays of wands of every shape, colour and size. Some were small enough for child to wield, and others were as tall as him, or were they staffs?

"Wands," came the Stevie Nicks lookalike.

He shot her a glance, then reined it back in. How did she know... He looked at her again, and one of her thick black eyebrows rose in curiosity. He pulled his eyes and his thoughts back to focus on the floor before him.

He bumped into Loggie, who stopped at a stringed instrument similar to his rebec. He leant forward and whispered, "This place gives me the creeps."

Loggie hmphed. "You're easily creeped."

"But she knows stuff." In a lower voice, he said, "I think she's a witch."

He chuckled. "She thinks you're a creep."

This was no time to joke. He saw Rosalind cross the shop and disappear behind a display. In the low lighting, he could no longer see her. "Let's not stay long."

"She has stirred a deep feeling?"

"This isn't my kind of shop."

"I'm surprised." Sarcasm dripped from his words. "I'm curious. Why are you travelling with Rosalind? You two are opposite sides of the moon. I understand you rescued her from the dungeon. If you honestly did do that, but what else?"

"I did."

He shrugged. "I have no witnesses, and you know as well as I do, she said that only because you told her you did." He glared at him. "For all I know, you lied to her, which makes me wonder why you're still with her. What's your motive?"

"We're friends."

"Truly? What do you have in common?"

"We like travelling."

"Give me something better than that. Do you think you love her?"

He baulked. "I said friends. There is no love."

"I see that."

"Why are *you* traveling with her? You can leave at any time." And he wished he would. Leave now. Today, and never look back.

"Rosalind and I are truly friends. You? Not so much. You give me the impression you're friend to no one but yourself."

He pulled away. He had friends, and he was trying to get back to them. His only way of doing that was through Rosalind. His task would be easier if Loggie left. Disappeared.

Rosalind approached the display of wands on the outer wall. The magical items were fused with different colours, some bright orange, others soft orange, some bright evergreen, others lime green. Walking slowly past, each one shone its true colour. She paused, held up her hand and saw the glow upon her skin and felt the subtle vibrating energy of each. They were truly magical, but none attracted her hand, and she walked farther, her hand floating along, feeling for a tug that would tell her one of these belonged to her.

"They do not speak for you." The shop keeper stood before her. "Wands are not your channel."

"What is?"

Her dark eyes considered her. "I believe these will connect with your energy." She gestured with her open hand towards a table with many colourful cards. "Come. Let's see if any know your name."

Rosalind stepped forward and gazed upon the table with the dark purple cloth. It displayed many decks of various sizes decorated with colourful images of unicorns, fairies, stones, celestial satellites, flowers, trees and fantastical creatures. "Are these tarot cards?"

"It is one name for them. In some circles, they are known as terra roots or Roots of Terra." Her pleasant smile generated calmness. "Embodied in each card is the quaint energy that transcends the earth below to the moon above and the solar beyond. Within its dance, we are given the opportunity to sense what others cannot. Do you wish to experience its life force?"

It sounded foreign to her ears, and she wanted to learn more. "Yes."

"Here." She directed her to a table, dark cherry in colour, that came up to her rib cage. It was the only surface that did not contain multiple items. The keeper picked up a deck that rested between two thick green candles and handed them to her. "Shuffle them slowly. Intentionally. Think of waking this morning. How your body feels at this moment. How it feels to sit next to a soothing fire. Push everything else from your mind and let this energy flow throughout your body."

Rosalind let her mind drift to her eyes opening in a warm, comfortable bed in soft moss beneath a large swooping branch of an evergreen tree with the sun shining on her as it rose. Nearby slept two men she did not know. When the person next to her woke, looked at her and smiled, she felt safe and welcomed. When he said her name and wished her a good morning, she felt a connection to him. Her body was relaxed, and the warmth of the fire in the tavern energized her nerves and soothed the doubts that lingered since waking.

"Now, place the deck on the table."

She set the cards on the table, and the keeper flipped the top one over. "I see you are in good company. While you..." She studied the card and her brow knitted. "This confuses me. You know who you are but..." She stared at Rosalind. "A veil of confusion separates... I've not seen this before." She flipped another card and studied it. "An unknown force shields you from the truth but in your heart, you know the truth. This shield prevents you from forming roots. It's as if you are adrift on the vast ocean, spotting land only to float away from it. Interesting."

"What does that mean?"

"You have a mystery to solve." She flipped another card and grinned. "Clues surround you. You will solve it." She flipped another card and her eyes widened. "You carry a magical item that will lead you to..." Her face bent in confusion. "Interesting indeed. The item was a gift mistakenly given or...not intentionally given but given just the same. By someone who will play an important role in your life." She smiled. "He will be a good friend. Maybe more." She winked. "We are not told all. We are left to wonder as we should. Life is about wondering and wishing and learning."

"How do these cards tell you this? Can I do it?"

"I believe you can. If patient. If you practise to understand and translate the messages given."

Rosalind saw movement to the side. On a shelf two feet above her head, tucked into the shadows were three sets of green eyes staring at her. She stepped back.

"Nothing to fear," said the shop keeper. "Peky, Piky and Poky harm only those with bad intentions. You are in no danger."

Her eyes adjusted to the lighting and three cats took shape. They were fluffy and varied in shades from light to dark brown. Tilting their heads to the side, they watched with curiosity the scene below.

The keeper moved to the table filled with decks. "Move your hand over the table." She demonstrated by opening her hand, facing it downwards and moving it slowly over the tarot cards. "Feel the energy vibrating from the Roots of Terra to learn if one calls to you."

Rosalind followed her instructions. At first, she didn't feel anything, then a soft force struck her palm. It tickled. Another force struck it. It felt like puffs of warm air striking her skin. The strength of the air depended on the deck she hovered over.

"Find the one that sends the strongest energy," said the keeper.

She paused over several decks, found a strong pull then was directed to another deck. Her nerves danced with excitement. She'd never done anything like this. Energy tugged her hand to the right, to a deck with several variations of the sun depicted on it. Here, her hand stayed and drank in warm, vibrant energy.

"You are solar energy," said the keeper. "An energetic energy. Adventurous. Serve it well, and it will reward you." She picked up the deck and placed it in her hands. "For you, a copper coin."

"How will I know how to use it? Read the energy? Translate it?"

"Intuition." She picked up a small book no larger than a slice of bread and gave it to her. "This will guide you to begin your journey but only through practise and tuning into the energy will you find the most benefits. Connect and read your energy first and only when you know it well, attempt to read the energy of others. If you are not familiar with your energy, you will not be able to distinguish it from theirs, and it will confuse the messages."

"Thank you. I will practise every day." She took a copper coin from the pouch attached to the leather strap securing her cloak and handed it to her.

"Come." She led her to the front of the store and went behind a narrow counter. "Take this." She placed a short pencil and a piece of paper on the surface. "Write yourself a note today about what to do with the Roots of Terra to remind yourself in the future. In case you forget."

"It will be done."

The keeper watched Loggie and Cormac approach and before they reached her, she leant forward to whisper. "One is wishy-washy. The other dedicated."

"Which is which?"

She smiled. "That is for you to decide. And to change if you wish."

"Have you found something?" asked Loggie.

"I have. You?" said Rosalind.

"Indeed. This." He held up a necklace with a sky-blue rectangular stone pendant. On either end of the stone was a decorative brass cap.

"Interesting choice," said the keeper. "Put it on."

He drew the leather strap around his neck and tied it. Once the stone settled against his skin, it glowed with morning light. "Is it supposed to do that?"

"Only when the stone accepts you. It will bring you fair luck."

Rosalind fingered the stone. "We have both been fortunate." She looked at Cormac. "Anything?"

He frowned. "I don't need trinkets."

She turned back to the keeper. "He's dedicated to being wishy-washy."

The keeper snorted and attempted to stifle the grin but was unsuccessful. "You are indeed a charm. I hope we meet again."

"I'll wait outside," grumbled Cormac and left the shop.

"The sign said two coppers." Loggie held out two coins.

Her eyes narrowed, and she grew serious. "Promise to guard her safety while you travel with her, and I'll accept one copper."

He glanced at Rosalind. "I need not be paid for that. I accept without compensation."

"What I needed to hear, and that is why one coin will suffice. Tuck the other in your sock to remind you of your promise today."

He handed her one coin and stuck the other in his sock. It settled near his heel. "Thank you."

"It has been a pleasure meeting you..." said Rosalind. "I do not know your name."

"Ashland of Ancient Moonshire."

"Not Lucinda?"

A sly smile creased her lips. "Not today."

"Rosalind of somewhere I don't remember."

"One day, you will."

She nodded, then led Loggie out the door. Leaning against the building, protected from the drizzle beneath the overhanging roof, stood Cormac, a sour expression darkening his face.

"Where to now," she said. "It is still early." She spotted Norn Sanctuary across the street and walked towards it.

"Where are you going?" asked Cormac, hesitating to follow.

"To see a dragon."

Loggie hurried after her. "A dragon. They live in sanctuaries?"

"Yes. And caves. Mountains. Forests." She marched up to the mammoth door and stopped abruptly before the steel ring surrounding the dragon head with its mouth open wide. Its deep eye sockets stared off into the distance.

"There's nothing here," said Cormac. "Besides a decent looking mini castle."

"I'll be the judge of that." She grasped the ring and tugged, but it didn't move. She pulled harder. Still, it didn't move. Drawing strength into her arm muscles, she prepared to yank it but froze when the eyes of the stone dragon opened. When the mouth moved, she jumped back.

"You do not need sanctuary," growled the dragon. "Go away." It twisted its head, then settled into its previous stone position.

She stared wide-eyed at the dragon, waiting for it to do more, but it lay silent. Taking one step forward, she hesitated to go farther.

"What the heck just happened?" gasped Cormac.

"Magic?" she said. She stepped closer but stalled mid-step when the dragon awakened, drew a breath and snorted fire.

She leapt out of the way, bumping into Loggie and Cormac, who couldn't move fast enough. "Now that's a dragon."

"One not to challenge," said Loggie.

"Or played with," said Cormac. "Let's do what it says and go away."

Rosalind stepped away from the doors. For the first time today, she agreed with him. A strong wind swept through the air, bringing with it a flash of lightning and rain. She stared up at the dark sky. Unless she wanted to get drenched, the best place for her was inside. Thinking about the Roots of Terra deck tucked inside her cloak, she didn't want to risk getting it wet. Then she thought about practising translating the energy, sitting on her bed in a warm, dry room.

"Back to the inn." She raced across the street, avoiding as much rain and as many puddles as possible, and ducked inside.

She spent the rest of the afternoon sitting cross-legged on her bed, examining each card, trying to read its energy and thinking about the messages they were sending. She also wrote herself a note to remind her of how to work the cards.

Loggie sat on his bed, back against the wall, playing soft tunes on the rebec. Now and again, he picked up her flute and played a tune. Cormac lay on his pillow. At first, he read a book from the bookshelf in the tavern, then he fell asleep.

7

Sanctuary

CORMAC YAWNED AND stretched. Rosalind had shaken him awake a few minutes earlier. It was nine o'clock, and she wanted to eat and thought he should, too, before they settled for the night. Approaching the tavern, he wished she had waken him sooner. The dinner crowd had left and the night crowd - the most dangerous of patrons - were staggering in. He had second thoughts about eating. His stomach chimed in, reminding him that all he had to eat today was the bread, piece of fruit and water at dawn and the toast and hot drink at elvesnes. He'd have a quick bite and then retreat to the safety of his room. That was all.

Loggie spotted an empty table along the wall next to the fireplace and pulled Rosalind towards it. Cormac followed. It looked like a safe place, out of the way of flying objects, which he was certain would strike those sitting at tables away from the wall. It would also be warm on this cool, damp night.

"What food interests you?" asked the server.

"Oh," crooned Loggie. "Do you have smoked pig tail?"

"We do. It comes with lentils, carrots and fried turnip."

"Sounds delicious. That's what I'll have."

"Anything to drink?"

"Ale?"

"Dandelion?"

"Certainly."

"And you?" She looked at Rosalind.

"Something simple. Fish and fried coins."

"Salmon or striped mongrel?"

"I've never had striped mongrel." She looked at Loggie. "Good?"

"Different. Taste like duck but less greasy, more like asparagus."

She twisted her face. "It tastes like broccoli stalks?" She turned to the server. "Salmon."

She grinned. "Drink?"

"Something fruity. With rum."

"Dragon's Punch, then." She winked. "It's got apricots." She turned to Cormac.

He thought of the only thing he had ever found in this realm that resembled a great hot meal, something that reminded him of home. "Mashed potatoes and pork roast. Carrots. Peas."

"No peas. Yellow long beans okay?"

He shook his head. "Carrots are fine."

"Drink?"

"Water." He had to keep his senses about him. While he waited for the meal, he cautiously surveyed the tavern. It was large, and he couldn't see it all from his viewpoint. Most of the tables were full. A cloud of grey smoke from pipes already lay in the thick air, adding to the smoke from the fire. Beneath the candles and lanterns, it blended into the ceiling and created a fantastic scene similar to those in movies he'd seen. Unlike sitting in a movie theatre eating popcorn and waiting for the action, here, living in the scene, he wanted only to escape any that happened.

Rosalind and Loggie chatted about different things, and Loggie asked her about the Roots of Terra cards she'd bought. She drew them from a leather pouch. A folded piece of paper fell from the book that came with them, and she quickly tucked it back inside.

Not interested in tarot cards, he watched three young men, all human, enter the tavern, shake rain from their slickers and fill an empty table. They were rugged, bearded and looked like they had just ridden into town. One caught his eye, and Cormac quickly turned away. He had no plans of making conversation with anyone in this room. Discretely, he looked around, first at the door where the server went, the lanterns hanging on the wall near it, the bar, then to another table. From the corner of his eye, he checked out the man who had made eye contact. He was engrossed in conversation with his friends and wasn't paying him any attention. When a server came to the table, he gave his order without even a glance in his direction.

The woman serving Cormac's table arrived with food, and his stomach sent an emergency message to his brain: eat. He dug in and forgot those around him. The hot food ignited sensations in his mouth, and all he could think about was eating the delicious meal. The mashed potatoes were similar to the way his mother made them, and images of her filled his mind. Most days, he tried not to think too hard of home and his family but right now, the corners of his eyes stung, and he wished he was jogging up the front porch steps, arriving home just as supper was being set out on the table. Unlike before, when he'd grumble about silly things that had ruined his day and eat like the food and his mother would always be there, he'd race into the kitchen and give her a big hug, thank her for the excellent meal she'd made and after eating, he'd tell her to enjoy her tea while he washed dishes and put away the leftovers.

"You okay?" asked Rosalind.

He stared at her through blurred vision. "Fine. Sore ribs."

She accepted the answer and resumed eating.

The thought of sacrificing Rosalind so he could return home made him feel horrible, like an evil villain, chaotic evil, but... He drew a deep breath. He had never hurt anyone in his life, but he couldn't live in this world anymore. He hated it. He'd do anything to get home. And his ticket to get there sat across from him, eating and enjoying the tavern atmosphere, oblivious to why he travelled with her.

His plate cleaned, he emptied the glass of water. Seeing Loggie and Rosalind also finishing up, he prepared to leave. Loggie pushed his empty plate aside and withdrew the rebec from the sack. Resting it on his shoulder, he plucked the strings, adjusted them, then picked up the bow.

"What are you doing?" he asked when Loggie grabbed his empty ale mug and stood.

"Playing for my adventures." He went to the fireplace, stood on a short square no larger than a sack pad for first base and struck the rebec with the bow. He played a sweet lullaby, catching the attention of most of the patrons. When the song ended, the crowd cheered. A few threw coins in his direction.

Cormac leant across the table to Rosalind. "Did he do this at the tavern in Maisa Ridge?"

"I don't know. I've never been there."

He stared at her, examining her innocent face. She had no idea who she was or what she was doing. On one hand, he envied her. On the other, he felt sorry for her. If he had a third hand, he'd curse himself. The object hanging around his neck would disrupt the spell. If he gave it to her, she'd remember today and every day forth and after a few weeks, she'd remember days leading up to this day and eventually, she'd remember her life on civilized Earth. But he couldn't do that.

"Were you there?" she asked.

"I was sleeping."

"You sleep a lot. Are you sick?"

"No." Was he? He slept because he'd been beaten pretty badly. He needed rest to recuperate. He thought about his days before the beating. Did he need more sleep than usual? He couldn't remember. He grasped the belt around his waist. It grounded him, broke the spell for him. Did it do the job completely? Or was he missing something?

"You look confused. Do you need to go to bed?"

"I'm fine." He was tired even though he had slept away most of the early evening but left this unsaid.

Loggie played tune after tune. He played a few fast ones, then slowed it down, then picked it up again. Almost an hour later, he removed the rebec from his shoulder and bowed, thanking the crowd. He no sooner sat down and put the rebec in the sack when a server came over with a mug of ale.

She leant close and over the boisterous crowd said, "Deary. On the house. The keeper thanks you. We doubled our sales while you played."

"Excellent. Thank you. A thirst quencher." He took a long drink.

"Is this your gig now?" asked Cormac after the server left.

"Gig? That sounds neat." Loggie took another drink, almost emptying the mug. "I love to play, and they love to listen, so we both benefit."

"You are an excellent player," said Rosalind. "Will you teach me?"

"Sure. Tomorrow."

"Wonderful. We will be a great team."

He chuckled, winked at her and drained the mug. "Now I'm ready for sleep."

Cormac left the tavern feeling relieved and satisfied. Relieved nothing dangerous had happened and satisfied with a full belly. He'd sleep well tonight. The lanterns in the hallway to the room provided just enough light to find his way. He unlocked the door, pushed it open for

Rosalind to enter first and prepared to unhook the lit lantern outside their door and move it inside.

She no sooner said, "Thank you," and stepped over the threshold when she was jerked into the dark room. Faint struggling drifted through the open door along with mumbled curse words.

Cormac grabbed the lantern and held it inside the room.

"Get in and shut the door." A man's deep, low voice came from the darkness.

Frozen in place, he considered running, but if he did, he'd lose his ticket home, and no one was going to steal that from him. He stepped inside and held up the lantern to illuminate the scene he had to face. Standing in the glow were three men, the same three humans who had eaten at the tavern earlier. One had Rosalind in a choke hold and held a dagger to her neck. The other two held daggers poised to attack.

"Why are you here?" asked Loggie. "What do you want from us?"

"Shut the door," demanded the one holding Rosalind.

Loggie moved the door into the closed position but didn't close it enough to engage the doorhandle. "We've nothing you want."

"You do." He leered at him. "A map. Give it now."

Cormac searched his memory. He didn't remember a map. Had Clive carried one in his saddlebags? He didn't remember seeing anything that resembled a map in anything taken from Clive or his men.

"You've mistaken us for someone else," said Loggie. "We do not possess a map." He glanced at Cormac. "Even though I can read one, I carry none."

"We know he gave it to you - to her - at Maisa Ridge." His eyes grew large, and he tightened his grip on Rosalind.

"I've no map," she said. "Nor have I ever possessed one."

"Shut up." He shook her. "It's your life or the map."

"Kill me, and you'll never find it."

"So, you know where it is?"

Cormac didn't like where this was going. "Look, she doesn't have a map. She's delirious. Drunk."

"I am not!"

"Sheesh! You don't have a map."

"I know. Trying telling them."

"Let's take her," said one of the other men. "We'll beat it out of her. She has it. She knows where it is."

"Wait!" Loggie pressed two fingers against his temple. "A map. Now I remember." He snapped his fingers and pointed at them. "I hid it beneath the leather flap of my saddle."

"Liar!" snapped the man who had yet to speak. "We searched the saddles, the saddlebags and sacks." He waved his hand around the room. The bags and sacks had been emptied onto the beds and their gear had been strewn across the floor. "It's not here, so that means one of you carries it."

"We tried to do this the simple way," said the one holding Rosalind, "without anyone getting hurt, but the map is worth more to me than your life."

"No map is worth more than that," said Loggie. "Let her go, and we'll talk this over like men." He pointed towards the tavern with his thumb. "I'll buy you a drink."

Cormac raised a sharp eyebrow when he heard the offer. These men weren't looking for conversation and ale. "We don't have a map. No one's life needs to end over a misunderstanding. Just go, and we won't say anything to anyone."

The three men roared with laughter. One tossed something on the floor between them, and smoke filled the air. From the billowy grey cloud, a violent force struck Cormac and threw him against the wall where he crumbled to the floor. The lantern flew from his hand, crashed to the floor and went out, leaving him in a haze of dark smoke. Heavy boots sped past, and he scrambled to his feet and reached out to find the wall and his bearings.

"Damn it!" Loggie's voice shot out of the smoke. "I can't see a thing. Cormac, you there?"

"Here."

"Rosalind?" Silence ensued. "Rosalind?"

"They've got her." He felt his way to the door. "This way. Follow my voice." He waved his arm in the air and finally struck a solid object. Grabbing hold of Loggie's shirt, he hauled him forward. "Come on." A few feet from the door, the hallway cleared of smoke. Searching the area in front of him, he saw the last man disappear at the end of the hallway.

"This way." He raced after the men. At the end of the hallway, he found a dead end. "What? I saw them. They were here. Where did they go?"

"No window," said Loggie. He banged on the wall. It didn't budge.

Cormac pounded on the wall where he had last seen the man. "It's hollow."

"A secret room. A hidden door." Loggie's hands flew over the surface, then fumbled with a hook that had no lantern. Pushing it to the left triggered part of the wall to slide open.

Cormac leapt in and raced down a set of steps. He turned and found another set of stairs. He glanced over his shoulder and found Loggie on his heels. At the bottom of the steps, there was a long hallway. Lit with lanterns for about 300 feet, it seemingly went on forever. At the edge of the last lantern's glow, he saw movement. "It's gotta be them." He ran to catch up and forty feet on, he tripped over something and slammed hard into the dirt floor.

Loggie tripped in the same fashion and crashed on top of him. He groaned and pushed himself to his knees. "Trippers."

Cormac looked to where he pointed. Where the lantern's light didn't reach, a piece of the wall on both sides extended into the hallway, leaving only a two-foot wide clear path. Veering off centre brought his foot into direct contact with it. He rose to his feet slowly, taking note of the extra bruises that were forming, then jogged towards the end. Mindful of his path, he avoided additional trippers. A moment later, he reached a steel door, breathing hard and feeling every ache in his body. He tried the handle. It was unlocked. He swung it open and rushed outside into the rain.

Not seeing anyone, he ran into the dark night and stopped in the middle of the road. He looked in every direction and saw nothing. He searched again, straining his eyes to see movement in the shadows, in the glimmer of scattered lanterns and the glow from windows lit from within. Nothing. She was gone. Along with the hope of getting home. "Rosalind!" he screamed, stretching it out for several seconds until his throat burnt. He listened with his ear tipped to the sky. Nothing. He shouted again. Still nothing.

His throat tightened, and he raked the area again and again, his eyes growing weary and vision blurry, searching for the slightest movement, the sound of someone splashing through puddles, the smallest hint of the direction they'd gone. His chest swelled, and rain dripped into his eyes and seeped into his shirt. She was gone. He squeezed his eyes shut with such intensity, he saw red. Dropping to his knees, he hung his head, not caring about the puddle he landed in, the rain beating on his back nor the chill that sought a home in his bones.

He felt a hand on his shoulder and looked up to see Loggie reaching out to help him off the ground.

"I believe I was too quick to dismiss the possibility of love." Loggie pulled him to his feet. "We'll find her."

He stared at him through the rain, trying to decipher what he said. When he grabbed his arm and dragged him, he let him lead him into the night and away from the secret tunnel to the tavern.

Rosalind attempted to call out to Cormac and Loggie, but the cloth around her mouth sealed it completely. It even covered part of her nose, making it difficult to breathe. The man dragging her through an alley had stopped long enough for the other two, who he called Reg and Matt, to secure the gag and her hands behind her back. His name was Guthro, and he appeared to be the one in charge, and he was the largest. Strongest. He shoved her against the wall, held her there and looked back from where they came.

"I think we lost them," said Guthro.

"Here ain't a good place," said Matt. "Let's get her out of town or at least not where someone might hear her scream."

Rosalind struggled to break free, but Guthro held her tighter.

"We ain't gonna hurt you," he said, then leered at Matt. "Keep that to yourself." He turned back to her. "Give us the map, and we'll let you go."

"I don't have a map," she said, but her words were stifled by the gag.

"Can't understand blabber," said Reg. "Let's get out o' here, so's we can get that rag out o' her yapper."

Guthro yanked her from the wall and dragged her down the alley. They made several turns, crossed a road, then ducked into a narrow lane that ended in a narrower pathway around to the back of a building.

"Here's good 'nough," said Reg. "We needs to get that map and skedaddle."

Guthro threw her against the wall so hard, her lungs expelled all the air. She struggled to draw a breath. After several gasps, she drew one, but by this time, she had collapsed to her knees.

"Easy," said Matt. "We can't get information from a dead woman."

Guthro dragged her to her feet and pulled the rag from her mouth. "No one's gonna hear you or care if they do. No point in screaming."

She licked her lips, feeling them swelling from the punches she'd taken. Gathering her senses, she thought of ways to escape. These men looked tough, but everyone had a weakness. She had learned that at... Her thoughts scrambled to finish the sentence, then stalled suddenly. The rope they'd secured her hands with was thick, which meant easy to ply with her thin wrists. She pretended to heave, acting like she'd vomit. All the while, she was wriggling her wrists, getting a hold of the end of the rope and following its trail with her fingers.

Matt and Reg stepped back, but Guthro kept a firm grip on her arm while avoiding the direction of her mouth.

"Makes me sick," said Reg.

"To see someone chuck their feedings?" asked Matt.

He nodded. "The thoughts o' it churns me innards."

Guthro forced her cheek against the wall and sprayed spit into her ear when he spoke. "Where's the map?"

"Are you deaf?" she spat. "I told you. I don't have a map."

He shook her. "I know you do. Unless you sold it."

"You're confusing me with someone else."

"You're the woman with the bard. There ain't many of them around, travelling with a skittish human that sticks out like he don't belong nowhere. Soulless, they calls him."

"Fine. I sold it," she lied. "To a pedlar I met on the way. Gone, it is. Never to be seen again."

He punched her in the gut and jerked her to face him. "No one with a stable mind would have sold that map."

"I have never claimed to have a stable mine even though I ride a fine horse."

Confusion swept over him, then anger.

Her eyes grew large, and she stared off into the shadows behind him. "Shit. He's found me," she mumbled. She let out a blood-curdling scream, and Guthro and the other two whipped around to see who approached. At this moment, she kneed him in the groin, punched him in the mouth, then sped down the narrow pathway at the end of the lane. Not looking back, she ran as fast as her legs carried her around discarded objects and crates. Seeing a glow up ahead, she ran to it and burst onto a lane. She didn't think, only went in the direction her legs took her, the most convenient route.

Stealing a quick glance over her shoulder, she saw the men racing after her and gaining ground. She sped faster with her heart beating loudly in her ears and drowning out every other sound. Rounding a corner, she saw a familiar sight: Blue Dragon Keep. Before she reached it, Guthro was beside her. She dodged to the right and ran towards Norn Sanctuary. Planning a quick left turn, then a leap onto the bench and then the wide frame above the window, she changed her mind when she saw the eyes of the dragon in the door knocker awaken.

"Sanctuary!" growled the dragon head. Drawing a breath, it shot fire over her shoulder towards the men in hot pursuit. The adjacent door swung open, and she dashed inside. It slammed shut behind her with a thunderous clap, and she collapsed to the cold stone floor, gasping for breath. For several moments, she lay on the floor, her body trembling and her heart recovering from the chase. When she looked up, she found herself in an empty room. Before her on a raised sheet of stone rested a table. No chairs. No decorations. Off to the right was a closed door. The same appeared to her left. She gathered her feet beneath her and slowly rose.

The only light came from the large candle secured in a bracket in the blue glass window above the door. It was the only window in the room. Narrow steps led up to it, and she climbed them to look outside. Guthro, Matt and Reg stood in the middle of the street, glaring at the sanctuary. No doubt, they were thinking of ways to get inside. Guthro took a step forward, and fire shot out from below, and he jumped back.

After several long minutes, the men disappeared into the night. Rosalind watched to ensure they didn't return, then settled on the mat below the window. She'd wait until morning, then return to the tavern and inn. She'd find Loggie and Cormac, and they'd get out of Romarin together. Until then, she'd sleep. She was tired. Curling up in a ball, enjoying the warmth of the sanctuary, she fell into deep sleep and wonderful dreams. She didn't wake until the sun shone brightly through the tinted glass and bathed her face in warmth.

Staring out at the street below, she watched someone walk by. A moment later, two men entered the building across the street and two more walked by. Stretching and yawning, she took note of her surroundings. A window ledge in a stone building. The window was as tall as her, and the metal bracket the extra large candle rested in looked strong enough to hold her weight. Several lines were carved above the window: three vertically crossing with three carved at an angle left to right and three crossing at the opposite angle. What it meant, she had no idea. The mat she had slept on was below the window and beneath the candle bracket. It was warm and soft. The sound of a wagon drew her attention back to the window. The two horses hauling it stopped at the building across the street and four people got out. She read the decorative sign above the door: Blue Dragon Keep. Searching her memory, she remembered what a keep was: a supply shop. No wonder it was busy.

Standing up, she stretched her back and shook each leg. The cloak she wore was slightly damp and in disarray. She removed the leather strap from around her waist and set it and the small sack attached to it on the mat. A gentle jingle sang from the pouch. She removed the cloak and found two additional pouches in an over-size pocket of the long-sleeve shirt she wore. She placed them on the floor. After shaking the cloak, she hung it on a hook next to the window and adjusted the shirt and dress beneath it, then sat cross-legged. The first pouch contained a small collection of coins. The next held a short flute. The last one contained a deck of pretty cards and a booklet. A piece of paper fell out, and she unfolded it.

The first line struck her, and she stared out the window feeling its meaning. *My name is Rosalind.* She hadn't thought about what her name was. If someone had asked her, what name would she have given? Rosalind sounded right. She'd give it.

She returned to the note and read it completely, smiling by the end. Picking up the Roots of Terra, she admired the decorations depicting the sun in various forms. Some were simply a yellow circle. Others were rays created in different shapes. She adjusted the wide leather band on her left wrist and found it moist like her cloak. Jiggling it, she pulled it away from her skin. Thoughts of untying it crossed her mind until she heard a door open.

An elderly man stepped inside the room below, looked up at her and smiled. His grey hair looked frazzled as did his beard. The off-white robe he wore touched the floor as did the hem of the sleeveless long vest. A rope belt kept the robe snug around his waist and when he walked forward, he exposed bare feet.

"You were granted sanctuary," he said in a gravely voice. "Well, are you hungry?"

"Yes, sir."

"Shall you break the fast with us?"

She felt her stomach. "If you will have me."

"Excellent." He pointed a crooked finger to the steps leading up to the window's ledge. "Make your way along, and we'll join the others."

She gathered her things and descended the stairs. When she reached the man, he bowed slightly.

"Shepherd Skuld at your service. And you, child? What does family call you?"

"Rosalind?"

A gentle smile creased his lips. "Timid. A good character trait in a place such as this." He turned and walked through the door. "Quick like a swallow before the door closes and you are trapped 'til morrow."

She leapt after him and slipped into the hallway past the solid wooden door that slowly creaked closed. The narrow passage, lit by only one candle, looked like it led to a dungeon. It even ended in a door. Shepherd Skuld opened this in his casual manner and held it in position for her to pass. Before she crossed the threshold, voices drifted to her ear. The brightness of the room highlighted the grey in his hair and dust that sparkled on his shoulders. Once inside, he closed the door gently, then turned to the occupants, who fell silent.

"I present to you Rosalind." He elegantly gestured in her direction. She felt the urge to bow or curtsy or something to acknowledge his formal introduction. "She has been granted sanctuary, and..." he winked at her, "wishes to break her fast."

The three women, similar in age and appearance stopped preparing the food and stared. They each had long, golden hair. One wore it loose.

One wore it in two braids. One wore it in a single braid. All three wore long slim white gowns that shimmered in the morning light pouring in the windows.

"Good morning," she said when the silence grew too long.

"Morning is good," said the one who wore her hair loose. "I am Claudia."

"Indeed, a good morning," said the one with two braids. "I am Cellach."

"Mornings are good for birds, not for those who wish to enjoy the sundown." The one who wore her hair in a single braid smiled mischievously. "I am Ashtrop."

"A pleasure to meet you," said Rosalind.

"You won't think so in time," mumbled Skuld. In his normal voice, he said, "Have a seat. You are our guest."

"Guest?" grumbled Ashtrop. "Not a cripple. Not a servant."

Almost to a chair to sit down, Rosalind stopped. She didn't need anyone to serve her. "I shall fix my own."

"Nonsense," said Claudia. "Ignore my sister. Moody, she is. Will be missing her cousin's child soon..." She eyed Skuld. "I foresee."

"Taking away the only fun within these walls." Ashtrop pouted.

"It was inevitable," said Ceallach.

"I know, but you have decided," said Ashtrop.

"Not I, but Muther."

At that moment, a young woman rushed into the room. Her golden hair was not as long as the hair of the sisters, and only sections on each side were drawn back and braided to rest on a blanket of gold. She wore a similar gown but shorter and no shoes. Her eyes were bright. Excited. When they found Rosalind, they sparkled.

"Aunt Urðr told me I'd meet my destiny today!" She squealed with excitement. "It is you. You've finally arrived."

"Sadly, she has," said Ashtrop.

The woman rushed to Ashtrop and gave her a great hug. "It is fate. I will keep you in my dreams, and I will return to continue our fun. Promise."

Ashtrop returned the hug. "I'll hold you to it."

Confused by all that was said, Rosalind made no motion to sit or collect food to eat. She remained still, watching and listening, wondering who this girl was and why they were expecting her to arrive.

"The first needs of the day must be met," said Skuld. He motioned to Rosalind. "Sit. We shall serve the one who will guide our Etain to her destiny."

Confused further, she sat in the nearest chair. The women chatted about the day, about Etain leaving and the supplies she'd take. Ashtrop continued to complain and speak over the others, and Etain giggled with every comment. Skuld sat next to Rosalind and smiled quietly, letting the women fill the room with noise.

Rosalind's bones shivered, and she thought about donning her cloak when she felt another presence in the room. A woman, aged but not much wrinkled, stood at the threshold of the same doorway Etain had entered through. Her gown was dark green and swept the floor. Grey was invading her golden hair but had made only small advances. Searching the room, her dark green eyes settled on Rosalind, and a barely noticeable smile touched her lips.

Skuld stood. "Lady Urðr. May I present to you Rosalind. Granted sanctuary and slept beneath the candle's glow."

"I sensed her presence." The woman's voice was smooth, confident. "I both dread and rejoice in her arrival." She glided to the table and stood across from Rosalind. "Hardly what I expected."

"That what we imagine is influenced by our desires, not what is meant to be."

Urðr acknowledged Skuld's wisdom. "Her attributes are well hidden. Beneficial to Etain and to those who wish to see her safe return." Her eyebrows rose and a subtle smile graced her features. "Confused, she is. Unaware of her fate."

"Have I been here before?" asked Rosalind. "Did you ask me to do something I said I would?"

"No and no," said Urðr. "The mind has tricks of its own as does those who work the land's energy. But we are confident."

"All... or..." Skuld's face turned a light shade of pink. "What needs to be known will be revealed after we eat."

"She'll need a bath," said Claudia. "Can't begin a quest smelling like one has already been through a stench pit."

"And suitable attire," said Ceallach. "A guardian must dress the part if they are to wield confidence."

"And a dagger or two," said Ashtrop. "To keep at bay those who challenge her." She giggled. "And a spell or two." She shrugged. "Everyone needs a spell, just for funimomes."

"Matig will take care of travelling arrangements," said Skuld.

"Then it is decided," said Urðr. "Etain sets out today." She gazed upon the young woman. "We feast to mark the occasion and create good memories to carry us through our time apart."

A plate of fried eggs and two slices of thick toast was plopped in front of Rosalind. On the table was butter and some type of red jam. These were pushed towards her, along with a cup of hot tea.

Etain plunked into the chair next to her. She radiated energy, making her unable to sit still. "We shall be great friends. Companions of the finest kind. We shall find great adventures together."

"Not too great," said Urðr.

Etain giggled, leant forward and whispered, "The greatest of adventures."

Rosalind returned the smile, then picked up her fork. She needed time to understand her role for the day. It sounded fantastic, but the exact purpose of these adventures left her guessing on whether or not she wanted to go on them. And then there was a nagging feeling that she had left something or someone behind. She felt the need to return to a certain place but a thorough search of her memory didn't tell her where.

8

The Mysterious Map

CORMAC DRAGGED HIS feet down the hall on the way to the tavern. He and Loggie had searched for Rosalind until well after midnight. By the time he returned to the room, he was exhausted, dispirited and drenched to the bone with waterlogged skin. He hung his clothes around the room and dropped into bed. His dreams were filled with running in a dark forest consumed by fog. It didn't matter how far or how long he ran, it was endless. Only trees. No people and more importantly, no Rosalind. When Loggie shook him awake at dawn, he'd felt like he hadn't slept.

He'd have complained, but it was vital they resumed the search early. The window for finding Rosalind was closing fast. The men who had taken her had their own plans, but it was the other problem that consumed him. If Rosalind had slept, she'd not remember him or Loggie, she'd wander off and be lost to them.

"A quick meal, and we start questioning people." Loggie led him to a corner booth. Given the hour, only about a dozen other people sat in the tavern. "Certainly, someone has seen her." He motioned over the server. "Eggs. Five. Fried. Tea. Yesterday, there was a woman with us. Have you seen her today?"

The server shook her head. "Only who you see here. I lives upstairs and haven't been outside yet." She looked at Cormac. "And you? Same?"

He considered what was ordered. "Sure. That's fine." He didn't feel like eating. His body needed sleep. His mind needed reassurance. Rubbing the sides of his head brought no relief, only pain from the newly formed bruises from tripping in the secret passageway beneath the tavern. He pushed back his hair that was in desperate need of a cut and cleaned sleep from his eyes. Yawning, he took in the scene around him.

The usual morning crowd occupied the space. The same soulless creatures he'd seen for more than five years.

His nerves jumped when a shadow passed before him and filled the seat beside Loggie. The young man with elven features rested his elbows on the table, clasped his hands and glanced around the tavern before turning his attention to Loggie and him. In a hushed voice, he spoke.

"We meet again."

"I've never met you," said Cormac.

Loggie's expression said otherwise. "You bumped into Rosalind at Maisa Ridge. Knocked her to the ground."

"That was you under the hood?" asked Cormac.

The man grinned. "A simple diversion. No one got hurt."

"Now you're here. Why?"

His mouth hesitated while he twisted his hands together. "You see, we thought you'd come through. Didn't happen. My mistake. I misjudged your abilities."

"What abilities?" asked Loggie.

He lowered his head and his voice. "To keep the map safe."

Cormac's eyes widened. "You have the map?"

"No, the woman with you does. Did." He shrugged. "Maybe still does in spite of capture."

He grabbed the man's jacket and jerked him halfway across the table. "Tell me where they took her? What are they going to do to her?"

"Calm down."

"He's not going to calm down," said Loggie. "He loves the woman."

"No, I don't."

Loggie rolled his eyes. "He's heart shy." He grabbed the man's head and shoved it to the table. "I'm angry. You put an innocent woman's life in danger with your foolishness."

"I can explain," he groaned. "Just give me a chance."

"Are you going to eat first or fight?" asked the server.

Cormac looked up. She balanced two plates and two mugs on a tray. "Eat. Then fight." He motioned for her to set the food on the table, and Loggie pushed the man's head aside. After she left, he dug into his eggs. "Who are you?"

"A man on a mission."

"Name?"

He hesitated.

"How can we believe anything you say if you won't give us your name?"

"I'm not the bad guy."

"Odd name. Was your father Not the Good Guy?"

He grumbled and spat out, "Jowsey. Look, Guthro doesn't want to kill anyone. He's out for treasure. Fame or fortune. I don't know exactly. I only know he wants the map. Bad."

"Bad enough to kill?" asked Loggie, who filled his mouth with eggs.

"I don't know. The two he's with are questionable, but they're not the brightest stars in the sky."

"The map leads to treasure?" asked Cormac.

"That's the thing. No one knows. The legend surrounding it says treasure. But of what type, I don't know."

"We're not interested in treasure," said Loggie. "We only want to rescue our friend."

"Great. I'd like to see that, too. Get the map back, and I'll be on my way."

"She doesn't have the map." Loggie took a drink of tea. "I'd have seen it."

"No, you wouldn't. It's disguised."

"In what way?"

He stared at the table and drummed his fingers. "I can't say."

"If she carried it, they've got it by now." He took another drink. "Our only concern is Rosalind. If they took her somewhere, found the map and left her, we need to know where that somewhere is."

"Okay, let's say they found the map," said Jowsey. "They'd take her to the edge of town and dump her." When Cormac's eyes grew large, he added, "Alive. Just so it would take time to return to the tavern."

"Wait," said Loggie. "I'm missing something. Why did you give her the map in the first place?"

"They were following me. Getting too close. It was three against me, and I couldn't escape. Fortunately, I saw you." He shrugged. "My plan was to hide it on your friend, get captured and released since I didn't have the map, and then track you down."

"Except?"

"They followed me to my contact, heard me tell him and then left Maisa Ridge."

"The other man in the alley that night?" asked Loggie.

"Maybe."

"What alley? When?" asked Cormac.

"You were sleeping," said Loggie. "Nothing important." He turned to Jowsey. "Why are you here? Why aren't you tracking this Guthro and stealing the map back?"

"It's still three against me. I don't like the odds."

"In other words, you want us to steal the map for you?"

"For you, it will be rescuing a friend."

"And you go off to find buried treasure," said Cormac.

"Not buried. Hidden."

"The same." While taking this man along evened the odds, he didn't trust him. "Maybe this Guthro didn't find the map on Rosalind, and you're here to find it for him. For all we know, you're working with him, not against him. You've hardly a scratch from this so-called confrontation with him at Maisa Ridge."

"A fair statement. I'm slippery. Fast. An opportunist, let's say."

"And you see opportunity with us." Loggie sounded unimpressed. "Our friend's life is on the line. We don't care about your map or your treasure, so tell us, where are they?"

He delayed replying. When he finally answered, it sounded like a lie. "I don't know. I didn't know she was captured until early this morning."

"How did you learn of it?" asked Loggie.

He fiddled with a short strand of thread and avoided eye contact. "You see, I set out to steal the map early this morning."

"And?" Cormac leant forward, his slow speed of talking irritating him.

"I saw she was gone."

"You were in our room?"

His nervous chuckle said it all. "I didn't steal anything. I was after the map. When I saw the state of the room and she not there, I thought there was only one reason she wasn't. Now I know."

"You didn't know when you sat down?"

He shook his head. "We're not enemies. We can work together. Each get what we want."

"I don't think so," said Cormac.

"So quick to decide," said Jowsey. "At least consider it."

"I have. No." He shoved egg into his mouth. The more awake he became, the hungrier he grew. He wished he'd ordered sausage or ham to go with the eggs.

Jowsey turned to Loggie. "You'll reconsider. You appear wiser than this sorry cut for kindling."

Loggie huffed. "Where do you suggest we start? Any place this Guthro might hide out?"

"I don't know him well. You might say we're enemies and as enemies, he failed to share his hang-out."

"A clue? Anything?"

"We're travellers through Romarin. The only reason he's here is because of you."

"Not me." Loggie jabbed Jowsey's chest. "You." He took a long drink of tea, staring at him over the rim. Setting it down, he smacked his lips. "Here's what we're going to do. We team up, find Guthro, and offer you to him in exchange for Rosalind."

Jowsey's face twisted. "He doesn't want me. He wants the map."

"You two can sort it out." He shoved the last bite of egg into his mouth. "You've disturbed my sleep. You've disturbed my morning meal. Don't disturb my entire day."

Cormac took the last drink of his tea. He was eager to get outside. Eager to find Rosalind before she disappeared from his life for good. If this world was a better place, he'd take the map and find the treasure. Now that would be an excellent quest, one he had successfully done many times with friends back home.

"Let's take the horses," said Loggie. "If she was dropped at the edge of town as this thief says, we'll be able to cover more ground."

"Good idea." Cormac stood.

"Can I ride one?"

He frowned at him. "What happened to your horse?"

"Lost it."

"Really?"

"Wasn't mine to begin with so..." He shrugged.

"Everything else and a horse thief, too." He was about to say more but caught Loggie's mischievous grin and remembered the horse he rode wasn't exactly his. Then he thought about Clive and how easily he could catch up to him if he lingered too long in town. With all the excitement, he had forgotten about that man.

He led them to the stable. It was quiet with only one man, who presumably stayed at the inn, outside the doors preparing his horse for travel. Walking into the large stable, he saw five horses held in crossties in the aisle, boys in their young teens grooming and tacking them up. They looked familiar. Then he realised they were the horses he had rode in on. He slowed his pace and glanced at Loggie. "Ours?" he whispered.

Loggie looked ahead, his eyes narrowing in the dimmer light. "They appear to be. But why?" He glared at Jowsey. "Your doing?"

He shrugged. "I've done nothing here."

Cormac stopped dead in his tracks. Who had told the stable hands to prepare the horses for a journey? Clive? He glanced around quickly, looking for the man and the three others who travelled with him. Thoughts of slipping out the door and leaving town invaded his mind. Avoidance of danger had kept him alive all these years. He didn't need a horse. Didn't need what was in his room. The itch in his feet directed him to turn around. He prepared to do that when Jowsey spoke.

"Why are we stopped?"

He ignored him, took a step back, but Jowsey stood in the way. Out the side of his mouth, he whispered to Loggie. "Clive?"

Loggie hung back, searching the area. The concern on his face increased the activity of Cormac's nerves and sped up his heart rate. It was possible. Even probable that Clive had found his horses and was reclaiming them. Clive would also look for him. In the short span of less than 12 hours, he was about to lose everything if he didn't run now.

"Risen and ready, I see."

Cormac whipped around to see who had spoken. It was the stable hand he'd met when he'd arrived. Marty Matig. "Are those our horses?" He swallowed to still the shake in his voice.

"Course. Dilly-dalliers we're no'." The man adjusted his grey flat cap. "Never too early, though..." he looked towards the large doorway, "mus' be near eigh'. Late morning."

"Who told you to prepare the horses?"

"Shepherd Skuld himself. Excited he is. Waited for this day." He grinned, revealing a missing eyetooth. "Fond of the young misses, but 'tis her destiny."

Loggie stepped forward. "This Skuld man is taking our horses?"

Marty eyed him sharply. "He's no' going along. Though there's an extra moun' for him. Wha' do you wan' me to do with i'? This man riding i'?" He pointed at Jowsey.

Loggie blinked quickly, then scratched the side of his head hard. "I'm confused. Can we start at the beginning? Where are we going?"

"North! To Delgrath."

"Why are we going there?" asked Cormac, ready to correct the man.

Marty stared. Hard. "That's where Sir Uwen the Noble is. He's the one who will train Miss Etain."

It was Cormac's turn to rub his head hard. "Can we start before the beginning? Who is Miss Etain?"

Marty shook his head. "You ain' had a nigh' sleep, have you? She and her escor' will be here soon." He looked him over, left and right. "No baggage? Packed, are you?"

"Is this an elaborate hoax to confuse me?" asked Jowsey. "If it is, it's working."

"Sir, we've no time for travel," said Loggie. "Our friend is missing, and we need to find her."

"Ah, the swee' miss..." He looked around. "No' with you. She should go, too."

"We're not leaving without her."

"No can wai'. Today. Fate has chosen. No one resists Fate."

"Watch us," said Cormac.

A ten-year-old boy ran up to Marty, grinning from ear-to-ear and out of breath. "She's here!"

"Wonderful." Marty gestured them forward. "Come. Mee' the one who deserves your protection."

"Protection?" mumbled Cormac. He'd meet the woman, explain that these were his horses, and she'd need to find others. Making the turn, he spied an older man wearing a robe and two women about the same height standing next to him. One had golden hair, part of it braided down her back. The unusual colour kept his attention for a few steps. She was beautiful, but she radiated something that confused his senses. Even in the dimmer light of the stable, her bright green eyes shone, and they found him and watched him approach. She was dressed in brown trousers with multiple pockets that tucked into knee-high leather boots. Her jacket was open, revealing a thick knitted shirt beneath. Across her chest was slung a purse. Not a purse. An Indian Jones type hip bag, but this one was adorned with jewels and a thin pompom of leather strips. Near her feet rested a backpack, half full, also with multiple pockets. The sheathed dagger on her hip and the smaller one tied to her calf piqued his curiosity. He was meant to protect her? She appeared capable of protecting herself.

She watched his every step, and he couldn't take his eyes away from her.

"It's Rosalind," whispered Loggie.

Pulled from his thoughts, Cormac deciphered what he'd said. Rosalind? Where? He looked to the left and right, into horse stalls and glanced over his shoulder.

"Miss Etain." Marty walked up to the golden-haired woman, grasped both hands in his and held them. "Wonderful to see you. You are well-prepared for your journey? If in need of anything, only ask, and i' will be granted."

"Thank you, Marty," she said. "All is in place."

Her voice wasn't as smooth as Cormac expected. Drawing nearer, he recognised elven features, yet he saw no trace of Rosal... He stared at the woman next to her and recognised the narrow chin, the sharp cheek bones and excitable brown eyes. Rosalind? He stopped before her, taking in her face as if he had never seen it before. She had bathed. Something she'd never done since he'd met her. Her hair was not dull brown, but golden brown with more copper than dark brown. She wore a slim-fitting outfit similar to Etain's, but it fit her better.

"These are the men who will deliver me to Delgrath?" asked Etain.

"Indeed," said Marty.

"As I have seen it in my visions," said Skuld. "And as Urðr has described them." He reached out a hand to Cormac, who accepted it but did not take his eyes from Rosalind. "Your name, man."

"Cormac, sir."

"This is Miss Etain, the one I place under your care." He motioned towards her. "Shake her hand as well."

Forcing his eyes away from Rosalind, he grasped Etain's hand. "Nice to meet you." Not really, he thought. He had no idea what was transpiring.

"And this is Rosalind, Miss Etain's guardian."

Cormac grasped her hand and held it gently. "Rosalind, I've been..." He couldn't say what he wanted to. She looked at him as he knew she would: like she didn't know him. An odd feeling surfaced in his chest and for the first time since they'd met many days ago, he wanted her to remember him. "Happy to see you."

"It is a pleasure to meet you," she said. "I am told you are skilled and will protect us on our journey."

He stifled a chuckle. This all felt like a cruel joke, one his friends, who he played Mediaeval Dungeon Adventures with, would pull for their amusement even if it saw their group thrown into the dungeon. "I will do my best."

"It is all that can be asked."

"Loggie." Loggie stepped forward, grasped her hand and kissed the back of it. "It is indeed a pleasure to see you."

Her cheeks turned pink. Something Cormac had never seen happen.

"It appears the guardian is to receive more attention than the future enchantress." Skuld raised an eyebrow. "Fine while safe in Romarin, but not on the journey."

"Isn't this the woman who was with you in Maisa Ridge?" Jowsey studied her, looking for something, probably the map. She was wearing new clothes, so if he had hidden the map in her cloak or shirt, it was gone.

Loggie shook his head discretely. "Rosalind. Etain. Our horses are at your disposal. Let's mount up and ride."

"I need to grab the saddlebags." Cormac needed help carrying the three bags that held their food and a few other items, but he didn't want to select Loggie to help and leave Rosalind in Jowsey's care. "Jowsey, help me get our supplies. We won't be long." He pulled the man with him. When they exited the stable, Jowsey spoke.

"That is your friend. While her style has changed, I recognise her."

"It's her."

"Why doesn't she know you?"

"Who says she doesn't?" He'd leave that in the air, letting him form his own opinion.

"What scheme are you running?" he asked.

"Can't say." He led the way to the room and opened the door. "Does she have the map?"

He grinned mischievously. "Can't say."

"She will not be harmed." He closed the door, threw Jowsey against the wall and held him there with his arm on his throat. "We don't want the map, but it will be taken gently so as not to startle or scare her. Understand?"

Jowsey huffed. "I get it. You love the woman."

"No, I don't."

"Heart shy."

"She's a friend."

"Whatever. I'll get the map and disappear...as soon as we get a good distance from Romarin."

"So, you won't be left here with Guthro and his thugs?"

"Exactly. The map is useless if I can't escape."

"Fine. We leave together, then you take the map and run." He released him and packed the belongings in the bags. Taking two, he gave the third to Jowsey, then looked around to see if he'd forgotten anything. After returning the room key, he stepped away from the counter and prepared to walk to the stable when a voice stopped him in his tracks.

His breath caught, and he held his swallow while he listened. It was Clive's voice. He was almost certain of it. Cautiously, he stepped towards the exit. From here, he couldn't see most of the tavern, only the tables near the entrance. The urge to glance over his shoulder to confirm it was Clive and to see if the other men were with him impeded his progress. Obviously, Clive hadn't seen him because he spoke casually to the server, ordering his meal and asking for a strong shot of rum in his coffee.

Jowsey nudged him forward, and he walked silently from the foyer and onto the boardwalk, making a bee-line to the stable. He breathed a sigh of relief when he saw the five horses fully tacked, two already with saddlebags, and Skuld giving final instructions to Etain, Rosaline and Loggie. He secured the final three saddlebags, then mounted.

"Let's ride," he said. "As a famous man once said, *We're burning daylight.*" Rosalind twisted her face as if searching her memory for the saying.

"Sounds about right," said Jowsey, climbing into the saddle of the spare horse.

Loggie shook Skuld's hand, bid him good day, then mounted. Rosalind did the same, then everyone waited while Etain gave Skuld a long hug, kind words and reassurance she'd reach her destination and return to meet him again.

Watching the exchange, acknowledging that he and the others in the party were supposedly her protectors, he marvelled at the circumstances that had led him to this point. In all his years of travelling this land, he'd never teamed up with anyone for very long. He remembered a few of their names but never knew them. Not like he knew Rosalind and Loggie, not that he knew them well, but he knew them more than anyone else in this fantasy land.

"Safe travels," said Skuld after Etain mounted. "I will send word of your departure and look forward to that of your arrival."

"I will have fantastic stories to tell upon my return," said Etain. "Keep Urðr, Claudia, Ceallach and Ashtrop with positive thoughts. Though they worry, it does them no good."

"While true, they will do so regardless."

She grinned. "I will not apologize for not sharing the worry."

"Blessed child. Nor should you." He waved as they rode off.

Cormac focussed on the road ahead, turning left out of the alley though he knew the route shorter by going right. The tavern windows overlooked the road that way, and if he could escape Romarin without being seen by Clive, he'd have a head start.

Jowsey rode abreast. He wore an odd expression but didn't air his question if he had one. Etain and Rosalind rode behind him, and Loggie took up the rear. They travelled in close formation until they left the town behind, then gave each other a little more space.

"Did you see any sign of Guthro?" asked Jowsey.

"No. Wasn't looking," said Cormac.

"Who were you looking for?"

"No one."

"Could ov fooled me."

He ignored him. Quiet chatter took place behind him, and he looked over his shoulder at Rosalind and Etain. They rode close to each other and while their expressions revealed they spoke of exciting topics, their voices were low. He heard the odd word but couldn't make out what they talked about. Turning forward, he focussed on the northerly road ahead and setting a quick pace to put distance between him and Romarin, him and Clive.

Rosalind sat cross-legged on the ground near the fire with the Roots of Terra cards. She'd read the note again before shuffling the deck. Focussing on the message and letting her mind drift to shifts in the soughing in the upper branches of the trees surrounding her, she waited for energy in the air to identify itself. Soft puffs of air brushed her fingers and made them tingle. Was this the energy? She hoped so. Shuffling twice more, she placed the deck on a smooth part of the saddlebag and flipped over a card. As the note told her, she stared at the colours, the design and followed the lines to see what the future held. A vision of water splashing against rocks appeared and faded just as quickly. She searched for the vision again, but nothing appeared. She flipped over another card.

"Have you worked the Roots of Terra before?" asked Etain, who sat a few feet away reading a book no larger than her palm.

"I think so."

"One should not dabble in the unknown. Urðr advises we stay away from that we do not know and are not trained in."

"How are we supposed to learn new things?"

"Through wise teachers. As apprentices."

"Is that why you're going to Delgrath? To be taught by Sir Uwen the Noble? To be his apprentice?"

"Yes, it's my destiny."

"Who said?"

"Urðr, Claudia, Ceallach and Ashtrop have all foreseen it."

She rolled that thought over in her mind. She didn't know these sisters or their mother or the powers they had, but she didn't believe anyone could predict a definite future for someone. One simple change could snowball into a completely different life. "Have they predicted it or planned it?"

Etain was about to speak but held her tongue. She searched the edge of the forest where they'd set up camp, her eyes roaming over the landscape as if she sought the answer in nature. When she turned back, her face was blank. "I have not asked that question."

"It's an important one."

She leant forward and viewed the card drawn. "Do your cards speak otherwise?"

"I have not mastered reading my own energy. I shall not do it for others. Mistakes will happen."

"Our journey is long. Perhaps we will discover the answer before we reach Delgrath."

"We should set a watch," said Loggie, interrupting the conversation.

"I agree," said Jowsey.

"I do not own a watch," said Rosalind. Cormac stared at her, and she wondered if he had one. He was a mysterious man, one who held his tongue instead of speaking his thoughts. Young and handsome, she sensed a seriousness about him the other two men did not possess. When he had held her hand, oh so gently, to shake it when they'd met at the stable, she thought she'd met him before but could not find him in her memories.

"I meant someone to sit up and watch while the rest of us sleep," explained Loggie.

"You want someone to stay up all night? They will be exhausted by morning."

"The way it works," said Cormac, "is, someone watches for a few hours, then wakes someone else, who sits for a few hours. Usually, three people watch during the night."

"Odd. What do they watch for? Falling stars? Raccoons?"

Again, he stared, hesitating to respond. Finally, he simply said, "People." His eyes, a mixture of green and grey in the glow of the fire, remained on her for a moment more, then he looked to Loggie. "Will you take first?"

"Sure."

"I'll take second," said Jowsey.

"I'll watch." She could continue working with her cards since she had no time during the day.

"Wait. No." Cormac grimaced. "If you do, you get first watch, and you..." he considered Jowsey, "I'm not sure."

"I can watch!" said Etain. She jumped up. "I've heard stories from travellers who have done such a thing. I could sit high in that tree." She pointed to a great pine on the edge of the campsite. "I will be well hidden but have a perfect view of the slumber area. Intruders do not attack from the road but from the bush. Those who know say it is useless to watch the road. Danger does not come from there. Unless a bear wanders down it."

"A bear," exclaimed Rosalind. "I will take first watch. I can smell bears before I see them."

Confusion raced across Cormac's face. "Bears. Yes. And other wild creatures that can eat us."

"Like dragons," said Rosalind.

"They come from the sky," said Etain. "Which I'll be able to see from my seat in the tree."

"Can I not sit by the fire and work my cards?"

"No, you must be vigilant. At the very least, sit beneath the pine to ensure you are not seen by those set on attacking us." Etain clasped her hands before her glowing face. "This is exciting. I am finally on my first real adventure."

"What do we do with them?" asked Rosalind. "Kill them or offer them food?"

Cormac's face twisted further and he prepared to speak, but Etain beat him to it.

"Food?!" Her eyes grew wide, then settled. "I suppose if they are hungry and that is all they want. Food might send them off. But if they are evil, you cut out their liver and shove it into their mouth."

"What if I can't find the liver? What if I use another organ by mistake?" Rosalind scratched her head. "This sounds confusing."

"You'll know," said Etain. "It will smell funny. And it has an icky feel about it."

"Wouldn't every organ cut fresh from the body smell and have an icky feel to it?"

"No, the liver is special."

"How do you know?" asked Jowsey, his eyebrows twisted in an awkward angle.

She shrugged. "I speak to everyone who enters the sanctuary. They know." She stretched out the last word and leant towards him.

"Sanctuary?" Cormac looked at Rosalind. "Did you get in? Is that how you escaped Guthro?"

She stared at him, wondering who Guthro was but more importantly, why she'd have to escape from him.

"She entered the sanctuary," proclaimed Etain. "She was worthy and in need, and she was destined to meet me."

"But the dragon fire," said Loggie. "How did she get past it?"

"Dorca protected her, aiming his fire at those who threatened her. He allows safe passage to those in need of sanctuary."

"Well, that answers those questions and created more," said Cormac. "We searched for you half the night. We thought, the w..." He grimaced. "We hoped you were safe."

"You saw me last night?"

"We did."

"You must have banged your head," said Loggie. "And forgot about us. We are grateful you are safe."

She felt her head. There was no bump. "I will work to remember."

"What were you doing in the sanctuary?" Cormac asked Etain.

"I live there."

"With Skuld?" asked Loggie.

"Shepherd Skuld is dragon master. He houses the family of Fate."

"Lady Urðr and her daughters?" asked Rosalind.

"Yes. They are like family."

"You called her aunt."

She grinned. "Of course. Family."

"Let's get back to watch," said Loggie. "Rosalind, you take first watch. If anyone comes, wake us up. You need not kill or remove organs. Together, we will confront them."

"I prefer that option."

"I'll take second," said Cormac.

"Are you sure?" asked Loggie. "You slept little last night."

"Positive."

"I had a full night's sleep," said Jowsey. "I'll take last watch, so I can watch the sun rise."

"What about me?" asked Etain.

"You will be first watch tomorrow night," said Loggie.

"Wonderful. We take turns. We all get sleep, and we all get adventures." She plopped down next to the fire, picked up her book and opened it where she'd stopped reading. "To sleep beneath the stars was but a dream until tonight."

"You've always slept in a bed?" asked Cormac.

"Yes. I've never left the sanctuary until today."

His mouth dropped open, and his eyes bulged. Rosalind knew how he felt. Staying in one place, one building all these years would have been a prison. She would never have survived.

One-by-one, the others crawled beneath blankets supplied by Shepherd Skuld. Before the sky darkened completely and the stars shone brightly, they were asleep and Rosalind was sitting at the foot of the great pine, hidden from view of travellers and wild beasts. The moon had set hours ago, leaving the sky dark and the stars bright. They provided enough illumination for her to see the thick symbols on the cards but not the fine details. She focussed more on sorting out the energy in the Roots of Terra cards than the sleeping area. They were under no threat.

Though she was appointed guardian of Etain. She glanced around the area and listened. An owl hooted, bugs buzzed and water flowed over the rocks in the nearby stream.

"All is well," whispered a voice. "Welcome back."

She smiled at the fairy sitting on the toadstool a few feet away. "Have I been gone long?"

She shook her head. "Learning Terra?"

"Trying. Do you know how to read the cards?"

"Very well." She flew to Rosalind's knee, sat down and gazed upon the three cards laid out. "Oooh. Dragons. There are many good ones and this one is..." She leant closer. "Questionable."

"Where?"

"There." She pointed to the card with the decorative cave entrance. "He appears to be stuck in a dungeon of some sort." Her voice grew sad. "Poor soul. He's been there an awfully long time. He's in misery. He longs for home, for those he loves." She looked up at her with sparkle in her eyes. "Maybe you will rescue him."

"A dragon needs rescuing?"

"There are always those greater than us, and those trickier."

"That is a fair quest."

The fairy hopped up, stood on the edge of Rosalind's knee and put her hands on her hips, creating a warrior pose. "And I, Lady Coraline Eldlow of Maiden's Way, will be by your side."

Rosalind giggled. "I am grateful for your friendship."

"Let us see what else is in our future." She plopped down and studied the cards again.

Rosalind flipped another card over, and again the fairy grew excited. With Coraline by her side, she felt grounded. She was the only familiar face in this strange land.

Around midnight, she woke Cormac. It took several shakes before his eyes fluttered open and he stared at her as if a stranger, wondering where he was. Then he sat up abruptly.

"Is everything okay?" he mumbled.

"Fine. Your time to watch the watch." She gave him the time piece Jowsey had given her to mark the hour.

He rubbed sleep from his eyes and shook his head. After a large yawn, he dragged his sleeve over his eyes and moved spit around in his mouth. "I guess so. Where'd you sit?"

"There, beneath the pine." Gazing upon her, she wondered if he had more to ask. His body suggested he did, but his mouth stood still. "Do you need water?"

He shook his head. "I wanted to say..." He surveyed those sleeping around him while his fingers toyed with an object beneath his shirt. Perhaps a necklace of some sort. "Thank you for waking me." He stood, gave his body a shake, then went to the spot beneath the pine.

Rosalind settled under her blanket, facing him. At this angle, she saw only his shoulders and head. He stared back at the campsite, possible at her, but the light was too dim to determine that. Time passed, her eyelids sagged and before constellations shuffled across the sky, she was asleep.

Dreams filled her sleep. Water crashing against rocks on the shore, a white dragon living deep within a mountain and... Something touched her, and her nerves came alive. Her hand moved under another power. Was she floating on a river? She opened her eyes and the person before her stared in surprise. He pulled away, and she sat up.

"What's going on?" She rubbed her eyes roughly. The sun had yet to rise, but twilight was spreading across the land. "Is it time to get up?"

"You were dreaming," he said. "I thought you were having a nightmare." His should-length brown hair looked like it hadn't been combed in days. It was parted in the middle with little sign of bangs. His eyes appeared dark in the dim light.

"I was... I think... I don't remember the dream."

"Did it scare you?"

She considered the condition of her body. It was calm. If the dream was scary, it had no effect on her nerves.

"What's going on?" Another man rose from a blanket nearby. "Rosalind, are you okay?" He scowled at the man next to her.

"I'm okay. I was having a nightmare." She glanced at the man beside her. He moved away and settled near the firepit where the fire had died to simmering coals.

The man who had called her Rosalind stood and reached for her hand. "Come with me, please."

She accepted his hand and rose. Walking away from the campsite, she surveyed her clothing. The trousers, thick shirt and jacket were foreign to her, but they kept her warm, so she wouldn't complain.

When they reached a fair distance from the others, he turned to her. "I am Loggie. Your friend. I will keep you safe."

"Thank you, but I..." Her tongue froze. Something in his eyes felt familiar.

"You don't remember me. A spell has been cast upon you."

Her eyes widened. "By who?"

"We don't know. But we're trying to fix it. Before we start the day, let me tell you of the people in our small group and what we are doing." He smiled. "Your name is Rosalind."

9

Midnight Excursion

CORMAC GROANED AND stretched, trying to shake the weariness from his body. He had slept well when he slept but breaking up the night with a watch didn't do him any favours. He was almost as tired as when he first lay down. He slapped his tongue on the inside of his mouth and gathered spit. It was going to be a long day.

He spotted Loggie talking with Rosalind at the edge of the clearing near the brook. No doubt, it was their morning conversation: reminding her of who she was. Today, it was vital she had that information. Given the men who searched for her to retrieve the map and Clive, she needed to understand who was a threat to her life.

Sensations he didn't recognise tingled in his chest. He was a good person, a law-biding citizen where he came from, and he had never caused anyone harm but right now, he questioned his integrity.

Etain squealed on the other side of the darkened firepit. Leaping from her bedroll, she stretched, did a whirl, then dropped onto her knees to dig into her backpack. "Mornings are the best. I shall have bread. Oats with cold water." She grinned and her eyes buzzed. "It is the food of the trail. My cousins ensured I had enough to do a five-day journey, the time it will take to reach Moore. Shepherd Skuld gave me coins to purchase the necessary supplies." She grabbed the bread from the pack. "Bread with adventures is the greatest."

He didn't say anything. He had no words to describe how he felt. How could anyone spend their entire life in one building? She was 19, maybe 20, and her first real experiences in life would be with him and the others on a road that took them north to some guy she'd never met. Was she to be locked away there, too?

Loggie and Rosalind returned. She went to her backpack, one similar to Etain's, and dug out a sack of food.

"Bread and oatmeal," said Etain. "Cousins have packed it well. Let us break this first fast together."

"I am your guardian." Rosalind's statement was half question.

"Yes. You are well prepared."

"I am?"

"Of course. You are the chosen one. The one I was destined to meet. Even Urðr cannot deny it."

Rosalind glanced at the others. "And they are to protect you, too?"

"Protect us both."

"Good." She broke off a piece of bread and took a bite.

Cormac dug into the food sack Skuld had provided and extracted bread. Bread. He ate it every day. Most days, it was plain. Not toasted. Not with anything on it. He released a long sigh. At least he had toasted bread with butter on it at the tavern a few times in the past week. One morning, he even had strawberry jam to put on it. Today, he'd have only water with it. Bread and water: a prisoner's ration. Perfect since he was a prisoner of this fantasy land.

He peeked into the sack and saw something green. A cucumber. That was different. He had been too tired last night to explore the sack and had eaten only a piece of bread. Taking the knife Skuld had provided, he cut off two pieces of bread, then sliced cucumber, making a sandwich. He bit into it and savoured the taste. Now this was different. He sat back against the saddlebags and watched the birds fly to and fro and listened to their song. This wasn't the best breakfast, but it was better than most he'd eaten in this land.

A short time later, when he was saddling his horse, Loggie came to him.

"The problem must be solved sooner than expected," said Loggie.

"What problem?"

"Rosalind." He leant close and whispered. "Things are getting too complicated. We need to find a paladin to remove the spell."

He baulked. "Remove what spell?"

"The one that erases her memory."

"Can a paladin do that?"

"I am told they can," said Loggie.

He searched the man's face. His eyes were serious, his expression determined. But Loggie was wrong. A paladin couldn't break this spell.

Harmon had told him there was only one way...two. But the second wasn't permanent and could end at any time.

"We will ask at the next settlement." Loggie turned angry and lunged towards him but instead of striking him, raced past.

Cormac spun to find Jowsey standing near the rear of the horse. Loggie grasped his jacket and jerked him forward.

"This is not for your ears," spat Loggie.

"Yet I heard it." Jowsey chuckled. "So that's why you need a paladin. You should have told Fuller. He may have helped."

"Who?" asked Cormac.

"The man with me in the alley," said Jowsey. "The one your friend won't talk about."

Cormac looked at him. "What were you doing meeting this man in an alley?"

"I wasn't meeting him. A thief had stolen my change purse, and we bumped into them while they were making a deal."

"He gave me the map," said Jowsey. "He expects me to deliver it to our contact."

"Guess he chose the wrong person to do that," said Loggie.

He huffed. "I'm halfway there."

"What does that mean?" asked Cormac.

"Just know when you no longer see me, I'll be on my way."

"Not with Rosalind."

"Not so heart shy now."

He cringed. He hated that phrase. It didn't apply to him.

"Just get me the leather bracer, and I'll be gone. Today."

Cormac and Loggie exchanged glances. "The leather armband is the map?" asked Cormac.

"Hidden in plain view." Jowsey pulled free from Loggie's grip. "She still has it."

"Maybe we want to find this treasure," said Loggie.

He grunted. "You've not the stamina nor the courage."

"Maybe we'll prove you wrong," said Cormac. What was he saying? He didn't want to hunt for treasure.

"Fine. Come with me then. Except..." He smirked. "I'm not the one following the map."

"Who is?"

"Shayde Thornheart."

Cormac laughed. "That's a made-up name if I ever heard one. Is he your brother or something?"

"You've never heard of the Great Shayde Thornheart?"

He shook his head. "Is he as good as Gandolf or as evil as Saruman?"

"Never heard of them, so I guess they're not so great."

"They're greater than your Shayde Thornheart."

"This isn't a competition," said Loggie. "A paladin. We need one. It sounds like you know where to find one. Tell us where, and we'll give you the bracer."

"He'll lie!" Cormac didn't trust either of them, and he didn't want a paladin involved.

"I don't lie. I manipulate the truth."

"The next village," said Loggie. "What is it?"

Jowsey shrugged, and his eyes darted between the men. "Hermit...something. Hermit's Hollow. We'll reach it today. Late today."

"Good. Will there be a paladin there?"

"I don't know. It's not like I've a paladin kammerat. And I've never courted their sisters."

"Your friend? Where is he?"

"On his way to parts left unsaid."

Loggie frowned. "So, he's meeting you there?"

"No."

"You don't sound convincing. Either way, let's get moving before trouble rides over us." Loggie marched to his horse and tacked up.

Jowsey leant close to Cormac and whispered, "You seem like a reasonable person, someone who cares about Rosalind's well being."

"Don't start."

"I mean, you don't want to see her harmed. If Guthro finds her, I can't promise he won't kill her to get the map. It's worth a lot to the right person."

"To get her, he has to go through us."

"Like he did in Romarin?"

His back stiffened. "I'm assuming you'll stand against him to protect your map."

"Sure." Sarcasm slid from his tongue. "Me and the metamorphosing nymph who's on her first *adventure...*" he raised his voice and eyebrows to say the word, "will be a great help." He got serious. "All I'm asking for is the map, and I'll be out of your life, taking Guthro and his henchmen with me. You and your ladylove can return to your boring life."

He grabbed him by the jacket and jerked him forward. "She ain't my ladylove, and my life is far from boring. And I don't make deals with weasels."

"Fine. Just know if we come under fire, I'm taking what's mine and abandoning ship."

"Like the weasel you are." He threw him backwards and turned to his saddle, watching out the corner of his eye as he walked away. He released a frustrating sigh. He didn't want the map. He didn't want Jowsey travelling with him, nor Loggie and that woman needing an escort. When he'd rescued Rosalind from the prison, he had a simple plan. How had it fallen apart so quickly?

Mid-morning saw grey clouds move in and threaten rain. It started to mist, but the rain held off. Entering a lush forest with ferns filling every possible space between the trees, a heavy silence filled the air. An odd smell seeped into Cormac's nose, and he sniffed in an attempt to identify it. Moist. Like toe jam or belly-button wax.

"What is that." Disgust laced Loggie's voice.

"Slime," said Jowsey.

Cormac stared at him. He rode abreast, mostly in silence, but now and again, he'd make a smart remark. "Slime? Nothing more? Is there a slime pit around here?"

"Slugs. They're in season."

"There must be thousands of them to make that smell."

"Not exactly."

"You've seen them?"

"Once or twice."

He frowned and turned back to the road. He didn't recall this section when he'd passed before. It must have been out of season for slugs. The mist continued, and low-lying fog lay over the road ahead. On either side was bog or swamp. He couldn't see much in the thick cloud. A few minutes later, the fog got so thick, he could only see a hundred feet ahead. The silence ate at his nerves, and the hair on his neck sprang up. Nothing made a sound. It was like everything was dead. The clopping of the horses' hooves against the soft ground echoed, and the squeak of saddle leather was ten times as loud.

"Creepy," whispered Etain.

"I feel like we're being watched," said Rosalind in the same hushed voice. After a short pause, she whispered, "I sense an unsettling. Do you see what causes it?"

"I can't see anything in this road cloud," said Etain.

Cormac strained his eyes to peer through the veil of fluff. A shadow took form and then another one. They were as large as seals, even had the shape of a seal. The farther he rode, the more he thought they were seals.

"Of all the pigs to butcher!" mumbled Jowsey.

"Why?"

"You've never seen a cornucopia have you?"

"I don't know what that is?"

"It's a large gathering of slugs."

"So. Slugs are no big deal."

"The slugs of Astro Pond are different than your usual slug."

"How so?"

"They can grow as large as a hauflin and when they're in season, they're hungry."

He let up on the reins and stared at the road ahead. Several large shadows appeared in the fog.

"Don't do that," said Jowsey. He turned to the others. "They sense fear. Don't slow down. We either turn back and run or charge through. They're easy to kill unless you're unable to defend yourself and there are four or five on you."

"We should turn back." Cormac didn't want to fight slugs. There was no need.

"When I say ride, follow me," said Jowsey over his shoulder. "Keep up. Run over them. They're soft. They'll fall."

Before Cormac could stop him, Jowsey brought his horse into a gallop and raced away. The others did the same. Not wanting to be trampled or left behind, he raced after Jowsey. The shadows quickly grew into solid forms. Prominent tentacles with huge black balls on the end swayed in the breeze, then turned towards him. Were those eyes? If so, every slug on the road was watching him. Sweat gathered between his fingers and the leather reins, and the voice inside his head kept yelling at him. "Turn around! Run!" He ignored it but its pitch grew as he neared the first slug.

Jowsey was four horse-lengths in front of him, and the nose of Rosalind's horse was at his knee. The pounding of hooves resounded in his ears, and all he could think about was holding on while his horse galloped blindly into the fog. Six shadows grew to ten, then a dozen, then he lost count. He passed the nearest ones in a blur but when one stood directly in his path, he tried to weave around it. The horse stumbled and caught its balance but not before veering into the soft body that struck Cormac's leg, then bounced off. A thick layer of slime coated his pants and boot.

Focussing on Jowsey, he sped forward, over-running a slim slug directly in his path. The impact released a gelatin substance that plastered the horse and his body. The horse shook its head frantically and snorted hard. Snot and goo flew into the air and onto Cormac's face. It stung his eyes and oozed into his mouth, making him gag. He wiped his eyes quickly with the back of his sleeve.

The fog thickened and visibility reduced to 50 feet that went by quickly at a gallop. Hoping Jowsey saw enough of the road to follow it, he trailed him, dodging snails if he could, but he was certain he hit one in every ten on the road.

A scream from the rear, made him glance over his shoulder. Rosalind was slowing down and quickly disappearing in the fog. "Stop!" He shouted at Jowsey and slowed his pace enough to turn. He didn't want to go back, but he needed Rosalind.

A riderless horse rushed by him. It was Etain's. Damn. He couldn't see her, Rosalind or Loggie, but he heard them struggling, shouting at one another. He kicked his horse into the fog and came upon Loggie and Rosalind stabbing slugs that swarmed Etain, who lay on the ground caked with thick slime. She shook and heaved, all the while trying to clean her face of the gelatine-like substance. Remembering how thick and resistant slug slime was on garden plants, he imagined it blocked her mouth and nose, making it impossible to breathe.

He leapt from the horse and sprinted towards them, dodging slugs that reached out to him. Falling to his knees beside Etain's head, he jerked a rag from his shoulder bag and roughly wiped her face, clearing what he could from her mouth and nose. She gasped for breath and clung to him with a death grip. Pulling her to her feet, he led her back to his horse. Jowsey had circled back and trampled several slugs with the front hooves of his horse.

"Let's go!" Cormac shouted at Loggie and Rosalind. He jumped onto the horse, kicked a slug away from the stirrup and pulled Etain up behind him. Once Loggie and Rosalind were on their horses, he charged forward. Once again, Jowsey led the way, and Loggie and Rosalind brought up the rear.

Cormac didn't know how long or how far they travelled. He knew only that by the time they emerged from the fog, he was exhausted and covered with a layer of slime so thick, it dripped from his hair into his eyes and ran down his shirt. White foam covered the lips of his horse and flew back at him, adding to his misery.

Behind him, Etain gripped him tightly around the waist. A quick glance told him she was in a similar state except he had block much of the slime from her face, which she buried in his shoulder. When she looked up, the eyes that had been so excited to be on this adventure were wide, almost pleading.

"You're okay," he said. He surveyed the others. "We're okay." He forced a smile. "All in a day's work."

"You are truly my saviours."

He wanted to laugh but didn't want to make her think he was laughing at her.

"Shepherd Skuld has chosen well and while Rosalind was not what Urðr had expected, she is who I need by my side. I am grateful for your service."

That struck him in an odd way. He wasn't her servant.

Jowsey came along side. "That's a tale to share with mates at the tavern." He hooted and wiped his face roughly with a cloth. "I hope Hermit's Hollow has a steaming hot bath house with buckets of soap. That's the only way to get rid of this." He coughed several times, then spit. "I think I swallowed a trough-load. Look along." He pointed to the road ahead. Etain's horse grazed peacefully on a patch of grass.

Cormac rode up to it, helped Etain down, then waited while she mounted. The scenery was drastically different than what they had just escaped from. Here, the forest was thick with evergreens and birch with low-growing shrubs lining the roadway. More importantly, it was bone dry. Not a cloud in the sky and not a swamp to be seen.

Late in the day, they entered Hermit's Hollow. He remembered passing through years ago. It hadn't changed. It was the same boring landscape populated with the same dull people. At least it was half warm with sunny breaks. Large puffy white clouds drifted through the sky, but they took up only a quarter of the space. His brain told him to keep riding, leave the village and camp outside of it. His body commanded him to rent a room for the night, soak in a hot bath to rid himself of the slime that had dried to a thick crust, eat a hot meal and lay in a soft bed where bugs wouldn't crawl into his ears. The sun low in the sky made the decision for him, not that those he rode with would have chosen differently.

Seeing a sign for The Nowhere Inn and Tavern, he was about to head in that direction but stopped. "I've heard of this place. It has a reputation."

"So do I." Jowsey shrugged. "I've stayed there. The only bad that ever came of it was the tavern wench who threw a pitcher of ale in my face."

"You bring out the best in people," said Loggie.

He grinned. "I do." He trotted his horse towards the tavern.

Cormac reluctantly guided his horse behind him.

Rosalind rode alongside, looked him over and half smiled. "Thank you. I am her guardian, but I can't do it alone."

"I don't think any of us could." He glanced at Jowsey. Maybe he could. He grumbled under his breath. The man was digging a deeper ditch under his skin.

"Still, I appreciate it."

"She shouldn't be out here. Not without proper protection."

"She's got us."

He was about to speak, but her expression stalled him. A gang of half-wits was not the protection Etain's family wanted protecting her, but there was nothing he could change about that now. The best plan was to get her to Delgrath as quickly as possible.

The Nowhere Inn and Tavern sat on the corner of Moonway and Sunset Lane. It was the largest structure in town though it was only two storeys. The fake roof front reminded Cormac of those in western movies. Gunmen usually stood behind the false front to shoot the good guys. Thankfully, guns didn't exist in this realm. Then he remembered the fireballs he'd used in the game. He shook his head. They were only in the game. Like magic, they didn't exist here.

Jowsey rode behind the tavern beneath a sign with neat letters that read: *Horse Bordin' - At your own risk.* That didn't give him much confidence his horse would be here in the morning. A solid wooden gate blocked the alley, and Jowsey stopped to ring a cast iron dinner bell. The dinging bounced off the stone walls, making the horses jittery. After the slug incident, they were nervous.

"Takes a minute," said Jowsey. "It ain't dark yet, so it ain't full."

Five minutes passed before a window eight feet above ground opened.

"Whatcha want?" came a rough voice.

"Bordin for the night," said Jowsey.

A middle-aged man with wiry grey hair, big nose riddled with pockmarks and a missing front tooth stuck his head out and looked over the group. "Five. Anymore?"

"Just us. Is there room?"

The man sniffed and huffed. "Supposin' so. Make it, I guess. Money, you have?"

"We do." Jowsey took out his coin purse and shook it.

"Fine, then. Fine. Give me time. Gotta get the key. The door must be opened." He froze and looked behind the group, and Cormac followed his line of sight. Not seeing anyone or anything, he returned his attention to the gateman.

"No more? Don't be lying."

"Only us, sir," said Jowsey. "I'm sure more will come later to stay at your fine establishment but for us, we are all there is."

"Fine enough." He withdrew his head and closed the door. Much clamouring went on behind the wooden gate before one door wide enough for a horse to pass was opened.

Jowsey passed through. Cormac followed. The man who had spoken to them stood off to the side, cane in hand, holding the door and rolling his teeth over his bottom lip. Up ahead was a barn that could accommodate two dozen horses, maybe more. Stable hands were feeding, watering and grooming horses. Many looked up when they rode to the door and dismounted.

"Feed and water included," said the old man. "Groomin' extra. Extra, I say. Pay or it won't be done. That's what I say, and that's what I means."

"Understood," said Cormac.

The old man stopped and stared. "You ain't from 'round these parts, are ya?" His wrinkled face twisted.

"No." He cleared his throat. "Not really."

"Either you are or you ain't." Darkness shadowed his eyes.

"Ain't." Cormac looked away.

"Ya smells like a slug assaulted ya in the worst ways."

"It's slug season," said Jowsey, taking over the conversation. "Have many arrived like we have?"

"Many, but not as filthy."

"We encountered a particularly bad batch." Jowsey led his horse inside. "Only by Hamingja's hand did we survive."

"Bet ya did." The old man shuffled forward, striking his cane on the dirt floor with a solid thud. "This way. More to come. Get ya settled. No time for layabouts. Here's a stall. Take that one." He pointed to one, then another. "That one. Your job to untack. I touch nothing. Take it to your room. Risky. Stay at yar own risk."

Cormac groaned. By the time he untacked, groomed the horse, then toted his gear to his room and had a bath, it'd be well after dark, and he'd be starving.

Rosalind stretched and yawned. With her belly full of warm beef stew, she was ready for sleep. The mug of wine and heat from the fire added to her relaxed state. The others around the table appeared in a similar manner.

"Not tonight," said Cormac. "Not here."

Loggie had pulled the rebec from his sack and was about to pluck a string. "Why?"

Cormac leant forward and whispered. "We don't want to attract the attention of this type of crowd. Not tonight. Let's break the routine."

Loggie conceded and returned the rebec to the sack. Then he rested his chin on his hands, elbows propped on the table, and scanned the room. When his eyes met Rosalind's, he smiled. She remembered that smile even if she couldn't remember him more than she knew him today. He was a handsome fellow, kind and generous with time.

A voice behind her stuck in her ear, but she didn't turn to see who spoke. The man whispered to another about Shayde Thornheart. That was the name Jowsey had spoken earlier in the day. She tuned her ear to hear more.

"Thornheart is expecting you. You know what awaits if you don't arrive."

"The old wizard will never find me," said a second man.

"You'll be found and when you are, you'll wish you'd crawled to the hinterland on bare knees. Do you not remember Ferris?"

"He was weak. Gave into greed."

"You will follow his shadow."

The voice travelled down her neck, into her spine and vibrated her ribs. She didn't know him, but his voice sounded familiar. It eventually struck her chest, and a slow, steady ache grew, triggering moisture at the corner of her eyes.

"Will you betray me?"

"You've betrayed yourself. Thornheart probably already knows. Senses it. You'll hang."

Rosalind gulped. That word created an image in her mind, and when the body swayed around and the face came into view, the feeling of someone's hands around her neck made it difficult to breathe. She fingered the dagger secured to her waist. Every nerve wanted to drive it into that man.

"Rosalind." Loggie reached across the table and grasped the hand that rested on the surface. "What's wrong?"

She stared at him through blurred vision. "I don't know."

"Are you in pain?"

She swallowed hard, her fingers stroking the handle of the dagger. She'd never killed anyone...or... A strange scene flashed before her.

There was more than one body below the woman hanging in the noose. Had she done that?

An arm fell across her shoulder, and Etain stared into her face. "You must tell us. We cannot aid in your recovery if we do not know what causes this pain."

"I need... I need to go."

"Where?"

"From here."

"Done." Cormac rose and held on to her arm to steady her balance when she stood. "It's late. We're tired. We need the rest."

She accepted his and Etain's help and turned to leave. But before she did, she glanced back to see the face of the man who had spoken. Fortunately, he was staring right at her. His scruffy beard, sprinkled with breadcrumbs, consumed most of his face. Blond hair pulled into a makeshift ponytail exposed his round cheeks and dark eyes that pierced the distance between them. The corner of his upper lip curled, and she returned the snarl.

"You are a demon," she whispered.

He grunted, splayed two fingers sideways and flicked them at her.

Cormac dragged her away, and when they reached the hallway leading to the rooms, he pulled her near. "What was that?"

She stared in the direction of the tavern, wanting to return and face that man... Instead, she turned to Cormac. "I don't remember."

"You don't remember what just happened?"

"Who he is." She rubbed her temple.

He directed her down the hall. "You're tired. When you wake in the morning, this will all be just a... forgotten." He removed the lantern hanging outside the door and entered the room. "Just stay in here tonight, and all will be fine."

Rosalind entered the room she and Etain shared. Their gear was placed neatly in the corner. Two beds rested against one wall with a small table and a tall, narrow window between them. Cormac hung the lantern on a hook near the door, and it cast an eerie glow. The outer wall was stone, but the walls separating the rooms were made from wood. The wood was rough cut, uneven and in some places, knots had fallen out, leaving tiny openings to the other side.

Loggie shut the door and went to her. "Rosalind." He held her by the shoulders. "What do you remember about that man?"

"I don't know." She winced from pain from an unknown source. "His voice. I've heard it before. I think." Her heart sank. "I think he hurt someone I know. When he said Shayde Thornheart would hang that man—"

"He mentioned Shayde Thornheart?" asked Jowsey.

"Yes."

"You're certain?"

"He said it twice. It sounded like the other man wanted to escape, and the one nearest me was trying to convince him to stay."

"He must be indebted to Thornheart."

"Are you indebted?" asked Cormac.

Jowsey's expression indicated he was insulted by the question. "I'm not foolish. It's a death sentence."

"So, Thornheart is evil like Saruman."

"Maybe they're cousins," snapped Jowsey.

"Did you see a paladin in the crowd?" asked Loggie.

"None. Only questionable individuals."

"Any contacts in the village where you might enquire?"

Jowsey pressed his lips together and twisted his face. "I can't say."

"You don't need to tell us. Go alone. Ask. Tell us one way or the other."

"I will sneak away in the morn. Too dangerous this time a night."

"Fair enough." Loggie turned back to Rosalind. "When we leave, lock the door. Don't leave until morning."

She remained silent, not wanting to voice the thoughts rattling around inside her head.

He looked to Etain. "Both of you. Don't open this door. Keep it locked. Okay?"

"Yes. We shall do that." Etain stretched. "I've no plans to leave. Only rest. I was not aware riding all day tired the body."

"The slugs didn't help." Jowsey grinned.

"None at all."

"We're just across the hall. If you need anything, bang on our door." Loggie released her.

"We are not to open the door," said Rosalind, lifting an eyebrow.

"No, you're not. Unless you absolutely need something." He led the way, and Cormac and Jowsey followed, closing the door behind them.

Etain locked the door and secured the wooden bar behind steel brackets. "There. No one shall enter. We will sleep like princesses in a..." She considered the room. "In a room suitable for stable hands." She squished her shoulders together and squealed. "We can talk now that the boys are gone." Jumping into the air, she landed squarely on the bed with her legs crossed. "What shall we do before sleep. We must do something. While tired, I strive to learn something each day before sleep. Shall we dabble in your Roots of Terra to see if we can learn about that man in the tavern? Or shall we read the spell book given to me by Urðr?"

"You have a spell book?" She sat on the edge of the bed beside her.

Her wide grin indicated she did. "I'm not supposed to break the seal until I am in the presence of Sir Uwen the Noble, but..." She giggled. "I made no promise. It tickles my mind and whispers for me to sneak a peek."

A breath of wind struck Rosalind's cheek, and she looked towards the wall on the other side of her bed. Several symbols and letters were carved into it, graffiti left by those who had stayed in the room. She turned back to Etain. "Roots of Terra. Tomorrow, we break the seal of the spell book."

For the next hour, she tried to decipher the message of the cards laid out before her. All six appeared to point to water, but she didn't know what that meant. Etain hovered over them and offered suggestions, but she'd never been allowed to play with Roots of Terra, so was not helpful. The more the girl talked, the more Rosalind believed she had been locked in a room and never allowed to see the outdoors.

Rosalind wished Coraline was here to help solve the mystery of the cards, but the fairy didn't enter villages. Large populations terrified her, so she stayed in the forest and waited for her return.

Eyes watering from yawning, she packed up the cards and turned down the lantern to as low as it would go. A little light would give her comfort while her mind raced to find the truth of who that man was. With images sweeping through her mind, she fell into a restless sleep.

"If rats were kings," cursed the voice near her ear.

Rosalind opened her eyes and stared across the space between her and the bed next to hers. Someone slept in it. The soft glow of light coming from the dying lantern on the wall illuminated shapes in the room but little else. Her arm stretched out before her, and she saw a leather bracer as wide as her hand wrapped around her wrist. The strap was coming loose, and she thought about remove it and fixing it in the morning when a floorboard creaked behind her.

A shadow leapt from the floor between the two beds, followed by a howl.

"Ah! Get back!" A man about her age held a dagger in a threatening manner but he wasn't looking at her.

She swung around and saw two large shadows coming from the wall. Scrambling out of the bed, she stood behind the man with the dagger.

"What is this mischief?" asked the woman in the other bed. She sat up and stared at the large men. "It is that man. I'm certain. Jowsey, you have predicted his evil ways and came to our aid. You are truly a brave soul." She grabbed her dagger and stood. "We shall chase you from this village," she said to the intruders. "You will regret the day you crossed Etain of Elridge Mountain and her faithful guardians."

Jowsey gave the woman a strange look. "Faithful guardians?"

"You are here, are you not?"

"By rotten luck."

"Yet, you stand at our side to protect us." She held the dagger higher. "We shall see to these evil men together."

"Just hand over the girl," ordered the man. "She's all we want."

"Did Guthro send you?" asked Jowsey.

The man squinted at him. "Never heard of him." It sounded like a lie. "The girl." He pointed his dagger at Rosalind.

"Why should I go with you?" she asked. "I do not know you."

"Yes, you do. You've forgotten. These people are not your friends. You must believe me. This illness you have. It steals your memory. I can help you."

She stepped away from Jowsey and Etain. "How do I know you are telling the truth?"

"You don't remember me," said the intruder, "but I remember you."

"He's lying," said Etain. "He is the evil man we met in the tavern this night."

"She's lying," said the man, edging closer. "She's going to sacrifice you. It's why I was sent to save you."

Rosalind stared at Etain. "Why would you sacrifice me?"

Jowsey swore under his breath and knocked his middle finger against his head. "Of all the people I could have involved. Each morning, the weeds thicken. I suppose overmorrow, I'll have to battle a dragon."

"Give me your hand, and I will lead you to safety." The man reached out to her, but she stepped towards the door. "Don't go that way. They've set a trap."

"Rosalind, trust me," said Etain. "I am your friend. I sleep here with you. I am not your enemy." She glared at the man. "He is. Do you not recognise his evil voice? Or need he say Shayde Thornheart to trigger your memories?"

Rosalind stared at the man. She didn't recognise him, but his voice did sound... She stared at the floor. There was something familiar in it. Arms wrapped around her, shaking her from her thoughts. The other man, hidden in the shadows, had grabbed her and was dragging her towards a door in the wall.

"Don't try anything," growled the man. "Or I'll slice her throat for her to bleed out here."

Jowsey and Etain stood down and watched with wide eyes as she was dragged away. Once inside the wall, Rosalind heard a mild explosion, and light from the room half blinded her. The man dragged her down a narrow flight of stairs. In the darkness, she didn't know where they took her. When her bare feet hit stone, he dragged her towards a door.

"Boote, get the door," growled the man who pulled so hard, she stumbled. "Get up. Of all times to find this wancol." He thrust her through the doorway and under the night sky.

Rosalind kicked him in the groin. He groaned and loosened his grip enough she was able to pull her arm free. She didn't get more than two feet before he pounced and threw her to the ground. He lifted his fist to strike her, but it was frozen above his head.

"Taper. Get off her," ordered Boote. "If you kill her, Thornheart will have you skinned alive."

Taper grumbled, grabbed her by the front of the long nightgown and jerked her to her feet. When Boote turned towards the horse, Taper slapped her so hard, it made her ears ring.

"A death wish is what you make." Boote turned with rope in hand. "Hold her steady." He forced her hands together in front and secured them with rope. After tying the end to the hitching post, he prepared his horse, and Taper did the same.

Rosalind dug her fingers between the loops of the rope, wiggling her wrists in an effort to loosen the knot. While she worked, she searched the area behind the building and the alleyway leading from it. Above the exit was a wooden beam with poles on both sides sporting flags. It was framed on either side by two-storey buildings. Footsteps caught her attention. Boote walked towards her. Their threat to kill her had been an act. Good for her; bad information for them. All she needed to do was increase the slack and hold the rope firmly in place.

Boote grabbed her by the arm and stood her by the horse. "Throw her up to me." He mounted and waited for Taper to throw her into the saddle behind him.

Once the task was done, Taper rushed to his horse. "This is where we part ways. I've done me part. I want nothing of this." He gestured at Rosalind, then turned his horse and brought it to a trot. Once he passed through the open doorway, he disappeared into the shadows.

Boote cursed under his breath and started after him.

Rosalind removed the rope completely from her wrists and let it fall to the ground. Drawing a breath, she steadied her nerves and grabbed hold of Boote's shoulders. Tucking her feet under her, she quickly lifted her body off the saddle. The quick movement of the horse and Boote glancing over his shoulder jostled her. She lurched forward but regained her balance by clenching her toes into the leather saddle. The horse pranced as it reduced speed, and she clung to Boote's jacket for extra security. A second later, she grabbed hold of one of the flag poles. She swung onto the pole and scurried onto the beam.

Boote brought the horse to a halt 10 feet away and rushed back.

Rosalind inched her way across the beam. In the dim light, it appeared larger than it was. Reaching the building, she searched for a route to one of the windows or the roof. She found a solid place to grasp the wall and lifted herself off the beam.

A solid thud against her side sent jarring pain to her shoulders. Unable to hold on, she slammed against the beam, then tumbled ten feet to the dirt. Spitting out dust, she fought to rise. She managed to get to her knees before a rough hand grabbed her hair and jerked her back.

"Nice try," said Boote, "but I've only two choices: return you to Thornheart or kill you. There's no escape for you."

She kicked and punched him, but he was too strong. He threw her against the ground face down and secured her hands behind her back. Her hands tied, he rose and jerked her to her feet. Then a force struck them, sending him crashing into her, and they both landed in the dirt. Gasping for air, she struggled to break free of his crushing weight. Constant thumping shook her body, and the man upon her was only partially off her. She wiggled towards freedom, but he gripped a chunk of her hair. Her head throbbed, and the dull sound of someone pounding on flesh and clothing filled her ears.

Finally, she managed to look around. It was Jowsey. She no sooner identified him when he was flung backwards. He hit the ground with a thud and released a loud groan. She felt another quick movement, and Etain landed near him. The girl rolled several times and came up on her feet.

"Release her," ordered Etain.

Boote grunted, rose to his feet and jerked Rosalind to stand beside him. "And if I don't, missy?"

"I shall bring the full wrath of the gods upon you."

Boote shook with laughter. "The full wrath, you say? Are you speaking with them now?"

"They will answer my call."

Jowsey stood beside her and rubbed his chin. Blood trickled from his lip. "Let her go, and we let you escape without injury."

"Jesters of the king, both of you." He tightened his grip on Rosalind.

Jowsey smirked. "If you only knew."

"You're missing your hat."

"If you don't release her, you'll be missing something a shade more vital to your well being."

"You shall heed his warning," said Etain. "He means it."

Boote reached for the saddle horn. "I'm sure he does, missy, but his only audience is weedy mooncalves."

She thrust her shoulders back. "I am not weedy, and she is my guardian. You will not escape with her."

"My plans are as such. She is not from this world. Thornheart has called upon me to deliver her so she can be sent home."

"That's a lie," said Jowsey.

"I should believe you instead?" He tsked. "You don't pay me."

"What do you want for her?"

"The deal's been made. She's a threat to this land and to all who live in it. She has to go."

"Nonsense," said Etain. "She remains. Release her before I am forced to wield my power."

Rosalind couldn't see Boote's face, but his laugh indicated he didn't care what Etain did or said. He put his foot into the stirrup, dragged her closer and prepared to mount. Something whizzed by her ear and landed with a solid thud near her head. Gargling sounds erupted in her ear, and his grip grew slack.

"Of all the rodents to fall," cursed Jowsey. He turned to Etain. "We were still negotiating."

"We do not negotiate with killers."

He put his hand on his head and shook it. "I do. It's in the rules. Even thieves have a code."

"Even killers?"

"Yes," he squealed. "We negotiate until there's no other option."

"There were only two options: I kill him or let him escape with Rosalind."

"We were getting to that, but I had other options."

"What?" She folded her arms and stared at him, waiting.

"Of all the nixies to travel with."

"I am not a nixie. That would be Cousin Esmerelda. She spends most of her days as a cat."

Jowsey groaned. "I need to get out of here."

"Could you untie me first?" Rosalind had watched the light slip from Boote's eyes. The dagger in his neck had extinguished it quickly.

"That is my next task." Etain walked with purpose to her and quickly untied the rope. "Are you harmed?"

"I'll survive."

"Wonderful." She ripped the dagger from Boote's neck and wiped the blood off on his jacket. "Let us search the body for valuables and dispose of it."

"Whoa, whoa, whoa." Jowsey stood before her. "That will bring more grief than you anticipate."

"I anticipate a lot."

He stared at her with a blank face. "I don't, nor do I want it. In my dealings with this..." he waved his hand over the body, "we leave it untouched, and exit the scene quickly. Let's go."

"That is odd. To surrender what might aid us in our quest is foolish. Fate has brought him to us. We must not ignore the gift." She flipped open the pouch on the dead man's belt and reached inside.

"She continues to ignite the fire within the opal. Great. We're all going to die."

"I light no fire. What of this opal?"

"You've not heard of the dreaded Lucia's Opal curse?" he said, and she stopped to listen. "Theft of the dead ignites it." He grasped her arm and gently guided her to stand. "I will tell you in great detail when we return to the room, but not here. Come." He reached for Rosalind. "We must go immediately, or we shall wear the opal's curse."

Rosalind saw Etain close her hand around an object. Curses didn't appear to concern her. Standing up, Rosalind brushed away dirt from her nightgown. Boote's actions had revealed who to trust, and she followed them towards the door that led to their room through the secret entrance. Glancing at the body, she wondered what he meant by her not being from this world. If not this one, which one? Once inside their room, they secured the secret door in the wall and placed the bedside table on an angle against it.

"Do you know of other worlds?" she asked.

Etain stared at her. "There are many."

"She means real worlds," said Jowsey.

"I assumed."

He grimaced. "Well, now that the threat has been disposed of, I should get back to my room." He went to the door.

"You have yet to tell me about the curse," said Etain. "This will not be the first life I take. I need to know why I should abandon what is rightfully mine." She sat cross-legged in the centre of her bed.

"For a girl who escaped a prison she had spent her entire life in, you're risking a lot by killing people. Maybe you should slow down. That was a real person's life you took tonight. I know you might not understand that, but out here in the real world, we appreciate life."

"I completely understand my actions. It's not the first time."

He dropped onto the corner of the bed and stared at her. "Impossible. You said you've never left the Sanctuary."

"The Sanctuary is large."

"Small."

"On the surface."

"And underground?"

"Much larger."

"And you wander about killing people lost in the catacombs?" He glanced at Rosalind, who crawled beneath the blanket and propped her head up on a bent elbow to listen. "How did you find her again?"

"We broke the fast together," answered Etain. "I do not kill needlessly. I am well trained by my keepers. Shepherd Skuld has left nothing out. Except this curse that concerns you."

"Yes, Lucia's Opal curse." He looked off into the distance, which was the far wall. The dwindling light of the lantern provided illumination only to distinguish him from a stranger. "Legend has it, a beautiful princess wore a colourful opal. It was a fine mixture of forest green and sea blue. One day while walking in the garden, a marauder attacked her. He took nothing but the beautiful opal necklace and left her there to die. The man who had killed her was later found. Dead. The opal necklace gone. Stolen by another. He, too, was found dead and the necklace once again stolen. Every thief who took it ended up with the same fate.

"Finally, the king recovered the opal necklace and locked it away. Not only as a keepsake from his daughter but to prevent further death. In total, 23 people, mostly men, died. This curse is inflicted on anyone who steals from the dead."

Etain twisted her face, considering the story. "You say the necklace is secure?"

"Secured in the kingdom."

"Which kingdom?"

"That remains a secret to keep the necklace safe."

"Sounds unbelievable," said Rosalind. "Who told you this?"

"It is legend. Passed down through the centuries."

"Yet," said Etain, "it has not reached my ear though I've heard many stories from men and women from across the land."

"I haven't heard of it either," said Rosalind.

"Not surprised." Jowsey stood. "You're not from here." He went to the door. "Secure the lock when I leave."

"Wait." Etain jumped off the bed. "I have more questions."

"Which will wait until morning." He opened the door and left.

Etain closed the door and slid the bar across the brackets. "He's an odd fellow, don't you think?" She crawled beneath the covers and placed a dagger under her pillow.

"Odd is one word. Crafty is a better one."

Etain grinned. "Both are intriguing."

Rosalind settled onto the pillow. Seeing the leather straps of her bracer loose, she secured them before falling asleep.

10

Tavern Talk

CORMAC STARED AT the menu board at the entrance of The Nowhere Tavern and considered the options. Cheese on milk-soaked bread that was then toasted didn't sound appealing. Lose the milk, add tomato sauce, bacon, onions and pepperoni, and he had an archaic pizza. What he wouldn't give for a slice to start his day. Boilt pig hock with a side order of asparagus, rutabaga and beet greens didn't appeal to him either even though it was smothered in gravy. Eggs it was. He had the choice between chicken and goose. He'd never eaten goose egg. He wondered if they tasted different than chicken eggs. Didn't matter. They were a coin more. He'd stick with chicken eggs, sliced ham and fried potatoes with garlic and thyme. It was the special and written in bold letters in the middle of the chalkboard: Nowhere's Morning Brew. It came with a mug of apple cider. More than likely, it was fermented.

Hearing footsteps approach, he looked and saw Rosalind and Etain. The two women, dressed in similar garb, were in deep conversation. When Rosalind looked up, he waited for the familiar expression. Instead, his attention was drawn to the scrape and bruise on her forehead.

"Fine foods to break the fast?" Etain stopped to look at the board.

"Sure, but I'm more interested in that." He pointed to Rosalind's head. "What happened?"

Rosalind shrugged. "I fell."

He looked to Etain. A more thorough examination revealed minor cuts and bruises along the hairline and the back of her hands. "What happened?" He swung around and stared at Jowsey. Something about him was off this morning. Looking back at Rosalind, he grasped her hand and pulled up her sleeve. The bracer was still in place. Releasing her, he marched to the table and looked Jowsey square in the face. Just as he thought. He had minor cuts and bruises, too. "Where were you last night? And how are they involved?"

Jowsey smirked. "A little this and that. Nothing we couldn't handle but I say, if our source for information is correct, we – I mean you have a bigger problem than me." He leant forward and whispered, "And it shant be easy to solve."

Cormac dropped onto the bench opposite him and beside Loggie. After glancing around the crowded tavern, he held his tongue. Rosalind and Etain joined them, the server arrived and took their order. While he waited, he assessed Jowsey, considered his wounds, his clothes and the way he looked at Rosalind. Thoughts of what he should do sparked in his mind. Then his thoughts tumbled backwards into a tangled mess. Everything was not going according to his simple plan. He worked out a new one. He'd steal the bracer, give it to Jowsey, and the man would be gone. One down. He'd deliver Etain to Delgrath, and she'd be gone. Two down. Getting rid of Loggie would be the most difficult task. He could sneak away in the middle of the night with Rosalind and feed her a story. After she slept, it wouldn't matter.

"How much do you know about her?" asked Jowsey.

"Know about who?"

He nodded towards Rosalind.

"Enough."

"So not much."

"We know she is good," said Etain. "That's all that's necessary."

"And spirited," said Loggie.

"And lost," said Jowsey.

"That's why we need a paladin," said Loggie.

"You need more than a paladin."

"What do you mean." Cormac leant closer.

Jowsey lowered his voice and all heads leant towards the centre of the table. "According to my sources, she is not from this land."

Spit caught in Cormac's throat, and he steadied his nerves and swallowed slowly. Controlling his facial movement, he worked to appear surprised yet not believing the claim. His fingers pressed against the table, and his mouth remained closed. He'd let someone else comment first, hoping they'd dismiss it as nonsense.

"Not what you thought, right? I reason the one who done the transferring is hunting her and has cast this spell."

"That doesn't make sense," said Loggie. "What land are we talking about? One across the sea?"

"Another realm." He gestured to Etain. "She knows of other worlds. That's what you said, right?"

"And we're to believe a naïve woman on her first outing?" Cormac held his breath, waiting for doubt to set in.

"Wasn't her who shared the matter."

"But I know of other worlds," said Etain. "There are many. Only those gifted with the power of Astro Vision can see them."

"Do you have that?" asked Jowsey.

"No. It is not my calling. I have met many paladins and when I next encounter one, I certainly will convince him to break the spell holding Rosalind." She put her arm across her shoulder. "We are destined to protect each other."

"What if your source is lying?" Cormac wanted to put his hands beneath the table, but he thought he'd give himself away if he did. Instead, he focussed on keeping them and his voice steady. "It might have been a trick to get you to... Why did they tell you this? Who told you?"

"One of my sources."

"It was the man who was here yesternight," said Etain.

Jowsey groaned, shook his head, then rested it in his hands.

"The one..." Cormac lowered his voice further, "she called a demon?"

She smiled and mimicked his actions. "Yes," she whispered. "He made the claim, trying to convince us he had to deliver her to this Shayde Thornheart. Surely, he lied."

He glanced around the tavern and didn't see the man.

"You won't find him," she said.

"Why?"

While she answered, Jowsey hushed her, but Cormac heard her response, and that horrible feeling in his throat returned.

Jowsey grew frustrated. "We don't talk about such things in a tavern. Right? It's not the place. Too many ears, an abundance of eyes and sneaks, who sell information to bidders with any number of coins."

Realising the probable reason Jowsey got caught up in the scuffle with the women, Cormac glared at him. If not for the so-called demon disrupting their night, Jowsey would have had the bracer and be gone. That wasn't a horrible thing, but.. If Jowsey had successfully escaped with the bracer, Rosalind would also be gone. Or not. He considered Etain.

"Be it lie or not," said Loggie, "she's my friend, and I stand by her."

Rosalind sat quietly, listening and looking into the faces of those around the table. If she recognised anyone, it didn't show.

The server arrived and after three trips, the meals, drinks and condiments were on the table. Cormac concentrated on the meal. It was hot, fresh and delicious. Not knowing when he'd have another meal like this, he wanted to enjoy it, but the nagging feeling something horrible was going to happen agitated his nerves.

The meals consumed, the server paid, they returned to their rooms to gather their gear. Once behind the closed door, he felt freer to speak. "This man Etain killed. You call him one of your sources. Did you know him?"

Jowsey shook his head. "He worked for Thornheart, but I've never seen him."

"That's who you work for?"

"I work for who pays."

"And at the moment?"

"That be the infamous wizard, who has more power than the average wizard."

"An evil wizard."

He tsked. "If I limited my contractors by reputation, I'd be a travelling serf, like you."

"Thornheart must be infamous elsewhere," said Loggie. "I've never heard the name."

"The wizard doesn't participate in street shows."

"It was luck..." Loggie simpered, "you were there when the women were attacked."

"That's what I'd call it. Be it good or bad." He threw his pack over his shoulder. "I hope to improve it either way."

"Find us a paladin, and I'll see to it you get the map."

"The deal of your choosing." He smiled mischievously. "With or without it in hand, my task is being carried out. Now let's get those horses saddled." He opened the door and left.

"I don't trust him," said Cormac.

"You think I do?" Loggie picked up the saddlebags. "But we need him. I'd not recognise a paladin though I may have spoken with one. I've no contacts. Our task would be near impossible. I know only that every day that passes with that spell hanging over Rosalind, danger grows nearer. We must rid her of it."

Cormac nodded. "We have to keep a closer watch on her."

"Easier said than done." Loggie left the room and Cormac followed.

An hour later, he was riding from Hermit's Hollow and travelling along the shoreline of the ocean. The salt air dusted his lips, and he licked them. It reminded him of the Eastern Shore, where he'd camped many times as a boy. Lawrencetown Beach was the most popular place to go. If he was there now, he'd race along the tide line, leaving footprints in the grey sand. He bet this water was just as cold as that at Lawrencetown. It was dark and smashed against the rocks, sending spray into the air.

Seagulls screeched and soared overhead. A large flock was following a fishing vessel into port. The men on the deck were far away and appeared like miniature figures. The nearer they got to the wharf, the louder the birds became.

The next stop was a place called Moore. He didn't remember it, but according to Etain, it was a town of about 20,000 people. That was a fair size settlement in this world. It was three days away.

Movement ahead caught his eye. It was a lone traveller. The hooded cloak hid their appearance. Given the size, he guessed it to be human. A man. He travelled with a walking stick. More like a staff.

"Beware," whispered Jowsey. "The cloaked man is the one to fear."

Cormac glanced at the man riding abreast. "You know him?"

"No. You?"

"No. Why should we fear him?"

"Because he's a cloaked man."

"That's all you've got?"

"All I need. Ready your muscles to grab your weapon but make no movement unless he does."

They were five against this one man. The stranger wouldn't try anything. He'd lose easily.

"He wears the boots," whispered Jowsey.

Cormac peered at the boots. They were black. Leather probably. They almost reached his knees. There was nothing special about them. He'd seen others wear them.

"Not a good formation." He whispered over his shoulder. "Single file. Follow me exactly." He nodded at Cormac. "I'll lead. Stiff back. Don't let him see you slouch." He cut in front of him and took the lead.

Annoyed by the odd behaviour, Cormac was about to curse at him when he saw the face of the approaching stranger. The shadow beneath the hood was dark and shapeless. It stared at the ground and kept a steady pace, never wavering. At every stride, the staff was picked up, moved forward and plunked down.

When Jowsey rode past, the stranger did not look up or deviate from his path. Cormac kept his back straight and watched the cloaked figure, trying to figure out what it was. Quickly leaving it to continue its journey, he picked up the pace to once again ride abreast of Jowsey.

"What was that?"

"A wayfarer."

"What is that?"

"Lost soul. Killed when it wasn't his time."

Cormac scrunched up his nose and glanced back at the stranger, who appeared more like an apparition than a solid form. In all his years of travelling this realm, he'd never seen one. "Are they dangerous?"

He hmphed. "If you cross their path, they can claim your body, reground their soul, live another life and mend their broken spirit."

"What happens to my soul?"

"Gets displaced, and you get to wander as a wayfarer. The advantage is you get to live forever." He chuckled. "If that's your thing." He half-turned. "You don't know much about much. Were you locked in a sanctuary all your life?"

"I just haven't explored like you have."

"The outside world? Where do your parents' dwell?"

"Around."

"An orphan?"

"No." He answered too quickly, but the mention of his parents caused the ache in his chest to reveal itself.

"Many good men are." He smirked. "Look at me." He laughed easily. He appeared carefree, swaying with the horse and travelling where the wind and path took him.

Cormac didn't like it. It was like Jowsey felt he couldn't die. Couldn't get into horrible trouble. Trouble and death awaited everyone eventually. Especially in a land as ruthless as this one.

At the end of the day, Cormac positioned his bedroll alongside Rosalind's. Loggie set up on the other side of her. He'd take first watch, Etain had second and Loggie took third. The surrounding forest was thick with deciduous trees and low-growing shrubs. The setting sun shrouded it in darkness. Once the fire was lit, its glow danced on the leaves and illuminated the faces around it.

Before they had left Hermit's Hollow, they'd stopped at the keep to purchase basic supplies. One item was a thick piece of beef. Jowsey had it in the pan, frying with lard, onions and mushrooms. Removing a small sack from his pack, he opened it and sprinkled white crystals over the pan contents. Salt? Then he constructed a bed of hot coals, placed a thin stone over them and set five potatoes on it to cook. He surrounded the potatoes with upright stones to capture and keep the heat.

While he took care of the cooking, the rest gathered wood for the fire and filled the watering flasks. By the time they settled, the food was ready.

Cormac sliced a thin piece of meat from his portion and poked it into his mouth. His tastebuds came alive, and his mouth watered. This was the best meat he'd ever tasted. He ate another piece and savoured it, chewing it until nothing was left. While he enjoyed his meal, he glanced at the others quietly eating with the occasionally lip smacking and sounds of satisfaction.

The quiet evening reminded him of nights long ago when he'd hangout with friends around a fire while camping. They were times he cherished. He never believed he'd find a similar feeling here, far from family and friends. His meal eaten, he set down the plate and lay back against his pack and bedroll and gazed into the fire. The flames danced and flickered, soothing his nerves further. His body relaxed and his eyelids grew heavy. Sleep beckoned him.

His eyes shot open, and he stared at Jowsey. The silence grew so strong, Jowsey spoke.

"What?"

Many things ran through his mind but the one at the top of the list was: Did he put something in the meat to make him sleepy? He sat up and gave his head a shake, then rubbed his hands roughly against his face. He couldn't sleep. He had to stay awake. "Nothing. Just..." He stood. "I need a drink." He grabbed his cup, went to the nearby stream and dipped it in. The water was cold and sweet. It tasted like the spring water at his grandparents' house. They lived in rural Nova Scotia, far from any great settlement. The natural spring on their property provided their drinking water. This stream tasted similar. His drink consumed, he returned to the fire.

One-by-one, the others fell asleep. Cormac paced. He wanted to sleep, but he would not leave the campsite unguarded.

Rosalind packed her gear. It had been a pleasant morning and while she wanted to play with the Roots of Terra longer to learn more of the dim tunnel she'd seen, the others in the group were anxious to travel. Grey clouds fueled their urge. It looked like it would rain, but it didn't feel like it.

"If we had a map, we could plan the trip better," said Cormac.

"Ah, the elusive map," said Loggie.

Etain pulled a folded piece of hide from her pouch. "Like this?"

Rosalind watched her spread it out. A detailed drawing covered the tan-coloured hide, and she leant forward for a better view. "It's pretty. Did you make it?"

Jowsey chuckled. "Cartographers make maps, and they cost more than most can afford."

Etain stared at him, then turned to Rosalind. "Yes."

Jowsey sat up. "Is it accurate?"

"I was taught by the best," she said. "I am told it is extremely accurate. Many places have never been visited before nor heard of."

Confusion blanketed Jowsey's face. "Then...? You didn't copy a real map?"

"I envisioned this one."

He grunted. "So, you dreamt up a map and drew this?"

"Exactly." She put her finger on a dot. "This is Moore. Moore Thyme. We shall reach it by the end of the day if we leave soon and ride late."

Jowsey leant over the map, searching one end, then the other. After a minute, he stood straight with hands on his hips. "While some places appear correct, this..." he leant to read the name, "River of Ancient Minds can't be right. And this whole section..." he drew an imaginary circle, "must be wrong."

"Have you been there?" asked Etain.

He hesitated. "No, but—"

"Spoke with those who have?"

"No, but—"

"You had a vision?"

He released a loud sigh. "No, but it doesn't make sense. The river flows this way, not between these mountains. I've been through Lakes of Green Skies, and there's no village there."

"Have you walked that land?"

"No, but it's—"

"Nothing you'd know."

He frowned at her. "I've been to more places than you; everyone here has."

"Only in body."

"As a rule, yes."

Rosalind ignored the conversation and looked closer at the trail ahead. Past Moore was a trail through a valley of lush forest. Following it, she read the names of several settlements before she reached Delgrath. It was a dim spot on the map, and she would have missed it if she'd not followed the line from one settlement to the next on the road heading north. Mercurial Road, according to the map.

What stood out was Engarland. The morning sun highlighted it. She squinted to clear the image and saw light flicker around it. She was going to ask Etain what it meant, but she was busy fine-tuning the discussion with Jowsey, who appeared to be equally enjoying the banter.

"If we are here," said Loggie, pointing to a spot on the map, "then we're... about ten days from Delgrath. Although this terrain looks rough. Might add a day." He looked up at Cormac. "Where does your friend live? Starlight Ridge? Past a blue field, a forest of lilies, a nodding dragon? I can't read that on the map."

Cormac huffed. "They might be too small for the map."

"Sure, they are."

"Forest of Wild Lilies," said Rosalind. "Right there." The River of Great Turmoil ran along its edge. "There's a place called Dragon's Noggin'. Is that it?"

Cormac leant closer. "Yeah." He fell silent for a moment, then mumbled, "That's it."

"Are you certain that's what it says?" Loggie pushed him aside and looked. "You only sounded like you were lying?" He hmphed. "Guess I was wrong."

"Does that make you a demon?" asked Etain in a loud voice.

Everyone looked at her, and it took Jowsey a second to regroup and reply. "Why would it do that?"

"While not an evil mastermind, you do Thornheart's work. That makes you a demon."

"That's not how it works. I'm a messenger for hire. I deliver goods. I am not to blame for any messes made by the person who hires me no more than a jester is responsible for what a king does."

"You're a jester? One that will be sacrificed on the battlefield."

His mouth hung partially open while he stared at her. "This conversation is over. Time to ride." He picked up the saddlebags and went to his horse.

Cormac chuckled. "If I didn't know better, I'd say you got the best of him."

Etain cocked her head. "I took nothing from him, let alone his best."

He grinned. "Just an expression."

One that sounded familiar to Rosalind. She watched Cormac walk to his horse and tack it up. Of all the people in the group, she felt most familiar with him. Why, she didn't know.

A short time later, they trotted their horses on the trail that traced the ocean shoreline. Yellow seaweed lined the shore and covered the rocks. She remembered having stepped on it in the past and hearing the pop of little pea-size pockets of air. It was slippery and if wet, needed to be avoided. A steady breeze blew off the water, filling her with a fresh, salty smell. It brushed her hair from her face, allowing the sun full access to her skin until a dark cloud passed before it. Seagulls flew overhead, squawking their complaints of whatever disturbed their day. Terns swooped overhead, dove, then skimmed across the water. She smiled at their antics.

What's the difference between a tern and a corner? Terns have wings.

It was something she had heard many times, but... from who? She didn't remember being here. She stared at Cormac riding ahead. Maybe he had said it. He was a peculiar fellow. This morning, he and Loggie explained who she was and what she would do today. Cormac warned her of the dangers following them: men who wanted to capture her. She had to be careful, yet she did not feel fear or an urgency to escape. Once the explanation was done, he avoided her. Not really avoided her. He simply went about his day without concern. His actions weren't unusual, but her senses expected more.

Feeling her watching him, he looked over his shoulder. His expression, first innocent, turned curious. He was handsome in a rugged way. Unkempt was more like it. If he had a home, he hadn't returned to it for some time. His dark hair had grown to his shoulders and was scraggly and dirty. It looked like he hadn't shaved for a long time, and his clothes were far from clean. In spite of that, there was an easiness about him. Most of the morning anyway. His moments of anxiousness surrounded the map and their destination. Maybe there was someone there he didn't want to meet.

He turned back around but glanced over his shoulder several times before deciding there was nothing she was going to say.

The sun rose high in the sky and began its descent. They stopped near a stream for the horses to drink but didn't stay long. Continuing, they left the seashore and travelled into thick forest with tall trees that cast chilly shadows across the road when late afternoon arrived.

Strange birds flitted across the road, spooking the horses. They were super fast, and it took several minutes to determine they weren't like any bird she'd seen. They were the size of a robin and had four wings, two layers on each side. The wings acted as one and at times tricked the eye into thinking there were only two. Their feathers were black but beneath the wings, a strip of red flashed in shadowy light. Their hooked beaks were also red. The birds emitted a low, sharp cry each time they flew in front of the horses and remained silent at all other times. The horses didn't like it, and neither did she. While she focussed on a particular group of birds, one from a dark shadow would shoot through the air, shaking her nerves. Several times members in the group mumbled under their breath or cursed the birds out loud.

This went on for more than two hours. The lower the sun sank, the more birds that darted from one side to the other. She couldn't travel twenty feet without at least one bird flying in front of her. Each time, she waited for a thud against the horse's chest, but it never came. The horses and their riders were growing frustrated, but the birds were too fast and too plentiful to do anything.

"If I had a stick," said Loggie, "I'd swat them as if scorpionflies."

Cormac quickly looked at him. "There's such a thing?"

"Never seen one?"

"Don't want to."

"Doesn't mean they don't exist. Their bite isn't fatal. But it leaves a nasty yellow bump that aches for days."

"Still don't want to see one."

Cormac's horse pranced sideways, almost throwing him into the shallow ditch. "What is this? You hear anything about these birds?"

"Flitting birds," said Jowsey. "An unusual happening, but..." He scanned the area. "I wouldn't worry about it."

"Should the rest of us?"

Jowsey chuckled. "Not unless you're undead."

"You're serious?"

"Always. Okay, most of the time." He glanced at Rosalind. "If she is..." He shook his head. "Can't be."

"What?"

"If the henchman was right, and she's from another world, I wonder if she's dead there."

"Another world?" asked Rosalind.

"Do you feel dead?" he asked.

"What a crazy question. I am as alive as you."

"Then we've nothing to worry about."

Cormac stared at her, his face twisted. Did he think she was dead?

Thirty minutes later, they exited the forest with nothing further happening. Planted fields separated them from the patch of buildings on the horizon. With the work day ended, the fields were empty of people. The buildings grew in height, the farther they travelled. Most were two storeys, but a few were three-storey buildings. Grey smoke rose from the many chimneys and created a low-lying cloud over the town.

Before they reached the first building, a sign constructed of thick timber painted forest green with yellow letters welcomed travellers.

Welcome to Moore Thyme
Population: Anyone's Guess
Home of the Giant Cockatrice

Rosalind read the sign twice. Both times, her eyes stalled at cockatrice. Somewhere in her past, she'd heard of this creature, but she couldn't access the memory.

"Giant?" Cormac's head jerked sideways, and he spoke to Jowsey. "Is it secured? How giant? Those things are deadly."

"Get a grip of your tongue." Jowsey spoke like he talked of the weather. "Cockatrices are more afraid of you than you are of them."

"I highly doubt that. We met one in a cave once, and it..." His mouth froze, and the long silence prompted Jowsey to speak.

"And what?"

He closed his mouth and appeared to draw inward. "It attacked us. My friend got turned to stone."

He brushed him off. "They only do that when they get excited or scared. You probably startled it."

"It startled us."

"Same thing. Did you get your friend into a milk bath quick enough?"

"What does that do?"

"Breaks the spell." He winced. "I'm guessing your friend is still stone."

"No. Deeper in the cave, we found a potion that saved him."

"That works, too."

"Or you could have plucked it," said Etain. Both men looked back at her. "It's another cure. They can't work their magic again until all their feathers are grown in."

"I'll keep that in mind." Jowsey turned back around.

"The one we encountered was as large as a deer," said Cormac.

"I'm told this one makes a moose look small."

"Insane. They should kill it."

Jowsey frowned. "Is that your answer to all threats? Like hers?" He nodded towards Etain.

"No, but... That thing is deadly."

"It's well contained. It's an attraction. Makes money for the town."

"I can think of better ways."

"Visit The Chamber then. Tell them how to run this town."

"I've got better things to do."

"Then don't criticize what they do."

Buildings soon blocked the final rays from the sun, casting them in deep shadow. Rosalind pulled her jacket closed to block the cool breeze. Her body was tired from riding. She looked forward to a warm meal and a comfortable bed.

Inhabitants catching sight of the travellers stared for a moment, then went on their way. They were mostly human with blond or white hair. All the men except for a few wore brown trousers with an extra piece of lighter brown material sewn across their buttock. Their shirts were cream-coloured, and they wore a short brown sash over their shoulder. The outfit was topped off with a short-brimmed black hat. The women wore knee-length dresses in the same colour as the men's trousers with a matching cream-coloured apron. They wore similar sashes except they rested on the opposite shoulder. Their hair was pulled up and under a small cap that barely covered their head. The people not wearing these styles stood out, and she wondered if they were visitors to the town.

"Let's get an inn that doesn't have a tavern attached," said Cormac.

"Skittish, have you become?" Jowsey laughed.

"I want a full night's sleep."

"Didn't you have one at Hermit's Hollow?"

"I—Yes, I did, but... Let's try to avoid encounters."

"There's one." Jowsey pointed to a sign. "Doesn't look to have an attached tavern." He looked across the road from it. "Not attached but nearby." He jerked his thumb in that direction and read the sign, "Lizzy's Liquid Lizards and Billiards."

"That's a unique name," said Rosalind.

"Sounds like they have a fetish for lizards," said Etain. "First the cockatrice, now liquid lizards."

"I hope that's not on the menu." Loggie made a face.

"We don't have to eat there." Cormac returned his attention to the inn and groaned. "Really? A Stumble Inn. That is so overused."

"Impossible." Jowsey steered his horse towards a sign that read *Stable*. "It's the only one I know."

They were greeted at the large doors by two stable hands who directed them to stalls for the horses. Once the animals were secured, they entered the inn. Jowsey went first, and Cormac followed. At the threshold, he stumbled but caught himself before he fell to the floor.

"Welcome to Stumble Inn," came a voice.

Rosalind searched for the woman who greeted them. To her right, behind a counter stood an aged woman. Beside her was a similarly aged man. Both wore the attire of those outside. Their hair was well on its way to greying but given the light colour of their youth, it didn't immediately stand out. Their wrinkled faces suggested they were well into their 60s.

"Thank you," said Jowsey. "We are looking for rooms."

"We have rooms," said the woman.

"Men on the bottom floor," said the man. "Women on the second. Couples on the top. Bathing room at the end of each hall."

"Four rooms or five?" asked the woman.

"Two," said Jowsey.

"Do you need three beds or four?"

"For us, three."

"Four would provide a place for your carry gear."

"Does it cost extra?"

"Certainly."

"Three beds are fine."

"And for the ladies? Two beds or three?"

"Two."

"Depriving yourself, you are." She picked up a pencil and held it over a piece of paper. "Name of your party?"

"Jowsey's Gang."

"Wait a minute," said Loggie. "I didn't agree to this."

"Neither did I." Cormac crossed his arms.

"Do we need to give everyone's name?" Jowsey made a face. "She said party. That's a group."

"Jowsey's Gang, it is," said the woman and wrote it into the ledger.

"Two keys," said the man. "This one is for you." He slapped it onto the desk. "This one is for the ladies." His voice softened, and he held the key out to Etain.

"Thank you, sir." She accepted the key.

"Room 204, dear."

"And my room number?" asked Jowsey.

"It's on the key," the man snapped. "The front door is never locked. Come and go as you please. Any marauding or silliness and Pithaul will intervene."

"Pithaul?" asked Jowsey.

"Our loyal wood woad."

"They're dangerous!" Cormac's face lit up. "High strung. Quick to attack."

"We do not have repeat offenders."

Rosalind swallowed hard and glanced around the small entrance way. She didn't know what a wood woad was and by the sounds of it, she didn't want to.

"Fifteen copper pieces," said the woman. "Exact only. We make no change. If you overpay, it is a contribution to the upkeep of our exquisite inn."

They each put three coins on the counter, and she quickly seized them and dropped them into a container.

"Can you recommend a great place to eat?" asked Jowsey.

"I can," said the man, "but I won't."

"Would you tell me?" asked Etain in a sweet voice.

"Dear, Lizzy's Liquid Lizards and Billiards is no place for a lady as fine as you." He glanced at the men. "They can eat there," he said gruffly, then softened his voice. "For you, I suggest The Lady of Shades Hostelry on Sapphire Lane."

"Thank you. Blessed be your evening." She nodded at Rosalind, who followed her towards the stairs.

"Yay, thanks a lot," said Jowsey and walked away.

Rosalind ascended the stairs and his voice faded into the distance. The Stumble Inn was old and showing its use. Chips out of the stairs, a cracked rail and worn paint on the walls indicated it had seen many days and few contributions to its upkeep. Etain found the room easily, and she led her inside. Rosalind stopped abruptly before she slapped her foot into the bed leg. The small room was large enough for the door to open all the way, two single beds and the small table separating them. That was it. No wonder they were encouraged to buy a room with three beds.

The long thin window over the head of the beds was horizontal. It was so low, she had to bend her knees to look out. She pulled across the curtain and put the saddlebags and her pack on the foot of her bed.

"The rain on the horizon will not wet us in here," said Etain.

"The room brings that benefit."

"I wish to bathe before I eat. It is one of only a few things I miss not being at the Sanctuary."

"Good idea. Then we'll decide where to eat."

"Not The Lady of Shades Hostelry?"

"It sounds formal. Do we want formal or adventurous?"

Etain grinned. "I think you know my answer."

11

Silently into the Night

CORMAC SCANNED THE crowd. It had grown since they'd arrived three hours ago. If all residents of Moore Thyme wore the brown and cream dresswear with the sash, that meant everyone in the tavern was from away. While he had strongly suggested they eat at The Lady of Shades Hostelry, the others chose Lizzy's Liquid Lizards and Billiards. The place recommended to Etain sounded safer, more civilized. Lizzy's was rough around the edges and growing rougher with each passing hour.

The décor fit the name. Solid wood construction with a large section of stone to create the fireplace no doubt kept the place warm in cooler seasons. The high ceiling with exposed beams allowed smoke to rise instead of sit on the shoulders of patrons. The 30-foot bar was lined with stools and each stool was filled, mostly with men. A few had their women with them. Others were being charmed by ladies of the night.

Behind the bar were the tools of the trade – bottles of intoxicating substances, glasses, mugs, swords, daggers, clubs – intermingled with images of lizards of various types. The three barkeeps stayed busy, pouring, giving advice and keeping order. They were large men, muscular and bearded. While they must have lived in town, they wore the clothing of travellers. They did, however, wear sashes.

Three billiard tables were off to the right of the bar. A steady stream of players kept the balls snapping. A few arguments had broken out but were quickly subdued by one of the barkeeps' gruff voice calling an end of it.

While the atmosphere was relatively calm, at moments it teetered on chaos. Cormac had never been much into the downtown bar scene in his own world where weapons weren't on display. Here, his nerves were on high alert, waiting for someone to say the wrong thing to the wrong person.

He wanted to leave, but Loggie was on the small stage at the end of the room playing the rebec and collecting more coins than he had at the Blue Dragon Keep Tavern and Inn in Romarin. The crowd loved him. They hooted when he played a fast tune, fell quiet for slow tunes and clapped at the end of each song. The crowd was enjoying themselves with a few patrons dancing, and Loggie was grinning from ear-to-ear, particularly when he tried to leave the stage five minutes ago and they begged him for one more.

Checking the clock on the wall, it was just after midnight. If he had been alone, he'd have already gone to bed, wanting to get up early to get on the road. If he was alone, he wouldn't have the funds to stay at an inn.

Across from him, Rosalind sipped a mixture of rum and berry juice, enjoying the show as much as the rest. She and Etain had played several games of pool. She was more experienced at the game than Etain, but both needed more practice. They tried to convince him to play, but he didn't want to be seen in the centre of anything. Sitting in the corner, cast in shadow by dim lighting was safer.

The music stopped and the crowd roared. Many banged their fist or mugs on the table. Some mugs still held alcohol, creating waves of liquid that splashed onto tables, the floor and those nearby.

"One more!" shouted someone near Loggie. Several others joined in.

Loggie bowed. "Thank you, kind ladies and gentlemen, but I'm due on the road at dawn. I must bid you restful night and fair travels."

The crowd didn't like that answer and many banged their fist and mugs harder. A wave of alcohol splashed against the face of a man, who had been sitting at the next table. Growling, he punched the man who beat the mug. The man retaliated, and they crashed to the floor, wresting and knocking over chairs.

A loud cheer rose, and others joined in.

"Time to exit," said Cormac. "Quickly."

"Don't need to be told twice." Jowsey was out of his seat.

Rosalind picked up the sack Loggie carried the rebec in and headed for the door, where Loggie met her.

Cormac tripped and fell into a solid woman, who turned to scowl at him. His first thought was, she's dwarf. His second was, she's strong. After she punched him in the face and sent him flying, the third was, I need to get up fast before she hits me again. Finally busting through the doorway and into the night air, he joined the others and hustled towards The Stumble Inn. Five minutes. If he had left five minutes earlier, he wouldn't have a sore jaw. He rubbed it, but it hurt either way.

"An excellent night," sang Loggie. "A great crowd." He leapt into the air and swung around. "If every tavern was as generous, my worries would be few."

"Less zest would be better," said Cormac.

"Less zest," said Jowsey, "equates to less spirit, less excitement and fewer coins. Am I right?" he asked Loggie.

"As right as any words spoken."

"Consider the extra as danger pay," said Cormac. "I'd settle for fewer with less danger."

"Where is the adventure in that?" asked Jowsey.

"It is his nature to play safe," said Etain. "Is it your lack of confidence or experience that makes you avoid adventure?"

The question smacked Cormac in the gut. He was confident, and before he entered this world, he had taken lessons in horseback riding, axe throwing and fencing. While he was no expert in any of them, he had a firm grasp of each. Shortly before he had cast the spell, he'd taken up archery. Experience meant nothing if he couldn't afford the weapons to use it. Not that he wanted to kill anyone. He'd defend himself but avoiding conflict was his goal. He'd not look for a fight and end his life prematurely. What he had come to this world to experience was the adventure of exploring, seeing new sights and finding unique items, like he had in the game. Except... This was far from a game and too risky to enjoy.

"I'd rather play another day," he said. "Unnecessary risk is foolish."

"You seek necessary risk?" said Jowsey. "Living is a risk. I accept it. Better than wrapping a woollen blanket over my lap and reclining in a chair with the old near the fire reminiscing about stories told by others who lived adventures."

Cormac kept his mouth closed. He couldn't win the argument with someone this carefree. Jowsey didn't care about anyone but himself and went where he pleased. Everything was a joke to him. If he took anything seriously, he hid it well.

He caught Rosalind staring. She appeared deep in thought, and he wondered if she thought him a coward. He wasn't a coward. He was reasonable. It was foolish to seek out danger. Before he reached the inn, she looked away. His throat clenched, and he shoved his hands into his pockets. Surviving this world was his goal. Nothing else mattered.

Passing over the threshold, he watched his step so he wouldn't trip over the extra piece of wood added to the bottom of the doorway. Once inside, his thoughts went to sleeping. Given the time, he'd get only five hours before the sun rose and shone in the window.

"Pithaul," whispered a raspy voice.

He slowed his pace and scanned the small entrance way. Rosalind had stopped at the display of stones in a glass case fixed to the wall. Her hand was on the glass but when she heard the voice, she removed it.

"Must be Pithaul," said Jowsey. "No dawdling, else the wood woad suspects you're up to something devious."

A bolt of lightning shot through Cormac's body. He had forgotten about the wood woad. Cautiously, he searched the dimly lit room for signs of the tree monster. There, in the corner, five feet from the edge of the steps, was a darker shadow. His eyes grew accustomed to the darkness, and the form took shape. It was about four feet high only because it sat with its trunk on the floor. Its legs – thick branches – were bent at the knees and tucked in close to the body. Its long arms wrapped around itself. If he didn't know better and if the dark eyes had been closed, he'd think it was a fancy side table. But he knew better.

"Good night, Pithaul," said Jowsey in a merry voice. He skipped by the steps and disappeared into the shadows. Loggie followed.

Grabbing hold of his nerves, Cormac focussed on the hallway leading past the steps and walked on the side farthest from the wood woad. Once away from the tree monster, he increased his pace and left the sentry far behind.

Once inside the room, he fell into bed and stared at the ceiling. His friends at home would never believe him. He'd come face-to-face with a wood woad and didn't have to fight for his survival. Incredible.

He heard the jingle of coins and looked at Loggie in the next bed. The bard was counting his coins with a big grin. In the end, everything worked out at the tavern. He adjusted his jaw. The ache was subsiding. In spite of that, the coins earned would ensure they had food and lodging for their trip. If Loggie shared. And so far, he was generous with his money. Skuld had given each of them a small sack with 20 copper and 20 silver coins. He still had almost all of it.

"One hundred and ten." Loggie grinned. "A fairer night I have yet to have."

"You're a fine player." Jowsey stripped off his clothes except for his shorts and crawled beneath the blanket. He lay on his back and rested his head on his hands. "Tis a dreamy life to spend it creating music. Sadly, I cannot pick a melody." He looked towards Loggie. "You have a gift. Use it wisely and if you ever come into possession of a magical instrument, use it stealthily."

"I am told such instruments exist," said Loggie, "but I've yet to see one in action."

"One day. If you keep your ears open and your foot to the path, you'll find one." He yawned and stretched his shoulders one way then the other. "As for me, I seek a magical pouch to carry many things yet weighs that of an egg and is scarcely much larger."

"Many things?" asked Loggie. "It would hardly carry anything."

"A bag of holding?" asked Cormac.

"You've seen one?" asked Jowsey.

"No... Not really. I mean. I've heard others talk about it." Both stared as if they knew he wasn't telling the truth. "I've never held one. Just know about them. It's like common knowledge or something."

"Or something," said Jowsey sarcastically.

"It's in the handbook."

"What handbook?"

Cormac sealed his lips. Neither of them knew about the Adventure Master's Handbook for this world. While not everything was right, most of it was. Or at least the parts he had experienced. Except the coins went further. He had forgot somethings, but he was pretty sure he couldn't buy a full meal with one copper piece. It was two or three in the game. Inflation, he guessed. It hadn't yet hit this time in the game.

"Do you have a copy of this handbook?" asked Jowsey. "I'd like to read it. See what else I might like to acquire in my travels."

Cormac frowned. "No. I didn't mean... I meant I read it in a book. Can't remember the title." He removed his boots, trousers and shirt. Before sliding beneath the blanket, he removed the belt from his pants and discretely fastened it around his waist.

"No matter," said Loggie. "If I hear of one, I'll let you know."

"How? I will be gone soon."

"Where are you going?"

"Away. Our paths will soon part." He yawned again and closed his eyes.

"Paladin," said Loggie. "No map before the paladin is found."

"That's a deal I never agreed to."

"But I'll hold you to."

"Good luck."

Cormac closed his eyes. He needed sleep, not discussion. Drifting off, he thought about the wood woad downstairs, the coins Loggie had earned and the treasure map. He didn't need treasure but finding it would certainly be an adventure. Thinking about this, he fell asleep.

Sometime later, he heard a thump. Hesitating to open his tired eyes, he ignored it. It was only noise in the hall. Probably.

"Shhh." The voice was soft, too soft for him to bother opening his eyes. Sinking deeper into sleep, the voice whispered again. "Follow me."

The creak of wood touched his ears and confused his thoughts. Was he dreaming?

"Wait!" A louder voice shattered his descent into dreamland. "Loggie!" It was Jowsey. "Loggie, wake up! Loggie!"

Cormac's eyes flew open. The scene before him confused his thoughts. Two beds away, Jowsey was jumping up and frantically putting on his pants. A second later, he pulled on his boots and grabbed a dagger. Loggie's head disappeared into the floor along with a soft golden glow. Rubbing his eyes, he tried to see clearer. A dark shadow fell forward and when he leant over the edge of the bed, a square section in the floor slammed shut.

"Get up!" shouted Jowsey. "They've taken Loggie."

He sat up. "Who? How did he get in the floor?"

"Trap door." He fell to his knees and tried to lift the wood with his fingers. It wouldn't budge. He drove the tip of his dagger at the edge. It moved but wouldn't lift. "Help me. Do the same on that side."

Cormac grabbed a dagger and forced it into the gap along the wood. Wiggling and pushing, they pried the trap door open enough to get their fingers beneath the lip. Jowsey wiggled his hand beneath it, fiddled with something and the door lifted. A set of narrow stairs led below. A faint light moved deep within, but the stairs were bathed in darkness.

"Get your pants on," said Jowsey. He removed the lantern from the hook by the door and turned up the wick. "Don't forget your dagger."

The brightness forced Cormac to squint and look away but allowed him to find his pants and boots easier. Then the light dimmed.

"Not much wick left," growled Jowsey and went to the trapdoor. "We'll keep it low."

Cormac prepared to follow until he realised what was transpiring. "No, no. This ain't happening. No tavern adventures. We can't go down there."

Halfway down the stairs, Jowsey stopped and stared up at him, confused. "We have to save Loggie. He's your friend. I assume you want to rescue him." He waited for a respond. "No? We let them steal him? Honestly? You'd let them take me, too?" He huffed. "We know where your morals are. Expect the same effort when you go missing." He continued down the stairs.

Cormac cursed under his breath. He hated it, but Jowsey was right. They had to rescue Loggie. It was the game plan. Descending the stairs, he wondered if an Adventure Master oversaw the action and planned this little night-time skirmish. Of course, they did.

At the bottom of the stairs, a passageway stretched for at least 50 feet. Fifty feet - wasn't that the measurement for... He shoved the thought from his mind and followed Jowsey with dagger in hand, not knowing whether he'd use it or not. Given the fact it might be life or death, he tightened his grip on the hilt. "We need to watch for traps."

Jowsey gave him a queer look. "You say you never do this, yet you know what to do. You act like you're not brave enough to enter a dungeon, but here you are. You're the weirdest man I know."

"Yeah." He half chuckled. "I read a lot."

"Reading is good but doing is better." Jowsey picked up the pace but came to an abrupt halt and put out his hand to stop him. "Did you hear that?"

"Yeah," he said softly and scrutinised the path ahead. "It's too dark for me to see anything past the lantern light. You?"

"Nothing, but..." He sniffed the air. "The gutting of fish," he cursed. "Cover your mouth."

"With what?" He was shirtless.

"Your hand. Hurry." Jowsey cupped his hand over his mouth and nose and hurried forward.

Before Cormac's hand went over his mouth, the odour reached his nose. It smelt horrible. He hurried after Jowsey, waving the blade of his dagger in front of him in a futile effort to disperse the gas quicker. His eyes watered and his view blurred. With only a shimmer of light from the lantern, his human eyes were practically useless in this tunnel. Dungeon. He assumed since Jowsey was elf, he'd have better vision and would lead him safely through it. Either way, he followed the shadow before him, listening for any change in gait. Careful not to jab himself, he wiped one eye with the back of his hand, hoping to clear up the blurriness. This only made it worse. His nose grew itchy, and he sneezed. The sound vibrated off the stone walls and pulsated in his ears. Anyone within the dungeon surely heard him. Then Jowsey sneezed. They weren't sneaking up on anyone.

"Stop!" Jowsey put up his hand.

Cormac stopped beside him. They had reached the end of the tunnel. It continued left and right.

"There." Jowsey pointed.

Cormac spotted soft light in the distance. "Loggie is dwarf. He can see in low light. So those with the bright lantern are...?"

"Human. Or they've not strengthened their natural ability." He tapped him on the upper arm. "Let's go." He walked quickly. More like a cautious jog. Not 30 feet along, he stopped too fast, and he almost lost his balance. He grabbed hold of Cormac's arm to steady himself. "Trap."

"Where?"

"Before us." Jowsey bent forward and examined the floor by holding the lantern over it, then inspected the wall. "It's an illusion. I smell it."

"Smell it?" He sniffed the air. All he could smell was the rotten odour of the previous trap, and he could barely see through watery eyes. "You smell magic?"

"No. Whatever's at the bottom of the hole. To the edge." He reached his foot forward and tested the ground. "Stay close."

He didn't have to be told twice. Feeling the wall, he did as Jowsey did and stayed as close to it as he could. Once they were past the pit, he saw it. Only a foot along each side was safe. In the centre of the passage was a deep hole. Peering into it, he couldn't see the bottom.

"About ten feet," said Jowsey. "Deep enough to be stuck and need help getting out." He pulled him along and increased his speed to a jog. The soft glow had disappeared. Another 50 feet and the tunnel turned right. Again, Jowsey slowed his pace.

"Another trap?"

Jowsey hesitated to answer. "I think..."

Cormac strained his eyes to make out the shapes moving in the light up ahead. Flames danced above four candles tucked into the rock walls, two on each side. Two people...or three small beings walked in an odd manner within the glow. A thought popped into his mind, but it was too outrageous to consider. No. It couldn't be. Only in fantasy games would they encounter—

"Skeletons." Jowsey didn't sound impressed. "Four. Two for each of us. Ever battle them?"

"Yes. No. Not really. Easy to kill?"

"Yes. Dagger at the ready. Take out the spine, and they're done."

Cormac rubbed his eyes, clearing the remaining moisture. Gripping the dagger, he prepared to face a foe that had already been killed once. Maybe twice and reassembled. He tried to remember what he'd done in the game, but the distance closed too quickly. Readying the dagger, he prepared to reduce one to bones with the first attack.

The skeletons turned towards them, clubs in hand. Their jaws chattered non-stop as if they were freezing or had plenty to say. With only hollow eye sockets, they looked menacing. Cormac thought of the skeleton in Mr. McNeil's biology class. It was scary when he had first seen it but harmless.

Jowsey set down the lantern, leapt at one of the skeletons and in seconds, the spine was severed. The skeleton crumbled into a pile of bones that clattered and jingled.

Cormac's turn. He advanced, focussed on the spine and slashed with the dagger. The skeleton swatted the dagger with its club and the weapon flew through the air, hit the wall and dropped to the floor. For a moment, he stood there, frozen, unable to do anything. They were supposed to be easy to kill. He should have taken them both out by now, yet they prepared to slaughter him.

"Get the dagger!" Jowsey exchanged blows with a skeleton as if they were jousting. Jousting? He could do that.

He sprang for the dagger, grabbed it and clambered to his feet. Remembering his fencing training, he struck a pose and swatted at the skeleton. It swatted back. It struck the blade but wasn't powerful enough to knock it from his hand. He jabbed between the rib cage, hoping to poke the spine hard enough it would break. No such luck. The skeleton was faster and knocked him over with a strike to the shoulder. He fell against the wall and lost the grip on the weapon. He scrambled to grab it but before he did, the skeleton brought the club down on his butt, sending him sprawling across the floor.

An eerie sound filled the tunnel. It sounded like laughter but by someone who chattered their teeth and had a burp stuck in their throat. He glanced at the skeleton. It was laughing at him lying on the ground. The skeleton fighting Jowsey joined in, filling the tunnel with an eerie noise. Laughing, they raised their clubs and brought them down on his bare back. The hits weren't powerful, but they hurt. They wouldn't break a bone, but they'd leave him black and blue.

"Skeletons with clubs will only kill you if you lay there and do nothing!" shouted Jowsey. "Get up!"

Cormac blocked the clubs with his forearm, crawled to his dagger and jumped to his feet. He was faster than them and taller. He needed only to get behind one of them. His days of playing hockey kicked in, and he faked going left. When the skeletons moved in that direction, he jumped to the right and got behind one. He swiped air with the dagger and struck the middle of the spine. It shattered and bones clattered to the ground. Sucking in a gulp of surprise, he grinned at the pile of bones. He had done it.

A solid wack to the jaw sent him flying backwards against the wall. Another skeleton advanced with the club ready to strike. Before it did, Jowsey side-kicked the spine, breaking it in two. The bones crumbled to the floor. That was the last one.

Jowsey frowned at him. "Next time, get behind them quickly. This was easy. There were only four and they had clubs. If you meet four with swords, it won't be so pleasant."

"Gotcha." He wiped a layer of sweat from his forehead. Ideally, he'd practice, but who would he practice with? Jowsey? He was probably faster and better than him even though he appeared younger. But he was elf, so maybe he was 30 or 50 years older.

A squawk interrupted the silence, and he whipped his head around. Before he could react, a brown chicken raced by him and into the darkness from where they came. Its squawking faded into the distance, and he wondered if it fell into the pit.

"Not the first chicken I've seen in a dungeon." Jowsey picked up the lantern and stepped over the bones. "Let's go."

Cormac followed him into the near darkness, leaving the candlelight behind. They travelled about 200 feet before encountering a side passageway. Jowsey peered down it, then looked down the passage that continued straight. Almost a minute passed before Jowsey decided.

"I'm guessing more than knowing, but I say this way." He pointed to the side passageway.

"You have more experience than me. I accept your decision."

Jowsey gave him a strange look. "Let's get to it then."

They travelled a good 400 feet before Jowsey paused. "You see that?" He pointed ahead.

Cormac squinted. In the distance was a shimmering light. "What do you think it is?"

Jowsey shrugged. "Don't know. It's bright. We'll sneak up on it. Walk where I walk." He started away. When he neared the light source, he hugged the wall with the largest shadow and slowed his pace.

Cormac tried to see what lie ahead, but light only illuminated the opposite stone wall. He couldn't see anyone or anything. Why would Loggie's kidnappers stop to ignite a light source? He tapped Jowsey on the shoulder and whispered, "Trap?"

"It crossed my mind." Jowsey slowed further and crept silently towards the mouth of the passageway.

Cormac followed so close, he could hear Jowsey's breathing. Or was it his own? He swallowed slowly and took a deep breath to quiet his racing pulse. Another five feet, and they'd be in the room. At the edge of the passageway, Jowsey stopped. The room measured about 20 feet by 20 feet. At one end rested a high table. No, an alter. His spit stuck in his throat. This was never good.

Jowsey nudged him and nodded his head towards the other end of the room where a thin figure in a blue robe that almost reached his knee-high boots stood peering into a second passageway. The hood hid the back of their head and their face. After a moment, the person turned and walked towards the alter. It was a man, a hauflin, with a thin beard, one worn by a teenage boy who had just graduated high school. When he saw Cormac and Jowsey, he jumped and stalled in place.

"We come in peace." Jowsey stepped into the room but went no farther. "We search for a friend. Did he pass by here?"

"Dwarf wearing shorts only?"

"That's him."

"Mia the Mystic has captured him. He is under her spell."

"Spell," asked Cormac. "Which one?"

"Mesmeric Melody. He will do as she orders."

"And what would that be?"

"Sing. Play. I assume he is a bard."

"He is, but..." Cormac scratched his head. "She kidnaps bards for a private concert?"

"She keeps them until she gets bored. Only then will your friend regain his mind and be set free. If he pleases her, his stay will be lengthy."

Jowsey stepped closer. "Where will she take him?"

"To her lair."

"Do you know where it is?"

The young man fumbled for words. "It is not my place. If she... I cannot say. I cannot wrong her. If I do..."

"We won't say anything."

"She will find out." He backed away. "I am here for simple healing. Then Matilda and me, we go home." He tilted his head. "Did you see a chicken?"

"I may have." Jowsey stepped closer. "Tell me where she is taking our friend, and I might remember."

"That threatens the life of an innocent hen. Surely you cannot justify this."

Cormac chuckled. "You're worried about a chicken when we have lost a friend."

He tsked. "Mia will do him no harm less he doesn't play and under her full control, he will play."

"That is evil," said Jowsey. "A woman cannot possess a man like that. He needs to be rescued."

"At what cost? My life? Yours." He shook his head. "I cannot help you."

"Then we go alone." Jowsey walked towards the passageway the man had been peering down when they arrived. "Good luck finding the chicken after the skeletons are finished with it."

He gasped and stared into the passageway where the chicken had gone. "Not Matilda. She is my only friend."

"Maybe if you didn't hang out in dungeons with a chicken," said Cormac, "you'd have more."

"And if you didn't cower in the face of mild danger," added Jowsey, "you'd have a loyal one, not a coward that runs off at the first sign of danger."

"Matilda is not a coward. She's a chicken."

Cormac laughed. In this land, chicken didn't mean afraid.

"Just the same, we're leaving." Jowsey stepped into the passageway.

"Wait!" The man rushed over to him. "You have seen Matilda. Is she good?"

"Where is this sorceress taking our friend?"

He hummed and hawed, battling doubt. "Her lair is...not far from here." He clenched his fists. "Around the corner and into a shallow door and... I cannot say more."

"You've said nothing."

"All right." He thrust his arms straight like a pouty girl. "Go straight down this passageway to the end. Take a left. Walk nimbly to avoid the light coming from the wall. Do not break it."

"A trap?" asked Cormac.

"Of course. Mild in comparison to the next one."

"How many?"

"Two I am aware of. Turn right at the turtle and crawl until you reach the bottom of the stairs."

"Something is going to swing?"

"Most likely. At the top of the stairs, step on only the green stones. The door swings open towards you, so... there's that. If you stand too close... Down you go."

"Sounds easy enough," said Jowsey.

Cormac stared at him. The biggest threat was the sorceress, not the traps. "What will she do to us if we show up at her door?"

"One of any number of things."

"Her weaknesses?" asked Jowsey.

"Music. Sing to her. Recite poetry."

Cormac cringed. He was neither a singer nor a poet.

"Got it." Jowsey walked away.

"And Matilda?" The man grabbed his arm to stop him. "Where is she? A deal we made."

Jowsey told him where they'd seen the chicken. "The skeletons are dismantled. You should be fine to catch her unless she fell into the pit."

"Eek. I will fetch her immediately." He hurried off and disappeared into the shadows.

Cormac fell into step behind Jowsey. They passed a tunnel to the right and kept going until their passageway ended, then turned left. The light was extremely low in this area, and he struggled to see Jowsey in the dwindling glow of the lantern. When Jowsey stopped, he almost bumped into him.

"See the beam?" Jowsey held the lantern to the side.

He squinted and found a thin yellow beam of light half a foot off the floor. "I do."

"Step over it." Jowsey went first and cautiously lifted his foot to clear the beam. Once on the other side, he waited.

Cormac stepped up to the beam, lifted his foot higher than he needed to and set it on the other side. A bead of sweat pooled on his forehead. At another place and time without fear of striking the beam, he could have done this without thinking. But here, knowing something horrible was going to happen if he struck it, his muscles hesitated. With deliberate moves, he lifted the other foot, carried it over the beam and set it down. He breathed a sign of relief and followed Jowsey.

"I can't see much," he said, squinting at a two-foot shadow about eight feet away.

"A tunnel with a stone turtle standing on its hindlegs guarding it," whispered Jowsey. "The stairs are 20 feet away. Let's crawl the entire way. We leave the light here." He set down the lantern and dropped to his hands and knees. "Keep your head down until you feel the steps."

He followed his lead and got as close to the floor as he could and still have the ability to squirm. The fact that something could swing down at any moment set his nerves on fire. What if the man had lied only to save his chicken? He inched forward at an agonising pace. The stone was cold, and dirt stuck to his arms and chest. Something crawled across his fingers, and he shook it off. It landed on his back. Tiny feet digging into his skin made him want to swat it but to do so, he'd have to raise his hand high, which might set off the trap. He pressed on, twitching his back muscles to encourage whatever it was to go away. Finally, his hand struck the first stair.

"You can stand." Jowsey's voice came from above. "The stairs curve. Stay close to the inside." Soft footsteps indicated he climbed the stairs.

Cormac stood, brushed the bug off his shoulder and placed his foot gingerly on the first step. The steps were randomly spaced, and he stumbled several times before reaching the top where a small candle illuminated a door with a rounded top. Between the top step and the door was a patchwork of colourful stones.

"Only the green ones," whispered Jowsey. He stepped on a small green stone. His foot covered it completely.

"Wait. We can't knock and ask to be invited in."

"Got a plan?"

"First, don't get too close to the door. If she opens it fast, you'll be knocked down."

"Good point." He stopped. "If she likes song, let's sing."

"I don't sing."

"Poetry?"

"I don't know any poems."

"We could make it up as we go."

"That always works." His sarcasm made him chuckle. He and his friends had often 'made it up as they went' and things never turned out in their favour.

"Song it is." Jowsey cleared his throat. "Join in if you know the words but if your voice sounds like a baby dragon screeching, don't." He turned towards the door and sang softly. "On the bank of the river green was the last place I had seen, the one so kind and fair and my heart wishes she were near."

The door creaked open a crack, and Jowsey kept singing. Inch-by-inch, the door opened wider until the opening exposed a woman his height. The glow of many candles made Cormac squint. Her long red hair, parted in the centre, hung to her waist. It was decorated with silver clips and ribbons. Dark eye shadow outlined her eyes and ruby-red lipstick painted her lips. Her pale skin made both look unnatural. She wore a black gown that dragged on the floor. White leaves decorated the shoulders of the material and the drooping sleeves that almost touched the floor. In her hand, she held a twisted stick.

Surveying the scene outside her door, she focussed on Jowsey, who was singing with such passion her expression softened. When he finished the song, he started another. This one was also low and sweet. While he had some talent, he was no Stan Rogers.

Cormac wondered what they'd do next. He looked behind the woman and didn't see Loggie. If she was a powerful sorceress, she could blast them with a fireball and send them tumbling down the steps. Jowsey was busy serenading and made no motion to go inside, so that left him. He stepped on a green stone, looked for another and put his foot on it. Three steps later, and he was on the threshold.

Mia the Mystic's dark eyes gazed into his. At first, they appeared welcoming, then they turned serious, and his mind numbed. His thoughts felt sleepy and... A solid whack to his bare back woke him up. He stepped over the threshold and scanned the heavily-decorated room for Loggie. Material of various shades and patterns hung from the ceiling and draped the walls. A collection of soft cushions filled one corner, and counters and bookshelves filled the rest. Various instruments were hung from the wall and balanced on stands. A door, that appeared to lead to the outside, was half covered with thick blue material. Illuminating the space were more than three dozen candles.

Seeing movement near the cushions, he found Loggie, stretching out across the soft mounds. His eyes were open, but he stared at the ceiling.

"You are not welcome," said Mia in a low, matter-of-fact tone. "But your singing friend is." She traced his bare shoulder with her finger. "Unless you sing. I've always wanted to own a trio."

"I do sing," he lied. "But I need a drink first." He stepped inside.

"There is no water for those who do not play or sing." She attempted to grab his arm, but he was too fast.

He raced to Loggie and smacked him across the face.

Mia laughed. "I am not a simple low-level sorceress. You'll need more than a slap for him to regain his senses."

Cormac cursed under his breath. Jowsey stepped inside but didn't take a break from crooning. In fact, he added to his routine by performing a simple dance. Cormac tried to think of other ways to break a hypnotic spell. If he had the Adventure Master's Guide, he could look it up if the sorceress granted him the time, and...

"Little man, if you don't leave, I shall turn you into a... chicken, so you can wander the dungeon searching for your only friend."

His mind snapped back to the man who had lost his chicken. Surely, she hadn't...

She smiled slyly and stepped towards him. "Let me ease your burden. Forget this nonsense and enjoy the night." Soft shock waves of white and black slowly radiated from her eyes. Around and around the colours turned until he felt his muscles relax and... He slapped himself in the face. The sting awakened his senses, and he looked away. If he couldn't wake Loggie up with a slap, could he... He glanced at Mia from the corner of his eye. If he was wrong, she'd surely blast him with fire. Yet, he had to try. Faking a shocked expression with big eyes, he stared at Jowsey at the doorway. His hand flew over his mouth, and he pretended to shield himself from an invisible attack.

Mia smiled mischievously. "You'll have to do better than that."

At that moment, Jowsey swung the dagger, catching her forearm. Blood seeped from the superficial wound, and Mia jumped back. Scowling, she grabbed a cloth from the counter and covered the cut.

Cormac grabbed Loggie by the arm and threw him over his shoulder. He jostled him and found a comfortable, balanced position.

"Whath's doing on..." Loggie stammered. "When am I?" He sniffed the air. "Whath's the flower?"

"Let's go." Cormac rushed to the door, where Jowsey continued to sing. He raced over the threshold, forgetting about the green stones. His foot went through the floor, and he stumbled, throwing Loggie onto the stairs. Jowsey grabbed his arm to steady him on the green stones that remained intact. Getting his bearings, he scrambled across the stones to the top step.

"I muth be dwunk," said Loggie. "The floor dithappeared." He rubbed his head and tried to rise but lost his balance and slammed against the wall.

Cormac heaved Loggie onto his shoulder and staggered down the uneven stairs towards the soft glow of the lantern. He glanced back to see Jowsey trailing him. So, too, was Mia, but she wasn't moving as fast. What was her plan? The turtle?

Then he remembered the trap. At the bottom of the stairs, he lowered Loggie to the floor. "Crawl," he ordered. "Stay low." He pushed himself across the hard, cold stone, dragging Loggie with him, until he reached the lantern. He rose and helped Loggie to his feet. His friend was still in a horrible state, so he lifted him onto his shoulder and held tightly to his legs.

"This isn't over." Mia descended the stairs into shadow. Her footsteps stalled, and yellow light grew and illuminated her hands.

Jowsey slithered quickly across the floor. As soon as he jumped to his feet, Cormac turned to run but something snapped at his buttock and held him. He groaned and swatted whatever it was.

"Turtle?" Loggie sounded confused. "Cute. Little turtle bites butt." He laughed in a high-pitched voice, then giggled.

"Get it off!" He slapped the solid object, but it wouldn't let go. Then something struck it, and it jerked away, almost taking him with it.

"Not waiting to see what happens." Jowsey pushed him forward.

"No, don't go, Turtie?" shouted Loggie.

Cormac raced down the passageway beside Jowsey, who gripped the lantern that swung back and forth. They stepped into the beam of light as one. A single snap reached Cormac's ears, and he remembered the trap. The ensuing thud and clatter made him glance over his shoulder. He couldn't see what it was, but it sounded deadly.

"Right!" Jowsey pulled him in that direction, and the bright light of the alter room came into view.

"I can see," said Cormac and picked up the pace. Jowsey beat him to the alter room, and he sharply took another right.

"Whither to do we rush?" Loggie's voice shook from bouncing on Cormac's shoulder.

"To our room. No talk. Only run." He sped through the alter room and faced the 400-foot passageway. He ran half blind, keeping his focus on the dim lantern. Jowsey's shadow kept him from hitting the wall. At the end of the passage, they turned left, and candles up ahead shed light on piles of bones. Not willing to slow down, he leapt over the piles and stumbled when his foot rolled on a bone. He caught his balance and kept going.

Loggie shrieked. "Skeletons! Cursed, we are!"

Jowsey disappeared around a corner, and when Cormac made the turn, he barely had time to stop before smashing into him. A low clucking sound reached his ears and a small shadow stood before Jowsey.

"You rescued him!" said the young man, who coddled his chicken.

"And now we make our escape," said Jowsey. He grabbed Cormac's arm. "Trap. Pit. Close to the wall." He pulled him forward.

"She chases you?" asked the man. Dim light hid his face, but his voice revealed his concern.

"We assume." Jowsey froze. "Did you hear that?" He stared into the darkness from where they came.

Cormac lifted his ear to listen. Had he heard feet on the...? What he thought was the wind blowing down the passageway turned into a long howl that shook his nerves. Yapping ensued. It was far off but growing closer. "What is that?"

"Of all nights to be in the galleries." The young hauflin looked towards the sound, then in the other direction. "I am... This won't end well."

"I'm not sticking around to find out." Jowsey moved forward.

"What are they?" Cormac asked the stranger while following Jowsey.

"Red wolves. Her pets. Hunters." The hauflin took a step towards the sound, then turned back. "Nowhere to go."

"Come with us," said Loggie, hanging onto Cormac's back.

"I cannot. If she learns I've aided in your—"

"Kneilot!"

His head whipped around at the sound of the voice echoing down the hallway, and he clutched his chicken tightly.

"You will regret all you've done since sunrise!" The voice and the wolves grew louder.

The young man squealed. "Must go." He quickly followed Cormac along the edge of the hole in the floor.

Once past the pit, Cormac raced after Jowsey, who waited for no one. He turned down the passage on the right and headed straight for the narrow set of stairs. Halfway there, he heard a puff, and a rank odour filled his senses. He cursed for not remembering the trap. The gas stung his eyes, but he was moving too quickly to absorb any great amount. He rubbed his eyes to clear the growing moisture. Jowsey was doing the same until he reached the stairs, then he quickly ascended and threw open the trap door.

The yapping wolves were gaining ground and by the time he reached the first step, he thought they had already passed the skeletons and were turning down this passageway. He squealed, grabbed the bar along the wall for extra support and raced quickly up the stairs, landing on top of Loggie between the beds.

"Quickly," ordered Jowsey, who held the trap door open.

Kneilot, with the chicken tucked firmly under his arm, leapt from the hole, and Jowsey slammed the door shut. "No latches," he said. "Grab a bed!"

Cormac squealed, then grabbed the bed post. One leg rested on the door, and he sat on the bed to make it heavier.

"This will not contain her." Kneilot raced to the door.

Jowsey grabbed a shirt and raced after him. Loggie grabbed his pants and shirt and did the same. Cormac didn't wait for an invitation and when the door opened, he ran after them, closing it behind him.

Kneilot sprinted to the entrance of The Stumble Inn and sat on the bottom step leading to the second floor, as close to the wood woad as he could.

"Pithaul," came the ominous voice in deep shadow.

Cormac went for the door but stopped when the others didn't follow. "What are you doing?" he gasped, catching his breath. "We need to get away from here. Far away."

"Where would we run to?" asked Jowsey.

"We are safe here," said Kneilot.

"Safe?" said Cormac. "That's a wood woad you're sitting by."

"I know. Mia is afraid of Pithaul. He protects the inn. Anyone who causes trouble is immediately dealt with. She will not come here."

Cormac eased his grip on the door handle. "Really?"

He nodded. "Safer here than anywhere else in Moore Thyme. Right, Pithaul?"

"Pithaul."

"He agrees." Kneilot relaxed and stretched out on the step, setting the chicken beside him. "We stay here for the night, Matilda. Morning will see us travelling with these fine folks."

"What?" asked Jowsey.

"Wait." Cormac sat on the floor against the wall. "You can't come with us. You can't trust us. For all you know, we are thieves. Assassins."

Kneilot half chuckled and half grunted. "Assassins don't squeal as you did when facing wolves."

He was about to respond, but his mouth froze open.

"He's not wrong," said Jowsey. "That was a horrible squeal."

He folded his arms. The squeal had been a natural reaction to the danger. All this was new to him, and he had been terrified of dying. Glancing at the wood woad, he still was. But Kneilot appeared comfortable on the step. He was so close to the tree monster, he could reach out and touch it.

Deciding to give the night a rest and think about things tomorrow, he settled into a comfortable position and closed his eyes. The chicken clucked softly, and the smell of the horrible gas from the dungeon lingered in the air.

"Pithaul." The soft voice blended with the noise of the night, and Cormac released a weary breath and fell asleep.

Rosalind closed the door to the room and walked down the hallway, following Etain. The woman was explaining what they had done yesterday and what they'd do today. The notes she'd found in her pouch alongside the deck of Roots of Terra shed some light on the situation but hearing it from Etain was easier.

"Make more notes," said Etain. "In case we are separated, and you need to find your way back to us." She pointed to a set of stairs going down. "We'll find a paladin and crush this spell."

Rosalind chuckled. "I like your spirit." She descended the stairs and checked the clock on the wall: 5:30. A few people stood next to a counter with bags in hand. Passing them, she caught a piece of the conversation about paying extra because they'd taken two lanterns off the hall wall. The elderly couple behind the counter paused to stare at her until she reached the exit door.

"There." Etain pointed across the street. "Lizzy's Liquid Lizards and Billiards. Fine food. Exciting entertainment."

"Did we play pool?"

"We did. You're very good, and I have lots to learn."

Rosalind surveyed the town. The sun was creeping over the horizon and casting bright golden sunshine across the land and creating long dark shadows. The town was quiet this early in the morning. Only a few people walked about wearing... She wasn't sure why everyone wore the same thing, and she had already asked Etain many things this morning and didn't want to add to the questions, so kept her curiosity to herself. Entering the tavern, she was drawn to the fireplace producing heat. It beckoned her to come near and promised to remove the chill from her bones. Since she'd awakened, she hadn't been warm even after putting on three layers.

"So much for our private chat over morning tea," said Etain. "They're already here. We had agreed to rise at six. Guess they couldn't sleep either." She led the way to a large table where four men around her age sat eating. They appeared worn out, scraggly looking with minor cuts and bruises on their faces and arms.

"You started without us?" Etain sat next to a man with tangled, messy hair as if he had been out in the wind on a ship for days. His eyes lit up when he saw her.

"Rosalind." One of the men gestured for her to sit beside him. "I'm Loggie. Cormac." He pointed to the man beside him, who was the tallest of the group. "Jowsey and Kneilot."

That name was new. Etain hadn't mentioned him. She sat next to Loggie and studied the faces around the table to remember them.

"You have gathered a new friend?" asked Etain.

"Not exactly," said Jowsey. "He's hanging around hoping we'll let him leave town with us."

"Oh," she looked closer at the man. "I am Etain of Elridge Mountain. And you?"

"A lovely name. I am only Kneilot. Failed blacksmith apprentice." He winced. "It was not for me. I near most burnt down the shop. Sent away, I was, without even a copper coin for the days worked."

"You've discovered blacksmithing is not your calling. What is?"

He hesitated, and his face turned a light shade of pink, making the brown freckles across his cheeks and nose stand out. "I am unsure."

"You do not look unsure, only ill prepared to voice it."

His face grew redder. "It is a fanciful dream. Nothing that will come true." He took a drink of ale and picked at his meal.

"Share with us your dream. We have our own, which we chase vigorously."

"Why bother," said Jowsey. "He's not coming with us."

"Do you wish to accompany us?" asked Etain.

"I can't stay in Moore Thyme because I helped your friends."

"Then you shall come with us."

"He doesn't have a horse," said Jowsey, "and he's not getting on mine."

"You shall ride with me." Etain smiled, and her eyes glistened.

"Hold on. We didn't agree to this." Jowsey appeared ready to fight.

"I do not need your permission."

"Yes, but..."

The server arrived at the table, and Rosalind and Etain placed their orders.

"You can ride with me, too," said Rosalind. "Adventures are better with friends." Cormac stared at her, and he looked like he was going to say something but remained silent. "Tell us what you pursue. Maybe we can help."

"It is too great a challenge." He bowed his head and ran his hand through his short dark-blond hair that stood on end when he was finished. "I will be 50 before a cleric I be."

"You're a cleric?" asked Cormac. He nodded. "Every adventure party needs a cleric, but you're untrained. Right?"

"Yes. I have only begun to search for Eir. The goddess is elusive, and I am told beautiful. Perhaps she does not allow me her time because I am no great person."

"Nonsense," said Etain. "Eir comes to those after many hours of meditation, studying and good deeds. She will see the light within your heart, and she will come to you when you are ready for the next phase of your training. Be mindful. She is listening though she may not make her presence known."

"Have you seen her?" His eyes widened and his mouth hung open.

"I have."

"You are a cleric?"

"No. But I have learned to tend injuries, to dress a wound, to encourage healing."

"You are indeed more magnificent than I first imagined."

"She's not interested in you," said Jowsey, "so you can stop with the flattery."

"I am a mere hauflin," said Kneilot. "I am well aware a woman of her statis is not interested in me. Even if I attract her attention, I could never betray the one I love."

"Oh, right. Matilda." Jowsey chuckled and poked a piece of egg and put it into his mouth.

"Thanks to you, I have no hope of Mia reversing the spell."

"Who is Matilda?" asked Rosalind. The conversation wasn't making much sense. "Is she coming too?"

"She must." Kneilot lifted his arm to reveal a brown chicken sitting beside him. "I cannot see her live the remainder of her life as a hen."

"Does she lay eggs?"

"Um, well, of course. She's a hen."

"We will have fresh eggs on our journey."

"And if we run out of food, drumsticks." Jowsey chuckled until Kneilot slapped his face. Then he growled.

"She is my lover you threaten to eat. I'll not tolerate such speak."

"You're bluffing," he spat. "That's not a woman in chicken feathers."

"It matters not what you think. It is what I know. And I will protect her with my life."

"The first lesson in the cleric handbook is to control anger," said Etain. "We shall work on that first."

Rosalind looked away, hiding the grin that escaped.

"All adventure groups need a cleric," said Cormac. She turned to look at him. As soon as the words escaped his mouth, he appeared to regret them. "It's just a thought. If he can heal us when injured, that's a good thing." He put food into his mouth and stared at his plate.

The food arrived and Rosalind focussed on eating. Not knowing who was who or what their purpose was, she didn't believe she had a say in who came and who didn't, but she'd still offer a seat on her horse. Etain's quick explanation before they'd left the room didn't provide enough information to make an informed decision. It didn't matter. She was happy wherever she went. Life was about living the adventure, not worrying about the details.

Just over an hour later, they rode out of town, leaving behind the citizens in matching clothing and the noise of wagons on dirt streets. The forest was where Rosalind wanted to be. As soon as they passed the many fields of crops and farm animals, they entered lush woodland. Birds of various colours and sizes sang, filling the morning with a melody that lifted the spirit.

Today would be a good day.

Rosalind enjoyed the leisurely trot through the ever-changing landscape with wildlife making their presence known by chattering, passing in front of them or stopping to stare from a branch or from beneath a bush. Occasionally, she heard the whisper on the breeze of a fairy familiar to her ear. When she stopped for a break and went into the bush to relieve herself, Coraline met her there. A sprinkle of fairy dust rekindled the memories they'd shared. They were many, and they reminded her of the inner strength she possessed. It also reminded her of their many conversations and the Roots of Terra visions. But it did not restore her memories of those she travelled with nor where she'd come from or where she'd been. They remained elusive to her. Knowing Coraline travelled alongside gave her the confidence she had been missing since she'd started the day.

Wispy clouds that reminded her of horse tails painted the deep blue sky. While riding, she'd stare at a collection and imagined creatures within them. Horses, dragons and silly faces abound. The forest rolled into grasslands and meadows by mid-day. To give Etain's horse relief, Kneilot rode with her with his chicken tucked comfortable under his arm.

"You are hauflin," he said to open the conversation.

"That I remember." She glanced over her shoulder at him. He was around her age. Wiry. A peppering of dark freckles across his face.

"Etain says you are her guardian. You must be skilled with the dagger. Brave in the face of danger."

She giggled. "She is a fantastic storyteller. I am no one special. I stand to face danger by her side." Her smiled softened. "That is all anyone can expect from a friend."

"Do you come directly from Spiritwood? Or did your parents?"

She searched her memory for the name. "I have not heard of this place."

"You have forgotten it."

"Why would you ask if I came from there?"

"It is where all hauflins originate. It is where every generation born elsewhere must return for the teachings. I was born elsewhere. My parents returned to Spiritwood and lived there until I was 12. Then we left, and I have missed it since. I loved it there and will return one day."

"And you haven't return yet because...?"

"I am in search of something I feel is missing in my life."

"Did you find it?"

"Not yet, but I feel I am closer today than yesterday."

She grinned. "Then you have made progress." She nodded towards the hen that slept with its beak tucked under its wing. "Is this truly a woman?"

"It is. A wicked sorceress has done this."

"And you love her?"

"Yes. As much today as yesterday."

"Progress and stability." She turned back around to face the road.

By the time Cormac and Loggie agreed to stop for the evening, they had left the expansive grasslands behind and returned to forest. A small meadow lay nearby, and a stream ran alongside it. She led her horse to the greenest of grasses and left it to graze after giving it an affectionate pat. It neighed and began eating.

The fire built and the meal consumed, she found a soft spot near the trunk of an old tree and dug out her Roots of Terra. She looked up and saw Etain leading Kneilot to a boulder resting beside a great oak. There, they sat cross-legged and conversed. They were too far away for her to hear even with her excellent hearing. She returned her attention to the cards and unfolded the note she'd written. The instructions were easy to understand. She cleared her mind of all thoughts and focussed on the energy. Shuffling the cards, she tried to see the energy in the air, dancing in the late day rays of the sun. If she stared hard enough, she saw the waves like those breaking gently along the shoreline, ebbing to-and-fro with a mesmerizing melody.

"It is strong here," whispered Coraline. "Nature's magic will guide you. Open your mind, and let your imagination accept what is in front of you."

Rosalind dealt the first card. Many golden lines crossed against a black background to create a five-pointed star. Star bursts of various sizes enhanced the design, and everything floated on a golden wing of a bird outside the image.

"The Ace of Pentacles," gasped Coraline. "A special card for hauflins. Much abundance lies ahead. You need only remain grounded to your intentions. Stay true to what you believe in your heart, and you will be granted your wishes."

"I have no wishes."

Coraline smiled. "Then you should make some."

"I could wish for a large bowl of apples."

"Silly. These wishes are meant to satisfy your soul, not your tummy."

"I will give it some thought." She drew another card. "The lone dragon. We have seen him before."

"We have. It reveals he is in your future."

The sun eased into slumber, taking its light with it and casting Rosalind in darkness. She gathered her cards and returned to the fire. Etain had also returned, leaving Kneilot at the stone.

"He is making his intentions clear and quietly meditating on them," she said. "He will make a fine cleric."

"Doesn't matter," said Jowsey. "He's staying at the next town."

"If he wishes to continue farther, he is permitted," she said. "I encouraged him to go to Delgrath. Sir Uwen the Noble will find him a teacher."

"Great," mumbled Jowsey.

"It is his desire, and I encourage it. Can you not appreciate his life aspiration?"

"I welcome his company," said Rosalind.

"You won't remember him in the morning," he snapped. "So, him being here has no consequences to you."

"Your comments were unjustified and now they are rude." Etain frowned at him. "Follow Kneilot's example and meditate to become a better person."

"I can't become any better than I am."

"You have set low standards for your life. You'll suffer greatly for it."

He jumped up and walked away, grumbling under his breath.

"Maybe he's right," said Rosalind. "I won't remember any of this in the morning." She looked around at the small group. She wouldn't remember any of them. Cormac stared at her with an uncertain expression. His fingers toyed with an object on his chest beneath his shirt.

"Nonsense," said Loggie. "You are part of this group, and your opinion matters." He draped an arm across her shoulder and pulled her near. "It's Jowsey who will be gone soon, and we won't have to put up with his nonsense."

"He was the reason we rescued you last night," said Cormac. "I would have slept right through your capture."

"He has some redeeming qualities. But he has his own quest, and that is his priority. When we veer from his destination, he'll leave."

Etain glanced in the direction Jowsey had gone. He was walking the road with his shoulders slumped, kicking random rocks. "Have any of you seen this map he speaks of?"

Cormac shook his head. "For all we know, he's lying."

"But Guthro wouldn't risk his life for a useless map," said Loggie.

"What map is this?" asked Rosalind. All three stared at her, making her think about the question. Was she supposed to know about this map? "Where is it?"

Loggie reached for her and slid up her sleeve, revealing the leather bracer. "Supposedly it is inside this."

"Why do I carry it? Is it mine?"

"The short of the long story is, he gave it to you for safe keeping from people who were chasing him. Now he's working to get it back and escape with it."

"Why doesn't he take it and run?" She winced. "I wouldn't remember."

"He has tried. Not lately."

"Honestly," said Cormac, "I thought he'd have succeeded and gone by now."

Rosalind unfastened the straps.

"What are you doing?" asked Cormac.

"Looking at this map."

"He says it's cursed. Only Shayde Thornheart can look at the treasure map." He glanced at Jowsey, who had walked out of sight. "We probably shouldn't."

"Treasure map? I'm not afraid." Rosalind removed the bracer and looked for a map.

"That's the spirit." Etain knelt beside her. "Is it on the back of the leather?"

She flipped it over and searched for marks. There was nothing. She checked the straps. Nothing there either. Sliding her finger along the edge, she found an opening. The straps woven through the leather kept it secured. She tugged on one, and it came free. She removed the other three and separated the leather sheets. There, folded several times to conform to the bracer was a piece of material.

"He wasn't lying," said Loggie, leaning in for a better view.

She unfolded it and at its full size, it was two feet by two feet. Seeing nothing of substance on one side, she flipped it over. This was barer still. She checked the other side again. "There's nothing but a few faint lines." She held it up and her eyes widened. With the fire behind the material, many lines became visible. "Look at that. Do you see the trail? There are other marks, too."

"I see them," said Loggie, "but there are no place names. No way to know where anything is."

"Etain," said Cormac, "your map is similar in size. Maybe we can identify places by finding similar road shapes."

She dug out her map and spread it on the ground. Rosalind hadn't seen it before. It was as dull as the map she held when the fire didn't illuminate it. She placed the map to the treasure over Etain's and it radiated soft golden light. "Fascinating."

"The perfect word." Loggie leant over it.

"Incredible," said Etain. "My vision did not reveal this."

"If we wanted to," said Cormac, "we could find the treasure."

Everyone looked at him. "It's guarded by magic," said Loggie. "Are we now willing to risk life for treasure? All because of a map we can read?"

"No, not really." He grinned. "But it might be fun."

"Fun, says the man who squeals when wolves nip at his heels."

"It was dark."

"Like a dungeon won't be."

"There's a short cut to Delgrath," said Etain, pointing to the map. "I am to take it. I am not told why, but I've seen it in my nightly visions."

"That's not far from here," said Loggie. He looked up. "Only a mile or so. It will cut two days off our travel time."

Cormac groaned. "I think you mean add two."

Loggie bent his brow. "Why would it take longer to cover a shorter distance?"

"Short cuts lead to...adventure. Unpredicted adventures."

"Are you a foreteller?" asked Etain.

He huffed. "No, I've just seen enough short cuts to know what we'll find on them."

"Excellent." She grinned. "We shall take it."

"Where is this infamous treasure?" asked Cormac. "I don't see a big red X marking the spot."

"Why would an X mark the spot?" asked Loggie. "Seriously, you make no sense at times. Treasure is marked with a circle."

"Right there?" Rosalind pointed to a spot with a red circle. Nothing around it for one inch – in map measurement – was indicated. No road or town. No indication if it was a hill, a forest or if a river ran by it. Just one red circle in the middle of nowhere.

"Possibly." Loggie studied it further. "That's not far from here." He hmphed. "Closer than Delgrath."

"Where is this Shayde Thornheart that Jowsey talks about?" Cormac sat back on his feet. "Did he hint at his location?"

"Thornheart is not on a map." The sarcastic voice came from behind, and everyone turned to see Jowsey walk towards them. When he saw the map, his head tilted. "Is that Etain's map? It didn't..." His voice trailed off as he examined it in the glow of the fire. "That looks like..." He scratched his head.

Rosalind waited for the explosion. Once he noticed his map lay before him, surely he'd be angry, maybe snatch it from her grip and ride off with it.

"Cool map," said Kneilot, who joined them. He leant over Etain's shoulder to see it. "Where'd you get it. I've never seen anything like it."

"I made it?" Etain's voice sounded innocent.

"I've seen the one you made," said Jowsey, "and this....this..." His eyes widened, and he reached for the map. "How did you make it do that?" He lifted the treasure map from Etain's map, and the lights went out, leaving only obscure lines. "What happened?"

"It only glows when laid against Etain's map." Rosalind reached for it, but he pulled it away. "It shows where the treasure is. We were thinking about rescuing it."

"You don't rescue treasure," he said, "and if we did that, Thornheart would hunt us 'til our bodies rotted in the sun." He folded the map quickly, grabbed the leather bracer and tucked it inside.

"He won't know."

"Thornheart will know. There are spies everywhere." Once the map was secured, he put the bracer on his arm. "No need to continue the charade. If you can't find me, don't bother looking." He pulled his sleeve over the bracer to conceal it, then plopped down on his bedroll.

Rosalind massaged her arm where she'd worn the leather. It felt naked. She wondered when she woke in the morning if she'd still feel it missing. It didn't matter. She wouldn't even remember wondering about it.

"I'll take first watch," she said. She wanted to live with these memories a little longer. She had room on her paper, and she thought about making a note about the map.

"Second," said Loggie.

"Third." Everyone eyed Jowsey. "I didn't watch last night."

"No one watched last night," said Cormac.

"Someone should have." He smirked and settled on his bedroll.

"Are we to trust you?" asked Etain.

"You think I'd bring you harm?" He tsked. "You've nothing to base that on. Good night." He rolled to his side facing away from her.

"I could take third watch if anything is in question," said Kneilot.

"No," said Cormac. "He gets to prove to us we can trust him." He looked at Rosalind for longer than usual with the fire dancing in his eyes. Thoughts were racing through his head. She could tell by his every-changing expression. In one way, he was an easy man to read. In another, he was a stranger, who hid his true thoughts well.

She lay her head against her folded jacket and stared into the fire, waiting for the others to settle, then she'd watch over the campsite. Beyond the flames, Coraline sat on a branch, watching. Given the energy flowing through the Roots of Terra cards this evening, Coraline said she'd stay by her side and not venture into the woods like she usually did. While the fairy could find her easily, being close was vital at this time.

12

The Short Cut through the Wood

CORMAC'S SENSES SLOWLY awakened, and light lit up the world beyond his eyelids. Morning. He stretched and felt every aching muscle. Some aches were from riding for many days, an activity he'd never done. The rest were from the beating inflicted by the skeletons he'd battled in the tunnel. Skeletons. He had fought actual skeletons and lived to talk about it. If he had encountered the four while alone, he might not have been so lucky. Without Jowsey's help and advice, he might have been beaten black and blue or worse.

Jowsey? He opened his eyes and stared at the fire pit with simmering heat rising from the fading coals. Sitting up, he searched the area. Everyone was sleeping. Everyone. Except Jowsey. Jowsey was supposed to be on watch, but he couldn't see him anywhere. Rising to his feet, he looked beyond the campsite, beneath tree branches and then the road. His head swung back to the horses. There were only four. He walked over to them and searched the area. Jowsey's horse was gone. So that was it then. The man had abandoned his post, leaving them sleeping and unguarded. At least no danger had arrived while in their vulnerable state.

Walking back to the campfire, he scanned the road one way, then the other. Nothing travelled it. If Jowsey had left shortly after taking watch, he was three hours away by now. He was glad he was gone but didn't wish any ill fortune on him. Jowsey wasn't a horrible person. He did things his way, which didn't align with the party. Party? This wasn't a game. He and the others weren't going out for drinks afterwards or catching a hockey game. This was for keeps.

He grabbed a stick and stirred the coals. Adding tinder to the exposed embers, he produced flames. He added more fuel and before long, it was a fire worth heating up water for tea over. By the time the others rose, he'd have a pot brewing and ready to be poured.

Seeing Rosalind sleeping peacefully, he tried to imagine what it was like for her. Horrible. That's what. He remembered those days of memory loss, but they had been short lived and long ago. The frustrated edge had worn off them and some days, he forgot about them all together. That was until someone tried to steal his talisman. Then fear gripped him. His muscles tightened and he pushed the thought from his mind. He couldn't live with that constant fear.

Loggie rolled over and saw the fire. He rubbed his eyes and yawned. "Has our loyal thief run off with the treasure? Map?"

"Gone like yesterday's wind."

He sat up and looked around. "I'm not surprised. And most of me doesn't care."

"Most of you?"

"A small percentage will miss his expertise. Knowledge about giant slugs and birds that attack the undead."

"That was useful." Cormac dug into his pack for the package of dry tea and the pot to heat water. "We're almost halfway to Delgrath. We'll make it fine without him." He went to the spring to gather water. With Jowsey gone and Etain and Kneilot left at Delgrath, it would be back down to him, Loggie and Rosalind. He'd also be only a week and a few days from Harmon's cottage.

He stared over the weeds towards the campsite and saw Rosalind stand and stretch. She was a beautiful woman, but he couldn't get atta... What was he thinking? He was already attached due to their shared experiences. He groaned. This was going to be more difficult than he had first thought.

After a brief discussion of Jowsey's departure, the group ate in silence, then packed up the gear. They didn't travel far before encountering the short cut Etain was set on following. Getting no support to continue on the road, Cormac conceded, and they left it for a path only those travelling by foot and horseback could traverse. It wound around large trees with trunks so thick, he couldn't wrap his arms around. High in the treetops, birds sang and squirrels chattered. Grey clouds moved in, but it didn't feel like rain in spite of the wind picking up. The soughing of the upper branches created a ceiling of sound and fluttering leaves.

Etain led the way with Kneilot on the back of her horse, his chicken tucked beneath his arm. This morning, the hen had clucked loudly for no apparent reason. Then an egg plopped out. Kneilot had said he felt uncomfortable eating the egg, but Loggie had no problem frying it up and eating it. Fresh eggs while travelling was a luxury.

The trail continued in a peaceful manner. Late in the afternoon, the sound of water reached Cormac's ears. The farther he travelled, the louder it grew. A watercourse had been recorded on the map, but there was no indication of how large it was. If the short cut was used as much as it appeared to be, it either didn't cross a river or there was a bridge.

The smell of water reached his nose, and he stretched his neck to see where it lay. The trees were thick but up ahead, more light was visible. When he reached the crest of a hill and looked down at the river, he stopped, mouth open, taking in the view as if it was something out of a fantasy novel. He swallowed hard. It was out of one, and he was living in it.

Three hundred feet below was the most intricate and unique bridge he'd ever seen. A tangled mess of thick tree branches and roots were woven together to make a link from one side to the other. The river was at least a hundred feet wide, and the bridge span had to be twelve feet wide, enough for two horses to ride abreast.

"I've never seen anything like it." Rosalind stopped her horse beside him. "Have you?"

"No. Nothing. No one will believe what we're seeing."

"Not in all my travels have I seen such craftsmanship." Kneilot stretched his neck around Etain's shoulder for a view. "Hauflins of Spiritwood have not created such a vision."

"Impressive." Loggie squeezed in beside them. "A true miracle of nature."

"You think this formed naturally?" asked Cormac.

"Probably not. Yet it is still a miracle. Magic. A work of art. A living bridge that grows stronger by the year. Never needs painting or repairs."

"That last part should encourage everyone to build bridges this way." Cormac thought of the bridges from his world. Some were beautiful, but none matched this.

"Let us not spend our day admiring it," said Etain. "A personal experience can be had only by crossing." She continued to the bridge, and the others followed.

While the bridge looked exceptionally strong, Cormac wondered if it was strong enough for his horse. All their horses at the same time. He hung back and waited for Etain and Kneilot to ride onto it. It didn't make a sound. No creaks, no cracks and no hint it would give way beneath the weight.

"Concerned about a bridge but wants to loot treasure from a dungeon while an evil wizard hunts those who would steal it from him." Loggie chuckled and rode past to join Etain on the bridge.

"Finding long stashed treasure sounds exciting," said Rosalind. "I'm in. If only we had a map."

"Etain said she remembers the spot," he said, admiring the graceful way she smiled.

"That's all we need. A general spot."

"But they're waiting for Etain at Delgrath."

"She says they expect her when she arrives. No sooner."

He thought about the meaning of that. It literally meant she could get there at any time. Certainly, that was not what Skuld had in mind when he appointed him and the others to escort Etain to Delgrath.

Guiding the horse onto the bridge, he looked to see if there were large holes between the roots a hoof could fall into. There weren't. It was as smooth as any wooden bridge. With the rest leading the way, he gave his attention to the details of the structure. Roots as thick as his torso held the platform in place. They grew along the sides and overhead to ensure the rails didn't separate and fall into the river. Smaller branches of the trees criss-crossed and made intricate designs. They took on shapes, and he wondered if they were created on purpose or randomly. Looking through one section heavily braided, it appeared to be an image of the moon with openings for stars. Coincidence. Farther on, the branches of various sizes appeared like a tower. He chuckled. This was like finding shapes in clouds.

He noticed Rosalind had stopped mid-span, and he halted beside her. She stared at a section of the bridge. Her lips were moving, but he couldn't hear what she was saying. She probably spoke in hauflin whissputter, but who was she talking to? The others were still traversing the bridge. A glint of sunlight near Rosalind's head drew his eyes, and he thought something flew near her. A bird? But... She glanced at him and closed her mouth.

"What do you see?" he asked.

"A dragon." She pointed to a section of the bridge wall.

He couldn't make out a form, so brought the horse closer. Studying the roots and branches, he tried to see what she did, but only saw a tangled mess. "Where?"

"Its mouth is there." She pointed to the left. "And its snout goes this way, and that thick branch there is its brow."

Drawing back his focus to see a larger section of the bridge, his eyes widened. The design consumed the whole side and its body stretched along the bridge to the point where he had boarded it. Stretching his neck back and looking up, he saw the wings expand overhead and come down the other side. "Dragon Bridge." He had heard that name before, but where? And why?

"What are you looking at?" asked Etain. She and Loggie had reached the end and were waiting for them.

"It's a dragon bridge." Butterflies or something dangerous fluttered in his gut. This bridge was known. Many had crossed it. He had heard whispers of it time and again in his travels. Yet, he couldn't remember its significance. He cursed himself for not caring to listen and remember.

Etain's face grew serious, and she trotted her horse to join them. "What did you say, and why did you say it?"

"I think this is what I've heard others call Dragon Bridge."

"It cannot be."

"Why?"

"I was warned to never cross it. Tell me why you think it is the Beguiled Dragon Bridge."

"I didn't say Beguiled Dragon, only Dragon."

"I believe they are one and the same. Now why do you think this?"

He pointed to the design of the dragon, starting with the head. The more she saw and distinguished from the rest of the bridge, the larger her eyes grew. He thought he heard her gasp, but she looked away from him, following the wings embracing the structure.

"We must leave immediately," she half whispered. "That way." She pointed to the trail behind them.

"You want us to return to the road? That will add two days to—"

"Go now!" She forced her way between him and Rosalind and trotted the horse towards the forest. Before she got there, flames shot up from the base of the bridge. The sudden blaze spooked the horse, and it rose to its back legs, throwing Kneilot to the ground. He landed with a thump, and the chicken flew from his arms, squawking. The bird raced past Cormac and headed for solid ground. Kneilot jumped up and gave chase. Etain held on to the saddle horn and brought the horse down with a thud. She got the animal under control and turned to the others. "We are not prepared for what awaits us."

"Elaborate." Cormac's voice squeaked, and he cleared his throat. "What is this bridge?"

"Somewhere in this land, a dragon is trapped. Legend has it, the poor beast has been imprisoned for a human lifetime. Its only connection to the outside world is through the stream that runs through its dungeon. Using it, he sends his magic forth. That magic built a bridge across a river. It is marked with the sign of the dragon." She gazed upon the intricate design. "Everyone who crosses the bridge is cursed. When the dragon is freed, the curse is removed."

"What kind of curse?" asked Loggie.

"Legend says the curse robs the traveller of taste. Eventually, they will lose their desire to eat, then drink."

"They'll die."

"If the legend is true, we have one full moon cycle to rescue the dragon before we no longer wish to consume sustenance vital to our survival."

Cormac's nerves danced under his skin. "One month? Wh... Where is it? Are you saying no one has found it after all these years? Has everyone who crossed this bridge died?"

"I have heard stories from travellers that speak of such tragedies."

"But how are we to know if this is true or not? It's just a story."

"I cannot answer that. I have spoken to no one who knows without doubt."

Cormac stared into the flames that blocked the bridge. The barrier was as wide as the bridge and about ten feet thick. Yet, it did not burn the wood. He was tempted to drive his horse through it, but it would probably buck him off instead of charge through the flames.

"We can't stay here," said Loggie. "And we can't go back that way." He turned his horse and trotted to the other side of the river.

Cormac followed. Slowly. He studied the design of the dragon, trying to remember if he had seen anything that resembled it. He also tried to replay the fragmented conversations he'd heard about it. Nothing stood out. No curse was mentioned. That he remembered. He hadn't even heard the legend about a dragon being imprisoned.

"If the dragon has a connection to this bridge through a river," said Rosalind, "would it not make sense that he is trapped up stream?" She stared at the flowing water. Beneath the bridge, it was relatively calm but upstream, it narrowed and flowed faster around rocks. "And wouldn't it make sense for the dragon to build the bridge near his prison?"

"That is sound," said Etain, bringing her horse alongside to view the river. "However, if the dungeon is far from settlements and roads, he'd build it where travellers would create a short cut between two settlements. If not, no one might cross it." She winced. "The dungeon could be up around the corner or ten miles from here."

"We must find him."

"We don't even know he's real," said Cormac. He'd search for treasure but getting tangled up with a dragon was nothing he wanted to risk his life on.

"He is." She looked at him. "It's a white dragon. He's extremely sad. There's a cave entrance that leads to the dungeon."

He didn't believe her. "Where did you learn that?" She had only a ten-hour memory, and they had met no one who had shared such a story.

"The Roots of Terra cards."

He was about to argue the fact that they were only playing cards, but he remembered the creepy woman at Lucinda's Enchanted Wands shop. She knew things she shouldn't have.

"What did the cards reveal?" asked Etain.

"It showed a dragon stuck in a dungeon for a long time. He is in misery. He misses his home. I saw water splashing against rocks." She looked to the river. "Similar to that but the water was rushing faster."

"And you saw someone else rescue it?" asked Cormac.

She stared at him for several long seconds, and he felt uncomfortable under her scrutiny. He wanted to know what ran through her mind. Was she thinking him a fool or a coward?

"No. I didn't see anyone rescue him." Her gaze fell to the ground, and her expression grew more concerned with each breath. "His heart is broken, and his spirit will soon follow. If he loses hope..." She looked up with sadness in her eyes. "Not man nor beast with a kind soul should suffer that fate."

"It's a dragon," said Cormac. "It will eat us."

"He will not eat me."

"Are you going to tell the joke where you don't have to outrun the dragon to be saved only outrun me, leaving me to get eaten by the dragon?"

Her bow bent. "I wasn't thinking that at all."

Loggie chuckled. "That's not a joke. That's a fact when any beast is chasing us."

"Rosalind, what are you saying?" asked Etain. "You want to free this dragon?"

Emotions rolled across her face like the ever-changing sky at sunset until it lit up with that pleasant smile he'd come to know. "Yes."

"It is a noble quest," said Etain, "but I'm unsure it is mine."

"Maybe it's mine."

Cormac wanted to tell her rescuing a dragon wasn't her quest. Finding her memory and returning home to her world was. "This is all coincidence. Tomorrow, we'll forget about it."

Kneilot returned to the group with the chicken under his arm. He climbed into the saddle with Etain. "Tonight, I will meditate and ask Eir for guidance."

"And Rosalind and I will explore the cards." Etain reined her horse onto the trail. "We shall not worry for what is out of our control."

Rosalind sat cross-legged beneath a giant oak. The ground beneath the limbs was dry and smooth with short weeds to cushion the seat. Six cards lay before her on the blanket she'd spread. So far, none spoke to her. She tried to block everything from her mind and focus on the energy, but the cards were lifeless. Silent.

"Unusual," whispered Coraline in her ear. "The energy hides from our eyes."

"Maybe reshuffle the deck." Etain sat on the other side of Rosalind.

"We did that." She gathered the cards and slipped them into the pouch. "The cards are silent for a reason."

"But why?"

"I cannot say."

"They are afraid," whispered Coraline.

"The cards may be afraid," said Rosalind.

"I've never heard of such a thing." Etain folded her arms. "If I were in the sanctuary, I'd seek an audience with Dorca."

"Who is that?"

"The dragon who guards the sanctuary. He's very knowledgeable."

"I have heard of Dorca," whispered Coraline. "He is wise."

Rosalind glanced at her. The fairy was barely visible to her and invisible to Etain. Her voice, no louder than a sweet summer breeze, was too low for Etain to hear. "I wonder if the energy in the air tonight is controlled by the dragon." She directed her question at Coraline but turned to Etain. "Is that possible?"

"Yes," whispered the fairy.

"If the dragon controlled the energy," said Etain, "he would surely use it to send a message to those who traversed the bridge." She sighed. "That message would save us and the dragon."

"I shall sleep on it." Rosalind stood, picked up her blanket and returned to the firepit. Etain followed, but Coraline remained within the branches of the oak. Rosalind spread her blanket and tucked away the cards. There was nothing more she could do.

Kneilot came to the fire. He had been meditating, hoping to seek guidance from the god he endeavoured to serve. He plopped down on his blanket, chicken at his side, and folded his hands. "Nothing. The voices of the gods are as silent as the night air, which is disturbing."

Rosalind lifted an ear. He was right. She heard no creatures of the night. Now that she noticed the silence, her hair stood on end.

Cormac added sticks to the fire, making it spring to life. The sun had set about 30 minutes ago and the lingering light was fading fast.

She yawned and crawled into her blankets. Catching Cormac staring at her, shadows dancing across his face, she wondered what he thought about. Treasure? Or the dragon? He was a peculiar man. One moment brave, the next avoiding all challenges. His expression this evening appeared to be that of longing. Like he missed his home or his family. What ever consumed his thoughts, he resolved to keep it secret, and he slowly lifted his gaze and looked into the cloudless, stary night sky. A quick glance at her, and he settled and prepared to sleep. He was taking second watch, Kneilot was first and Etain was third. Apparently, she had watched the night before and would get a full night's sleep this time around.

She closed her eyes and used her other senses to feel for energy. For a long time, she felt nothing. It was elusive, dodging the energy she sent forth. Her mind grew weary, and sleep beckoned. On the cusp of it, a voice whispered her name. Her body drifted off, leaving her mind vaguely aware of energy invading her.

Where once was darkness, a shimmering green glow lit her way. She crept forward, dagger in hand, searching for... What was it? Her feet did not hesitate. They crossed the cool damp floor eagerly, her toes feeling every uneven surface and pebble. Deeper into the cave, she found it branched off. One way was well travelled and lit with eternal torches. The other was smaller, not as bright and had cobwebs crossing the pathway. The illuminated path tugged on her feet; the less travelled path spoke to her in whispers of foreign tongue. She chose this one. With less light, she travelled slower, weaving around stalagmites and stepping over fallen chunks of limestone. The ceiling sloped, and she was forced to walk bent over. But not too far and after 25 feet, she was able to stand upright. Her eyes adjusted to the dimmer light, and she travelled onward confidently, not knowing where she was going but knowing this was the way. She passed a stalactite and looked up to find its base covered in bats. One took flight but soon settled. She continued.

Not ten feet away, a soft click froze her in place, but it was too late. The floor gave way beneath her, and she tumbled into the black unknown. Her heart raced, and she fought to find solid ground. Arms and legs flailing, she screamed and her voice vibrated her ears.

Her eyes flew open, and she screamed again. Jumping to her feet, she ran into the night, away from the gaping hole and onto a winding trail.

"Rosalind!" a voice cried out, but she didn't turn around. The name was called again. Still, she ran. Into the forest and up a hill. She had to get away from the abyss before it swallowed her.

"Rosalind, stop!" A different voice was beside her head. "It is Coraline. Stop running!" The voice flew beside her, and she frantically tried to escape it, swinging her arms to make it go away.

Tackled from behind, she crashed to the ground. She fought the monster from the pit before it claimed her, slapping and kicking blindly.

"Rosalind!" came the voice. "Rosalind! It's me! Cormac. Open your eyes!"

Looking up, she saw... him. It was the same man she'd spoken with... She couldn't remember when.

"I'm your friend," he gasped, trying to hold her arms away from his chest while he straddled her. "I won't hurt you."

Other faces looked over his shoulder. They appeared friendly. She stopped struggling and lay on her back, panting. "Who are you?"

"Cormac. Your friend."

"Loggie," said the man beside him. "We are friends."

"Etain," said the woman with the beautiful golden hair. "What haunted you? A dragon?"

She searched her memories. Dragon. A bridge. Her eyes widened. "He is trapped. In a dungeon." Her throat tightened. "It's a trap! He can't be freed."

"Did you see him?" asked Etain.

She shook her head. "He called to me. Told me which way to go. But the trap." She gasped for air.

"Let her up." Loggie pushed Cormac aside and helped her to stand. "You were dreaming?"

Was that all it was? A dream? Nightmare? She rubbed her eyes and looked around. The trees hummed with an unnatural sound. It was coming from... She whirled and stared into the dark shadows of the woodland. "He's that way. Each day he grows weaker. His magic is slowly dying and when it does, so will he." She looked at Cormac. "But the bridge will live on and curse every traveller who crosses it. We have to save him."

"He spoke to you?" asked Etain.

"He sent his life force, and it gave me a message. The caves are treacherous. Everyone who has entered has died."

"And you expect us to go there?" Cormac stepped away. "You said it yourself: it's a trap. I'm not throwing away my life on an impossible mission."

"You're going to die anyways."

He stared at her with his mouth open. A question teetered on his tongue for a breath, then was swallowed.

"We are all cursed. Whether we go or not, we will die. It is our only chance to survive."

"You know the way?" asked Etain.

"Not exactly, but he will guide us."

"How?"

She searched the forest, then the ground before looking up. "Through dreams."

"Your dreams?" asked Cormac.

"Yes."

"This keeps getting better." He groaned and looked away. She wasn't sure if he was mad at her or himself.

"Now that we know, let's get sleep." Loggie put his arm around her and guided her back to the campsite. "Will he contact you again tonight?"

She shrugged. "We are a few days away. Four, maybe five."

"Then rest. We'll talk more in the morning."

"She won't..." Cormac clamped his mouth shut. "I've got another hour of watch. I'll keep an eye on her." He settled against a rock 20 feet away. From there, he watched her.

Rosalind found her blankets and lay down. Her mind was wide awake, but her body was exhausted. Each time she looked at Cormac, he was watching her. She checked on him countless times, and he wore only one expression: apprehensive. Finally, her mind slipped beneath the blanket of slumber and tumbled into the shadows of sleep.

Her sleep was peaceful and when she woke, she felt rested. Yawning and stretching to shake away the cobwebs of sleep, she looked over the campsite. A man near her smiled. He looked familiar, but she couldn't remember his name.

"Rosalind, did you sleep well?" he asked.

"I did. You?"

"Fine except for your nightmare. Do you remember it?"

She searched her memories. While she often dreamt, she didn't always remember them. "What was it about?"

"Rescuing a dragon. You woke us up. You were scared and ran. Cormac," he gestured towards another man digging in his pack, "caught you and calmed you down."

"Loggie helped," said a woman who came to stand next to him. "He and Kneilot were great help."

"So was Etain." Loggie put his arm over the woman's shoulder and jostled her.

"We work well together." Etain rustle his hair, then stood. "If you want to read the Roots of Terra cards in your sack after we break the fast, I'll help."

Roots of Terra cards? She pulled the sack near and looked at the cards. Along side them was a piece of paper. She read it silently, then looked up. "I don't remember many things, but... I remember feeling scared." She looked at Cormac. "You tackled me. Held me down until I came to my senses." His surprised expression made her grin. "Thank you. I hope I didn't give you those bruises."

"No. Skeletons. Mostly." He looked away shyly, and she didn't understand why. "I should have woken you when you started to toss and turn. Maybe I could have saved you from the terror."

"Only remnants of fear remain, not what horrified me."

Loud clucking interrupted the quiet conversation, and she looked to see a chicken rise and walk around. It continued to cluck, shouting to the world its good morning.

"Excellent," said Loggie. "Breakfast." He picked up a freshly laid egg.

An hour later, Rosalind mounted her horse and settled into the saddle. The Roots of Terra cards were silent today. Fairy dust reminded her of the conversation she'd had with Coraline the night before and the many times before then. This dragon that haunted her sleep was not an ordinary beast. It was intelligent and crafty. It was also kind. She felt that in its energy. But it was desperate to escape and return to its clan. That desperation scared her, but the warnings delivered through her dreams terrified her.

"I have asked the woodland animals about the cave," said Coraline, "and they know little. They advise asking the squirrels that live closer to the mountain."

"Any help we can get will go towards saving us and the dragon."

Cormac rode beside her and gave her a strange look. "Talking to yourself?"

"I do it to work things out in my mind."

"I sometimes do that. Especially when I've been travelling alone for long periods." He fumbled with the reins and after he solved whatever problem he was working on, he added, "If you ever..." he hesitated, looking her up and down, then to the trail in front of them, "You can talk to me if you like." His face turned pink. "You know. If there's no one else."

"Thank you."

"You're welcome." He looked back at the others, then again to the trail ahead. "You riding up here with me?"

"Sure. Maybe I'll remember something."

"Great." He nudged the horse forward. "The map is an interesting piece of art."

"Etain's?"

"Yeah. Every time I look at it, I see something different."

"It's because she's added many details. It's kinda like reading a book the second time. You learn things you didn't the first time."

"Like a movie."

"Precisely." Her mind stalled. What was a movie? She was certain she'd said the word before, but she was unsure of what it was.

"I noticed the treasure was this way. While we don't know for certain, Etain said it was on the other side of the mountain. If Jowsey hadn't taken his map, we'd know for certain." He pointed ahead to a white-capped mountain. It was a great distance away and part of a small mountain range. "But it could be buried in any one of these mountains. It's a large area to cover."

"The dragon is more important than treasure. The treasure will last indefinitely. The dragon will soon die. I believe it's white because it is sick."

"If your dreams are accurate, we'll know soon enough."

Less than an hour later, they came to a fork in the road. One direction led towards Delgrath. The other into the mountains. The one to Delgrath continued on in a similar fashion, through the woods on a narrow path winding around large trees and bushes. The one towards the mountains silenced the group for a long moment. A warm breeze brushed back their hair and as seconds ticked away, excited energy crept beneath Rosalind's skin.

"If I didn't know better, I'd say it was the road to doom," said Loggie.

"Don't say that," said Cormac.

"It doesn't do anything for my nerves," said Kneilot, "and the gods have not given me any indication it is safe."

"You contacted them?" asked Etain.

"No, and they've said nothing about this."

"I think it's intriguing." Everyone looked at Rosalind. "Think about it. We're in the middle of wild woods and this exists. A straight as an arrow road that goes on for as far as I can see. The beech? They're beech, right?" Etain nodded. "With large beech trees lining both sides and creating a canopy to block the sun."

"To make it dark and sinister," said Cormac. "It's not like someone was worried about us getting sun burnt."

"It is safe," whispered Coraline. "Fairies live within it."

Rosalind raised an eyebrow. "Really?"

"Really what?" asked Etain.

"I thought I saw fairies flying about. Maybe this is a fairy village."

Cormac grunted. "There's no such thing." His laughed turned into a screech. "Ouch! What was that?"

Rosalind heard faint giggling. "Maybe it's the fairies disagreeing with you."

He shot her a look of irritation and rubbed his ear. "We should seriously reconsider travelling it."

"Follow me." Rosalind guided the horse onto the narrow road.

"Wait! We didn't decide." Cormac remained in place.

"It is the only way," she said over her shoulder.

"Loggie?" He looked to him for reassurance.

Loggie shrugged. "She's the one in communication with the dragon. And he controls our fate." He fell into line behind her.

"But..."

"We cannot change fate." Etain went next.

"But should we tempt it?" asked Kneilot, holding tightly to his chicken as he was led away behind Etain.

"No, we shouldn't." Cormac hung back. "We really shouldn't."

"He'll come," whispered Coraline in Rosalind's ear. "He's a stubborn man but reasonable. Fear has ruled his life for too many years. He knows no other way."

"That way of living puts him in danger," Rosalind spoke in whisputter.

"Only until he finds his courage."

"I hope he finds it before we find the dragon."

"The whispers on the wind of the hidden fairies say he will need to." She flew off and was gone for several minutes. When she returned, her voice was excited. "Many have come this way. Some have returned. This place is called Merlshire on Loft. It is home to ancient tree fairies of Beech, cousins of fairies of Oak. I have not met them before."

"Friendly?"

"Friendly as fairies are to strangers. They say this goes for one mile. There is no break in the trees. No way to leave it, only forward or return from where we came. It leads to marshland. You must travel the east side of it. Less treacherous. Choose your course wisely and do not stop until you reach the forest."

"Why?"

"They said while day travel is tormented by black marsh flies and dank odour from the heat, the night is tortured by mosquitoes, daring muskrats and boars that will charge for no reason. There was mention of shoebills. A large bird. Large enough to carry away a chicken."

Rosalind glanced over her shoulder at Kneilot riding with Etain. The marsh didn't sound safe for his hen. "We should hurry then and reach it sooner rather than later, so we cross it before dark."

"I was hoping you'd say that. I dislike shoebills."

Rosalind brought her horse to a lope, and she heard those behind her do the same. Coraline rested between her horse's ears and held tightly to its mane. With her hair whipping in the wind, she appeared to enjoy the ride. Every time she glanced back, she was smiling.

The beech trees grew so close together, she imagined they were a sight from the outside. Within its tunnel, she could barely see the sky. Sunlight seeped in, creating dappled ground. Mixed with the beating of hooves and the wisps of wind, she heard whispers of Merlshire on Loft fairies. She was travelling too fast, and their voices were too low to decipher what they said.

Five minutes later, she saw the end of the beech trees. Bright light illuminated the exit. Beyond it, lay grass waving in the breeze. She closed the distance quickly and was bathed in bright sunshine. Slowing to a walk, she surveyed the marsh. It went on in every direction for as far as the eye could see. The only solid ground was back from where she'd come. Only a few hundred feet separated the beech trees from the first pool of water. Large bugs - dragon flies - zipped across the grass and over the water. They were numerous and mingled with the clouds of black marsh flies. A large bird flew over. A crane? A great blue heron in all its glory sailed overhead and into the distance. Its wingspan measure at least six feet.

Given the time, she had ten hours of daylight to cross this wetland. Checking the location of the sun, she found her directions and turned the horse to the eastern edge.

"Great," said Loggie. His sarcasm floated on the air. "Water. Lots of it. This is the kind I dislike. Hate even. Too many bugs. Errr. Bugs in the nose. Bugs in the ears. There'll be bugs in my bread if they get the chance."

"We should check the map," said Etain. "To find the best route."

"This is it," said Rosalind. "The east side. Then straight on 'til the end. We waste no time. Only ride."

"Who made that decision?" asked Cormac.

"I did." She kept a steady trot, avoiding the waterholes and soft ground. In doing so, she found a solid path, but it took her far off centre from the starting point. "Are you certain?" she asked Coraline when doubt set in.

"Certain." She rose from the horse's head. "I will scout ahead. Stay the course." She flew away and quickly disappeared.

Rosalind rode north as straight as possible, but many times, she had to go around water holes, always choosing the right side of them. She wondered if she went directly east if she'd reach the edge sooner and perhaps follow a river northward. Not willing to risk it, she kept to the plan. A fair amount of time passed before Coraline returned.

"It goes on for longer than I imagined. Several miles I covered and did not see an end."

"Not good."

"But it can't go on forever."

"Hopefully not into the night." She focussed on the path, keeping a steady pace and not wasting time. When the others wanted a break, she encouraged them to go a few more miles.

"What is the rush?" asked Etain.

"I want to be out of this by dark," she said.

"I agree," said Loggie. He slapped his arm. "The bugs are infuriating. And the stench makes me not want to eat ever again."

She turned to him. "You have lost your desire to eat?"

His head shot in her direction. "No. I didn't mean that."

"Good." She went another three miles, found a solid piece of land and halted. "Fifteen minutes," she said. She dismounted and allowed her horse to drink and graze.

Etain came to her. "Tell me. You are set to escape this place for a reason." She slapped her arm to kill a bug and then scratched the bite.

"The fairies in the beech. They whispered warnings."

"What kind?"

"Not to linger in the marshland. To get out before dark."

"Fairies?" Cormac was about to say more, but clamped his mouth shut. He scanned the air around him, then pulled his water flask from the saddle and drank.

"Fairies or not," said Loggie, "this is not fit for dwarfs. Stinky. Soupy water." He slapped the side of his neck, then scratched the bite. "Bugs of all types." He growled. "I need full armour to defend myself."

"Something stirs." Kneilot stood at the edge of the water with Matilda in his arms. "It hides and watches." His voice was subdued. "We should linger not." He stretched out his arm and spread his fingers. Soft humming escaped his lips.

Rosalind watched closely. Was he casting a spell? What spells did clerics possess? She thought only healing spells.

Kneilot gasped. "Winged creatures."

She scanned the marshland. Everything she saw had wings. The black marsh flies, the beetles, dragonflies and even the herons she'd seen. "Could you be more specific?"

"Larger than that which we've seen so far." He turned to the group. "Large. Very large." He held the chicken closer. "I need to secure Matilda." He went to his pack and withdrew a food sack that was half empty. He stuffed the remaining food into a saddlebag, then placed the chicken inside with only its head out. "For your safety, my love." He secured the sack to his chest with cloth ties.

When he was done, Rosalind mounted. "Let's reach the trees before the sun sets."

"Ask me twice and I'll think you crazy," said Loggie, jumping onto his horse and gathering the reins.

They travelled many hours and Rosalind still did not see the edge of the marshland. The mountains grew in size, and she scanned each one, wondering which one held the dragon. From their path so far, she believed a trail led to the cave opening. At least she hoped one did.

The afternoon came and went, and the sun dipped towards the marshland. Its low position highlighted everything that buzzed atop the water and tall grasses. Staring into the bright yellow light illuminated hundreds of thousands of bugs, small birds, dragonflies, flower seeds, debris and other things flying about. Some zipped to-and-fro. Others gathered in swarms. Occasionally, something leapt from the water to snatch a meal. Each time she heard the splash, she looked in its direction but always too late. All she saw were the rings where the creature had surfaced and disappeared.

"How can we cross this safely in the dark?" asked Cormac from the rear. "We could end up in the water."

"I will be able to see enough to guide us." She then remembered he was human. The only human in the group. With the sun going down and the quarter moon obscured most of the time with clouds, he'd be blind. She slowed her pace. "Let him behind me," she said. "The horse should follow but if he faulters in the dark, we will see."

They switched positions, putting Cormac second, Etain and Kneilot third and Loggie last.

"Dawdle not!" Loggie shouted from the rear. "The mosquitoes are dining on the finest meat. A bard cannot play if he is too busy scratching welts."

Rosalind returned to a steady pace. The sun disappeared from the sky, and her eyes gathered light from the few stars that poked out of the breaks in the clouds. She pulled her hood up to block the chilly wind as much as to protect her from mosquitoes. Her feet twitched when she felt bugs on them, and she wished she had boots or socks, anything to ward of the pests. As long as she kept a steady pace, they weren't too bad, but when she slowed to navigate a tricky section, they swarmed her. It was a constant battle of keeping the reins steady and swatting bugs. Several times she heard Loggie slap and curse. The language he used was colourful even for a bard.

A splash nearby made her search for the source.

"That was large." Cormac's voice sounded small in the darkness.

"Nothing to worry about. Probably an otter or fish jumped."

"It sounded like something landed."

She replayed the sound in her head. It was a possibility. She hadn't been looking in that area, so something could have dived into the water unnoticed.

A dark shadow scurried in front of her horse, making it rear up. She held onto the horn and brought it down safely. "It's okay, girl." She patted its neck for reassurance. The shadow passed nearby again, and the horse side-stepped away from it.

"What is it?" asked Cormac. His horse had bumped into hers, and he calmed it. Whatever was scrambling from one point to another was spooking it, too.

"It looks like a giant rat." She peered closer. "A beaver?"

"Muskrat," said Etain. "They resemble beavers."

"Daring muskrats," she said. "I was warned about them. Hold tightly to the reins, and let's get away from here." She forced the horse forward. It danced sideways but eventually walked on. Leaving the rodent behind, she returned her attention to the trail. She peered ahead, trying to distinguish the horizon from the mountain. It appeared to reveal trees, but there was not enough light for her to see that distance.

The next two hours were filled with slapping, cursing and avoiding aggravating muskrats that tested the patients of riders and horses.

Rosalind's arms and legs grew weary by the many encounters and while she thought about stopping, she convinced herself to keep going.

Another large splash in the water, this time nearer to her, forced her attention to it. She searched for the source but again, didn't see anything.

"Muskrats?" offered Cormac, his voice strained.

"Possibly."

"I'm learning to hate muskrats!" shouted Loggie. Then he commanded the attention of the clouds in the sky. "Did you hear me?" He shouted upward. "I! Hate! Muskrats!" He slapped his arm and cursed. "And mosquitoes! Nothing will take away this itch. Bathing in vinegar and goat's milk will only give short relief. Curse you flying rats. How much longer must I tolerate these evil creatures?"

"An hour?" replied Rosalind. Truthfully, she didn't know.

"Ah! I shall never play again. My fingers will be swollen beyond playing all but a flute."

"Dear, Loggie," said Kneilot, "while I understand your plight and I share it, your voice attracts larger creatures than mosquitoes."

"I'd sooner fight a muskrat than a thousand pesky bugs."

"Larger than muskrats."

Rosalind grinned at the silence that followed. If not for the bugs eating her alive, the night travelling wouldn't have been so bad. Sure, she had to be more caution, but the trail wasn't that difficult.

A great shadow loomed towards her, and she blinked several times to bring it into focus. It travelled fast. It was at least eight feet—no ten feet wide. That was a wingspan?

"Shoebill!" Coraline shrieked and ducked into Rosalind's hood. She scrambled around inside and clung to her shoulder. "They can smell fairies."

Rosalind snatched a dagger from the sheath on her waist and held it, ready to defend herself and Coraline.

"What is that?! A small dragon?" shouted Cormac. His horse rose up, and he slipped off the saddle.

"It's a bird!" exclaimed Loggie.

"Shoebill!" Etain flung a dagger at its chest. When it struck the bird, a cloud of feathers exploded into the air. It faltered and slammed into the ground, rolling several times and crashing into Cormac who fought to regain control of his horse. He was thrown to the ground and lost hold of the reins.

Rosalind acted fast and caught hold of the horse. Bringing it under control, she turned to find Loggie helping Cormac to his feet and guiding him away from the water's edge and the giant bird.

The shoebill flapped frantically, flopping around, trying to get its feet under it.

"Let's get out of here," said Rosalind. "Loggie, bring him to his horse." She held it steady while Cormac climbed into the saddle. "Hold on. I'll get you past here." She held onto the reins and led him away.

Loggie grabbed the reins of his horse from Kneilot, jumped in the saddle and followed. "Hurry, hurry," he said, out of breath. "I shall die here in the marshlands half a man for the flesh these buggers have eaten."

"Safe?" whispered Coraline.

"Safe." Rosalind felt the fairy climb from the hood. "Stay near."

"I am as near as possible." Coraline settled on her shoulder, still covered with the hood.

Behind her, the shoebill continued to flap its massive wings. By the sound of it, it had reached the water's edge and was splashing in it. Whether it would live or not, she didn't know. That was a fatal shot by Etain. The sound of struggling faded and eventually disappeared while the marshland continued. The temperature dropped further, but it did not deter the mosquitoes. Fearing she'd not see the end of the marsh this night, she was surprised when trees loomed from the thin fog that had developed. Relief washed over her, and she hurried her pace, crossing the last 400 feet with joy easing her aching muscles.

"We'll travel half a mile more before we stop," she said over her shoulder.

"Anything to escape the demons," said Loggie.

She looked for a path that continued the journey but saw nothing. Eventually, she settled for a break in the trees and left behind the marshland, the buzzing of mosquitoes, trilling of frogs and the squeals and snarls of muskrats lurking in the reeds.

Picking her way between trees and bushes, she came upon a small clearing, large enough for them to build a fire, sleep and secure the horses. There was even a small patch of weeds for the horses to munch on. Dismounting, she felt pain shoot through her legs. Her muscles ached. By the sounds of the others getting off their horses and walking around, they shared in the pain.

"I'd help gather wood, but I can't see a thing," said Cormac.

"We know." She directed him to a tree. "Stay here. I'll take care of your horse."

"Thanks." He felt around the tree, found a good sitting spot and sat down. "I'll stay out of the way."

Within an hour, a fire was lit, water was heating over the flames for tea and the bedrolls were spread. Rosalind was too sore to make a full meal, so snacked on bread toasted over coals and dressed with strawberry jam. "I will take first watch." She yawned.

"How will you dream of the dragon?" Etain bit into dried meat.

"The dragon will have several hours to contact me if it wants." She drew a steadying breath. In truth, she didn't want to sleep, didn't want another nightmare. While the feeling of dread was minimal, fear lingered. Yet, she knew the only way to find the dragon was to allow it into her dreams.

"I'll take second," said Loggie.

"Given Cormac's lack of vision on this dark night," said Etain, "I'll take third."

"I'll save my turn for tomorrow night." Kneilot held a piece of bread out to Matilda, who pecked it from his fingers and ate it.

With that, they settled, leaving Rosalind alone with her thoughts.

"The birds sing," whispered Coraline.

"I hear them. Does that mean the dragon's magic does not touch this land?"

"Not sure. The cards will tell us."

She pulled the Roots of Terra cards from the pouch and shuffled them. While doing so, her thoughts drifted to the note inside the pouch, telling her to focus on the energy and to allow it to speak to her. When she was ready, she laid one card on the ground before her. The flames illuminated it. She stared at the upside down tower on a hill surrounded by stars, the moon and the sun. Forgetting what it meant, she opened the book and found it. "Inverse," she read. "Illness, losses, obstacles, volatile situation." She looked up. "That doesn't read well."

"Learn from the energy." Coraline flew near the card. "I see a path. It is difficult. There's no indication of loss. Only change."

She stared at the lines of the tower, looking for the energy within. Releasing a slow, long breath, she deflated and focussed. The lines were there in bright blue, not the green she'd seen before. They flowed around the tower, then touched the moon, then the sun. "I see the... He sleeps. He is the dragon we saw. It must be him."

"The patterns are similar. But not exact. Strange."

"I do not remember as well as you." She scratched the side of her head where two mosquito bites caused an itch. "Is it because he grows weaker?"

"Possibly."

The next card was one she'd never seen before. It was faint, showing only the moon and stars. "I see little but feel much activity."

"Confusing. It is as if something is there, and it is filled with nothing. Invisible beings?"

"Confusing beings." Rosalind pulled three more cards and each one was more elusive than the last. Growing weary, she put away the deck and took a walk around the campsite. The forest felt calm. A lone owl hooted in the distance followed by the yap of some canine, a coyote or wolf. She couldn't tell the difference. Going to her horse, she stroked its neck and scratched behind its ears. It neighed softly, setting off the other horses in a chorus of soft neighs. It soothed her, and she recalled this sound in a barn long... She tried to think where. Not here. Not this horse. Her mind went around in circles, and she ended up back to where she began. She remembered the sound.

Leaving the horses, she sat beneath a tree, waited and watched. When two hours passed, she woke Loggie.

"All quiet?" He yawned and stretched.

"Just the hoot owls to keep company."

"Great." He stood and shook off sleep and grabbed his water flask. After taking a long drink, he wiped his mouth.

Rosalind crawled beneath the blanket and pulled it close around her to ward off the chill. Her eyelids were heavy and before Loggie settled into his watch position, she was asleep.

13

From Foggy Air

AN ODD SOUND disturbed Cormac's deep sleep. His body refused to wake, so he lay in limbo until a scream pierced the tranquillity. Tossing sleep aside, he sat up and opened his eyes. The sun was still below the horizon, but twilight was on the land. A woman screamed again, and he searched the landscape for her. It was Rosalind. Etain was chasing her.

He leapt from beneath the blankets, yanked on his boots and ran. His long strides closed the distance between him and the women, but he didn't catch up to Rosalind before Etain tackled her and threw her to the ground. They wrestled until he arrived and grasped Rosalind's hand. The look of horror on her face shook him to the bone. It was worse than the morning before. She was drenched in sweat, her face was flushed and her eyes bulged from their sockets. Her grip on him was like death, and though he was tempted to pull away, he held on to reassure her.

"Rosalind." Etain spoke with her face only an inch from hers. "Do you hear me? Say something." She shook her by the shoulders. "Wake up!" She slapped her across the face.

"Stop!" He pulled Rosalind into his arms. "Don't hit her."

"She's in a trance. It's the only way to break it."

"No," said Loggie, who knelt beside Cormac. "She'll come around." He brushed hair from Rosalind's face and caressed the cheek Etain had slapped. "Do you hear me, Rosalind?"

"I hear. I see." Her bottom lip quivered. "It is the dungeon of death. One wrong step. Spell his name wrong, and..." She closed her eyes and shook.

"Whose name?" asked Etain. "We need to know. Who?"

Rosalind's eyes flew open. "The evil wizard who created this deadly trap."

"What's his name?"

She searched their faces, her eyes growing wider until she looked at Cormac. "Stay by my side." Her voice was ominous. It was an order, not a request. "Death awaits you. It waits for us all if we cannot solve Kragen Darkmoore's riddles."

Cormac's stomach muscles clenched. This was not how he had imagined living in the fantasy world. Certain death was never part of the game. The Adventure Master always provided an escape. That was the rule. He looked around at the landscape and the people who populated it and wondered if he, too, was living a nightmare. If so, why hadn't anyone woke him? His mom should have been in to check on him long ago. What about his Dad? He'd have been home from work by now. His little brother and big sisters should have sought him out for a baseball glove or a loan of money. Where were they?

"His name is Kragen Darkmoore?" asked Etain. "Do we spell both names or only one?"

"Darkmoore. Two Os."

"Make a mental note," she said to the others. "Anything else?"

"Gylph of Warding." She looked into Cormac's eyes and silently pleaded with him. "Take the torch offered. It is not a trick. Remember the spelling. D-A-R-K-M-O-O-R-E. Two Os. We *must* remember this."

"Rosalind, are you seeing predictions?" asked Etain. "Not a pathway to the dragon but what will happen?"

She turned to her, her mouth partly open. After much hesitation, she said. "I don't know." She stared at the ground and tilted her head. "I had a dream..." Her face twisted as if she fought for words to say. "I can't remember."

Cormac gulped. Her forgetfulness was starting to seriously threaten the lives of everyone. Details in her dreams were meant to guide her, but if she couldn't remember them... The dragon had targeted the wrong person to send his messages to.

"Can I have a few minutes alone with her." He swallowed hard. It sounded awkward. Suggestive.

Loggie stood. "Come on, Etain. Kneilot. Let's get the fire started." He gave him a long look before turning and following the others.

Once they were a fair distance, Cormac resolved to do what he should have done the day he'd met Rosalind. He reached behind his head and untied the leather strap from around his neck. Hanging from it was his high school ring. "This is my good luck charm," he lied. It wasn't a full lie. He did consider it lucky, but that wasn't the reason he was giving it to her. "I want you to keep it safe for me."

She fingered the ring with a blue stone. "It's pretty. Does it fit you?"

"Yes, it does." He wrapped the leather around her neck and secured it. "It's brought me luck, and I want it to give you the same."

"But you're the one who needs the luck. Everything we can give."

"I'll be fine. You're my lucky charm." He half chuckled. Since he'd met her, many things had gone wrong, but many things had gone right. After more than five years in this realm, he had finally found travelling companions, ones he considered friends. People he trusted.

In that moment, he realised he could never sacrifice her to return home. In all honestly, from the start, he questioned whether he could go through with it. It wasn't in him. Together, they'd find another way. Gazing upon her while she admired his ring, his smile came easy. While she didn't remember him each morning, he remembered her. Waking up and seeing her had given him purpose, someone to share his day with and now, they would share the memories of their time together. From this moment forth, she'd remember her days and in the coming weeks, more of her memory would return. Or at least that was what Harmon had said about the talisman. Looking back over their time together, a twinge of fear surfaced. Would she remember anything about him he'd regret? He didn't think so. From here on, he'd live fully understanding she would hold in her memories what he did and said.

"When we're done here, I'll give it back."

"No. Keep it until I need it." He tucked it inside her shirt to hide it from view. "Never take it off. Okay?"

"Okay."

"Hungry?"

"I think so."

"Good." He stood and offered her a hand. She accepted, and he pulled her to her feet. "Let's eat. I'm starved."

He ate a hearty breakfast. The nerves in his chest invoked a tingling sensation that suggested it might be his last for awhile. This thought kept rattling around in his brain, keeping him on alert and waiting for a deadly force to take him out. Feeling his uneasiness, Loggie offered his morning egg to him, rounding out his meal of toasted bread and heated dried pork. Everyone cautiously glancing at him in discreet ways didn't help matters and by the end of his meal, he had to say something.

"If you want to make me nervous so I make mistakes that lead to my early death, your stares are working."

Loggie grinned, but the rest quickly diverted their eyes. "If my eyes were that dangerous, you'd already be missing a few limbs."

He chuckled at the comment, and it settled the nerves but not completely.

Etain unfolded the map and studied it. After a few minutes, she released an intense sigh. "This was not on the map yesterday. I am certain of it."

"What wasn't?" asked Cormac.

"The only way I can explain it is...fog." She looked up with bent eyebrows. "And it keeps moving. Nothing is supposed to move on this map. It's ink on the highest quality vellum. It's supposed to be permanent."

He studied the map where she pointed. "I don't see it moving."

"Not like that. Look here," she pointed to another spot on the map. "Now look back. Look here, then look back."

His mind twisted. It moved without him seeing. The move was so subtle that if she hadn't pointed it out, he may have missed it.

"What does the fog reveal?" asked Kneilot.

"You mean hide," said Loggie.

"It reveals there is uncertainty ahead," said Etain flatly.

"Can we go around?" asked Cormac.

"No." Everyone looked at Rosalind. "We must face the test," she said. "It will prepare us for what is to come in the caves. The dragon's doing." Her eyes wandered, as if she was thinking, then they widened. "Nothing is real." She stood and looked in the direction they were to travel. "It is all an illusion. An elaborate illusion. The body reacts to what our eyes see. It doesn't know the difference between real and fake. It relies on our thoughts to guide it. We cannot allow ourselves to believe what we see." She scanned the group. "If you can't do that, close your eyes. Hum a pleasant song. Think pleasant things. A lovely sunny day. A purring cat. Eating pizza."

"What's a pizza?" asked Loggie. "Does it taste like horned melon? Or gac?"

"A delicious mixture of dough, tomato sauce, cheese and toppings." Cormac's mouth watered.

"A tomato pie?"

"Yes. Exactly. Almost. Not as much tomato."

"I would like to try that."

"Once you've eaten it, you will never forget how it tastes."

Etain huffed. "We are being tricked into believing we are in danger?"

"Yes." Rosalind knelt next to the map. "Show me the fog."

Etain pointed to the small, grey area. "It was not there yesterday. I am certain."

"You made the map, so I don't doubt you. It leads us towards this mountain." She winced. "Still three days away." She looked up. "Dreadful but necessary. It gives us time to learn more."

"If we're going to face death," Loggie stood, "might as well get to it." He rolled up his bedroll. "I like facing uncertainty in daylight. Fewer bugs."

"I won't argue with that." Cormac scratched a lingering itch on his neck. What he wouldn't give for a can of Deep Woods with 30% deet.

Within a half hour, they were saddled and riding through the forest towards the map location with the fog. Cormac wondered if the fog would be there only if conditions were right. He looked up at the sky. A few puffy clouds floated by. The sky was the bluest he'd ever seen it, and the sun shone brilliant yellow. The morning was warming from the overnight cool spell. It was a perfect early summer day. The inhabitants of this land didn't call this season summer. The name depended on the territory and the race. Humans in this area called it Apricus. Translated it meant *full of sunlight.*

His mind turned over many things as he travelled. Everyone else must have been doing the same because no one spoke. There was no real trail only a faint deer run. He picked his way around bushes and trees, searching for the clearest path. Occasionally, he glanced over his shoulder. Rosalind appeared deep in thought. If their eyes met, deep concern tensed the muscles in her face, then she forced the hint of a smile. It was as if she didn't want him to lose hope.

He travelled for more than two hours before the landscape ahead brightened. The farther he travelled, the more he wondered if they were exiting the forest and entering an open area. Peering into the distance, his teeth pressed together, and his hands held the reins tighter. Sweat gathered on his brow and the breeze cooled it, sending a shiver down his spine. Sweat on his hands made the reins slick. It wasn't a clearing that brightened the landscape; it was fog. Bright, illuminated fog. The kind he'd never seen before. The closer he got, the more he felt the world closing in on him. How thick was it? So thick he feared he'd lose sight of Rosalind who was only five feet behind him.

It flowed across the ground towards him, billowing out like smoke escaping a structure fire. His pace slowed, and he questioned the logic of entering it. They could go around. They could wait until it dispersed. Above, the sun shone brightly. If it was going to burn off the fog, it should be doing it.

Rosalind came alongside and stopped. "It feels ominous."

"It looks that way, too." He winced. "You're certain we have to go through?" The fog creeping low to the ground curled around the horses' legs, yet they waited patiently like any other time.

"It's a test. A practice run. If we avoid it, we will be ill prepared to face the actual challenge in the cave." She peered into the fog. "The nightmare terrified me but now that I've distanced myself from it, I can think about it logically." She stared at him. "I feel the dragon will help us when we need it."

"He won't eat us?"

She grinned. "He hungers for freedom, not human flesh."

"Are we waiting for a boat to emerge from the fog?" asked Loggie. "Or shall we ride out to it?"

"We'll go slow," said Cormac. "Stay close together. The last thing we want is to be separated."

"No, the last thing we want is to die in it." Loggie frowned.

"Remember what I said." Rosalind looked each of them in the eye. "Nothing is real. It's all an illusion. Think happy thoughts."

"Happy thoughts," sang Loggie. "Like the happiness a good book can bring. The happiness of a lively song I sing."

"Keep it up," she said. "We'll not only be happily entertained, we won't lose you."

"I have my rebec to keep the mood."

"And I have my flute."

"Piccolo flute," he corrected.

With this silliness in his mind, Cormac took a deep breath. "Stay close. Close enough to smell my horse's farts." He guided the horse forward, looking for the faint trail he had followed to this point. The fog swallowed him, and he glanced over his shoulder. Rosalind was still visible but details were obscured. "If you lose sight of me, holler." His voice sounded thick and not as loud as he thought it should.

"I'm right behind you," she said.

He focussed on the trail and every 50 feet or so, he glanced back to confirm she was still there. A solid breeze blew against him, brushing hair from his face and rustling the horse's mane. It died as quickly as it had come. Shadows of tall trees lined the trail. He couldn't make out what type. They were faint shadows though they were only ten feet away.

The farther he went, the thicker the fog became. He slowed his pace to ensure Rosalind would not lose sight of him. He glanced over his shoulder. She was there, her horse's nose almost bumping into his horse's rump. Turning forward, he met another blast of air. This time, it smelt like wood smoke.

Spit stalled in his throat. His thoughts raced so fast, he couldn't hold one long enough to gauge its possibility. If this was wood smoke, and it was getting thicker the farther they travelled, was he riding into... No. That didn't make sense. It was on the map!

Someone shouted from behind. He thought it was Kneilot but wasn't certain. He couldn't see past Rosalind's saddle. "Should I stop!" he shouted over his shoulder.

"No!" said Rosalind. "He's fine."

In the distance, he thought he saw a spark. No flames. If this was a forest fire... the horses would be nervous. They'd run. They'd never ride into a forest fire. His horse was calm. If she was jittery at all it was because of him. He glanced again at Rosalind. She was there. He turned around and almost fell off the horse.

An old man in a long grey robe sat on his horse's head. He stared back at him. When he smiled, he had no teeth. "I am the undertaker." He held up a dagger. "And I need customers." He swung the dagger forward.

Cormac dove sideways and fell from the saddle. The horse stopped and stood quietly. The old man leapt off the horse with dagger in hand.

"It's an illusion!" shouted Rosalind.

He scrambled away and avoided the blade. Grabbing his own dagger, he prepared to tackle him.

"It's not real!" Rosalind jumped off the horse and leapt at the old man. She passed through him and landed on the ground, rolling to a stop. "It's an illusion. Happy thoughts. Pizza!"

His mind snapped back, and he thought of his favourite meal. The more he thought about it, the more opaque the man became. Rosalind stood behind the old man and waved her hand through the fog.

"Not real," she repeated.

"He had a dagger." He sucked in a breath. "I thought he was going to..." The old man completely disappeared.

"If you believe it, your body will react to it. Understand? If he had stabbed you with that dagger and you thought he did, your body would react as if he had. This is not a game."

He swallowed hard. "But it was so real."

"You allowed it to become real. Next time, wave your hand and imagine it going through the illusion."

"Get it off me! I hate snakes." It was Kneilot. Cormac couldn't see him.

"It's an illusion!" shouted Rosalind. "Etain, show him it is."

"Ahh! It's biting!"

"Come." She led her horse by the reins to where the voice shouted. Kneilot lay coiled up in the body of a giant yellow snake. Its mouth was wide enough to consume the hauflin's head. Kneilot's arms were pinned to his sides, along with Matilda secured to his chest in a sack, and he struggled to get away as the snake lowered its mouth. The chicken was calm, but it eyed Kneilot with a questioning look.

"Close your eyes!" Rosalind rushed over and put her hand between his head and the snake's jaws. "Close 'em. Think of your god. What's her name? Eir?"

"Yes." He was losing his breath, and he gasped to draw in more.

"Close your eyes. Think of her. Say her name. Say it."

He closed his eyes and mumbled the goddess' name over and over. After the fifth time, the panic subsided and his body relaxed. "The snake is gone? It left? Eir made it go? Can I open my eyes?"

"Do you believe the snake is gone? If so, wave your arms in the air."

He did that and grinned. "Gone." He opened his eyes and stared at her. "How did you do that?"

"It was an illusion."

"I felt it."

"You believed you felt it. Your body reacted to that belief."

"This is bad magic," said Etain, holding the reins of her horse and peering into the fog. "What does this, controls the mind."

"We must learn to distinguish between what is real and what is not before we enter the caves," said Rosalind. "When you see the next illusion, examine it. See the mistakes in it." She turned to Cormac. "If that man was really sitting on your horse's head, would your horse tolerate it?"

He stared at the horse. "No. It was impossible."

"Where did the snake come from?" she asked.

"From Etain's hood." Kneilot inspected the hood closer. "Impossible. A trick of the mind."

"These were easy ones. I expect more difficult ones the farther we go. Let's move. As Loggie said, we don't want to be in this at night."

"Ah, someone who admires my words and appreciates them." Loggie mounted. "It's all a bard can ask for."

Cormac climbed into the saddle. When everyone was mounted, he found the trail. Keeping a steady pace, he hoped to escape this fog before more old men attacked with daggers.

Strange noises reached his ears and the wind that had blown against him before returned. This time, it smelt like garbage. Twilling sounds came from the trees, then the ground. A small frog hopped onto his horse's head. It's not real, he told himself and swatted away the illusion. It flew through the air and slammed into... He squinted and tried to see the person clearly. It was a woman dressed in rags. Her hair was knotted and hung in an odd fashion. He thought there were twigs and dry leaves in it, but it was difficult to see in the fog. She moved slowly with outstretched arms. Her long, crooked fingers fumbled in the air. The closer she got, the more dishevelled she appeared. If he didn't know better, he'd swear she crawled from beneath a pile of brush and leaves. He tilted his head to think. Her skin was pale, parts of it on her face had peeled away.

"What are you seeing?" asked Rosalind.

He wanted to look at her, but he couldn't take his eyes off this woman. When he realised what he stared at, his blood ran cold. "Draug. She's a draug."

"What's that?"

He swallowed hard and didn't believe what he was about to say. "An undead. She's dead. Buried. And here she is."

The draug gripped the frog. In one smooth motion, she bit off its head. The legs squirmed and swatted the air.

Cormac gagged and rubbed his eyes. That didn't just happen.

"It's not real."

Rosalind's voice came to him, yet he couldn't take his eyes off the woman. Not until someone screamed. He turned and found Rosalind had been thrown from the saddle. She wrestled with a... He blinked several times. "Troll?" He halted, dismounted quickly and ran over to her. "It's not real. It's an illusion. Stop fighting."

The troll struck her face with its big fist, and blood trickled from her lip. She pounded its face with her fists, but it had no effect on the monster. It hit her again, and her head snapped back.

"Close your eyes," he said. "Think happy thoughts. It's the only way to defeat an illusion that feels this real."

Loggie tackled the troll and punched it. Once he got on top of it, he drove a dagger into its chest. It screamed and rocked in spasms. It threw him off, got to its feet and staggered away. It disappeared quickly into the fog.

Stumbling over to Rosalind, Loggie helped her sit up.

Cormac squatted beside her. "Why didn't you close your eyes?"

She frowned at him. "It was real." She wiped blood from her mouth with her sleeve.

"What?" He half stood and looked to where the troll had gone. "Real? I thought these were all illusions."

"What test is that?" She rubbed her head where the beast had hit her.

"How did you know it was real?" asked Etain. "What gave it away?"

"It leapt from the fog without warning," she said. "There was no hesitation, no trying to trick my mind into believing it was real. I had closed my eyes for a second, but it didn't take it away."

"I thought trolls were larger," said Cormac, staring into the fog where he'd seen the draug. It had disappeared.

"Larger?" said Loggie. "They're big enough. I think that was a mountain troll. Bridge trolls are smaller than hauflins."

He turned to stare at him. Bridge trolls? They were an actual thing? "Are goblins real? Hobgoblins? Orks?"

Everyone except Rosalind gawked at him, mouths open, eyes wide. Seconds ticked by and he wondered if they thought him crazy for asking.

"Why do you speak of such evil creatures?" asked Etain.

"Just wondering if they were real." He jerked his thumb in the direction the troll had gone. "I didn't think trolls existed."

"Never speak of them again. Never say their race name." She stood and cautiously scanned the area. "Have you not learned as a child to never speak of them, not even to mutter their name under your breath?"

He leant back. "Why?"

Her eyes settled on him. When she spoke, her voice was low as if in a library. "Though I have spent my life in the Sanctuary, even I know the dangers of their names on my tongue. You have travelled the lands yet are ignorant of them. To them, the mere mention of their name is reason to seek out that person."

His insides tightened. "What do you mean?"

"You have called them."

"No, I didn't."

"By muttering their names, you have. They will come for you to ask why. You better have a good answer."

"That's crazy. How are we supposed to discuss them if we can't say their names? Call them what they are?"

"You use what we have been taught to use: green shadow creatures, mischief imps and barbarians of the swamplands."

"And I'm to know what you're talking about?"

"If you have had half a lesson in your life, you would." She offered Rosalind a hand. "Let's move. Illusions in the fog are tiresome; unspeakable creatures stalking us in it is deadly." She marched to her horse and jumped into the saddle.

Cormac watched, frozen in place. This was nonsense. He hadn't called such beings. Mentally creating an image of each creature, he wondered which versions lived in this realm. Were goblins big and green? Or small and crafty? Were hobgoblins blood-thirsty ape-like creatures, or were they short sneaky pests that—

"Get on your horse!" demanded Etain, impatiently.

Jerked from his thoughts, he mounted, and brought his horse onto what he thought was the trail. He set a steady pace, one Rosalind could follow. Concentrating on going straight, putting all his focus on the trail, he hoped it deterred illusions. Minutes passed, he glanced over his shoulder to see if the rest were still with him. They were. He turned back and saw a shadow on his horse's head. Not again. He ignored it, looked to the trees and swerved around them. The shadow formed into the back of a head. It was small with pointy ears. The creature's shoulders rocked with the gait of the horse. He ignored it, saw bushes and went around them.

"Zippy, zippy, zippy," sang the creature. It clapped its hands and sang a happy little tune, one that made it dance on its seat, wiggling back and forth.

Ignore it, he told himself. He leant to the left, looking around it and watched the trail.

"Hobby, hobby, that is me," it sang. "O'Robin a jolly hobgoblin be."

Cormac fought to keep his eyes on the trail, but the mention of hobgoblin pulled them to the creature. It turned around and grinned, revealing two rows of shiny silver teeth. Its eyes were large, its nose larger, and it stared right at him.

"Hippity, hoppity, can it be? I am here because you called me." It threw its arms in the air and clapped, then grabbed hold of the horse's ears to hold on. The horse nickered loudly.

The creature was no larger than a six-month old child, but it was thinner and had a complete head of black hair. It wasn't viciously ugly like in fantasy movies he'd watched, but it wasn't a thing of beauty either.

"What do you want?" Cormac's voice shook, and he cleared his throat to steady it.

"A gem for me; a gem for you. Let's find gems that shine bright blue."

"I have no gems."

It whirled with eyes big, staring at him. "We find!"

He shook his head. "I don't know where to find."

"That way." It pointed into the fog. "See them I do. You should too. Find them, we will before we get killed."

His mouth went dry. "Would you settle for something gold?"

The hobgoblin whirled again. "Gold, you say. Tell me which way."

"Far ahead. At the end of this fog. Help me get through it, and I'll show you." He clamped his mouth closed. Making false deals with such creatures went against everything he'd ever done.

"This fog is endless. Can't you see. It is created by you and your friends, not me."

What did that mean? He caused the fog? How?

A grey shadow passed beside him. Then it swooped over his head, leaving a cold breeze that chilled his ears. "What is that?"

"Ghosts of want to be."

"Wants to be? Who?"

"For you to decide."

He heard loud cursing behind him, and he looked to find Rosalind gazing into the fog behind her. The cursing came from Loggie, who was lost to him in the fog.

"Of all the silliness to send forth!" he shouted. "You are not real! Leave me be!"

"His mind, your friend has lost," sang the hobgoblin. "And everyone pays the cost."

"You say this fog is endless," said Cormac. "But it does not cover this entire land."

"It does!" It leant closer, and its eyes grew larger. "In your mind."

"It's not in my mind; it's..." He looked in one direction, then the other. "It's in my mind?" More cursing erupted from behind, and someone shrieked. He half turned and yelled to them. "Imagine a bright sunny day. Just like when we entered the fog. The fog is the illusion."

"Are you serious?" asked Rosalind.

"That's what the hob—Mr. O'Robin says."

"Who is..." She leant sideways and looked at the hobgoblin sitting on the horse's head. "Incredible." She turned in the saddle. "Imagine a bright sunny day. The fog is an illusion. Say after me: it's a bright sunny day. Look at that blue sky."

Cormac turned forward and painted a clear sunny day in his mind. He imaged the green of leaves fluttering in the wind, wildflowers growing along the trail and birds singing in the trees. A warm breeze caressed his cheeks, and the fog slowly dissipated. Within five minutes, the skies had cleared leaving a bright sunny day.

"And they say there is no wisdom in the fighter," said Loggie. "I have found a drop."

Cormac shot him a glare. "I abound with wisdom." Loggie broke into fits of laughter, and he smiled. Having escaped the fog, he was in a good mood and didn't care what the bard had to say. He caught Rosalind watching him, and he smiled at her. She returned the smile, but it faded fast when she looked past him and saw the hobgoblin.

"That is real," she half whispered.

"What is?" asked Etain. She stretched her neck and when she saw the creature on his horse, she squealed and halted her horse. "Keep it away. I warned you. And this is what has come from your lack of knowledge."

"He's not going to hurt anyone." He cautiously looked to the hobgoblin. "Right? You just like to sing and dance."

"Gold, you promised," it sang. "Or are you dishonest?"

"Oh, gold." He looked up at the sun. "It is the biggest golden orb I have ever seen. Let us gaze upon it and soak in its worth. I am a richer man for basking in it." One eye was on the hobgoblin, waiting to see if it satisfied him. "See it? Feel it? It gives us life."

The hobgoblin stared into it, then sank away. "Blind, I am and cannot see. This gold you found is not for me."

"You do not want it? Then I shall keep it."

The hobgoblin frowned. "I came to your pitiful call, thinking not big but small. Linger, I will for days on end until you give me something to spend." His eyes widened, and he drew near. As quick as lightning, his hand shot out and grabbed the small pouch of coins from around Cormac's waist. It leapt off the horse and ran cackling and prancing and quickly disappeared into the trees.

Shocked, Cormac stared at the hobgoblin stealing his only coins. He wanted to give chase, but he'd never catch him.

"Could have been worse," said Rosalind, who halted beside him.

"A lot worse," said Etain.

"Think of it as payment for escaping the fog," said Kneilot.

"Or the cost of your stupidity." Loggie leant against the saddle horn and looked into the forest where the creature had run.

"Let's hope the other creatures you beckoned to your side don't show up. This one was the calmest of the bunch." Etain reined her horse onto a clearly-cut path. "I'll lead for awhile."

He watched her go. He didn't doubt what she'd said, and now he wanted to put as much distance between him and this place as he could before dark.

"You can be last for awhile." Loggie jogged his horse past him. "Rosalind."

She smirked and guided her horse onto the trail. "It is a beautiful day. Best to enjoy it."

He followed her. She was right. While he was penniless, the day was beautiful. He gazed up and took in the expansive sky, then the landscape. In the five years he'd been here, it had never looked this serene. Odd how it affected him now that he was struggling to save his life. And that of his friends.

He considered every rider before him. While there were different degrees of friendship, he considered each one his friend. He hoped they considered him the same.

The landscape slowly changed, and trees grew smaller. Lower growing shrubs were transforming the view, and he could see farther ahead. The sound of water touched his ears. Ten minutes later, they reached a river. It was fast flowing and came directly from the mountain ahead. His eyes followed it for as far as he could see. Somewhere along its path was a dragon.

"We need to head west for a short time," said Rosalind. "It's too rugged for the horses."

He nodded and followed when the rest moved on. Leaving the river behind, he heard the chatter of birds, squirrels and other woodland creatures. For the rest of the day, they travelled west, into the setting sun. An hour before it disappeared, they stopped to make camp.

Gathered around the fire with tea in hand, he sat up when Etain unfolded the map.

"We're about here," she said, pointing to a spot on the map. "I think this faint line is the trail. I did not draw it."

"It magically appeared?" asked Cormac.

"I believe the dragon is revealing the trail, one section at a time."

"Is the fog still there?" He searched for it but didn't see it.

"Gone." She shook her head. "The map continues to change at will. I have no control over it."

"Did you make the map with magic?" asked Rosalind.

"No. Ink on vellum. No magic."

"Were you thinking of magic when you drew it?" asked Kneilot.

"Not at all."

"Thinking of a god?"

She shook her head. "I cannot explain it. Urðr has viewed the map. She said nothing about magic."

"Could she have cast a spell on it?" asked Kneilot.

She hesitated to answer. "I cannot say. I will ask her upon my return." She released a sigh. "Her instructions to me were clear. Reach Delgrath and continue my studies. She gave no indication I would be on this quest."

"Then it must be the dragon." Rosalind took a drink of tea. "Am I to watch tonight?"

"No," said Loggie. "Rest."

"I'll take first," said Kneilot.

"Second." Cormac finished his tea.

"That leaves me third," said Loggie.

Cormac settled in his bedroll on his stomach. His arms folded beneath his chin, he watched the flames lick the air. Beside him, only two feet away, Rosalind settled. The expression on her face revealed her thoughts: she was dreading the dreams that awaited her. She caught him watching, and she tried to remove the strain from her features, but they remained.

"Think of these nightmares as illusions," he said. "Be the observer, not the participant."

"I have tried, but the horror is too real." She closed her eyes. Her face lay on her hands that clenched and unclenched.

Needing sleep, he closed his eyes and tried to get at least a few hours before either Kneilot woke him for watch or Rosalind woke him with screams.

Rosalind fell in the dark. The hard cave floor was cold and damp. Many hands beat on her back and legs. She tried to rise, but there were too many. They pulled at her shirt. They pulled on her pants. They pulled off the dagger fastened to her leg. Then her vest was ripped off. She turned to fight and swung the dagger wildly. A yelp pierced her ears, but the faces, so many faces consumed her space. Animated faces with large eyes, large noses and large flappy ears that ended in a point. They wore clothes of various colours and material. Their fingers were long and ended in sharp claws that scratched her. Their hissing and ranting weighed her down as much as their bodies.

Swinging the dagger frantically in front of her only removed half of the small creatures from her body. Then they returned. Kicking, screaming and swinging gave her enough room to get to her knees. There, she was tackled again and thrown to the ground. Her body ached from the pounding fists, toes digging into skin and claws that constantly scratched her. Overrun and thrown to the ground, she could neither get up nor stop the onslaught. Darkness swirled around her, and she swallowed it with every breath. Swaying on the edge of consciousness, she slipped deeper into the bleak unknown.

"Rosalind," came a soft whisper near her ear. "Wake up."

Her mind snapped awake and with every muscle in her body, she leapt to her feet. She didn't complete one step before she slammed into the ground, screaming. Her feet were bound; she couldn't run. Muffled sounds exploded around her. They had found her. She flipped to her rump and grabbed at the rope binding her feet.

"Rosalind!"

She turned. Cormac? He had fallen next to her. Scanning the area, she saw everyone on the ground. Everyone except Loggie. He rushed over to the campsite and stared at them, confused.

"What did you do?" He scratched his head. "Why did you tie your feet together?"

"I didn't." Cormac unwrapped the binding around his ankles. "It's..." he held up the stringy cord, "tree roots?"

"Who did this?"

"You were the only one awake. You tell me." He threw the roots aside and stood.

"I didn't do it," said Loggie.

"If not you..." said Etain. Her fingers gripped the roots she'd removed from her feet, and she scanned the edge of the campsite. "Then who? Or what?"

"The dragon that controls trees or the hob—" Cormac slapped his hand over his mouth. "Would it follow us?"

"The creature that stole your coins?" asked Rosalind. Everyone stared at her in silence. Feeling it had gone on too long, she spoke again. "The thing whose name we're not supposed to say. That thing."

Etain fell to her knees before her. "You remember yesterday?"

"Shouldn't I?"

"You should." She turned to the others. "The dragon has broken the spell."

"At least something good has come from this ordeal." Loggie sat next to Rosalind. "What is my name?"

"Loggie?"

His grin reached both ears. He grasped her head gently and kissed her forehead. "You, my dear, give me hope." He wrapped her in his arms and squeezed. "We shall see this through and be on our next adventure together. Once Etain is delivered, we shall visit his friend in the woods," he waved his hand at Cormac, "then kingdoms far and wide to entertain kings and queens with our spirit."

"Kings and queens? Far and wide? Sounds like more than one adventure."

"Certainly does." He leapt to his feet. "Today will be a great day. Unless I have no breakfast." He winked at her. "Then it will only be a good day."

"Before we start this day," said Etain, "Rosalind, tell me about your dream."

She replayed the scene that had haunted her. "Small creatures. Too many to escape from."

"Hob—?" Again, Cormac's tongue froze on the word. "Small creatures. Like we saw yesterday?"

She shook her head. "Smaller. Thinner. Big ears that flopped. Claws. More human-like."

"Kobolds?" He visibly winced and looked to Etain.

"No worries," she said. "They do not hear their name."

"Make a list of those that do," he said. "I need to know."

Etain spoke to Rosalind. "What was the trigger this time? What brought them to you?"

Rosalind thought about the dream. It was a mish-mash of short clips. The falling in the dark. The pounding. The tearing of clothes. Where had it started? "It was only one. Watching me. Following me in the cave. I..." She stared at Cormac. "You told me it was an illusion."

"Was it?"

Her thoughts rambled on. "I don't think so, but..." she thought harder, "they came from cracks in the wall, the shadows, from behind rocks. They came so fast. They overwhelmed me with number." She shook her head. "They had to be. It's impossible for them to step out of rocks."

"That was the lesson we were to learn yesterday," said Etain. "They are illusions. We must remember this and clear our thoughts of them."

"There were so many. So hard to think when I was being attacked from all sides." Her eyes widened. "They even rose from the floor."

"Definitely sounds like an illusion," said Loggie.

"Does the map show anything in our path today?" asked Cormac.

Etain pulled it from her pouch and unfolded it. "Nothing unusual. Grasslands, then woodland. We should reach this large lake by nightfall." She pointed to the blue spot on the map. It was in the shape of a peanut.

"Nothing like taking a cool bath in mountain lake water," said Loggie. "Let's get the day started."

They packed their gear and rode west. The terrain was mostly low bushes with a scattering of deciduous trees. Mid-morning, they entered the grasslands. Rosalind stared across it and watched seed heads on long stems swaying in the breeze. Small birds flew over it and disappeared into the blades. She recognised a few: sparrows, yellow finches and black-capped chickadees. Their songs came together in nature's choir. The easiness of the day relaxed her muscles, and the horse's gentle trot lulled her further into the joy of the moment.

Quick movement one hundred feet away made her look off to the left. She tried to make out what it was, but it happened too fast. It looked like a hand rising from the grass, snatching a bird and disappearing. No, that couldn't have been what happened. She stared at the spot. Nothing appeared unnatural, and the birds continued to fly and sing.

"Did you see something?" Kneilot followed her line of sight.

She glanced over her shoulder at him. This morning, he and his chicken Matilda were riding with her to give Etain's horse a break. "I thought I saw movement, but there's nothing there."

"Do you observe a god?"

She looked into his hazel eyes. "No."

"May I suggest one?"

"Who would you suggest?"

"I feel you love nature. The soil is your home, like all hauflins. You feel a deep connection to the woodland. Jörð is our goddess of all the lands. She keeps it in order."

"What would she do for me?"

He stared, confused by the question. When he spoke, his voice was small. "She has done all this for you." He waved his hand across the grasslands. "From the mountains to the valleys. The streams and the forest. She has provided a home for us, all of us, to live in."

"And if I observed her...?"

"You would sing her praises. Live within your basic needs and cherish that which feeds and shelters you."

"But what would she do for me specifically?" His bow bent, and she reworded the question. "What do you have to gain by meditating and connecting with Eir?"

"Nothing."

"Nothing? Not even a little help with your healing?"

He stumbled over his words for a moment, then, "Eir is to aid me with attaining a healing spell to help others."

"And what would Jörð aid me with to help others?"

"You are not a cleric."

"I don't need to be a cleric to help others."

"I am unsure. Etain may know the answer."

"Maybe influence the weather? Or talk to animals? Control plants?"

"That is extreme."

"Curing a dagger wound isn't?"

"It is assisting healing, not curing. And it is for others, not me."

"Talking a bugbear out of eating you is beneficial to who?"

His surprise turned to a grin. "You, of course, so I can heal you when you are injured."

She laughed and turned to face the front, giving her full attention to the trail ahead. For as far as she could see, the grasslands stretched before her. Bordering it to her right was the mountain range. White caps indicted winter weather on top. Given the early summer temperatures, they also revealed the height: high.

The sun reached its highest point and slowly began its descent, moving into their line of view as they travelled. Still, no end to the grasslands was visible. Rosalind removed her jacket and draped it over the saddle in front of her. An hour late, she unbuttoned the shirt to reveal another shirt below. The day grew warmer still, and she wiped her brow and removed the button shirt.

Kneilot had also stripped down to his first layer of clothing and took drinks often. "We shall fry in the heat before we reach shade."

"Or run out of water." She held up her flask. There were only a few mouthfuls left. "If anyone sees water, let me know. I need a refill."

"So do I," said Loggie from behind. "Yet I see no water in sight."

"The water in Spiritwood is sweet," said Kneilot. "Sweeter than honey."

"Sweet or sour, I'd drink a mug now."

The horses plodded over the terrain, their pace slowing with every mile. Mid-afternoon, she told the others to stop. She dismounted, poured the remaining water into a pot and allowed her horse to drink it.

"You need the water more than the horse," said Kneilot.

"I'd rather this horse carry my weary feet from these grasslands than have to walk to a point I can't see." She thought about their earlier conversation. "If Jörð allowed me to influence the weather, I could make it rain, and my horse would have water. That is helping another, and who better to help than the greatest creature on the land." She scratched the horse's nose.

"You are thinking of connecting with Jörð?" asked Etain.

She jerked her head in Kneilot's direction. "He says I'll not be granted anything if I do."

"You do not recognise a god for what they can give to you, but how you can serve them. In the process, you will receive gifts, but that is not why you dedicate yourself to them."

"So, I will get something in return. What? Control weather? Talk to animals?"

She chuckled. "That is not how you are to look at it. Do the work, then you may be granted special abilities. Or, if you are there only for the gifts, you'll receive nothing."

"Sounds like a gamble."

"Only to those who seek something in return."

The horse licked the pot dry, and she put it away. "Let's walk a piece to rest my horse."

"Walk?" asked Kneilot. "In this heat."

"Yes." She followed the trail. It was faint but still there.

"She's to bury me in this land that knows no trees," said Loggie. "You have taken me far from home, my gentle daisy. I'm told you were to return me to Popa. Promised him you would. Please, do not break this vow you have made to him."

She stared at him. "I've never met Popa."

"He has met you, and he remembers you well."

"Does he like me?"

He chuckled out loud. "That depends on you returning me to him." Then he got serious. "The dragon's magic has its limits if you can remember only yesterday. I wonder tomorrow if you will remember ereyesterday."

"Maybe it takes time to work," said Cormac.

For the next hour, they walked. The ground wasn't too difficult to cross, but the blazing sun directly in their eyes was slowing their pace.

"That's enough," said Loggie. "We want out before dark." He climbed into the saddle.

Rosalind quietly agreed and mounted. Waiting for Kneilot to get into the saddle, she scanned the grasslands. The higher viewpoint provided a glimpse of a shadow up ahead. She squinted and strained her eyes to identify the blur. "Are those trees?" she said.

After a long silence, Cormac answered. "Trees. Bushes. It's something besides grasslands."

"Let's take a closer look," said Loggie.

The breeze created by faster movement dried sweat that had gathered along the hair line and in her armpits. It pushed her hair back and curled in around her shirt to cool her further. The short rest rejuvenated the horse, and it had more spring in its trot. Looking up, she saw a thick dark cloud hanging over the grasslands. That would provide relief from the sun, shading them in the final mile of their trek to the forest.

The closer she came to this cloud, the more attention she gave it. It appeared unusual. She thought she saw sparks within it but when she stared at the spot, there was nothing. Finally, they entered its shadow, and a cool breeze whipped around her ears. Thoughts of putting on her button shirt crossed her mind, but she'd have to stop to do that because she had put it in a saddlebag.

A speck of rain fell on her nose. It was a solid speck. The wind picked up, rattling the seed heads of the tall grass and sending loose plant material hurdling through the air.

"What is happening?" Kneilot's strained voice broke over her shoulder.

"Not sure!" The wind speed increased and whirled around, flinging dirt in her face and lifting dried grass and faded wildflower buds into the air. What had been a clear, blue day was now dark with debris swirling about.

Another drop of rain struck her face, and she saw it bounce off. A half a minute later, two more objects struck her. These were slightly larger than rain drops, and they stung.

"What is this?" asked Kneilot. "Rain doesn't hurt."

"I think it's ice." She stared at the ominous cloud. From this point of view, it looked like it was alive. The cloud was in constant motion, folding into itself and unfolding as if someone was stirring a great bowl of chocolate pudding. A rumbling deep inside echoed over the grasslands. Solid rain struck her cheek, then another hit her. "Yup. Hail. That's what I'd say."

"Hail!" Cormac looked back at her. He was in front of Etain, but he had heard her. "We gotta go!" He kicked his horse and rode away. Etain did the same.

Rosalind didn't want to over strain her horse with two riders on it, but she didn't want to stick around and see it pummelled with hail either. What she knew about this weather phenomenon was hail could be the size of golf balls. That wasn't good for her or the horse. She encouraged it to go faster. Once the hail picked up, this wasn't a problem. It raced to escape the projectiles.

"Of all the weather to be caught in with no shelter to find," gasped Loggie. He was hot on her tail.

"Pass me!" she shouted to him.

"No!"

"You can run faster." She was losing ground to Cormac and Etain. They were now fifty feet in front of her. But Loggie didn't pass and remained a horse-length behind her.

What started slowly picked up fast, and soon hail was falling like rain. The sound of it shooting through the grass and striking the ground sounded like a rock dropped into water. It struck her face, and she shielded it with her arm to reduce the number of impacts. It pelted her bare arms and the skin around her neck, making her flinch and curse. The horse snorted and whined, fighting off the projectiles. It flicked its mane from side-to-side. A few times it stumbled but regained its footing quickly.

Scanning ahead, she saw the shadow of trees growing larger. It was still a great distance away, and she wouldn't be out of the barrage of ice pellets soon.

"If I could control the weather," she shouted over her shoulder to Kneilot, "this wouldn't be happening."

"Speak to your god about this." He was ducking behind her, protected from most of the onslaught. His chicken was tucked between them, the most protected of all.

"I'm yelling at her now." She looked up into the swirling gut of the cloud. "Enough! Make it stop!" But it didn't stop. The pellets got larger and hit harder.

She raced towards the point in the distance, hoping the trees were large enough to shelter them. An ice ball the size of a fist struck her horse in the neck, and it stumbled sideways. After it regained its balance, she stroked the spot and encouraged the horse to keep running. Another chunk struck her hand, sending a shot of pain up her arm.

Barrelling down on the forest, it started to take shape. She could make out distinct trees, a mixture of deciduous and evergreen. It was about a half mile away. Seconds ticked by, and the onslaught of ice continued. There was nothing she could do to protect her or the horse until they reached the safety of the trees, so she just let it all go and sped as fast as she could.

At 400 feet away, she saw Cormac reach the trees and disappear into shadows. Etain was on his heels.

Rosalind's horse stumbled again and this time, it didn't recover. It slammed into the ground, and she flew from its back and landed in a mound of grass. Jumping to her feet, she raced back to it lying in the grass and struggling to rise with hail beating down. Kneilot rose from the grass, took one look at the horse and ran towards the forest with one hand over his head and the other shielding the chicken in the cloth sack strapped to his chest.

"Leave it!" Loggie stopped and reached down for her.

"No!" She yanked on the reins. "Get up. Come on! Get up!"

"It won't make it!" he shouted. "Ah!" He winced in pain from being hit with ice. "Come with me!"

She ignored him, went to the side of the horse and kneed it in the shoulder. It scrambled to its feet and staggered, but it didn't fall. She held the reins tightly and dragged the horse towards the forest. Once she saw it capable of moving, she ran, pulling it along behind her.

"Go!" she shouted at Loggie. "Get to cover!"

He hesitated, but then turned and jogged towards the trees.

She covered the last 300 feet of the grasslands and ducked beneath thick evergreen branches. Wiping sweat and ice chunks from her face, she looked for the others.

"This way," said Loggie. He was on the ground, leading his horse forward.

She followed. The tree branches deflected most of the ice pellets, but some still broke through. She travelled for a few hundred feet and found the rest gathered beneath a large pine with a branch span of at least 60 feet. The ice whacked and smacked against the branches, and she felt like ducking, but the impacts broke up the hail into smaller, less damaging chunks that rained down on them. Pulling her horse near, she dug the button shirt and jacket from the saddlebags. She pulled on the shirt and draped the jacket over the horse's head. It spooked, but she held on and once it was in place, the horse settled.

"Freak storm," said Cormac. "I've never seen anything like it."

"Nor have I." Etain drew her horse near and inspected its head.

"They usually don't last long," said Rosalind. "It should have ended by now."

As if the gods were listening, the thump, thump, thump of large hail stones decreased. Within a minute, it stopped completely, and the sky brightened, indicating the dark cloud was moving away.

"Thank the gods," said Kneilot, who clutched the chicken in his arms.

"Some cleric you are," said Rosalind. "Abandoning a poor animal to the storm."

"I could do nothing for it."

"You didn't try. If I were your god, you'd get no benefits."

"My god will understand. My life was endangered."

She frowned. "That's the whole point of your mission in life: to help others in need even when your life is in danger."

He was about to speak, but his mouth opened, then closed without words passing over his tongue.

"There are seeds of truth in her words," said Etain. "Eir will not look favourably on your decision. But you are young, untrained. With time and experience, you'll have the wisdom to do what is right." She addressed the others. "We'll rest here for a short time for the horses to recuperate. If I'm understanding the map correctly, we are only an hour away from the lake. We'll walk some of it." She stepped closer to Rosalind. "How is your horse? Ridable?"

"Not sure. It took a hard fall."

"Hold the reins." She handed off the reins of her horse and inspected the legs of Rosalind's horse. After a quick check up, she frowned. "I don't think it's lame, but we'll take it slow. Kneilot, you'll ride with me."

After ten minutes, they started walking, leading the horses by the reins. The first objective was to find a stream to quench their thirst. They found it 20 minutes later. It was only six feet wide and a foot deep, but the water was cool and refreshing. Rosalind let her horse drink first. While it sucked up water, she wet a rag and wiped it down. She found several marks made by the ice projectiles. These, she ran water over to ensure they were clean. The horse was favouring its left front leg, and she gave that special attention, soaking the rag and rubbing it gently on the tender spot. The horse watered and tended to, she filled her flask and took a long drink. Then she filled it again, capped it and hung it off the saddle horn.

When Cormac prepared to leave, she and the others did the same. Without a word, they moved on, walking the horses. Less than an hour later, they overlooked a lake. Its water was the bluest she'd ever seen. No wind blowing left the surface like a mirror, reflecting the trees on the opposite shore. Protruding from behind the trees was the mountain range with numerous peaks. A small island no larger than a tavern rested three hundred feet offshore. It consisted of mostly rock and had one large evergreen growing on it.

"Looks good enough to rest by," said Loggie. "When we get to Delgrath, I'm sleeping for a week."

"Let's say 24 hours." Rosalind looked for a place to let her horse graze.

"Nah. A week."

The band settled in for the night and soon, a campfire was burning. As the sun sank into the west, the moon rose full and bright orange in the eastern sky. Loggie took out his rebec and played a few tunes. Rosalind examined her flute and wondered if she knew how to play. She blew on it and Loggie reached for it.

"Can I see that?" he said. She handed it to him, and he threw it over his shoulder and continued to play the rebec. "While your face is as lovely as the moon," he sang, "to save your life, your lips couldn't play a tune."

Cormac chuckled. "She'd certainly not earn copper at a tavern."

Rosalind hmphed, collected the flute and tucked it into the leather pouch on her belt. She sat back in a relaxed position and looked across the peaceful lake. Her belly full and music filling the air, she felt at ease. While her bones ached from the tumble from the horse and bruises covered her arms from the hail, she felt good. She was surrounded by friends in a magnificent world. It was everything she needed.

Her head slowly rolled into a relaxed position, and she feared she'd fall asleep. Her eyes closed and for a moment, all was peaceful. An image appeared in her mind. It was a glass door framed by thick steel. Her vision zoomed in quickly, and she saw her hand grasp the steel handle. She tugged on it, but it wouldn't open. She pulled harder, but the door wouldn't budge. Her heart rate increased. She had to get the door open. Fighting with it, she collapsed to the solid black ground.

Gasping, her eyes flew open, and she saw the rest staring at her.

"What happened?" Loggie had his bow poised over the strings but didn't strike them.

"A steel door I couldn't open." She swallowed hard to regain her breath, then she described the door.

"Nothing like that exists in Lachspeur of Yore," said Etain. "Glass doors would be easily broken. Did you visit another realm?"

"I don't know," she said. She caught Cormac's gaze. "Have you seen a door like this?" He shook his head and looked away.

"It must be the dragon," said Etain. "Another message for us."

She silently disagreed and resettled in a comfortable position to enjoy the evening.

14

Swallowed by a Time Capsule

THE COOL MORNING air on the side of the mountain and the ice-cold lake water kept Cormac's bath short. He, Loggie and Kneilot had jumped into the lake to wash away yesterday's sweat. The short swim also cleansed and removed the itch of the many mosquito and fly bites he had sustained while crossing the marshland. His teeth chattered by the time he ran from the lake and wrapped a blanket around him. Standing on the shore, shivering and admiring the view of the mountains, he paused to contemplate his circumstances. While he wasn't home and his life was in danger, right now, right here, he felt pretty good.

After a quick meal and evaluating the condition of the horses, they started riding towards the mountain. Rosalind's horse was in the worse shape, and she wouldn't push it to injure it further, and she wouldn't abandon it. The pace she set was a quick walk. Kneilot rode with Etain.

Once again, the early morning had been disturbed with Rosalind waking from a nightmare. This time, it didn't make any sense. She said she dreamt of drinking from a large mug of water. She tipped up the mug and found herself swimming in it. Something was dragging her down, and the fear of drowning had awakened her. Her attempt at connecting the three days of dreams didn't produce further insight. When she remembered ereyesterday, the word in Lachspeur for the day before yesterday, everyone took note. Cormac stifled a grin and busied himself with putting on his boots. Her remembering him every morning was his reward for giving her his high school ring.

Like yesterday, everyone sleeping had their feet bound with roots. His first suspect was the dragon. It had convinced the trees to build the bridge. What were a few roots around feet? Then he thought of the hobgoblin playing tricks. Considering both, he didn't think one was worse than the other. The real question was: why were their feet being bound?

They skirted the lake for almost an hour before turning directly towards the mountain. This time, Etain led the way. She read the trail better than anyone. Cormac could only see it in spots. He wondered if it was because she was elf and he human, or because she was trained in magic. Didn't matter. The path was clear for her. Instead, he went to the back of the line. Rosalind was in front of him mollycoddling her horse.

The trail took them along the base of the mountain on a gentle incline, then it bent back on itself. It hadn't felt like he had climbed any great elevation until a break in the trees revealed the view. From here, he could see the entire lake, it's crystal blue water shimmering in the morning sunshine. The deep green of the forest, the one they had travelled through, was the richest green he'd ever seen. Beyond that lay the golden waves of the grasslands that went on for as far as his eye could see. His eyes drank in the scene, marvelling at the wonders of nature. If ever there was an enchanted sight like this on Earth, he hadn't seen it. In all his travels in Lachspeur of Yore, he had never seen such a sight. Was the dragon enchanting this land, painting it with its magic?

Trees obscured his view, and he focussed on the trail and the woman ahead of him. Now and again, she glanced back. He didn't know why. It could simply be to know if he was still there and had not fallen behind. Or was there more to it?

Rounding a bend in the trail, he looked ahead and found the incline steeper. The higher they went, the slower the horses travelled. By noon, they approached a sharp face of the mountain. The sound of water tickled his ear. The trees had thinned, and more grass, weeds and bushes covered the ground.

A sound from the front of the line caught Cormac's attention, and he leant to the side to see what was going on. Etain was riding straight for the rock face of the mountain, and she had said something to Loggie.

"A cave for a dragon." Loggie's voice drifted on the air.

They were here? Cormac swallowed hard. While he had explored many caverns in the roll playing game, he knew at the end of the day, he would go home. He'd be safe. Entering this cave and meeting the challenges set forth to rescue a dragon wasn't what he'd call a guarantee to return home. The closer he got to the rock wall, the quicker his breathing became. When he saw the mammoth hole in the mountain, a chill raced across his neck and down both arms. Sweat gathered in his palms, making the reins greasy. If Rosalind's nightmares were predictions of what was to come, he'd never make it out alive.

"That's it," said Rosalind over her shoulder. The muscles in her face were strained. "The wait is over."

He'd prefer to wait a few more days. A few more months. Another century of waiting would suffice. Then he thought of the dragon that had been trapped in this mountain for much longer. Its suffering was endless unless they survived to free it. Still, he'd give anything to sit on the chesterfield at home, eat popcorn and watch *Dragon Slayer* with his family.

Etain stopped and Kneilot dismounted and took a step away from the mouth of the cave. He clutched his chicken as if a great hawk would swoop down and snatch it from his grip.

Cormac slowed his horse. The elongated hole in the mountain had rounded edges. A giant, 30 feet tall, could walk in without hitting its head. The width was only ten feet. Vines and weeds grew from rock crevices and encircled the opening. The entranceway was smooth except for a few rocks no larger than a basketball scattered about. Sunlight pouring into the opening illuminated the first twenty feet. Beyond that lay darkness.

His horse stopped behind Rosalind. He stared into the cavern and thought about his adventures exploring Hayes Caves. The limestone caves were a must-see amongst his friends. The first cavern was huge. It had a 50-foot ceiling and a pool of murky water looming from the darkness. Several flashlights didn't create enough light to illuminate it completely. The climb down was intense the first time he had entered. He had no idea what to expect. The cave stretched for about half a mile. The limestone floor was covered in red mud, and water dripping from the ceiling made it slippery. Escaping at the end meant climbing up a 50-foot chimney, twisting to one side then the other to get around the moulded limestone. Not everyone could do it, but he had. Many times. He hoped to do it again one day.

The cave before him didn't hold the same appeal. He'd offer to wait outside and tend to the horses but that would be cowardly. These people who had become his friends depended on him as much as he did them.

Rosalind dismounted and gave him a long look. A hint of despair shadowed her face, and she dropped her gaze to the ground. She had seen glimpses of what lay inside. If she was wracked with apprehension, it didn't leave much room for discussion on what they'd encounter.

Etain led her horse towards the patch of forest. "We remove tack and leave the horses near the brook."

"They will run away," said Loggie, following her with his horse. "Then we'll be forced to walk down this insidious mountain."

"A little faith," she said.

"Faith in a beast that would sooner run to the next field of grass than stick around to carry my weary bones away?"

She grinned, and her eyes sparkled in the sun. "Faith in me."

Rosalind followed them. She glanced back at Cormac, but he was in no hurry to dismount. If something came charging from the cave, he'd... What? Escape and leave them behind? He dismounted and followed in silence.

Etain led her horse to the stream, and it drank eagerly. Then she removed the tack and saddlebags. From her shoulder bag, she withdrew a flimsy stick, half the size of a drumstick. "Take only a light pack," she said. "Water, enough food to ward off hunger and your weapons. Leave everything else beneath this tree." It was where she had placed her gear. "We travel light. We travel fast."

"But not too fast," said Rosalind. "We search for seven traps."

"Seven?" Loggie cringed. "Simple ones like dusty air?"

She stared at him, her mouth closed. Then she looked away without answering and removed the equipment from her horse.

Once everyone gathered what they needed and the horses were free to graze and drink, Etain held up the stick. Mumbling words too low for Cormac to hear, she held the stick at waist level and walked a large circle around the horses. By the time she returned to where she had started, she had included part of the stream. She flicked the stick, and it floated in mid-air. A faint glow traced the path she had walked.

"What magic is this fair maiden?" asked Loggie. "For a maiden told not to cast spells until she was instructed to do so as an apprentice, you have created something truly interesting.

"The Enchanted Rope of Esmerelda." She giggled. "A gift from my cousin. It will keep the horses within it and keep predators out."

"My faith in you is strong."

If Loggie joked to ease the tension, it wasn't working for Cormac. He moved methodically, knowing what he had to do but not thinking past it. The slim pack on his back held a jacket, a small packet of food that would sustain him for a day, dry socks and 20 feet of rope that was strong enough to hold his weight. Over his shoulder, he hung his water flask. On his belt, he had three small pouches with various items, including flint to start a fire, a bandana and gloves. His only weapons were two daggers: one on his hip and one fastened to his calf. Thinking about everything he carried, he realised he had travelled Lachspeur for five years without anything but the clothes on his back and the occasional sack of food.

"Ready?"

He turned to Rosalind, whose expression told him she wasn't. "As I'll ever be."

"I'll lead the way."

"I'll be right behind you."

She nodded and walked to the cave entrance. The others fell into line, including the chicken, wrapped securely to Kneilot's chest.

"Maybe she should stay with the horses," said Etain.

He stopped and looked back at the enclosed grazing area. "Can she escape?"

"No."

"Can a flying predator swoop down and snatch her?"

"No. Nothing in or out but the tiniest of insects."

He stared at the horses, glanced at the chicken, then stared at the horses. "What if we don't return? I mean, what if we...?"

"If I die, they will be set free. The magic is tied to me."

He stood silent, contemplating the option. Then, he said quickly, "I will speak to her in private." He walked away, mumbling to the chicken. He stood 30 feet away, his back to them. After a moment, he returned. "No. Matilda said she will live with me as well as die with me if that is the outcome."

Cormac stared at the chicken. It really wasn't a woman. It couldn't be. Kneilot had some sort of issue he connected with it but whatever it was, it wasn't going to be solved inside that cave.

"Then we proceed." Etain turned towards the cave.

Rosalind stepped up to the entrance and peered in. "Looks dark, but..." She turned to Cormac. "You can't see."

"That's why I've fashioned this torch," said Etain. "The fat and oils on it should burn for a long time. It won't be extremely bright, but it should provide enough light for us to see where we're going." She held the tip out to Loggie and gave him the fire starter. "Please."

Loggie worked the flint and steel. The torch lit easily, and a bright orange glow surrounded it. "Battle by candlelight," he said. "How romantic."

Cormac held the torch in a comfortable position. He was the tallest by three inches, and the light benefited Rosalind in front and those behind him. The first 30 feet of the cave intrigued him. The high ceiling gave him the feeling he was walking into a cathedral. The floor was relatively smooth. The few rocks littered about had been kicked to the side. Cool air greeted him and the deeper he travelled, the more visible his breath became.

Darkness swallowed the areas the torch couldn't reach, and from somewhere in the distance came the sound of soft clicks.

"Bats," whispered Rosalind. A cloud of frost breath escaped her mouth.

Deeper into the cave, the ceiling sloped and the passageway narrowed. Where once four could walk side-by-side comfortably, now only two could, yet they remained single file. Adding to the clicks was the sound of dripping water. Every few minutes, he heard a different noise. It sounded like someone tapping a wooden table with a stick.

"A light," whispered Rosalind.

"Where?" he asked.

"Up ahead." She pointed into the cave.

He directed the light of the torch behind him and strained his eyes. "I can't see it."

"It's green. Like something is glowing."

"A hole in the cave?" That was impossible. A mountain sat on this cave.

"No... Magic." She crept forward, her bare feet not hesitating on the smooth floor. In her hand, she held a dagger close to her side.

A moment passed before he caught a glimpse of what she spoke of. The green light shimmered and glowed from around a bend in the passageway. It looked like the glow of a streetlight, but that was impossible. Nearing the corner, light flooded the passageway and while there was no longer need for a torch, he held tightly to it. When he reached the bend, he saw a different type of torch. Its handle was stuck in a hole in the wall. It released a steady flame, making the glow unison around end. It didn't dance like the one he held. But it wasn't the torch that illuminated the entire passageway. The source of that light was not obvious.

"Remarkable," gasped Etain. "I wonder if this is the dragon's doing or the wizard's who imprisoned him here."

"There's a fork," said Rosalind. She stopped at it and gazed down one passage and then the other.

"This one is well lit with a green glow," said Cormac. It appeared to be the most practical one and safest. It was wider and smoother than the other one, which was barely visible.

"But that is not our way." She turned towards the narrower passageway. The ceiling was lower, the lighting nonexistent and cobwebs stretched across it. Symbols in the wall above the entrance caught her attention. She reached up and wiped away the cobwebs and read the strange words slowly. "Bi mar mhaighstir air do dhàn. What does that mean?" She turned to Etain. "Do you know?"

Etain examined the letters. "I think it means master your fate. In other words, control your destiny."

"Our choices in life dictate our destiny," said Rosalind. "Choosing to take this path leads us to our fate." Her voice trailed off.

Turning to the unique torch that helped illuminate the well-lit passage, Etain said, "I believe this is an eternal flame." She lifted it from its resting place. "It is." Seeing movement from where she'd plucked the torch, she jumped back. A torch exactly like the one she held materialised to replace the one removed. "Lighting for those before us, and we will never know how many have passed through."

"And everyone has failed." Loggie's voice lacked the usual humour.

"Let us not dwell on that," said Rosalind.

"I will take another," said Etain. She grasped the newly exposed torch and tugged, but it wouldn't budge. Handing off the one she'd already plucked from the wall to Loggie, she used both hands. Still, the torch wouldn't detach from the wall.

"Let me try." Loggie returned her torch and grasped the one on the wall. He tugged and jerked it sideways. "It won't move. It's like it's a part of the wall."

"Only one provided per session," said Etain.

Rosalind stepped into the passageway.

"Are you certain?" asked Cormac.

"Yes. It tugs on my feet and my heart." She continued, slower than before, and wove around stalactites and stepped over broken stalagmites to enter it.

Cormac had to duck to follow. After travelling more than 25 feet, the ceiling rose, and he could stand upright. Drawing in a long, deep breath, he tried to relax his nerves that were running wild. A soft thud behind him drew his attention. Kneilot, Etain and Loggie also stared into the darkness behind them. When nothing more than the click of bats and the drip of water were heard, he continued. The sound of wood on wood sounded closer, but he couldn't see what made it. It was followed by a vibration, quick and sharp. Like the buzz of a bee growing louder, stopping abruptly and leaving an eerie silence. The passageway widened and again, two people could walk side-by-side. Another odd sound touched his ear.

"That sounded like a bow striking a string," said Loggie. "Just once. One string."

"I was thinking the buzz of crickets on a hot day," said Rosalind.

To Cormac, it sounded like both. The air took on a dank smell, like that of a rag left for weeks on a damp concrete floor of an unfinished basement. Musty. Rosalind paused to look at a stalactite and he stepped around her and held out the torch to see what lay ahead. Odd shadows cast by the torch drew his eye, and he stepped closer for a better view, ducking to avoid the bat that had been disturbed. There was a statue of—

"Stop!" Rosalind's voice echoed in the cold air, freezing him in place. "Trap!" She seized his arm and jerked him towards her. She pointed to the bats gathered at the base of a stalactite. "This was in my dream. The floor," she pointed to a spot in front of where Cormac had stood, "will fall away. It is an endless pit."

He held tightly to her arm. "How are we to pass it?"

She winced. "I don't know."

"Great," said Loggie sarcastically. "Our first challenge."

"Stay here." Rosalind directed Cormac near the stalactite.

"And you?"

"I'll look around. Find the trigger and see what I can do."

"Here." He handed the torch to Kneilot, slipped off his pack and dug into the sack for rope. "Rosalind. Wrap this around you."

"It's unnecessary."

"Please. For me."

She hesitated, then reluctantly gave in.

"Just in case." He fastened the rope around her waist, tested it to ensure it wouldn't come undone, then gripped it firmly. "Search away."

She stepped closer to the questionable spot on the floor. "Hold the lights at different angles." Etain held the eternal flame low and Kneilot held the handmade torch high. The combination of lights revealed faint crevices in the floor. "There's a line. I think that's where it breaks away." She pointed to a spot six feet in front of her. Stepping closer, a soft click sounded in the cool air.

"Rosalind!" shouted Cormac.

She had no time to move. The floor disappeared, and she dropped over the side. He gripped the rope tightly, bracing for the weight. It jerked him forward, but he held on. Regaining his footing, he pulled with all of his might. Loggie grabbed hold of the excess rope behind him and together, they dragged her to the surface. "Help her," he said to Loggie. "Pull her up!"

Loggie jumped forward, grabbed hold of the back of her jacket and dragged her over the side. Once she was on solid ground, he drew her into his arms and held her tightly.

Cormac watched the pair. Ever since he'd met Loggie, he had sensed his fondness for Rosalind. They were good friends. If her memory returned, they might turn out to be more. He swallowed, and the lump in his throat made his eyes water. Blinking it away, he shoved the thought from his mind.

"Did you see what triggered it?" he asked.

"No," said Rosalind, out of breath. "It was too fast. Wow!" She slid away from the opening, and the floor slammed shut.

"At least we know where it is," said Etain. She stood behind Loggie and shone the light over the floor. "There's no ledge, so that means we have to avoid the trigger."

"Or find a way around," said Kneilot. "I don't feel safe walking over it even if the trap isn't triggered."

"There is no way around," said Cormac. "This is it."

Rosalind got to her feet and went to the wall. After examining closely, she went to the other side of the passageway. When she turned around, she was grinning. "He's right. There is another way." She slipped the tip of a dagger into a crack, and a narrow door slid open. "Bring the light over."

Etain held the light to the opening. "A secret passage. Well done."

Rosalind started to untie the rope, but Cormac stopped her. "Wait until we reach the other side. Please."

Her fingers froze on the knot. "Just to the other side. Give me six feet head start." She stepped into the opening and picked her way through the narrow passage.

Cormac stepped in with Etain close behind him with the magic torch, lighting his way. He coiled the rope and left slack for Rosalind to move forward. An odd smell lingered inside. It smelt like fox or...skunk. Sometimes it was hard to tell the difference between the two.

The passage went for 25 feet and ended in a solid wall. But he knew it couldn't be solid. There had to be a door. Rosalind searched around while he stood back in case the floor disappeared and Etain held the light so it shone on the wall.

"I feel a breeze," said Rosalind. She ran her fingers along a crack. They stopped on a stone four feet above the floor. It stuck out farther than the rest. She tugged on it, then pushed it. A door slid open. She turned to him and smiled. "There must always be an exit."

"That's the rule," he said.

She stepped into the main passageway, and he followed but not too closely. Just outside the door, on the side towards the trap, was the statue that had caught his attention. It was four feet tall, the same height as the stone inside the secret passageway.

Etain held the light closer. "It's a dragon. Not surprised."

"Neither am I," he said. He felt the top of the dragon's head. It was smooth and had a shallow dip in the centre, as if it was meant to catch water.

"One down; six to go," whispered Rosalind.

"We don't count the steps to death," said Loggie.

"Steps to life," she said.

"Not from this angle."

The sounds of the cave continued in the same manner as before. The bats clicked and the water dripped. The sound of wood against wood mixed with the buzz sound.

Rosalind untied the rope and gave it to Cormac, then she crept deeper into the cave. She travelled cautiously but the farther she went, the quicker she became. Cormac scanned the walls, floor and ceiling, trying to detect the next trap. The wizard who installed them wasn't fooling around. He didn't want anyone to rescue this dragon.

They travelled for at least ten minutes, taking gradual turns before they came upon a set of stairs. He held the torch forward but couldn't see the bottom. "Do you think they're safe?"

"We'll see." She pulled a stone the size of a baseball from the pouch she wore over her shoulder and tossed it onto the step. It bounced on five steps before it came to a stop. "I think these are." Before he could suggest the rope, she stepped onto the first one. Then the second. When she reached the rock, she picked it up and rolled it down the steps.

Cormac descended, keeping two steps back of her. She continued to throw the stone until it hit the bottom. By this time, everyone was on the staircase. He looked up. The top was bathed in shadow.

This passage went far beyond what he could see with the torch light. He proceeded, weary of sounds that indicated a trap had been sprung.

Not a minute later, Rosalind stopped and stared at the floor. "Hand me the torch." She held it over the floor before her. "It's a detailed design with dragon heads, symbols, letters and stars."

"Did you say letters?" asked Etain. She squeezed up alongside her and held the eternal flame over the floor. "Is this where we spell the name? Darkmoore with two Os?"

"Kragen Darkmoore," whispered Rosalind.

"A Glyph of Warding," said Cormac. He'd encountered one of these in a game. Everyone in his party survived, but someone got injured. He couldn't remember the details. His eyes roamed over it, taking in the many symbols and letters carved into the floor. The outline around each one wasn't straight or uniformed. It was more like a jigsaw puzzle. His eyes wandered farther, and he saw a glove. "Hold the torch to this side," he said.

Rosalind and Etain both held the torch closer to the wall. The light uncovered not only a glove, but an axe. He reached over, caught the handle and brought it to him. It was a small battle axe, a little too small for him, but... He turned to Loggie. "This may come in handy."

Loggie took it and flexed his wrist. "Sound. Like the one I used to throw for entertainment at the market in Doorock."

"Where did it come from?" asked Kneilot.

Everyone looked at him, and while Cormac wanted to tell him it was probably left behind by someone who was killed crossing this section of the cave, he kept his mouth shut.

"Someone may have lost it," said Etain softly.

"Then we shall bear it until we find them."

Cormac stared, his thoughts frozen on that option. Then he turned forward and reconsidered the Glyph, then the walls and ceiling five feet above. Seeing writing, he said, "Shine the light here." The torches highlighted letters as big as his head. He stepped back to read it. "THE GREATEST WIZARD OF ALL TIME." He hmphed. "Self-proclaimed."

"His ego was his undoing," said Etain.

"That's the clue to solving the riddle. I wonder if the symbols indicate anything. Do you know what they mean?"

"They're ancient. I've seen a few on items brought to the Sanctuary, but I don't know what they represent." She leant closer. "If Rosalind's dream is correct, we must step on the letters only. No symbols."

"The only way to know is to try," said Rosalind.

Cormac pulled off his pack to get the rope. "Not before you're secure." This time, she didn't hesitate and helped fasten the rope.

Then she turned. "D." It was in the second row of symbols and letters, next to K.

"Did that stone sink?" Cormac watched it closely.

"It felt like it did." She looked around. "I'm still here."

"Just go slow." He held the rope tightly, and he felt Loggie grab the end for extra support.

Rosalind reached for the A, stepped on it, then brought her other foot to it. She adjusted the torch, got her balance and stepped on R.

Humming mixed with the sounds of clicking and dripping water slowly grew louder. Cormac ignored it and focussed on Rosalind, watching where she stepped because he was next. She landed on K, and behind him Kneilot gasped. He ignored him. The stepping stones were always two levels apart. So far. When she stepped on M, Kneilot squealed.

"Spider!" Kneilot shrieked.

"Big spider," said Loggie.

Rosalind looked back at them, and her eyes grew wide.

"What?" said Cormac.

Her mouth dropped open and she pointed. "Quickly."

He looked at the ceiling and spit caught in his throat. It was alive. The letters that had given them the clue were consumed with spiders. One dropped on his shoulder, and he swatted it away.

"Quickly," said Etain. "Go now!"

"Take the torch!" demanded Rosalind. She prepared to toss it to him.

"You need it," said Cormac eyeing up the first letter.

"No! Take it!" The fierceness in her voice reminded him of the morning she'd awakened from the nightmare. She demanded he take the torch.

"Throw it." He caught it and held it over the stones. Seeing the D clearly, he stepped on it, then confirmed the position of the A. Glancing ahead, he saw Rosalind had almost reached the end. He reached for the R, then K. Darkmoore. M! He stepped on it.

"Two Os," she reminded him. "Two." She took up the slack of the rope as he advanced.

Behind him, he heard slapping and stomping. He wanted to check the condition of the others but instead focussed on the letters. Two Os. R and E. He leapt onto the solid floor beside Rosalind, then turned to light the path for the others. Kneilot skipped across the letters quickly, but he missed the R and struck the circle with the dot symbol beside it. He gasped and fell forward. In one motion, Cormac thrust the torch into Rosalind's hands, stepped on the E and grabbed Kneilot before he hit the floor. Dragging him onto solid ground, he sat him against the wall.

"Coldddd." Kneilot shivered. "Verrrry Coldddd."

Cormac yanked his jacket from his backpack and wrapped it around him. The shivering increased, and he rubbed Kneilot's arms briskly. The chicken cowered in her sack, watching him with dark, beady eyes. "A cold spell?" he asked Etain when she crossed.

She beat off the last spider and came to examine Kneilot. "Has to be. There's no logical reason he is this cold."

Loggie squealed, and Cormac half stood and looked in his direction. The dwarf had made the crossing and had pulled a spider from the back of his neck and threw it. "Nasty!"

Rosalind gave him a hug. When she saw another spider on his shoulder, she swatted it away. It scurried across the Glyph along with the others that had fallen. "I think they like you."

He frowned. "I dislike them. Strongly dislike."

"What do we do?" asked Cormac. He didn't have a warmth spell, and he doubted anyone else did.

"Rosalind, bring the torch closer," said Etain. "Kneilot, cup your hands, but don't touch the torch." She held his hands steady. "He should slowly warm up. Another jacket will help."

Loggie pulled off his and laid it over Kneilot's legs. Then he sat beside him, shoulder to shoulder. "Feeling any warmer?"

Kneilot nodded his head, but his teeth still chattered.

Cormac held the eternal flame higher. It illuminated a statue of a dragon on this side of the Glyph. "This statue is like the other one." He stood to see if the top was smooth with a dip in the centre. "Exactly. I wonder what goes in this indent." He looked around and shone the light farther into the passageway. Seeing a shadow, he was tempted to step back. "What is that?"

"Hold the light higher," said Loggie. He did, and he heard Loggie gulp. "Whichever block he stepped on, it wasn't the right one."

Cormac stilled his nerves and took a few steps forward. Lying in the middle of the passageway was a man. The skin had wasted away long ago, but his tattered clothes and equipment were intact. Another shadow farther on indicated another explorer had met his demise in this cave. One more step and the torch revealed the body had been pushed to the side. It appeared older than the first.

He looked back at Kneilot. Had the cold killed them? Or had they stepped on another stone that did worse damage? "Any improvement?"

"Yes," said Etain. "A few more minutes, and we'll continue."

"Never been so cold," said Kneilot, his voice shaking. "A hot tea would warm the blood and the spirit."

"We don't have time nor the ability to make a warm drink," she said. "Once you start walking, the blood will flow and warm."

The constant dripping consumed Cormac's senses. It was growing louder. But another noise was trying to overtake it. In one sense, it sounded like his stomach growling. In another, like a strong wind blowing through the crack of a window. What unsettled his nerves most was, it sounded like the growl of a large creature.

Rosalind held the torch steady until Etain waved it away. Kneilot's teeth had stopped chattering and his shaking was barely noticeable. She stepped closer to Cormac, who stood a few feet away, staring into the passageway they were to travel. The body sprawled across the floor looked like it had desperately tried to get away from the Glyph. Hearing a dull roar deep in the cave, she listened for more.

"Creepy, isn't it?" said Cormac.

"Not something I want to hear." She held the light closer to the dead man. "A dagger." She reached down and pulled it from beneath the arm. After inspecting it, she looked for a sheath.

"We're not supposed to take things from the dead," he said.

"Who said that?"

"Jowsey."

"A friend of yours?"

He was about to answer but closed his mouth.

"It seems a waste to leave it. He'll get no further use of it." She untied a leather sheath and stuck the dagger inside. With a dagger on her left hip and one on her right calf, she wondered where a third would fit comfortably. Right hip. She secured it, then tested the fit to see if she could slide it in and out easily.

Hearing noise behind her, she turned. Etain and Loggie were helping Kneilot to his feet. The hauflin shook off the shock of the cold and wiped his face with his hands. He checked on Matilda, found her safe, then held out Cormac's jacket to him. "Your generosity is greatly appreciated."

Cormac stuffed it into his pack along with the rope.

"Shall we continue?" said Etain.

Rosalind gave her the torch and stepped in front of Cormac, who held the eternal flame. She stepped around the body and walked past the second dead man, who lay against the wall. Twenty feet along, the flame illuminated another shadow.

"Three," whispered Cormac.

"Probably many more," she said with a quick glance. She wondered if these men had travelled alone, together or were with other companions who went farther. So far, she was yet to see the body of a woman. Another shadow up ahead revealed one more unsuccessful explorer. Passing it in silence, she made an unspoken wish that her fate would not be the same as theirs.

She walked for more than 30 minutes before she came upon an unusual sound. Mixed with the clicking of bats, distant howling of wind and water dripping was the clink of steel. It sounded five times, stopped, then repeated the pattern.

Seeing a soft shadow up ahead, she halted. "Hold the light ahead of me," she said.

Cormac stood next to her and held out the eternal flame. "What do you see?"

"Just a guess, but it looks like another dragon statue." Her face twisted. "Every time we see one, there's a trap."

"Why would he do this?" asked Etain. "It gives away the trap's location."

"Maybe locating the traps isn't the challenge." Loggie leant over her shoulder. "The question is, what will we encounter between here and there."

"That's 50 feet of uneven ground," said Rosalind. "Things are scattered about as if..." The objects strewn across the stone floor took shape. They were boots, a rucksack, sticks, a shield, even a sword. But no bodies. "This isn't good." She thought she saw movement near a pile of material but when she focussed on the spot, there was nothing there.

"What is it?" asked Cormac.

"I don't know." Movement caught her eye again.

"What did you see in your nightmare?" asked Etain.

She whirled around. "Kobolds," she whispered, her eyes wide.

"No," Cormac corrected her. "They were illusions."

"Just like on the plains," said Kneilot.

"But the troll was real." Loggie rubbed his chin and stared into the space.

"Somethings were real. Others were not." Rosalind wondered how to tell the difference between the two. She couldn't close her eyes if the kobold was real. The shadow near the lump of clothing moved. It crept close to the wall and approached the light. It was no more than a foot tall. Drawing closer, she saw its mouth with a full set of teeth grinning at her. Its big nose overhung the mouth, and its large, pointed ears flapped when it moved. The creature was bald and wore only a one-piece outfit, similar to a smock, that was tied at the waist. In its hand it cared a pick-axe. The eyes, cast in shadow, appeared deep and round.

She wanted to close her eyes to prove to herself it was an illusion, but she feared it would pounce and drive the axe into her.

"Do you see it?" she asked. "That thing?" She pointed at the kobold. "If only I see it, it's an illusion."

Cormac cleared his throat. "I see it."

"Unfortunately, so do I," said Loggie.

"Still, it may be an illusion." Etain held the torch in its direction. "There's more than one."

Rosalind swallowed slowly. "More than ten." She gasped. "There was more than a hundred in my dream."

"We can't do that many," said Cormac.

"They weren't all real." Loggie prepared the axe found earlier in the cave. "But how do we tell?"

"Focus," said Etain.

"Focus she says," Kneilot wrapped his arms around the chicken.

"Dagger ready," Etain said to him. "Prepare to fight. We must reach the dragon statue."

"Yes." Rosalind grasped a dagger tightly. "Focus on the statue and charge through."

"Running a gauntlet," quipped Loggie. "My favourite tavern entertainment."

The kobold drew nearer. Another popped out of the wall behind it. That had to be an illusion. There was only one. Or none. Or ten. "Let's go." She marched forward, dagger in hand. The kobold smiled, so did the three behind it. Three? Four. Now there were six to add to the others she'd already counted. She quickened her pace and slashed at the kobold when she passed. The pick-axe slammed against the blade of the dagger sending a shockwave up her arm.

Once past it, she slashed at the others following it. Ten feet down. Forty to go. Two kobolds fell from the ceiling, and she jumped back, banging into Cormac. He pushed her to the side and slashed at the creatures. One hollered in pain and fell to its knees. The other grinned and threw itself at her. It passed through but in the fear of being hit, she stumbled, tripped over a pile of clothing and fell.

By the time she got to her feet, the passageway was swarming with kobolds. Their shrill pierced her ears and the dozens of flopping arms confused her thoughts. Behind her, the air was filled with the clink of steel, grunts and shuffling feet.

"Keep going!" Cormac shoved her forward and swung the eternal flame at the creatures. They scowled and hissed at him.

"Faster," cried Etain. She ran alongside Cormac, dragging Kneilot behind her.

Rosalind returned her focus to the statue and raced ahead. Twenty feet down. A body landed on top of her shoulders, and Cormac grabbed it by the neck and thew it down. Two jumped on his shoulders and one wrapped around his leg. She kicked the one on his leg, sending it crashing into the wall. Stumbling over a kobold, she slammed into the floor. Before she could rise, they swarmed her, swinging their axes and striking her. Yet, she barely felt the weapons. Illusions! She threw them aside and jumped to her feet.

Etain and Kneilot were in front of her. Cormac and Loggie behind her. She pressed on, tripped, got up and ran. Thirty feet down. A kobold swung his axe and struck her calf, sending pain up her leg. She stumbled but regained her balance and kept running.

Cormac was keeping the creatures at bay with the eternal flame. The kobolds despised this more than the daggers. They swarmed around him, hissing and snapping their teeth at him. Loggie was three feet behind him, fighting through a mass of what appeared to be only illusions.

Etain and Kneilot reached the dragon statue. There, the kobolds stopped harassing them and turned on her. With ten feet to go, she charged through, tripped over an axe and slid to Etain's feet. She scrambled to stand and turned to see Cormac had 15 feet to go. Loggie a few feet more. A snap of string, a whistle and a thud stole the breath from her. She watched Cormac baulk and sway until he collapsed, the flame flying from his hand. The kobolds pounced, swinging their axes and screeching in victory.

"No!" Rosalind ran forward. Seeing the discarded sword from a previous explorer, she grabbed it and charged at the kobolds. She beat them off, both the real and the illusions. When she reached Cormac, he was on his hands and knees, trying to rise but unable to. Eight inches of an arrow stuck out of his side. His hand cupped the wound, and agony blanketed his face.

She tried to lift him, but he was too heavy. Loggie got beneath his arm and dragged him to his feet.

"Go," Loggie ordered. "I've got him." But he didn't have him, and he sagged under his weight.

Etain ran up and grabbed the other arm while Kneilot held the torch.

Rosalind swung the sword. It passed through the illusions and sliced through the real kobolds. She picked up the eternal flame and carried it back to where the others had stopped. The kobolds stood on their claimed ground, growling and hissing.

"Put him down," said Etain, and they rested him against the wall. "We have to stop the bleeding." She ripped open Cormac's shirt to examine the wound. "Hold the torch. The flame. I need both lights."

Rosalind rushed over and held the torch above Cormac. Blood had saturated both shirts he wore. The arrow had struck just below the ribcage.

"It needs to come out." Etain gave Cormac a grim look. "It must. It can't stay. This will hurt immensely."

Cormac gasped for breath, and his face twisted in pain. Sweat dripped from his forehead and tears left pathways through the dirt and dust on his cheeks. "Just... I know," he wheezed.

"Hold him down," said Etain. "Rosalind, sit on his arm. Loggie his legs. Kneilot, his other arm." Everyone got into position. "Bite on this instead of struggling." She rolled a bandana into a thick wad and put it between his teeth. His eyes grew wide and gawked at her.

Rosalind stared into his eyes, wishing this wasn't happening. She hadn't seen the arrow in her dream. At least she didn't remember it. If she had... What could she have done?

"Ready." Etain spoke quietly to herself.

Rosalind wondered if she was casting a spell. Catching Kneilot's gaze, she wondered if he had earned a healing spell yet. She was going to ask when Cormac jolted forward. She did her best to hold him down, but he was strong and threw her across his body into Kneilot, and they tumbled into the wall. He cried out and lay back gasping for air.

Etain had removed the arrow and held it up to the light. "It's intact." She tossed it aside and covered the wound with a rag.

Rosalind thought she heard whispering but when she looked around, there was nothing there. Even the kobolds had disappeared.

"Allow me," said Kneilot. He gently removed Etain's hand and placed his own over the cloth. "The noble and worthy Eir speaks to me and is granting me a gift." He bowed his head and mumbled words Rosalind didn't understand.

Waiting in silence, the cave sounds intensified and echoed off the stone walls. Their frosty breath mingled and formed a cloud. Cormac sighed and his expression relaxed. He kept his eyes closed and rested his hands on his chest. He appeared to want to sleep.

"Gracious, Eir," mumbled Kneilot. "I thank you for your amazing gift. I am humbled you chose me to deliver it. I am in your debt." Kneilot lifted his hand from the wound and removed the cloth. "It is truly a miracle." The wound had stopped bleeding and a scab had formed over the opening.

"You will make a great cleric," said Etain. She soaked a cloth in water and washed around the wound. Cormac groaned when she pressed too hard. "Time will heal it completely." She placed a clean dressing over the wound, then secured it by wrapping cloth around his torso.

Kneilot placed his hand on Cormac's forehead. "Eir has given the gift of healing. Honour it by leading a good and fair life."

"Thank you." Cormac's voice was hoarse. "Thank you. I was afraid..."

"Be not afraid. You are surrounded by loyal friends and watched over by gracious Eir. She is a goddess worthy of your acknowledgement."

Cormac's eyes watered but a smile graced his lips.

Rosalind picked up a discarded shield. "Next time, use this." She set it beside him and went to the sword.

"I don't want there to be a next time."

"None of us do," said Etain. She stood and surveyed the area. When she locked eyes with Rosalind, she half smiled. "Three down."

"The dragon statues mark the traps," she said, picking up the sword and examining it. "And what is left behind by the failures of others will aid in our quest." She rested the sword next to Cormac. "Every great fighter needs a sword."

"I am far from a great fighter."

"That which we act as and aspire to become are one and the same." She looked around. "I bet amongst these discarded belongs, I find a sheath for it." She held the eternal flame higher and searched through the items left behind by the dead. No bodies lay about, which made her wonder what or who had toted them off. She picked up a dagger and gripped the handle. It felt hot to the touch. An odd sensation travelled through her fingers and sent a shockwave through her hand. She dropped it and when it struck the ground, a red spark flew from it.

Seeing a long strip of leather, she pushed aside a tattered shirt and uncovered a scabbard. The design was simple, but the leather was still good. A belt pouch lay beside it, and she took that, too. Returning to Cormac, she slid the sword into the scabbard. "A perfect fit. When you're ready to stand, I'll help you fasten it."

His expression suggested he was confused, but it soon turned to embarrassment. "I am..."

"Perfect for this sword." She placed it in the scabbard across his lap. "You have proven to me you are worthy of this weapon."

He stumbled over words and finally said, "Thank you."

"You're welcome." She returned to the discarded and lost items and picked through them. Holding up a strip of leather, she examined it closely. "It's a bracer." She tilted her head. "I used to own one of these." She slapped it against her thigh to knock off dust and debris.

"Treasure." Loggie came to stand beside her and looked over the items. "There's a pair of boots for you."

"I don't need them. I prefer bare feet."

"A hat."

"Nope."

He picked up a pouch and opened it. "More treasure." He dumped the contents into his hand and held them below the flame light. "Two keys, flint, a ring and three playing cards. Hmph. I wonder why he kept only three." He moved the cards and found a small glass ball. Holding it up to the light, he turned it slowly. "Interesting."

"Looks like a marble."

"A marble? What is it used for?"

"Games. You need more than one."

"A child's toy." He was about to toss it back into the pouch with the other items, but she stuck out her hand.

"Can I have it and the ring?"

"Not the keys and cards?" She shook her head. "Discarded treasures for someone else." He gave her the ring and marble, stuffed the other items into the pouch and tossed it onto the pile. He lifted another item and held it up. "Still in working order." He glanced at Cormac. "A fighter needs a pauldron." He chuckled. "Who needs a keep. By the time we leave here, we'll have everything we need."

Rosalind took the leather shoulder protectors and dusted them off. They were solid with only a few scuff marks. Holding them up, she checked for size. The only person they would fit was Cormac. It was constructed in four layers over the shoulder and upper arm to allow full movement. The piece around the neck even had a thin stiff collar.

"There's something you don't see every day." Loggie held up a necklace with a silver cross hanging from it. The cross was two inches long with a blue stone in the centre. "I've only seen two in my lifetime."

"Aren't they common?" It looked extremely familiar.

"No. Popa says they come from a foreign land few visit."

"Where is this land?"

"I don't know. Not even Popa knows." He turned to her. "I think it's across the Neverending Sea, a place where some go but never return."

"Yet, this is here."

"A mystery." He set the necklace on the pile.

"You're not taking it?"

"It's meaningless to me, and I fear it brings bad omens with it. As I said, they are rare. Those who go, never return. There is no greater bad luck than never returning home."

She stood and went to Cormac. "I bring you protection." She held up the pauldron.

"You wear it," he said and took a drink from his water flask.

"It won't fit me."

"Again, robbing the dead," said Etain. "You'll curse us all." She smirked and helped Rosalind fit the pauldron over Cormac's shoulders. "We should all be so lucky to find such treasures."

After a short rest, they helped Cormac to his feet. He was a little unsteady but able to walk. He adjusted his added gear and stood with torch in hand, ready to go. Rosalind picked her way around the items strew across the passageway. One eye was on the path ahead and one scanned the floor to see what treasures she could find. After a hundred feet, the floor was clean of fallen objects and her full attention returned to finding the next trap. This section of the cave had many twists and turns. Most of the time, she felt like she was walking on a level surface but other times, if felt like she was walking down hill. Additional weird noises interrupted the usual sounds of the cave. Some sounded like screeching animals; others like whispering humans. If the intention was to keep her nerves on alert, it was working.

The homemade torch cast light up to 20 feet, and her hauflin vision extended that to 50 feet. When she saw what looked like a solid wall in the distance, she wondered if the passageway turned left or right. Forty feet away, a low grinding noise whispered to her. She slowed her pace but didn't stop. There was no sign of a dragon statue, but she didn't want to grow complacent in case the wizard had planned it all along, and there was no dragon at the next trap.

Her feet slid forward without warning and without any way to stop them. Her rump slammed against the stone floor, and her spit slapped against the roof of her mouth. Low shrieks and groans sounded behind her and when she glanced back, she saw everyone sliding towards her. The floor dropped quickly, and there was nothing to hold onto. The closer she got to the bottom of whatever this was, the more she stared. The floor was moving. Half a second later, she plunged into ice-cold water. Fighting to reach the surface, she was taken down when Cormac slammed into her.

She kicked and splashed and came to the surface, gasping for air.

"How do we escape?" Loggie was trying to cling to the wall, but it was smooth. "Quickly, before something else happens!" He searched the wall with his hands, running over the surface in a desperate attempt to find the solution.

Rosalind looked up. The ceiling over the floor that had collapsed disappeared into darkness. The ceiling directly above them was only a foot higher than the water.

"There," said Cormac, pointing towards an exit. He clung to the shield, giving him the extra support he needed to stay afloat. The torch he had held was extinguished in the water and floated near him.

"No," said Etain. "There." She pointed in the opposite direction at another tunnel.

"How do we choose?" Rosalind swam to the one near Cormac and tried to see down it. The water splashed over her face. The ceiling was getting closer. "It's rising!" Blood coursed through her veins.

"Wait," said Etain. She dove beneath the surface, taking the eternal flame with her and leaving them in the faint glow of its shine.

"Help." Kneilot was struggling to untie the sack on his chest.

Rosalind rushed over and helped, freeing the chicken. It squawked and floated on the water like a duck. "Chickens can swim?"

"They can," said Kneilot, out of breath.

Etain popped up, sucking in air and casting light on the ceiling. "This way." She pointed to where Cormac had said.

"How do you know?" asked Loggie.

"There's a dragon statue."

"Good enough for me." He swam towards it.

Rosalind and the others followed. The chicken swam past her as if it was doing the most natural thing a chicken could do. The water was cold, but it smelt fresh and tasted sweet.

"I can't swim much longer." Cormac gulped the words. He struggled under the weight of the sword and his clothes and against his injuries. If not for the shield, he'd have gone under.

Loggie swam over and supported him. "Let's say this is a short swim, and sunshine awaits on the other side." He banged his head on the ceiling and cursed in a language Rosalind did not know.

"Let it be truth you say," sputtered Cormac.

Etain led the way with the eternal flame. She swam at an awkward angle, tilting her head up to keep her mouth out of the water. "A little farther," she gasped.

Rosalind reached the statue. She dove down to view it and found it exactly like the previous ones. Back on the surface, she watched the others arrive. The chicken paddling around, dipping its beak into the water, lifting it up and smacking it as it drank.

When everyone reached the statue, Rosalind hoped the water would drain, but it didn't. Seconds passed, and when nothing happened, she turned and swam forward.

"Honestly," said Loggie. "We've done our bit. We've had our bath. It's time to end this deception."

But the water didn't drain away and kept rising. Rosalind swam farther. With the light cast by the eternal flame, she thought she saw an opening up ahead. The nearer she got, the more certain she became. Eager to travel the last 20 feet, she swam faster. Arriving at the corner, she found a flight of stairs going up. She breathed a sigh of relief and called to the others. "Here! Stairs." She climbed onto them, then turned to help.

"It is times like this I wish I had ignored my calling and had gone back to bed." Loggie dragged his sopping body onto the stairs and lay against them, catching his breath.

"And miss all this excitement?" Rosalind grinned.

The chicken clucked, stepped out of the water and shook its feathers, spraying everyone with mist.

"It's excitement like this..." Loggie wiped his face with his hand, "that will make me run back to Popa."

Her grin widened until she looked at Cormac. He was in visible pain. He sat on the step and rested his back and head against the wall. He stared at the ceiling and gulped air. She tried to find words of encouragement, but nothing came to her. Instead, she put her hand on his leg and rested it there. His gaze fell to her, but he didn't say anything. He was a strong man, but he needed rest. That wouldn't come until they escaped the cave.

"Let's move," said Etain. She stood, adjusted her wet clothes and considered the stairway.

Rosalind rose slowly. Her body was tired, and it ached. She had bruises where she'd never had them before. Reaching out a hand, she offered it to Cormac. He was in worse shape. If he could do it, she could. "This pizza you speak of," she said, and his eyes fell upon her, "we will make it when we reach Delgrath."

"I will help." His voice had lost its energy.

"The flame," she reached for it, and Etain gave it to her. She then passed it to Cormac. "You need it more than we do." Drawing a deep breath, she started up the stairs. It was a short flight, and 20 steps later, she was on level ground and peering down a long passageway. It looked endless, yet she knew it wasn't. Somewhere down its twisted path was a dragon in desperate need of saving.

15

Puzzles in a Cube

CORMAC PAUSED AND leant against the wall to catch his breath. Kneilot and his goddess had removed the greatest pain with the healing spell, but the ache surrounding the injury throbbed. Standing still eased it and if he could sleep, he might forget about it. But moving constantly and holding up the eternal flame gave life to the damage.

"A moment to rest," said Rosalind. She took the flame from his hand. "Drink."

He removed the cork from the flask and took a log swig of water. His parched throat craved the liquid. He should have filled it at the bottom of the stairs with the water flooding the dungeon, but he had been too weary to think of it and no one else had thought to fill their flask. His water was half gone, and he feared he'd not get a chance to fill it until they retraced their steps to the cave opening.

All his other thoughts gathered around and focussed on that one thought: retracing his steps. If the traps worked the same coming from this direction, he didn't... He brushed them aside. Dwelling on them made his body heat and his heart race.

"I'll hold the flame for a spell," said Rosalind. "Give your arm a break."

"Or give it to me," said Loggie. "Not to say you're the shortest but..." he surveyed the others, "you are the shortest."

She gave him the torch. "Then you'll be second."

"Of course, my lady." He bowed ceremoniously. "A jester and the princess. I shall play for you when the day is done."

After a few minutes, Cormac came off the wall and stretched his shoulders. The leather pauldron was a neat touch to his outfit. If he survived this nightmare of an adventure and returned home, he'd add it to his character's wardrobe. He grimaced. Thoughts of playing the game now felt strange. It would be like playing a roll-playing game around teens in high school. Once you lived it, how could you play it?

His hand rested on the hilt of the sword. In all his time in this realm, this was the first time he'd gotten to wear one. Own one. Yet, he preferred roaming the land without one now that he would be forced to use it in a life or death battle. Unlike what he had imagined, it felt awkward. It wasn't heavy, but he knew it was there and the added weight played with his balance. For now, Rosalind carried the shield. More to rest his body than for protection.

"Let's go," said Loggie. "I will not see sunshine standing here."

Rosalind walked on, and Loggie followed her. Cormac fell into step behind him, then it was Kneilot and his chicken, then Etain.

Twenty minutes later, the passageway narrowed. It became so tight, he had to turn sideways to continue.

"I feel like a sandwich," said Loggie.

"I am hungry, too," said Kneilot. "Perhaps at the next rest, I could eat the bread and carrot I have."

Cormac felt hungry, too, but he'd rather get this over with than eat. Loggie looked back at him with an eyebrow raised. "What?"

"I actually feel like a sandwich," he said. "Squished between two slices of rock."

He grinned. "Let's hope the sandwich doesn't grow thinner."

"Can we still stop to eat?" asked Kneilot.

"If you can eat in the time of five minutes," said Etain. "I feel no hunger, only apprehension for that which awaits us."

"And that does not sit well in my gut," said Loggie. "Vomit, I will. Share it with the bugs inhabiting the floor, so they can share my misery."

"Is it truly your dream to play for kings and queens?" asked Cormac.

He hmphed. "It's my popa's dream. I'll not be of any success less I play for royalty. In his eyes."

"What about you? What do you want?"

His face brightened beneath the eternal flame. "To play for the common working man, the one who thinks not of castles and trophies but of family, home and joyful times."

"At taverns."

He shrugged. "It is the drinking man who compensates me for entertaining the working man."

"It's getting a wee bit narrower," said Rosalind over her shoulder.

"And here I thought I'd not experience the joy of being squeezed into a boot too small." Loggie held the flame higher so his arm wouldn't bang against the stone.

"A passage this narrow is an effortless defense against the fat man." Cormac's back brushed against the stone.

"And possibly humans." Loggie had more wiggle room. He wasn't as short or as stout as dwarfs in fantasy movies. He appeared as strong yet more agile.

"It's getting wider." Rosalind's voice bounced off the stone.

"Excellent," said Loggie. "A break from breathing in the moist breath of others."

Cormac grunted. The man had something to say about everything.

"Escaping this flue without the release of flatulence has given shine to this otherwise dreadful day." Loggie adjusted the flame again.

"While I had not thought of that," said Rosalind, giving him a hard look, "I am also pleased particularly since I caught whiff of your inner gas release this morning."

Cormac laughed but not too hard. Laughing made his side hurt. With the widening of the passageway, he had room to walk straight. Another 20 feet, and the passageway widened to six feet.

"Hold the light higher," said Rosalind. "Slow down."

Cormac stretched his neck and looked through the glow of the flame. The first 20 feet were clear, but something rested just beyond the edge of the eternal flame. "What is it?"

Rosalind stopped, and everyone squeezed around her. "Bodies. Several."

"Do you see a dragon statue?" His muscles stiffened. He wasn't ready for another challenge.

A long pause followed. "That might be it, but it's at the extreme of where I can see." She adjusted the wooden shield. It was almost half her height.

"Anything from your dreams?" asked Etain. "A hint of what's to come?"

"I can't think of anything. We've done the disappearing floor. The Glyph and the illusions." She fell silent. "I hadn't seen the sliding floor, but I had imagined water."

"The illusions weren't in your dream," said Loggie. "They were on the plains."

Cormac considered that. No, the illusions were in both: her dreams and the plain. "Hail," he said. Everyone looked at him. "The hail was unusual. What if the dragon caused it to give us a hint?"

"Hail indoors." Loggie chuckled. "It will be followed by sunshine."

"He might be onto something." Etain leant forwards. "There are piles of small things around the bodies. It's starts about 20 feet this side of them."

"Hail would melt," said Loggie.

"We assume it would." She took the eternal flame and walked a few feet forward. "There's something beside those bodies."

"Can we go around it?" asked Kneilot.

Rosalind gave him a hard stare. "That won't work every time."

"But maybe here it will." He clutched his chicken and gave her a hopeful look.

She turned back to the passageway and reconsidered it. "Let's get closer."

"Said the hangman to the doomed man." Loggie walked behind her.

Cormac followed but kept a few steps behind. He wanted a clear view of what was to happen. She stopped ten feet from the first pile of debris.

"Pebbles," said Rosalind. "Small ones. Like marbles." She held the shield over her head. "We need four more."

"When in need, we improvise." Etain removed her pack and held it above her head. "Not a shield but it should soften the impact. But first." She dug gloves from a side pocket and put them on.

Cormac did the same and donned his jacket. While pulling on his gloves, he wondered if it was going to be this easy. "The stones must be moving fast to take down those men." He winced and already felt the pain in his gut from the thought of moving quickly.

"They must be shot like an arrow." Etain adjusted her pack.

"They will go through the pack," said Kneilot. He buttoned his jacket to the neck, turned up the collar and tucked the chicken's head inside.

"Let's hope not." Etain faced the passageway. "Run. Fast. Just go. Loggie, keep the flame moving to guide us around the bodies."

"Remember my faith in you, fair maiden," he said. "We shall dance amongst the flowers to hear bees buzz."

"I'll settle for seeing the sun," said Cormac. "No dancing. No flowers."

"A celebration without dancing is hardly a celebration."

Rosalind held the shield high. "Ready?" She glanced behind and beside her. "Let's go. Jog until we reach the pebbles, then run like you're making the dash to home plate." She led the way.

Before Cormac reached the first piles of pebbles, a strong breeze blew in his face. His hair flared to the sides, and he kept his eyes on the ground ahead, waiting for the stone hail to fall. The floor rumbled below him, unnerving him more than he already was. It was followed by sharp pinging sounds, like the sound of pellets flying from an airgun. A sharp pain on his cheek made him swat his skin, fearing a bee had stung him. Something struck him in the arm, making him wince.

"Not from above!" shouted Rosalind. She moved the shield to the side of her body.

"I feel that!" Loggie drew his pack down to guard his side and held up his free hand to protect the opposite side of his face.

Cormac felt multiple impacts on the sides of his body before he brought down his pack. Unable to protect both sides, he held the pack on the side that had taken the arrow. He kept running, absorbing the pain, knowing it would end when he reached the dragon statue. He couldn't see the statue, but he knew it had to be there.

Before Rosalind reached the first body, the air filled with a high pitch sound. It made her stumble and lurch forward. She tried to cover her ears but couldn't do that and hold the shield. Leaping over the first body, she tripped over the second. Loggie helped her up and cried out in pain as the assault of the pebbles increased.

Kneilot shouted behind Cormac, and he turned to see the young cleric had fallen. He stopped to yank him to his feet. Etain rushed by with horror written on her face.

"Side-by-side," Cormac gasped. "Ow! Protect that side." He held the pack to protect his face and dragged Kneilot along on the opposite side. Together, they were protected from the harshest of stones, but the screeching sound numbed his ear drums.

Rosalind, seeing what he was doing, latched onto Loggie and copied the move. She attempted to include Etain, but the woman raced past her, tripped over a body, rose and ran again. Whatever possessed her, it blocked logical thinking. She sped from the light of the eternal flame and disappeared into darkness.

The stones increased the farther he went, and if not for Kneilot blocking the left side of his face, he was certain he'd be on the floor with the dead. Shielding his face, he didn't know how far he'd travelled nor how much farther he had to go. He ran blindly. When Kneilot stumbled, he steadied him and dragged him along.

Finally, the projectiles ceased along with the horrendous screeching, and he staggered forward and collapsed to the cold, damp floor, taking Kneilot with him. He lay against his pack, fighting for breath and grappling with the agony in his side. Squeezing his eyes shut, he braced his muscles, which only increased the ache from his injury. He coughed and sputtered, and his body shook. His ears throbbed and sent shockwaves of pain into his temples. The natural sounds of the cave were barely a whisper as was the groaning and gasping of his fellow companions. It was worse than any rock concert he'd attended. Not even standing next to the speakers while Aerosmith jammed on stage had felt this horrible. At that time, his ears rang the entire next day, but they didn't ache.

Gulping in air, he opened his eyes and stared at the dim floor. He glanced up to see where the eternal flame was. It lay next to Loggie, who rested on his hands and knees, panting with spit dripping from his mouth. His face was blotchy with red welts. He groaned and cursed in his dwarven language.

Rosalind lay on her side next to Loggie, staring off into the distance. Her face wore the same red patches, and blood oozed from her forehead. She flinched and closed her eyes. Her shivering increased, and a low whimper escaped her lips.

Kneilot rolled to his butt and inspected the chicken. It clucked loudly, as if it wanted to disturb the dead.

Cormac glanced back at the bodies scattered across the floor. He didn't have to wonder how they died. If they were ill prepared, they would have succumbed to the onslaught. If they had travelled alone, they'd have no one to help if they stumbled. Though their skin had rotted away, he imagined their faces wore the scars of being peppered to death with stones the size of playing marbles. As they lay in their final moments of life, they'd have been driven completely mad by the horrendous sound, shattering their ear drums.

He pushed himself to his knees and slid back to sit on his feet. Digging a wet rag from his pack, he wiped his face. It came away smeared with sweat, dirt and blood.

"I will never cross another bridge 'til my bones are rotting in the ground, and I am dead of feeling," gasped Loggie. His face contorted, and he wiped his brow with his wet sleeve. "A curse is too kind a word to describe this torture."

"I shall reach Delgrath and never leave," said Kneilot. "Though I would like to settle in Spiritwood amongst peaceful hauflins where dragons and curses don't exist nor torture chambers like this cave."

Rosalind stood on shaky legs. Lifting the shield, she staggered and fell against the wall next to the dragon statue. "Etain!" she shouted, then held her forehead and closed her eyes as pain ripped across her face. She regrouped and called again. When no answer came, she stumbled forward.

"Wait for us." Cormac got his feet under him but lost his balance and slammed against the wall. Pain erupted all over his body. He gathered his senses and steadied himself on his feet. He wabbled side-to-side. If he had a walking stick, he'd use it, but he had nothing but the wall.

Rosalind disappeared into the shadows before Loggie was ready. Her voice, calling out to Etain, floated down the passage.

"Come on." Loggie stumbled forward holding the eternal light.

Cormac waited for Kneilot to stand, then they both followed him. He travelled at least 60 feet before he heard voices. Another 30, and the flame cast light upon Rosalind and Etain. Rosalind was rocking her in her arms and speaking softly. Etain clung to her. Tears streamed down her blotchy face. She gulped air and shivered uncontrollably.

Loggie rushed forward and dropped to one knee. "What evil is this?"

"She said it was like a thousand voices wailing in pain," said Rosalind. "Women and children crying out for help."

"That's not what I heard," said Loggie. "The pitch was screeching. Painful to the ears."

"She heard something different."

"Her connection with magic must have induced those voices." He gave Cormac the eternal flame. Then he drew a rag from his rucksack and held it to Etain's forehead. She jumped and held onto Rosalind tighter. "It's okay." He spoke softly and caressed her cheek. "They were not truly there. An illusion to terrify you."

She blinked several times and stared up at him. "My heart shivers from their cries." She sucked in air, and her bottom lip trembled.

"I have nothing to dull the memory but time." He patted her face, wiping dirt and tears from the many red spots.

"A drink." Kneilot held out his flask to Etain. "It will help ease the suffering within."

She took a sip and wiped her mouth. "You added herbs?"

"It's a diluted herbal tonic to refresh you."

She took another drink, this time longer. "Ahh. It possesses a sweet, lovely taste. Thank you." She handed him the flask.

Cormac sat to rest next to Rosalind. It felt like he'd been in the cave for days. Thinking about time, he wondered if night had fallen. Or was it the next day? His body was exhausted, but that was probably due to his injuries and escaping the traps. Could they have entered the caves only three or four hours ago?

Rosalind waited until Etain was breathing and talking normal before suggesting they move on. When she stood, she felt sorer than when she'd first escaped the onslaught of stones. She rubbed several spots that were especially sore, ones that were hit multiple times by the projectiles. After taking a drink, she shook the flask. Almost empty. She slung it over her shoulder, threw on her rucksack and picked up the shield. Cormac held the eternal flame. He was battered and bruised and walked with a limp. Surveying the small group, they looked like they had been in an horrendous battle. Bruises and cuts marred their faces and hands. No doubt they suffered similar bruises beneath the soiled, wet clothing.

Turning to the passageway that led to the dragon, she waited until everyone stepped in line. Cormac was behind her, then Etain, Kneilot and finally Loggie. Drawing a deep breath, she stepped forward, leaving the dead far behind.

Reaching the end of this passageway, she turned right, then left, then took a flight of stairs down, then turned left again. All the while, she listened for sounds other than clicking, howling winds, dripping water and the squish of wet leather boots. She searched for tripwires, cracks in the floor and the ominous dragon statue.

The passageway turned right, and she stopped. Six feet away, it opened to a larger space.

"What is it," whispered Cormac.

"A room."

"Where the dragon is?"

She looked at him over her shoulder, considering the possibility. "We passed through only five traps."

"Maybe there are only five."

She walked to the threshold. "Shine the light in front of me." Cormac held the flame inside the room. "There's a walkway down the centre. On either side is water."

"Is there a dragon statue?"

"I can barely see the far end, but it looks like a door. No statue."

"Just a walkway?" asked Loggie.

"It appears to be. The ceiling is high. At least 30 feet."

"Take a real good look before stepping forward," said Cormac. "Etain, another set of eyes." He moved aside and let her stand beside Rosalind. He held the flame above their heads.

"It appears...safe," said Etain, her voice still quivering. "Yet, I feel it is far from it. A dragon statue is not visible."

"And the door?"

"Closed."

"Are you sure it's a door?"

"Impossible to know unless I touch it."

Rosalind stepped into the room and stopped. Nothing happened. She took another step. Everything remained still.

"The dragon must be behind the door," whispered Kneilot. "It is a sight I fear will give me nightmares."

Rosalind stared at him. "Has nothing this day provoked the possibility of those?"

He clamped his mouth shut and looked away.

She walked on. With every step, she scanned the room, looked ahead to the door and glanced at the water lining the walkway. The sounds she'd come familiar with, the clicking, howling winds and dripping water, faded into the background. In this room, there was nothing but silence. She strained her sore ears, hoping to hear the whispers of the dragon that haunted her dreams. If he rested beyond this door, they had met the challenges offered and would escape.

But a large dragon could never travel the path through the cave she had to reach this spot. If magic put him here, then magic had to remove him. She hadn't considered this problem until now. How was she to get the dragon out of the mountain? Was that why he remained a prisoner within it?

Twenty feet from the door, she saw writing upon it. "Etain, can you read it? It's a mixture of..." She stared at the cube resting on the ground outside the door. It looked like it had been dropped or thrown there. It was the size of a softball. Nine colourful squares decorated each side.

"Colours galore," said Etain, reading the writing above the entrance. "Make them solid to open the door."

"What does that mean?" Rosalind picked up the cube. Before she stood upright, the doorway they had entered through was sealed by a thick slab of rock. A four-foot section of the floor sank into the water.

"What's that?" Kneilot pointed at ripples on the water.

"Something I'd prefer not to meet under any circumstances," said Loggie.

"How can we make the colours solid?" asked Etain. She held up the block. "There are six different colours spanning the cube."

"Let me see that." Cormac stepped closer and stared at the cube. "This can't be."

"Be what?" asked Rosalind. She'd never seen it before, yet it looked familiar.

"A Rub—" He looked up. "I used to have one of these."

Another section of the walkway sank into the water, creating a six-foot span between it and the entry point. Something large swam through it, leaving a small wake.

"You know how to make colours solid?" asked Etain.

"If you do, do it quickly," said Loggie. "No time for pleasantries when my life grows shorter by the second.

"I can. I have." He took the cube and twisted a row of colourful blocks. "The blocks are painted." He looked up grinning. "Impossible to move stickers and cheat."

"Incredible," said Etain. "They move."

"My friends and I would challenge each other to see who could solve the puzzle fastest." He grinned and spun another row. "Seth always beat us." He turned another row of colours one way, then the other. "My best time was 45 seconds. Our cubes were made of plastic, but this feels like stone."

Another chunk of walkway slipped into the water.

"Less talk; more solving," said Loggie. "If my calculations are correct, we have less than a minute before we are devoured by the monster swimming laps."

Rosalind watched Cormac's fingers fly over the cube, moving the colours one way, then the other. Already, he had most of the colours lined up.

"Damn." He ran through another series of moves. "It's been more than five years." Another chunk of walkway sank, and he stared back at it.

"Ignore what's happening here," said Loggie, who squeezed against Kneilot to escape the edge of the advancing walkway. "Solve the puzzle. I'll watch as death approaches."

Cormac's hands moved swiftly over the cube, trying one way and when that didn't work, a different way. Another chunk of walkway disappeared beneath the surface of the water. Click, click, click. "Done!" He held up the cube. Each side was a solid colour. "What do we do with it?" He watched another section of walkway disappear. Only six feet remained.

"Here." Etain grabbed it and stuck it into a square hole next to the door. In a flash, the door in front of them and the door they had entered through slid open, and the walkway that had sank resurfaced.

Rosalind saw a dragon statue on the other side of the door and was about to step over the threshold when Kneilot spoke.

"Who is that?"

She turned and moved her head to look around everyone. A tall woman and a man equal in height entered the room. The woman wore dark clothing, tight pants topped off with a flimsy skirt shorter in the front than in the back. A black jacket trimmed with white and pulled tight around the waist flared over her broad hips. Black hair was pulled back and hung over one shoulder. The pasty skin in the dim light gave the impression she had never seen the sun. Her eyes were as dark as the image she projected.

The man beside her was larger and taller than Cormac. He wore dark clothing typical of rugged men travelling in such places as this cave. In his hand, he carried an eternal flame. The closer they came, the more she recognised the smug expression on his bearded face. He knew a vital piece of information she didn't, and he knew she didn't.

Looking past him, she saw three other men but couldn't make out many details as they were mostly blocked by those who led the procession across the walkway.

"A miracle you all survived the Caves of Darkmoore." The woman's raspy voice resounded off the water and stone walls. "An impressive feat."

"Who is she?" whispered Rosalind.

"If I knew, I've forgotten," said Loggie.

"She looks not like a witch I've met." Etain stared intently as if she was picking apart the woman with her eyes.

"She reminds me of Mia." Kneilot wrapped his arms around his chicken.

"Guthro," mumbled Loggie.

Etain gasped. "A sharp eye to recognise degenerates."

"He was working against Jowsey," whispered Cormac. "And they were..." He paused. "This doesn't make any sense." He lifted his head and raised his voice. "Who are you?"

"The beautiful and enchanted mistress of the magnificent Thornheart Fortress." She stopped five feet away and crossed her arms. Her dark eyes raked over the party of adventurers. "The most wonderous Shayde Thornheart. If I must introduce myself, I gladly do."

Cormac scrunched up his face. "Shayde Thornheart is an old woman?"

She hmphed. "As if a man could do what I've done." She ushered them towards the open door with the flick of her long, black fingernails. "Let's take this discussion into the master's suite, Darkmoore's palace within the stone."

Rosalind glanced behind her. It was a large room with furniture. She backed away and searched beyond the glow of the eternal torch to see if a dragon lurked in its recesses, but the room was longer than 60 feet. In width, it was only about 30 feet. One side held the standard furniture for living: chairs, table, double bed. On the other side, several tables crammed with jars, bottles and sacks rested against the wall. The walls were decorated with tapestries depicting dragons, castles and fireballs shooting through the sky. Beneath them hung various containers and weapons: swords, daggers, shields, staffs, bows, arrows and spears.

"Fascinating," gasped Loggie. "Truly a treasure not of a dragon but of a desperate man's need to feel important."

"A fair assessment of the man who killed himself in his work." Shayde Thornheart stepped over the threshold. Her eyes grew wide as she gazed at the interior of the room. "A treasure worth the hassle of the inconvenience of organising the demise of many."

Rosalind stared at the woman. There was something vaguely familiar about her, but she couldn't place her. "Have you seen her before?" she whispered to Loggie.

"No, you?"

"I feel I have, but...it was long ago and beyond my memory."

Thornheart's eyes settled on Rosalind. "What do they call you?"

"I am Rosalind."

The woman raised an eyebrow. "More fitting than Ruth. I've always hated that name."

"What do we do with him, your highness?" asked one of the men standing behind her.

She didn't bother to turn, merely flicked her hand to the side. "Toss the garbage in the corner. He's served his purpose."

Two of the men dragged a tattered young man across the floor. He appeared only half conscious. He groaned and moved his head, but he had no strength to stand or struggle. They dropped him near the wall and walked away.

"Jowsey!" Etain squealed and ran to him. She helped him to sit up and gently leant his head against the wall.

"You remember the scoundrel." Thornheart cackled. "He's all yours. No payment required."

Etain turned on her. "You're a dastardly person."

The sorceress placed her hand over her heart. "I'm crushed you'd think so horribly of me."

Rosalind didn't know who this man was but if his name was Jowsey, she wondered if he was the same man her friends had spoken about. Loggie and Cormac stood next to her, rigid, as if they were attempting to hide their injuries. Kneilot went to Etain and knelt on the other side of Jowsey. They spoke in hushed voices.

Shayde Thornheart sauntered around the room, dragging her finger along the edges of furniture and leaving a line in the dust, lifting an item to inspect it closer and flicking things out of the way.

Rosalind's nerves were on fire. The more she watched the woman, the more she despised her. But she didn't know why.

"Why are you here?" asked Cormac. "Did you get cursed by crossing Beguiled Dragon Bridge?"

Her chuckle triggered irritation in Rosalind's ears. The way she strolled around the cavern suggested she'd been here before or had enough knowledge of the place to not be surprised by its contents.

"No curse necessary." Thornheart stopped at a table, picked up a wand and waved it around. She hmphed and tossed it aside. "Archaic magic not worth my time. However..." she turned and slowly scanned the room, pausing on an ornate door near an elaborate armchair, then her gaze settled on Rosalind, "there's a bounty of treasure in this horde that *is* worth the effort."

"This is the treasure Jowsey's map led to?" asked Cormac.

"He spoke of it to you?"

"In a round about way."

She mulled around the table, then went to another. "Coincidence, or is it ironic? I can never distinguish between the two. That the treasure exposed by the map is the same that brought you here to escape the curse. One and the same."

"Are you here to free the dragon?" asked Rosalind. "Or just the treasure?"

"The dragon is the treasure."

"Not all this?"

She huffed. "Kragen Darkmoore was an inept magician. It's why he was killed by his own trap."

"Who told you that?" Rosalind adjusted her weight and eyed the many weapons on the wall. They were designed for people of various sizes. Swords with four-foot blades as well as two-foot. Bows easily used by tall humans as well as shorter hauflins. The largest staff was six feet tall. One she eyed was only four feet; perfect for her. She imagined she could take someone's feet from under them if she struck the back of their knees with it.

"People. Here and there." Thornheart stood in front of the ornate door and studied the pattern.

"Are they still alive?"

She half chuckled. "No one lives forever." She slid her hand along the frame of the door, grasped a stone and pushed it in. The door slid open. "And there is the most pathetic participant in this cave of tricks. Unable to complete the final eight steps of his own design. What a fool."

Rosalind came closer and Loggie and Cormac followed. She peered through the opening and saw a short passageway five feet wide and eight feet long. Sprawled across the floor was a skeleton in dark pants, bright blue shirt and black cape that had flopped to the side. All that was left besides the bones was a head of thick blond hair.

A step closer brought into view glass balls that would fit comfortably in her hand. They were strewn across the floor as if the man had been carrying them and they had flown from his grip when he fell. The balls weren't clear. Something swirled within. They looked like an enlarged marble.

"Is that Kragen Darkmoore?" Rosalind's voice sounded small, and she cleared her throat. "The man who created this torture chamber?"

"That's him. In all his glory."

"How do you know?" She looked up at Thornheart. The woman was late 50s, maybe early 60s. A thick layer of make-up tried to obscure her age, but the wrinkles were too deep.

"I've hunted the right people. Those with secrets they didn't want to take to the grave."

"Like Jowsey?"

She laughed. "A useless pawn fulfilling dreams of adventure. I'm talking about those of great wisdom who can be bought." She looked down at her. "How much are you?"

"Priceless."

"I recall a time when you'd sell your soul for less than the boots you wear."

Rosalind didn't look down. She wore no boots. "Liar. You don't know me."

"I may know more about you than you do."

She wanted to call her on it, but given the lack of memory, she wasn't sure if that was a lie.

"Ah, hesitation. It reveals the truth of your history." She leant forward and whispered. "Do not worry, child. I am here to help."

Rosalind stepped back. "I do not want nor need your help."

"You'll get it anyways." She straightened. "But first, we need to clear away the dead, open that door and rescue my bondservant. I need a volunteer."

"For what?"

"To open that door." She pointed past Darkmoore's body.

"Not interested."

"Oh, I wouldn't accept you." Thornheart surveyed the others in the room. "I need someone brave. Someone disposable."

"We're not here to help you," said Cormac.

"Oh, dear, sweat boy, I don't—"

"I'm a man, not a boy." His eyes narrowed.

"So, you are." She admired his body and slowly licked her top lip.

"What killed Darkmoore?" asked Rosalind.

"Stupidity." Thornheart laughed at her joke. The rest stood silent. She collected herself. "His own doing, of course. The last challenge was to walk through this passage. It is the simplest of the traps. One either reaches the door with ease or dies right there. There is no in-between. No survivable injuries sustained. Once the door is open to the other side, anyone can enter. However, to open it, one of courage must do it. If an ounce of cowardliness exists within the heart, a thousand rays will shoot down and kill him." She chuckled. "Maybe not a thousand rays. No one knows for sure what is the final stab to the heart. We know only he did not pass the test."

Cormac stepped back.

"No, don't go. You're the perfect subject. Young. Handsome. Courageous."

"While I do not doubt he is capable of passing the test," said Rosalind, "what's in this for you?"

"Knowing I have freed a helpless dragon." She laid the back of her hand on her forehead and feigned sympathy. "This poor dragon has suffered enough."

"Liar!" Jowsey stumbled forward with Etain's assistance. "Liar! She can never be trusted." His face was strained, beaten black and blue, and blotchy, as if he had no protection when he crossed the hail of stones nor when encountering kobolds. One eye had been swollen shut, and blood dripped from the corner of his fat lip.

"Ah, he lives." Thornheart frowned. "Thought the torment of a thousand elves being massacred would have done him in."

Rosalind reconsidered him. He was elf. Had he, like Etain, heard the screams of women and children? Had it been her race, not her magic that inflicted the torture?

"Would you like me to finish him?" asked Guthro. "Reg and I could feed him to the moat monster."

"Later." She turned towards the passageway leading to the dragon. "Business before pleasure." She pointed at Cormac. "Bring this boy to me."

Cormac drew his sword and held it in a defensive manner. Loggie held his axe at the ready.

Thornheart laughed. "I did not come this far without breaking a sweat to lose a drop now." She rolled her hands over one another, mumbled foreign words, then directed her fingers at Rosalind. "Kneel."

An unseeable force dragged Rosalind to her knees. She tried to get up, but the force held her arms to her sides and kept her on the ground. Cormac rushed over and tried to lift her, but he couldn't move her.

"Wasting your energy," said Thornheart. "Only I can free her." She strolled over to Rosalind and grasped her chin. "Your prince charming will open that door, or you won't live past..." she checked her imaginary wristwatch, "let's say five minutes." She flung her chin to the side and straightened. "This crushing spell will slowly increase pressure. Bones will snap under the strain. Eyes will pop." She shook her head in disgust. "You get the picture. A mess no one wants to clean up." She went to the passageway. "You have five minutes to open the door. If you die on the way, that reduces the time for the next person. She will not be released until that door is open." Her final words were growled, then she pasted on a smile. "Now go."

Cormac dropped to one knee before Rosalind. His battered face was strained, his eyebrows bent in pain. "I can't do it," he whispered. "I'm just not..."

"Yes, you can," she said. "I believe in you."

"I don't believe I can."

"Don't let fear control you. A good man once said, *Courage is being afraid and saddling up anyways.* You saddle up every time."

"If I don't make it..."

"Tell me when you get the door open."

He stared at her with longing in his eyes. When she thought he'd stand, he leant forward and brushed his lips against her forehead.

"I thought you were going to kiss me," she grinned. "For luck, but then I realised you don't need that. You have courage."

Surprise ripened on his face, and he leant forward and kissed her lips gently. "A kiss for courage," he whispered.

"Good grief," said Thornheart. "Puppy love makes me sick."

Rosalind felt the force holding her increase in pressure. She was able to breathe, but it felt uncomfortable.

Cormac sheathed the sword, glanced back at her then went to the passageway. His shoulders stiffened, and he stared at the door.

"Waiting until death crushes your crush?" asked Thornheart.

Cormac frowned at her and stepped forward.

"May the gods walk with you," whispered Etain.

"And the goddesses," said Kneilot. "Together, they will help you defeat this evil."

Cormac shot him a quick look, then took another step. Two feet from Darkmoore, he paused. From this point of view, Rosalind couldn't see his face, but she imagined it was filled with worry.

"Wait."

Everyone looked at Loggie.

"I must be daft, but I cannot watch when my fate lies with yours." He entered the passageway and stood beside Cormac. "We meet challenges together."

Etain gasped and held her hand over her mouth. "It is our destiny." She released Jowsey and joined them in the passageway. "Together, we are strong. If one faulters, we are there for them."

Kneilot looked between Rosalind and the others, then slowly walked into the passageway.

"A package deal," said Thornheart. "All or nothing. I like these odds."

Jowsey stumbled over to Rosalind and knelt beside her. "You don't remember me. I'm Jowsey." His voice sounded parched, and some words sounded different because of his fat lip. "I know your friends."

"They've spoken about you." She returned her attention to these friends, who were preparing to walk deeper into the passageway. Cormac led the way, but they walked together as one. She wished she was with them. Though she was no hero and had many fears, their fate was hers.

They reached Darkmoore and took another step. Cormac glanced back at her, his face resolved in what he was about to do. Another step and another. They reached the skeleton's shoulders. Then they stepped past it. If Darkmoore had been struck where he lay, they had passed the test. Cormac must have thought the same because he walked the remaining steps without hesitation. He threw open the door and bright light flooded the passageway.

"Well done!" Thornheart clapped and stepped into the passageway. Unfurrowing a sack, she picked up the glass balls that lay beside the body. Before she continued, she spoke to Guthro. "Bring her."

Guthro walked to Rosalind, picked her up and threw her over his shoulder. Jowsey scrambled to his feet, but he was left behind by the men who quickly followed Thornheart passed Kragen Darkmoore and entered the dragon's chamber.

16

The Dragon of Darkmoore Caves

RELIEF WASHED OVER Cormac. If asked, he would have never considered himself brave, but whatever evaluated his courage for this trap considered him worthy enough. He stepped over the threshold with his friends by his side. The light inside the dungeon was bright as daylight, and he shielded his eyes from it. Waiting for his eyes to adjust, he searched for the light source. Something on the ceiling more than a hundred feet above illuminated the entire cavern. It was like the sun, but it produced white light, making everything bright and pale.

The sound of water drew his attention to a stream that flowed through the dungeon on the far edge. It was about ten feet wide and flowed with a gentle current.

"There it is," whispered Etain, pointing towards a large white mound.

Cormac stared at the mound. He would have mistaken it for a hill, a hill out of place in this cavern. It was as white as the light and as still as the stalactites. The only indication it was more than a hill were the dorsal crest of spikes but even those had flopped over. Its neck blended into its body and the stalagmites.

Was it dead? The thought shot through his heart. If it was dead, it meant he couldn't rescue it. Did this mean he'd suffer the curse and die after all he'd been through? He placed a hand on his stomach. He hadn't eaten for hours, yet he didn't feel hungry. He didn't even feel thirsty.

"It's still breathing." Etain's hushed voice broke the silence. She stepped towards it. "My hand trembles," she said, "but my heart breaks to feel it suffer."

Cormac grasped her arm. "We should see if its friendly from this distance." He drew in breath to raise his voice. "Hey, Mr. Dragon, can you hear me?"

Thornheart laughed. "Children of this world are so naïve." She walked towards the dragon, but Cormac recognised hesitation in her steps. She wasn't as brave as her words. Twenty feet away, she stopped. "Cursed dragon," she said, "what is your name?" No movement came from it. "Dragon! Do you not hear me? I am here to rescue you!" Still no movement. She looked to the man named Reg. "Come here."

Reg hesitated but when she scowled, he hurried forward. "Your highness." He cowered beneath her glare.

"Shake it," she said. "Stir it from its nap."

"Me?" Horror raced across his face. "I can't. It's a dragon."

"Which do you fear more? This dragon or disappointing me?" The smirk on her face revealed a crack in her make-up.

He ducked past her and cautiously approached the dragon. At five feet, he stopped, looked back at Thornheart, then took one more step.

"Closer," she said. "Your arm isn't that long."

He shuffled forward and stopped to reach out his hand. He was barely able to touch the dragon, but that's where he stood his ground. "Mr. Dragon," he said softly, "can you wake?" He tapped the side of the dragon, then recoiled.

"Harder," ordered Thornheart. "Its skin is thick."

Reg was forced to draw closer. He tapped lightly, then drew away in fear. The dragon didn't move. He tapped a little harder. Still nothing. "Is it dead?" he asked Thornheart.

"The heart still beats. Hit it harder."

Reg hesitated with his hand hovering over the dragon, then he whacked it hard and jumped back. Still, the dragon refused to move. Feeling more confident, he stepped closer and hit harder. The dragon snorted, and he ran back to Thornheart's side.

"I should have sent you through the passageway," she sneered. "The test would have done wonders."

He grumbled at her but didn't say anything.

"Dragon of Darkmoore Dungeon, do you wake to acknowledge my presence?"

Another snort broke the silence and rumbled across the stone floor. Its head moved slightly, then settled.

"It has suffered dreadfully," said Etain. "Even if it escapes this dungeon, it may not recover."

"A dragon lives on hope," said Thornheart. "Give it hope, and it will give you everything."

Cormac didn't like the sound of that. All he wanted was to be free of the curse; she sounded like she wanted a lot more. He approached the dragon warily. Part of him wanted to move silently, to sneak up on the beast. The other part wanted to make noise, lots of it, so he wouldn't startle it and it'd turn and snap at him. He cleared his throat louder than he normally did. Hearing footsteps beside him, he found Etain. Loggie and Kneilot tailed along behind.

If his only way to survive this curse was to wake the dragon and escape, he'd do it. He was dead either way.

"I hear your heart," said Etain. "It is strong but in despair. We are here to rescue you. To return you to the sky."

The dorsal crest of spikes that once lay flat inflated enough to lift off the body, and the neck shook as if the dragon dispersed cobwebs of sleep.

Etain placed a hand on its side and caressed it. "Your imprisonment is over," she whispered.

Cormac stared at her. This was a large dragon. It was not fitting through the door let alone the passageways he'd travelled. He glanced at Thornheart. He bet she knew how to set the dragon free, yet... that wasn't what she wanted to do. He felt it in his bones. The dragon had something she wanted. She had picked up the glass balls that lay on the floor next to Darkmoore. There were six. Each one held something. He'd been too focussed on not being struck down to take much notice, but he was certain whatever was inside moved. Slightly.

Looking past her, a dragon statue lay against the wall beside the door he had entered. Resting on top was a glass ball, just like the ones that had been on the floor. This one looked empty. He wanted to think more about this, but Thornheart walked past Guthro, who held Rosalind over his shoulder, gave the mesh bag of balls to the third man who had come with her and removed the glass ball from the statue. When she turned, the expression on her face shot a bolt of fear into his spine.

His eyes shifted to the letters over the door: DRAGOUN GLEIDHEADH. He was going to ask Etain what it meant but Thornheart ushered them aside.

"Move," she ordered. "It's time to complete this quest and start anew." She held the glass ball in the palm of her hand and lifted it into the air. "Inside out. Outside in. Encase this dragoun in glass skin." She hmphed. "A poet, he was not."

The dragon shook and took on a green hue. Its head lifted and swung in Cormac's direction. Heavy eyelids slid open and dark eyes watched him, then turned to Thornheart. It appeared unimpressed by the woman.

"What are you doing?" demanded Etain. She kept a steady hand on the dragon.

"Claiming my prize." Thornheart cackled like the wicked witches in cartoon shows. "Step aside or join the dragon within the glass."

"Oh!" She moved away and stared at the dragon. "I will ensure she releases you into the wild. You have suffered enough."

The dragon's snout swooped down and came within a foot of Etain. "Your name?" Its voice sounded dry and raspy.

"Etain of Elridge Mountain. And you?"

"Kiefwind of Sweetgrass." His body shuddered, making his words tremble. The green light around him shimmered and grew brighter. "Where are my loyal yswains? They were imprisoned when..." His eyes narrowed, and he peered at the mesh bag made from rope carried by the man who stood by the door.

Etain followed his line of sight. "What are yswains?"

"My protectors. Where I go, they follow."

"Dragons?"

"What else?"

"Are they encased in those globes?"

He roared, and his eyes widened. "They are to be set..." He winced in pain. The wind snapped around him, and his body vibrated.

Etain stepped away, and Cormac pulled her behind him. He moved away with the others and watched the dragon squirm wildly, then implode. The giant mass shrunk, and the glass ball drew the particles into it.

Spit caught in Cormac's throat, and he fought to free it. Gasping, he drew a breath and watched the remaining sparkling dust settle where once the dragon lay. "Did you kill it?"

"A dead dragon is useless to me." She turned and walked towards the doorway. Guthro had already turned and retraced his steps to the living quarters, still carrying Rosalind on his shoulder.

Cormac quickly caught up to Thornheart. "Let her go."

"Who?"

"Rosalind. I've opened the door, now release her."

She laughed. "My, dear boy, she's part of the treasure."

He grabbed her arm and spun her around to face him. Her expression made him instantly regret his actions. Her hand flew up and slapped him.

"Never touch me again," she growled. "I will take what I want when I want it."

"I won't let you have her." His cheek stung, but he ignored it.

"You and what army will stop me?" She grinned. "Even an army can't stop me."

Cormac's mind froze on that phrase. No one in Lachspeur of Yore used it. He hadn't heard it since... His blood ran cold. If Shayde Thornheart was from his world and knew Rosalind was, too, there was only one reason she wanted her.

"What's wrong?" She dropped the dragon trapped in the glass ball into a sack and fastened it to her belt. "Cat got your tongue?" She laughed and turned away.

He chased her through the passageway, past Kragen Darkmoore and into the wizard's chamber. Etain, Loggie and Kneilot followed. No sooner had he entered the room when he heard a battle scream. Guthro bent over, then collapsed to his knees, spilling Rosalind onto the floor.

Jowsey stood with sword in hand, his eyes as wild as his hair. Before anyone could react, he brought the sword down on Guthro's back, sending him to the floor permanently.

"Ah!" screamed Thornheart. "We should have fed you to the mote monster when we crossed." She grabbed a spear off the wall and threw it at him.

Jowsey dropped like a rock, and the spear sailed over him.

Thornheart braced her feet and rolled her hands over each other. Her lips mumbled silent words and before Cormac could tackle her to the ground, she released a spell from her fingertips.

Cormac felt his feet lift off the floor. Beside him, Loggie, rose, too. So did Etain, Kneilot and Jowsey. Once they were four feet off the floor, they moved in a circular motion around the room. He passed Reg and tried to knock him over, but he was too unsteady and missed. When he came close to the wall, he tried to grab a weapon but again, missed the opportunity.

Thornheart was moving towards the exit with the two remaining men. Reg was carrying Rosalind and the other was carrying the mesh bag of glass balls.

Cormac tried to break from the spell, but it was no use. Whatever he grasped, he couldn't hold onto. Etain was working her fingers, but if she was casting a spell, it wasn't working. Kneilot released his chicken, and it flew to the floor. It was unaffected by the spell. Running around and squawking, it was doing nothing to help Cormac's head from getting dizzy. In fact, its movement in the opposite direction was making his head swoon.

Thornheart stood at the threshold and looked back. "Pity. But we all can't make it to the surface." She chuckled. "We can but I won't let that happen. Enjoy your imprisonment. I doubt you'll last as long as this dragon, and no one will come to rescue you." She turned to leave and was knocked onto her back. The pouch on her belt broke free and slid across the floor. The screech she released was higher in pitch than that of the hobgoblin that had pounced on her. It sped away, jumped onto one of the tables filled with items and ogled its contents. Joy radiated from its face.

The fallen woman cursed and struggled to get to her feet. Before she did, Kneilot's chicken flew into Reg's face. It pecked with such viciousness, the man screamed in pain, dropped Rosalind and fought to get away. His eyes bulged, and blood dripped from the many wounds on his face. He turned and ran blindly from the room and onto the walkway, wiping his eyes to clear away blood.

The man disappeared from view, and Cormac heard a splash. It was immediately followed by a blood-curdling scream and the sound of bones snapping. A larger splash sent water through the doorway, then everything fell silent.

Once Thornheart was on her feet with the globe in her hand, she scowled at the chicken. She prepared to throw a spell at it when a staff flew through the air and knocked her in the head. She staggered but didn't fall. The hobgoblin danced on the table, rejoicing in hitting the mark.

Cormac's pace slowed, and he dropped to the floor, rolled and came up on his feet. The spell holding Rosalind was also broken, and she grabbed the staff the hobgoblin had thrown and swung at Thornheart. The woman stepped back to avoid the weapon.

The lone surviving man who had come with Thornheart ran for the doorway, carrying the mesh bag of orbs. Frustration, then anger painted Thornheart's face. She marched to the door, then turned to face them. "Good riddance." She pulled the cube from the stone, and the door slid shut.

Rosalind raced to the door and tried to push it open, but it wouldn't budge. Cormac joined her but together, they couldn't move it. Loggie shoved her aside, and he and Cormac pushed with all their might, but they failed to open it.

"There must be a way," said Etain. "There's always another way."

Cormac stopped pushing. He wiped sweat from his brow and surveyed his surroundings. "If there was another way out, wouldn't the dragon have found it and escaped years ago?"

"The dragon was trapped in the cavern," said Kneilot. "We have access to all of this." He waved one hand around the room while the other clutched the chicken. "There must be something here to aid our escape."

"At least the dragon has been rescued," said Loggie. "The curse is removed. The dragon will deal with that spawn of darkness."

"No, it won't." Jowsey had flopped into the ornate armchair next to the doorway. He held a rag to his forehead where blood oozed from a cut.

"What will she do with it?" asked Etain.

"Enslave it."

"How? A dragon is mightier than her."

He huffed. "It's cursed." He wiped blood and sweat from his forehead, then returned the rag to the cut. "Who ever rescues the dragon controls it and its followers. Thornheart now has an army of dragons to wield her power."

"Followers? Yswains? The dragons trapped in the orbs?"

"That's them. Kragen Darkmoore was more elaborate than anyone knew. His goal was to command an army of dragons. He captured Kiefwind and cast a curse on him. Then he imprisoned his yswains in the orbs. He placed them as his reward for successfully beating the challenges." He chuckled. "It was a game to him. One he thought he could win." He glanced at the passageway where the old wizard's bones lay. "His ultimate goal was to reach Kiefwind and set him free. Kiefwind's curse was he had to serve whoever set him free."

"And the yswains?" asked Etain.

"They are sworn to obey Kiefwind."

"Surely, they have free will."

He shrugged. "I'm not sure how that works in the dragon world, but Darkmoore and Thornheart both believe if they command Kiefwind, they command the yswains." He eyed Rosalind. "Apparently, Boote wasn't lying."

Cormac glanced between the two. "Lying about what?"

"From what I overheard, she's not from this world."

Rosalind's brow bent. "What do you mean?"

"You won't remember this," said Jowsey. "One night a man tried to kidnap you and deliver you to Thornheart. He had said he was rescuing you. That you weren't from this world."

"What world is she from?" Etain stood beside Rosalind and put a hand on her shoulder.

"Thornheart called it Earth. I think she's from there, too."

"Incredible. What does she want with Rosalind?"

Cormac swallowed slowly and bent his brow to hide any expression that might indicate he knew what Jowsey was talking about. Well, he knew half of it. He had questions, such as how long had Thornheart been in Lachspeur of Yore, but he kept them to himself.

"Not sure. It has something to do with revenge." He smirked. "Even she has enemies stronger than her. A man named Harmon. Richard Harmon, she calls him when she's cursing him. I believe he's from Earth, too."

Loggie turned and stared at Cormac. "Is that who we were going to see? Harmon of the Wood?"

"That's what she called him," said Jowsey.

Cormac's mouth went dry, and his thoughts tumbled over one another. He questioned why Harmon had sent him in search of another from Earth. He had thought it was for his own benefit but now, nothing made sense.

"Well?" Loggie stood in front of him. When no answer came, he pressed him further. "Why were we going to see your friend? Or should I ask, where are you from because your accent is the same as Rosalind's."

He stepped back. "I'm not trying to hurt anyone."

"The answer is in code." Loggie thought for a second. "I have decoded it." He frowned. "Coming clean now with your intentions may salvage friendships that will be lost otherwise."

He stared at Rosalind. She looked to him for answers she'd forgotten. "I am never going to hurt you."

"You knew I was not from here?"

He hesitated, knowing his answer would make him look bad. He drew a deep breath. "Yes."

"For how long?"

"Since I first saw you. It's why I rescued you from the prison."

"I was in a prison?"

"You rescued her to help her, not for some evil scheme, right?" said Loggie, his face growing red with every passing second.

"Yes. Well..., yes. I couldn't hurt her. I'm not that kind of person."

"You're the kind who strings people along, making them feel like friends when you have an alternative motive. Maybe you gain pleasure from knowing things others don't." He glanced at Rosalind, then back at Cormac. "Is this the source of her memory loss?"

He inwardly groaned. This would make him look extremely bad. "No." His word sounded pathetic. "I don't think so. She's under a spell." That sounded better, and it was true.

"Are you under this spell?"

"I remember everything."

"So, you broke it." Loggie turned to Rosalind. "You began to retain your memory a few days ago. We assumed it was the dragon's doing, but..." He glared at Cormac. "What did you do?"

"Nothing."

"You gave me this." Rosalind pulled the necklace from beneath her shirt and held up the ring. "You told me it would bring me luck."

"It has."

"Is it magical?" Loggie held out his hand for the ring.

Rosalind reached behind her neck to untie the leather strap, but Cormac stopped her. "Wait. Never take it off."

"Why?" Loggie stood facing him. Cormac stumbled over his words, and Loggie scowled. "It *is* magical."

"No. It's nothing like that. It's just a school ring. It's nothing special." He released a heavy sigh. "It's special to me, and I wanted her to have it."

"Sentimental," said Loggie sarcastically. "How are we to trust you?"

He released an exasperated sigh. "I come from a peaceful world. Nothing like this. We get up in the morning, go to school, work or just hang out. Our life isn't constantly threatened by swords, giant slugs, the undead or hob—" He glanced at the hobgoblin playing with items on a table.

"So, like in Doorock."

He paused to think about that. "Similar, but not really. There's no magic in my world."

"There must be," said Etain. "You're here because of magic."

Again, he stumbled over that point. "There are only humans. No dwarfs, elves, hauflins, orks or anything else."

"No dwarfs? So, truly no magic," said Loggie. "Life must be boring. Is that why you came here?"

"I didn't think the spell would work. I was playing around." He rubbed the side of his head hard and winced from striking a cut. "If I had known it was going to be like this, I wouldn't have cast the spell."

"How did I get here?" Rosalind stood at a distance as if she didn't want to be near him.

"I don't know. I don't know anything about you."

"Wait a minute." Loggie stared at Rosalind. "You're hauflin." He turned to Cormac. "You said there were only humans in your world."

"There are. It's difficult to explain. I played a game. I assume Rosalind played the same one. We pretended to be characters of different races. She must have played a hauflin, but she's really human."

Loggie again stared at Rosalind, looking her up and down. He went so far as to check her ears to see if they were fake. "She is pureblood hauflin."

"I can't explain it. I don't know what she did to get here. I just know she's from my world. When I first arrived, I tried telling people where I was from, but I gave up. No one believed me and worse, they thought I was crazy."

"Are you hired by Harmon?" asked Jowsey, who still relaxed in the armchair.

"No. I met him in a small town near where he lives shortly after I arrived. He discovered where I was from. He believed me. He took me to his cottage, and I stayed there for a few weeks. All that time, I didn't know he was from Earth, too. He never said anything. Now I'm wondering why. Why didn't he tell me?"

"Maybe for the same reason you didn't tell us." Loggie raised an eyebrow and waited.

Many thoughts ran through Cormac's mind. If Harmon wanted an Earthling to sacrifice to return home, why hadn't he used him? Or did he need two? Or a hauflin? Or a female? Maybe his plan didn't involve returning to Earth.

"While you mull over something intelligent to say," said Loggie, "I'll point out the obvious. Harmon and Thornheart are friends. Acquaintances. Or enemies if she plans to destroy him."

A loud crash made them jump and drew their attention to the hobgoblin. It had knocked over a glass bottle. Steam rose from the blue liquid that covered the floor. Perched on the table, the hobgoblin stared at it. The steam encompassed its head, and it fell back onto the table, knocking several more jars to the floor. Three broke, release more liquid and steam. The hobgoblin didn't move.

"Is it dead?" asked Kneilot.

"I see its chest moving," said Etain. "Maybe it's sleeping."

"You replaced me with that mischief imp?" asked Jowsey.

"We thought it an improvement," said Loggie. He turned back to Cormac. "First, we get out of here. Then, we learn more about what you know about Rosalind. She's our first concern. If I don't like your answers, I'll return you to the wild to wander alone. Rosalind stays with us."

"He is a good man," said Kneilot. "Eir would not have saved him if otherwise."

"At least you have one on your side," Loggie said to Cormac. "Now, an escape route." He turned towards the door leading to the entrance of the cave. "I fear this is sealed to us."

"Maybe Darkmoore has something we can use." Etain went to one of the tables and poked around.

"I will help," said Kneilot. He went to a different table and read the labels.

"I'll check the shelves." Loggie went to one of many shelves that contained bottles and books.

Cormac wanted to search a table but couldn't remove his gaze from Rosalind, who stared at him. Words that came to mind felt weak. Cheap. He dismissed each one. He could never reveal his initial motives for wanting to take her to Harmon's. She'd hate him. Never forgive him. Never trust him again. It would destroy what they had. What they had? By the look on her face, the feelings that had started to grow for him had dried on the vine. Shrivelled into an unrecognisable mess.

"Were we friends in this other world?" she asked. She sounded uncertain.

"No. I would have remembered you."

She nodded and scanned the room. "When we escape, will you tell me about our world?"

"Yes. Everything. I believe in time, you will remember it yourself."

"Because of the necklace?"

"I... I'm not sure. I don't know anything about magic."

"Can I trust you?" Her voice trembled on the last word.

He stepped closer, so they were only a foot apart. "You can. I promise. I will do nothing to bring harm your way." He wanted to say more, but his tongue wouldn't release the words. His brain agreed. Regardless of what he said now, it would sound like a lie to her.

"I want to trust you."

"You can."

She looked around. "We should help. The sooner we escape, the sooner we can save Kiefwind."

He stood rigid. "Save the dragon? How are we to do that if Thornheart controls him?"

"I don't know. But I can't do it from down here."

He watched her walk away, his mouth still. Chasing after the evil sorceress and her enslaved dragons wasn't what he considered safe. It wasn't even sane.

Rosalind scanned the many items on the table. She still carried the staff that had been thrown at Shayde Thornheart while she stood in the doorway. It was made of strong wood and fit her hand perfectly. When she'd first picked it up, she felt a warm sensation upon her skin. After carrying it for a few minutes, the feeling went away. An intricate swirling design decorated the top of the staff and words she could not read encircle it just below the design.

The hobgoblin that had passed out from breathing in the steam stirred. Sitting up, it shook its head, checked its body, then leapt to its feet. Unphased by what had happened, it continued its happy search of the table.

Considering the magic items, a thought occurred to Rosalind. "Etain, you said that when a magic-user dies, their magic goes with them. You said it of the Enchanted Rope of Esmerelda."

"Yes, that is truth." Etain held a flask in her hand.

"If that is so, why does Kragen Darkmoore's magic exist here? The traps should have been disarmed. These potions should turn to water or something harmless."

Etain stared at her. From her deep focus, she could tell she was rolling this problem over in her mind. "I have no answer. I have been taught this is so, and I've witnessed it firsthand, but..." She stared in the direction of Darkmoore's skeleton. "Perhaps it wasn't entirely his magic."

"Do you think these are magical weapons?" asked Jowsey, propping himself up. He winced in pain and resettled in the armchair.

"I'm unsure," said Etain.

Jowsey forced himself to his feet and limped to the wall to examine a dagger. "If they are, they'll be valuable."

"Money is your motivation?"

He grinned. "It helps."

"Get you into conditions that threaten your life," she finished the sentence for him.

His grin slipped, and he stared at her. "I've luck on my side."

"This time." She walked away.

Rosalind examined a dagger next to the one Jowsey looked at. "It has a lovely design."

"Nice bracer." He pointed to her wrist. "It will go well with the dagger."

"Thanks, but I don't think I'll take it. I have three."

"It's pretty though."

"I'm taking the staff."

"I'll take it then. This one, too."

She put her hand on the hilt. "No. I think I will." She lifted the dagger from the bracket. It fit her hand perfectly. She removed the sheath and looked down the shiny blade. "After all these years. Incredibly clean."

He removed the sheath from the one he picked up. "Incredible indeed."

Rosalind was about to speak, but glass smashing on the floor drew her attention to the hobgoblin. It giggled in its unusual manner and picked up another bottle, peered inside at the liquid and threw it at the wall. A puff of green smoke erupted and filled the room with an obnoxious odour.

"It's going to poison us before we starve to death." Jowsey held a blood-stained rag over his mouth.

The hobgoblin howled with laughter until Etain stomped over and shook her finger at it. "Stop!" she demanded. "Enough of this nonsense." She swept her hand over the floor. "Look at the mess you've made. If you've nothing better to occupy your hands, sit." She pointed to the ornate armchair.

The hobgoblin pouted and slunk off the table and into the chair, where it crossed its arms and stuck out its bottom lip.

Rosalind raised an eyebrow at Jowsey. "She's got a commanding voice."

"I pity her future mate."

"I doubt he'll throw magic potions at the wall."

"One never knows what a mate might do when frustrated." He grinned.

Rosalind returned the grin and stepped closer to a table to see if she could discover something that would open the exit door or provide another way to escape the dungeon.

Two hours later, Etain released a squeal. She had been sitting in the ornate chair reading a tattered book. "Listen to this. Thee who hath been rescued shall encapsulate the ever present and attentive servant of his rescuer until that time the servant saves the vital force of the rescuer, at which point he has paid his debt and becomes a free soul." She looked up. "This is a spell book. I'm certain this is the spell Darkmoore cast upon Kiefwind. If the dragon saves Thornheart's life, it's free. I wonder if she knows that."

"She wins, but she loses," said Rosalind. "I wonder if Kiefwind knows. If he does, he'll take the first opportunity to save her. Then turn on her."

"It also states that if the rescuer dies before freedom is earned, the servant shall meet the same fate."

"Nasty. Horrible if the enslaved was nowhere near to prevent the death."

"Does that tome have a magical verse to transport this weary dwarf to the surface where sunshine will once again grace his skin?" Loggie dropped to his knees beside the chair.

"Nothing yet," said Etain, "but I'm looking."

"Ah!" He flopped back onto the floor and lay as if asleep. "I shall never see the sweet sunshine again. Never shall I entertain the good and fair crowds of a tavern with my talent nor gather their coins in my empty mug. I am doomed."

Etain giggled. "You're entertaining us."

He sat up. "Yet, I see no coins flung my way."

Rosalind laughed. Of all the wonderful people she could have discovered in this land, Loggie was the most entertaining. She glanced at Cormac, who searched a cabinet on the opposite side of the room. He had stopped to watch Loggie's performance, then looked to her. She returned her attention to the bottles on the table and read the labels. Eye of Newt. It was a real thing. Breath of Fresh Air. Cure for Corns and Bunions. Attract Mosquitoes. She thought about that one. Who would want to attract them? Frogs. Tasha's Hideous Laughter. Again, she

paused to consider why she'd want to make anyone laugh hideously. False Life. Comprehend Language.

The possibilities were endless, but she didn't know what half of them did and none so far would help her escape the caves. Most of the spells were in liquid form. She assumed she'd have to consume the drink to use the spell. However, Detect Magic and Feather Fall were encased in what looked like shredded bark. They were in leather pouches. When she opened them, the smell was overwhelming. After all these years, would they retain their potency and still work? Feeling they may come in handy, she tucked them into the pouch on her belt.

Reconsidering Comprehend Language, she removed the lid and sniffed. It smelt like smoked bacon. She lifted it to her mouth, hesitated, then had second thoughts. Before she could remove it from her lips, something forced it up, and she drank a large mouthful. She swallowed, coughed and sputtered. Through watery eyes, she saw the hobgoblin dancing and giggling on the table.

After wiping her mouth with the back of her sleeve, she capped the jar and put it down. She blinked several times and each time, her vision grew brighter. The eternal flame and the two torches they'd lit to illuminate the room glowed brightly with orange flames. Scanning the room, she noticed all writings glowed. Some were yellow, others green. They glowed like sunshine. She picked up her staff to take a closer look at the glittering letters, and the scrolling wrapped around the end of the walking stick ignited in blue light. Twisting it around to read the inscription, she pondered over the words: *A calm hand wields sleep.* She was certain the words had been written in a language she'd never seen before.

Holding tightly to the staff, she made her way around the room, reading everything that attracted her eyes. While the letters glowed, she had to touch the item before she could decipher it. An hour passed and the spell wore off.

Tired, hungry and frustrated, the small band of adventurers gathered around the table to consume the remaining food in their packs. They ate quietly, having discussed many possibilities while they searched for something to aid in their escape.

The food gone, Rosalind tipped the water flask to her mouth and drank the last mouthful. Glancing around, she didn't see a source for water. The sound of the stream registered in her ears. She slipped from the chair and left the room, giving a passing glance to Darkmoore sprawled across the floor in the tunnel. Once in the dragon's dungeon, she squinted and allowed her eyes to adjust to the bright light. Then she walked the hundred feet to the stream. The water was clear and when she dipped her cupped hand in and sipped it, it tasted sweet. She held the flask in the water and filled it. Resting on a nearby rock, she drank and watched the water flow. It wound around a soft bend and left the cavern through a cave cut through the wall. The water splashed against the walls, but the ceiling was about six feet taller than the surface. With her thoughts meandering with the stream, she didn't hear Cormac come up behind her.

"Does it taste good?" He squatted near the water's edge and held his flask to fill it.

"It does."

"This is a lifesaver." He took a long drink, then dunked the flask again. "If we can't find a way out today, at least we won't die of thirst."

"I imagine it kept the dragon alive." She glanced around the cavern. "Though I don't know what he did for food. Unless dragons eat grass." There was a large patch of grass growing directly beneath the bright light source.

"I thought they were meat eaters."

She returned her attention to the water, unsure of what to say to him though many questions raced through her mind. Brushing them aside, she calmed her nerves. "Where do you think this water goes?"

He looked down stream. "Weren't we told it flows into the river that goes under the bridge?"

She considered that fact. It was just one stream that fed the river. This was only ten feet wide. The river was ten times that. She picked up a stick half the length of her arm and threw it to the middle of the stream. The current gently carried it away, and it soon disappeared into the darkness of the cave. Standing and resting against the staff, she caught the last glimpse of the stick. "Crazy." She walked along the water's edge.

Cormac followed. "What are you looking for?"

"A way out." She stopped where the water entered the cave. "What are the chances this cave continues and carries that stick from the mountain?"

He leant forward and peered into the cave. "If you're wrong, we'll drown."

"If I'm right, we escape." She paced the water's edge. "The current isn't too strong. We could come back if we had to."

"It might get stronger the farther it goes."

"The tables will float." She stared in the direction of where the others sat eating. "We can remove the legs. Use the tops as rafts. This might work." She hurried across the cavern.

"This is crazy." Cormac walked quickly to keep up.

"Do you have a better idea?"

"No, but we have time to think."

"Do we?" She stopped quickly to face him, and he bumped into her. "How much time should we wait until we try it? Until we are weak from hunger?"

"No, but..." He put his hand over the place where the arrow had entered.

"You're worried your injuries will inhibit your success?"

He half nodded. "It still hurts a lot. I can't use half my strength, and," he pointed to the others, "Jowsey is in worse shape. Everyone is suffering." He eyed her with sympathy. "Even you. You look exhausted."

"So we wait until we've had a good night's sleep?"

A crash sounded through the passageway, and she stared at the doorway. Cursing and grumbling escaped along with a billowing cloud of grey smoke.

"That mischievous imp will kill us." She marched towards the doorway and into the smoky room. The others were covering their mouths and coughing.

"Of all the insufferable companions to be encases with in a grave!" Loggie gathered his things quickly and ran towards the dragon's dungeon. The others followed.

"Best to get our stuff and join them." Cormac grabbed his rucksack.

Rosalind covered her mouth with her sleeve and rushed towards the table, where she had left her gear. She gathered it quickly, stuffing everything inside the rucksack. Coughing and sputtering she raced to the door. Seeing a small sack of items on the edge of a table, she grabbed it. Cormac waited for her and when she passed, he followed.

"What the...?"

She turned to see what he spoke of and baulked. "You're an..." She tilted her head one way, then the other. "Old man?"

"You're an older woman." He felt his head, found it bald and frowned. "You're hauflin, so the years are kinder."

Etain walked back to them, wiping her eyes and coughing. "You've aged. Both of you."

Rosalind looked at her. "So have you."

She looked at her arms, then at the others. Everyone had aged many years. "I don't feel old."

"You're an elf, so..." Cormac shuffled towards the stream.

"Ah, to be human," said Loggie. "One moment suckling at mawmaw's teat, the next, swaggering towards the grave."

Rosalind stifled her grin. It was unfair humans aged so quickly. Seeing the stream, reminded her of the plan. "I think I found a way to escape," she said.

"Inform us of our route," said Loggie, "before the imp turns us into trees and we're cursed to grow here for a hundred years."

She told them her theory about the stream and what she thought they should do. They listened with interest until she said, "It has to leave the mountain some how."

"Possibly through an underground spring," said Loggie. "Since the imp has turned us into mature beings and not sea monsters, I hesitate to accept your plan."

"It's a sound plan," said Etain, "but..." She stared at the water. "We could consider alternative ideas, but I'm not willing to spend half my life doing that."

"Looks like you already have," said Jowsey, grinning.

She frowned at him. "Rosalind, your Roots of Terra cards predicted the rescue of this dragon, which has happened. It also foresaw water splashing against rocks." She looked to where the stream flowed into the shallow cave. "I believe this is it. Sitting around talking about it won't get it done." She looked Jowsey up and down. "Your mouth is healthy enough for idiotic remarks. Let's see if your muscles can lift a table."

"I don't want to go back in there."

"Come." She walked away.

Jowsey squished up his nose at her but followed.

"Cormac, help me with a table?" asked Rosalind. He turned, considered her request, then agreed.

"That leaves you, me and that egg-layer to gather a table and risk our lives on a plan not half thought out," said Loggie to Kneilot. "It's a good thing your chicken can swim."

A half hour later, the legs removed from the tables, they gathered at the shoreline to test out the floatability of their makeshift rafts. Given their size and thickness, they had fair buoyancy.

Rosalind held the raft in place and reconsidered the plan. It was solid. Yet it was something she'd never try if given other options.

"Who shall be the first to plug the drainage hole?" Loggie stood poised on the shore, a pole in hand to help guide the raft.

"I'll go." Rosalind climbed onboard and waited for Cormac. He was slower in his old age, and she worried he'd not have the strength to swim if they were thrown into the water.

"Might as well," he said. "Life's too short not to take risks. Shorter than I first believed it was." He tried to joke about it, but she saw his limited abilities were frustrating him.

"The spell won't last long," she said and handed him the eternal flame.

"How do you know?"

"I don't but...I'm sure it won't." She pushed off from shore, and the gentle current carried her towards the cave mouth. Casting a final glance at the cavern, she spotted the hobgoblin standing in the doorway watching them. Given its craftiness, it would escape on its own terms. Or remain here and live out its life casting one broken spell bottle after another until they were gone.

Etain and Jowsey pushed their raft into the stream, and Loggie and Kneilot did the same.

Once Rosalind reached the middle of the stream, she sat down and let the current push the raft. There was nothing she could do now. Her fate lay with the water and this crazy mountain. Entering the cave, the sound of the enclosed water increased. The bright light faded away and they were left with the glow of the eternal torch.

"So far, so good," whispered Cormac. "My fingers are crossed."

"We'll be fine." She sat in the middle of the raft next to him to balance it out. "It can't be more horrible than what we've already experienced in this mountain."

He gave her a cautious smile. "You do realise you just jinxed us."

She laughed. "Let us not think of such things. Just sit back and enjoy the ride." The ceiling was high enough, she could sit cross-legged. She hoped it would always be this high and the current this speed. Anything else, and she might regret thinking of this escape route.

17

Time to Cast Off

CORMAC LOWERED THE torch. It was only two feet long, but he didn't want to scrape it on the ceiling of the cave. He rested the base against the wooden table to give his arm a rest. The bottle the hobgoblin had broken added 50 years to his life. He was now in his 70s. Much of his strength was gone, yet the wound in his gut remained, making quick movements painful.

Glancing at Rosalind, he envied her youth. He wasn't certain, but if he remembered what the *Adventure Masters Guide* stated, she could live to be 250 to 300 years old. Which meant, her 70 years were more like 25 – the prime of her life. Her copper-colour hair shone richly beneath the eternal flame, and her dark eyes were like bright orbs that danced with excitement.

"We must have travelled at least a half hour," she said, breaking the silence.

"Can't be much farther." He'd think positively even though the ceiling was slowly lowering. If the clearance reduced to zero, they had a long, tiresome swim ahead of them to return to the dragon's dungeon. He glanced over his shoulder at the others. They were relaxing on their rafts, floating along on the calm current.

"Do you know how to get home?"

He stared at her. "I have no idea." That was the truth. He'd never sacrifice another to escape this world. If that was the only way, he was stuck here for the rest of his life. "Maybe we can find a way together."

"Yes. We should." She fell silent and the slosh of water echoing off the cave walls was the only sound. After a few minutes, she spoke again. "Are you certain my memory will return, that I will remember who I am and where I came from?"

"Yes. I believe you will. I do."

"Does the necklace break the spell?" Her eyes looked up at him, pleading for the truth.

He swallowed slowly. "I believed it would help your memory, but I didn't know for a fact, and I don't know if it will return all your memories."

"Without the necklace, will you forget?"

He shook his head. "It's why I want you to wear it. Keep it until we can break the spell. Don't let anyone take it from you. Best that it remains hidden." He noticed she hadn't tucked it back into her shirt, so he did. "What can't be seen can't be stolen."

The ceiling was getting lower, and he ducked to avoid hitting his head. He could see only 20 feet and at this speed, that distance was covered fairly quickly. "It looks like the cave is narrowing. What do you see?" She could see at least 30 feet farther than he could.

"It is, and..." she peered into the darkness, "the current is getting faster." She adjusted her weight. "Maybe this..." She glanced up at him but didn't finish the sentence.

She didn't have to; he knew what she was going to say. He braced himself. A drawn-out death by drowning awaited him up ahead. While he hadn't lived 75 years, his body looked like it had.

"Hold on!" Rosalind shouted over her shoulder to the rest. "It's getting faster."

"A quick death!" said Loggie. "Much preferred over a slow one."

Cormac braced himself. The current was picking up faster than he anticipated both because the cave narrowed and because the incline increased. "If we get through this, promise me you'll forgive me."

She furrowed her brow. "For what?"

"For being an idiot."

She chuckled. "If we don't get through this, will you forgive me?"

He looked at her, then the water, then back at her, realising what she meant. "Forgive you for a premature death? Sure. I don't take grudges to the grave."

The faster the current flowed, the more unsteady the raft became. He lay on his stomach to lower his centre of gravity and held the eternal flame before him. Rosalind lay beside him, facing the danger head on. The stream bed dropped suddenly, and they shot forward. The ceiling was so low, he had to keep his head on the raft to prevent it from smacking against the rock as they bobbed up and down. They should have turned back ten minutes ago. Now was too late.

"I see a light!" shouted Rosalind.

"I was told not to approach such lights!" shouted Loggie, the rush of water almost drowning out his voice.

Cormac strained his eyes but couldn't see it.

"It's getting closer," she said. "It's not that big."

"But it's something," he said.

"I'll take anything right now."

They sped forward and the light came into view. At first, it was small, but grew the closer they came. They wouldn't drown in an underground spring. Then another thought came to him, and his blood ran cold.

"Hey, the spell has broken," she said.

"What?" His mind was on what lie ahead.

"You're not an old man anymore."

He glanced at his hands. The wrinkles and age spots were gone, and his muscles felt strong. Excellent timing considering he'd need his remaining strength to swim.

The opening came fast, so fast he hardly had time to draw a breath before he was launched into the air. For a second all was still, giving him exactly half a second to see the river 100 feet below before he plunged towards it. Behind him, he heard a scream followed by clucking. A quick glance and he saw the chicken flapping its wings and gliding towards the water.

The raft hit the surface of the water and bounced, sending him slapping against the side. Unable to hold on, he was tossed overboard. He tumbled and rolled in the current of the river. Once he found his bearings, he swam to the surface. He shook the water from his face, sending his hair flapping from side-to-side.

"Here!" Rosalind clung to the raft, then hoisted herself up. She turned and reached for him.

He swam towards her, struggling to keep afloat wearing boots, the sword and rucksack. Pain exploded in his side and if not for her grabbing hold of his hand, he may have gone under. He scrambled onto the raft with her help, then flopped to his back and gulped air. "We did it," he wheezed, coughing and sputtering.

Rosalind half stood, searching the water. "Over here!" She reached out to Kneilot, who swam towards her, and pulled him onboard.

Cormac half sat up. "The rest?" He wiped water from his face and searched for the others. The waterfall they had crashed over was fast flowing, spraying mist into the air. It appeared taller now that he was looking up at it. The pool beneath it was fairly large and calm. The river flowing from it was about 20 feet wide. Loggie was dragging himself onto what was left of his table. Etain was on her raft, but Jowsey was nowhere in sight.

"Jowsey!" Etain cried, panic lacing her voice. "Jowsey!" She wiped wet hair from her face and peered into the water.

"There!" Loggie pointed, then dived into the water. He disappeared beneath the surface for what seemed like forever. When he surfaced, he held the unconscious thief by the back of his jacket.

Etain used her hand to paddle towards them. Once there, she grabbed Jowsey and with Loggie's help, got him onto the raft. Loggie climbed on with her.

Cormac could only watch as Etain worked on Jowsey. She didn't do mouth-to-mouth, so he guessed Jowsey was breathing. Or they didn't know about that in this world. "Etain! Is he breathing?"

"Yes!" She rubbed his face and tried to wake him.

Rosalind used the staff and paddled towards them. Before they reached them, Jowsey was sputtering and coughing up water. He half sat up with Etain's help.

Kneilot's chicken swam closer, dipped its beak into the water and lifted it to drink. When it neared the raft, it hopped on and squawked, no worse for the ride.

"How's he doing?" asked Rosalind.

"He's survived to thieve another day," said Loggie. He sat with his legs partially bent and his arms resting on his knees. "If only that was the sun shining and not rain clouds approaching, we might dry off before nightfall."

Cormac looked to the sky. The sun was low and dark clouds were moving in. East? "Is it the next day? Surely the sun is not setting but rising."

"That would be my guess." Loggie brushed wet hair from his forehead.

"We were in the caves all night. Almost 24 hours." He yawned, suddenly feeling exhausted.

Jowsey sat up. He looked groggy. "We made it?"

"You didn't," said Loggie. "Sorry to have to tell you that. You're an undead."

Horror raced across Jowsey's face, and he grabbed his chest. After a few seconds, he came to his senses and frowned. "You're undead, too?"

"I feel like it." He started to paddle towards the shore but stopped. "Which shore? Which will be closer to the horses?"

Cormac tried to find his bearings. He had no idea where he was. The many twists and turns, stairwells and then the stream leading from the dragon's dungeon confused his senses completely.

Etain stood and surveyed the landscape. After much consideration, she pointed to the shore. "The cave mouth was on the south side of the mountain. The sun was shining into it when we entered. That means, we need to go along the east side."

They reached the shore, and Etain brought out the map. "If I am correct, we are here." She pointed to a spot on the map, then rechecked her surroundings.

"That's a fair piece away," said Cormac.

"If we walk steady and if the terrain isn't too rough, we should reach it by dark."

Jowsey moaned and lay back on the grass. "I'll never make it. Leave me. Save yourself."

Cormac frowned. If the thief wanted sympathy, he wasn't getting it from him. "Suits me. You'd only slow us down." He stood and removed his rucksack and jacket. He rung out what he could to make it lighter, then emptied his boots. Trekking over the mountain was going to be difficult enough with his injuries. Adding 50 pounds of water would make it torturous.

Rosalind stopped on a crest to catch her breath and to let the others catch up. They had been walking for the better part of six hours. The going was rough on the side of the mountain without a trail. They took breaks often. She was tired and sore and knew the others were in worse shape. Jowsey slowed the procession the most. Everyone but Cormac took turns helping him over the terrain. Cormac was lucky to keep himself upright with the multiple injuries he had sustained. What they needed was a long, quiet sleep at an inn. What they'd get if they didn't reach the horses and their equipment by nightfall, which was less than an hour away, would be a cold, hard sleep crowded together in the crevice of a rock.

"We must stop soon," said Etain. "We will not reach our destination before dark. Jowsey is near collapse. Cormac trails closely behind."

"We look for a suitable spot for the night?"

"A wise decision. Sleep and rest will rejuvenate us, and we shall begin again on the morewen." She scanned the terrain. "We should be there by noontide."

Rosalind waited until everyone caught their breath, then continued. She searched for a spot with shelter. The clouds that threatened rain all day had grown thicker and darker. Less than half a mile on, she found a spot tucked beneath a large protruding rock. She ushered Cormac in, and he stumbled and fell onto the ground, where he lay to collect his breath.

Loggie and Kneilot directed Jowsey to the deepest section and sat him down. Rosalind organised rocks in a circle, then gathered fuel for the fire. Before nightfall, the fire was casting a warm glow over the small band and thunder rumbled overhead. The clouds had yet to disperse their accumulated moisture. Cormac and Jowsey had fallen asleep and Loggie played a soft tune on Rosalind's Piccolo flute.

"A watch is unnecessary," said Etain. "No one shall find us here, and we all need sleep."

Rosalind didn't argue. She was exhausted and sleep beckoned her. After adding more wood to the fire, she settled next to it, the staff beside her. Laying awake and considering all that had happened in the days since retaining her memory, she saw the first flash of lightning. The rains quickly followed. It crashed down, filling her ears with water pounding on rock. Tucked beneath the overhang, she did not feel the rain, and the fire took the edge off the dampness. The weather was another deterrent to anyone or anything that might threaten them. Feeling safe and satisfied with her day, she drifted off.

When she woke, the sun lit up the forest below. She stretched and found Etain sitting next to the fire with a book on her lap. It was the same book she'd been reading inside Darkmoore's living quarters. The others still slept. Wiping the cobwebs of slumber from her face, she sat up and took a drink of water.

"Was your sleep restful?" asked Etain.

"It was. No dreams. No images. You?"

"Not as peaceful."

"What disturbed it?"

Etain cast a gaze at the others, then settled on the flames leaping into the morning air. "I fear we have released a destructive force that will destroy many."

"The dragon?"

She nodded. "It was not our intention, but it matters not. Shayde Thornheart must be stopped."

"What did you see in your vision?"

Etain locked eyes with her. "Urðr called out to me. She felt a ripple in my destiny." She played with the corner of a page. When she looked up, her expression was cautious. "Her heart was set on my arrival at Delgrath, but..." she moistened her lips, "she says that will be delayed. She fears for me. I felt it though she would not share these thoughts."

"What if we deliver you to Delgrath and continue on alone."

"That is not my fate."

"We can change it."

"Others will suffer."

"Someone always suffers. It is not our duty to prevent all suffering only negate that which personally affects us."

"Yet you wish to rescue the dragon."

"I do, but that is my choice. I make it freely knowing the possible outcome."

Etain smiled. "Urðr's concern has disturbed my thoughts. I wish to accompany you. Adventure is what I seek. I was sheltered, given the map to my future but for too long, I was told to wait. Without question, I was told I must follow it. I have not made those decisions. Others have for me." She grimaced. "Though I love them dearly, I wish to possess life in my own hand. For to live the life chosen by others is not a life at all."

"Then come with us. We shall seek adventure together."

Etain stuck out a hand and grasped Rosalind's. "We shall. Though others will tell me it is wrong, I must follow my path, not one designed by those who create it to fit their own destinies."

The chicken clucked loudly, announcing to the morning she had laid an egg. Loggie stirred, sat up and rubbed his eyes. "The call to break the fast. I will answer it."

18

Informal Introductions

THE GRUELING PACE the women set to reach the horses had Cormac groaning in pain by the time he collapsed in the grass near the Enchanted Rope of Esmerelda. From his resting spot, he gazed at the horses and the gear piled beneath the tree. Nothing was touched. The horses looked well rested and grazed peacefully. With his weary legs, he'd never seen a sight so beautiful.

"We'll rest for an hour," said Etain, "then we'll travel to a spot down the mountain. Away from the cave mouth."

Cormac groaned. "How far?" Physically, he couldn't go another foot. Considering the time, it was already late afternoon. They wouldn't get far before nightfall. Logic told him to stay here until morning.

"Three miles." She grasped the small stick floating in the air that charged the enchanted rope, twisted it and tucked it into her pouch. "An hour travelled today is an hour saved tomorrow."

One hour. One hour? Cormac inwardly groaned, rolled to his back and closed his eyes. He needed a week of doing nothing, just sleeping, eating and watching TV to recover from what he'd endured.

As if Etain had a watch and counted down the seconds, when she thought an hour had passed, she gathered her horse. "Tack up. No thinking. Only do what is necessary. You will feel less pain."

Cormac doubted that statement. In fact, he'd call it a lie if he had the energy. But he didn't. He forced his aching body to a sitting position, groaned, then forced it to rise. Every nerve begged him to lay down. But the others were preparing the horses. Kneilot was helping Etain and anyone else who needed assistance. Jowsey was still sprawled across the grass, sleeping. Or at least pretending to sleep. He wondered how fast the thief would rise if they trotted away without him.

"I will get your saddle," said Kneilot. "Can you manage the blankets?"

Cormac snapped to attention. "Yeah. Thanks." He stumbled over his words. The two of them had the horse ready to leave in 15 minutes.

"Loggie, can Jowsey travel with you?" asked Rosalind. "My horse still favours a leg."

"If I must." Loggie threw the saddlebags over the saddle blanket. "I can spare an hour but nothing more for a thief who brought us to this destiny."

They mounted and set a slow pace to descend the mountain with Etain leading the way. Cormac looked up at the large puffy clouds floating by. It was a stark contrast to the thunder storm that had passed overnight. The rain had made everything fresh and slick. He encountered mud on several parts of the trail and avoided it where possible.

He didn't keep track of time or distance, so when Etain halted at a level clearing, he was surprised they had arrived. A small stream ran along the trail at this point. He remembered passing it on their way to the cave.

Here, they set up camp for the night with a small campfire. He ate a warm meal, soaked in the stream to remove dust, sweat and blood, and then sat back, satisfied and feeling better than he had since before entering the cave. There was still daylight left, but he didn't want to do anything, only rest, relax and enjoy the view.

Etain spread her map on the ground and studied it for a long time. He had almost fallen asleep before she spoke.

"Jowsey, do you know where Thornheart will go?" she asked. "Where does she call home?"

"I've been there a few times." He came to sit next to her and looked over the map. "It's near a place called Haggle's Spring. She calls her place Thornheart Fortress." He smiled mischievously. "It's next to the lake she renamed Thornheart Pond."

"That's not on the map," said Etain. "I can't find Haggle's Spring. Can you give me an idea?"

He pointed to a dot on the map.

"Tempered Passage." She looked up. "It's near here?"

"Just north of it."

"And this Harmon of the Wood," she said to Cormac. "Where is he located again?"

"Beneath a dragon's nodding nose," said Loggie. "Deep in the heart of a meadow in full bloom." He smirked at Cormac.

"Haven't we already established these places?" said Rosalind.

Cormac stared at her. "You're starting to remember more."

She shrugged. "The places sounded real. What were they?"

"It was Starlight Ridge. Past Fields of Blue, beneath Dragon's Noggin', cross the River of Great Turmoil and into the Forest of Wild Lilies.

"I've found Dragon's Noggin'," said Etain. Her finger traced the route.

Loggie hmphed. "I swear you added that after he told you."

"According to the map," said Etain, "Thornheart's location and that of Harmon are a week's journey apart. Both rest beyond Delgrath." She hesitated, then, "The natural course is to pass through the town and then decide if we go northeast to Starlight Ridge or northwest to Thornheart Fortress."

"Why do all the wicked witches live in the west?" Cormac aired the question aloud.

"What other witch lives in the west?" asked Jowsey.

"It just seems that way." Cormac couldn't explain the Wicked Witch of the West to him.

"It's because of the wicked west wind," said Loggie. "While the north is bitter, the west is unkind, torturous, unexpected, unwanted and unlike the north wind that cools on a warm spring day, the west wind has teeth. It bites, cutting into the body like that of a gnawing weasel."

Etain stared. "So, we go to Delgrath?"

He huffed. "Ah, one place is as good as the other. Adventure calls in every direction."

It was decided. They'd travel to Delgrath, rest, gather supplies, then decide what to do.

Rosalind halted the horse and stretched her back, bending one shoulder forward then the other. Four days in the saddle to reach Delgrath had kept her from getting the rest she needed to fully mend. She looked forward to a night at the inn. Given the dark clouds moving in, the solid roof would keep her dry and warm.

Since they had left the side of the mountain, Etain spun stories she had heard from visitors to Norn Sanctuary who had visited the town. While Etain had never been here, she had been educated on it because she was to live here for five years or more, working as an apprentice beneath Sir Uwen the Noble.

She confided in Rosalind that she had learned more about the people in the town from the travellers than her cousins and aunt simply because her family had filtered their version. Their version of her future saw her confined to Oracle Tower of Enchantment, the sanctuary of Sir Uwen the Noble, for the duration of her stay. There, she'd live the pristine life they wanted, never coming in contact with the everyday citizen.

Delgrath was a town ruled by three clerics with years of experience. Once reaching this position, they remained until death or a more powerful cleric challenged for the prestigious position. The same three clerics – Pr. Sycamore, Pr. Alexandrite, Pr. Regulus – had held them for more than 40 years. They were elves in the prime of their life, so no one anticipated them leaving any time soon.

Order was maintained by the Dredgemen, an elite force of elven men trained in magic, sword and long bow. The many travellers to Romarin had told Etain the Dredgemen were more for decoration than anything. No one was foolish enough to challenge them.

"But what is unseen, goes on," said Etain. "Under cover, in darkness and behind sealed doors, the adventurous seek their pleasure and those who want it, find a way. It is the way in every town, every world."

"I smell a thirst-quenching drink and fresh vegetables." Loggie stopped beside her and gazed upon the town in the shallow valley, currently in shadow by the sun sinking behind a mountain. "It is long overdue. My spirit is drained, and it needs reinforcements." He glanced at the darkening sky. "My spirit doesn't want rain."

"It is more beautiful than I anticipated," said Etain. "Words cannot describe the serenity it emanates."

Jowsey, who rode on the same horse, raised an eyebrow. "Looks the same as when I last saw it."

"It indeed looks marvellous," said Kneilot, who sat behind Rosalind. "It is a wonder on the eyes."

"Not after you lose count of the times you've seen it." Jowsey chuckled. "You'll know what I mean after a few days here."

"But you are elven," said Etain over her shoulder. "Surely, an elven settlement is sweet to your spirit."

"Sure, it is, but the Dredgemen stifle it."

"Perhaps you should not draw their attention."

"Strangers draw their attention for no reason."

"We will?"

"You and I will, but not so much as them." He looked at the rest. "Dredgemen have no pleasantries for other races."

"Why is that?"

"Dark elves. Many disguise themselves as dwarf, hauflin and human. They can't take the shape of light elves."

"I've not heard of such nonsense."

"Are you calling me a liar?"

She sputtered, shocked by his accusation. "No. I've nothing of the kind. I am only questioning the reasoning. My elders nor the visitors who I was audience to spoke of dark elves in such a manner. They've nothing but praise for the Dredgemen."

"All of them? Not one spoke negatively about them?"

Her eyes darted between the town and Jowsey. "My recollection is fine, and it has not captured this news."

"Then you'll see firsthand and bring the news to the Sanctuary."

"Let us meet these men of rank and see if they enjoy a pleasant evening at the tavern," said Loggie. "And see if they have spare copper to donate to a starving bard's coffers that garnish him sustenance."

"Onward then," said Rosalind, not wanting to linger longer. She was hungry and tired. She had also felt the first drop that introduced the coming rains.

She rode abreast of Etain, leading the way. The road to Delgrath was well groomed. Two passing wagons could traverse it easily and smoothly. Before they encountered the first dwelling and its fields, a sign, handsomely designed from dark cherry wood and embellished with scrolling white letters, announced the town:

Delgrath
Home of the Elves
ELFER BUDT VELKOMMEN

"What does that say?" asked Cormac.

"Delgrath," quipped Loggie, who rode abreast of him.

"I don't mean that."

"Oh! Home of the Elves. I didn't know you were illiterate. Do they teach you how to read in your world?"

He groaned. "I meant the last line."

Loggie smiled mischievously. "Elves Welcomed. In other words, you, me and hauflins should pass through quickly."

"I've been through without hassle."

"Great. Let's see how you do when you spend a night."

"I'm sure it will be fine."

Rosalind watched the exchange, smiling to herself. Both men entertained her, and she'd grown fond of them.

"Don't talk about where I'm from," said Cormac. "No one needs to know."

"Why? Embarrassed about the illiteracy in your world. I bet the people where you come from can't even read a map."

He frowned. "Thornheart wanted to capture Rosalind for a reason."

Rosalind tuned a more attentive ear to the conversation.

"If she knew I was also from Earth," said Cormac, "she may not have considered me disposable. Thornheart called Rosalind a treasure, someone special. I've been thinking about that. Maybe she'll use her to perform a spell or something."

Loggie raised an eyebrow. "You're not that special."

"No, but Rosalind is. Let's just not talk about it."

"Not so heart shy now." He smirked.

Rosalind stared ahead and waited for Cormac to respond. He didn't. She thought of Thornheart. The woman was set on kidnapping her. For what, nothing was said. However, no one kidnapped anyone for good intentions.

By the time they entered the town, it was drizzling. Jowsey suggested an inn he'd stayed at before, so they let him direct Etain. The streets were busy in the early evening. Most of the people riding, driving wagons and walking were elven. The other races stood out. So did the Dredgemen.

Rosalind spotted the first one at the entrance of the town. Arms folded, he leant against a post supporting the overhanging roof of the boardwalk. He looked lean, tough, not pleasant at all. He wore a uniform of forest green trimmed with black. A short sword hung from his hip. His golden hair was pulled back in a single braid. The vibe she felt when passing made the hair on her neck stand up. She forced her eyes away, hoping to not draw more of his attention but each time she glanced back, he was watching her.

Jowsey turned down a lane and the Dredgeman left her sight. Scanning the boardwalks in front of the shops, she spotted another. He didn't look as mean, but he gave off a similar vibe. The people going about their business seemed friendly enough. Elves of all ages walked in small groups or alone. Some carried parcels in sacks. Some had baskets laden with goods. They wore similar dress as most people in Lachspeur of Yore.

"The sort of location I'd have guessed you'd stay at," said Loggie. "Being the weasel you are."

Rosalind looked ahead to the building he spoke about. The large sign outside the establishment read: Eldritch Tyde's Weasel Inn and Tavern. She smiled at the name. The large sailing vessel in the middle of the sign looked out of place with no ocean in sight.

"Should we choose another?" asked Cormac.

Etain stared up at the rain, increasing in strength. "One night won't kill us."

"It's a fair price," said Jowsey.

Loggie frowned at him. "Cheap doesn't equate to good."

"They're fair people. I've met Eldridge. He's a good man. Lots of stories to tell."

"About guests waking in the middle of night to torment?"

"No." He shook his head and grimaced. "He was a sailor."

"Explains the ship. Pirate or fisherman?"

He held his tongue, and Rosalind studied his face. He didn't want to say. That meant he didn't know, or Eldridge was a pirate.

"Stable." Etain pointed to a gateway beyond the entrance of the establishment. "One can judge an inn by its accommodations for horses."

Rosalind guided her horse into the gateway. Her weary bones didn't want to think about finding another inn. That which lay before her looked suitable. The young stable hand who rushed out to great them was friendly and eager.

"Take your horse," said the young man. "Staying at Tyde's, are you?"

"Yes, we are." She waited for Kneilot to dismounted, then swung her leg over the horse and dropped to the ground. "A stall for this mare. Will you groom her for me?"

"Yes. I do everything." His bright face and smile revealed large teeth. Though he worked outside, his skin remained linen in colour. His lips were only a slight shade darker. His hair, the colour of wet pearls, shined in the evening light.

Rosalind dug out a copper coin. "To show my appreciate." She placed it in his hand. "Take good care of her."

"Me will. The best, I am." His pale blue eyes sparkled.

"I know you will." She pulled off the saddlebags and slung them over her shoulder. Holding the staff, she waited for the others, then followed Etain and Jowsey as they walked towards the entrance.

The threshold of the inn was level with the boardwalk. Next to the door rested a six-foot wood carving of a sea monster. The head and wings were that of a dragon, its front legs of a horse and its torso and hind end that of a serpent. It balanced upright on its bent tail. Its hooves flailed in the air, and its mouth opened wide in an attacking manner to distract the light of heart. Its eyes of red stones watched Rosalind as she passed, putting her on edge before she set foot into the building.

The entrance of the inn was dimly lit with only two lanterns hanging above the counter to illuminate the small, enclosed room. The counter, no more than four feet long, was on the opposite side of the room. A closed door was off to the left and three chairs rested against the wall on the right. A man well-seasoned rose from a chair behind the counter and greeted them.

"Welcome to Eldridge Tyde's Weasel Inn and Tavern. Looking for a room for the night?"

"Yes," said Etain. "Two rooms."

"One for the ladies and one for the gentlemen?"

"Yes."

"We've no room with four beds," said the innkeeper. "Three will be necessary." He picked up an ink pen. "Each room is six copper pieces. Paid in full when booking. Names of the young ladies." He looked to Etain expectantly.

"Fernwind," said Jowsey. "She's my sister." He slung his arm across her shoulders and jostled her. "Younger sister. And this is our friend," he pointed at Rosalind, "Apricusal."

Rosalind remained quiet. Jowsey had his reasons for giving false names. She'd ask him later, but Etain was not happy with the lie and prepared to protest. "Fernwind, we should hurry," she said. "Let Knuckles get us registered. I haven't eaten all day, and my stomach complains like never before."

"Great food at the tavern," said the innkeeper.

"Excellent. As soon as I drop this gear, I'll visit your fine eatery." She caught Jowsey's gaze, and he turned back around to speak to the keeper.

"Fernwind, Apricusal, Knuckles." The keeper recorded the names. "And you?" He looked at Loggie.

"Tharsong Runedelver, the Great Bard of Moore Thyme, at your service."

"A bard?" asked the man. Then he looked at Jowsey. "Any good?"

"Not the best but a fair player," said Jowsey. "Though his selections are limited."

Loggie discretely jabbed two fingers into Jowsey's back below the rib cage, making him jump. "I'll share my quarters with this fine man," he gestured to Kneilot, "Olo Brandywood."

The keeper recorded the name. "And you, young fella?"

Before Cormac had a chance to answer, Loggie answered for him, "Snaig Oatbiter." He grinned at Cormac, pleased with the name he'd chosen. Cormac crossed his arms, appearing tired of the game.

The money paid and the keys given, the keeper gave directions to the rooms and the tavern. They were on the second floor, through the door to the left.

Jowsey led the way, opening the door and stepping through.

Rosalind was near the end of the line. When she passed through, she was met with a foyer dimmer than the previous room. Light glowed farther on. Walking deeper into the inn, she found the entire left side of the hallway opened up with stairs leading down alongside the stone wall. Large wooden barrels were stacked near the bottom of the stairs. Adjacent the stack was a three-sided bar with a keeper busy pouring spirits for those sitting on stools. The floor was divided into two levels, one three steps higher than the other. Tables spread across both sections. A fireplace on the opposite wall held a small fire. Countless lanterns hanging from the ceiling illuminated the large room. Where the walls weren't stone, they were dark plank wood. The only windows were those that ran the two outer walls near the ceiling. The room was decorated with paraphernalia from the sea: crossed oars, fishing nets, flags, miniature replicas of ships, ship's wheel, shields, spearing rods, sails and various other items.

Rosalind could almost smell salt air. Whoever owned this tavern loved the sea. Her eyes drank in the sight and soon she had reached the end of the hallway, and the scene below disappeared behind a wall.

"We should not linger in there this evening," said Cormac.

"We'll leave after I've earned enough for my keep," said Loggie.

"It's a fine crowd," said Jowsey. "As long as Mad Morgan Swett doesn't show up."

"Who's that?" asked Rosalind. "A friend?"

He winced. "No friend of mine nor anyone else who enjoys a quiet drink. Elven blood is tainted with that of sturgeon."

"He eats fish?"

"Not exactly."

She was going to ask further but his expression suggested she wouldn't like the answer. Finding her room, she went inside and stretched out on the bed, savouring its softness. While she lay there, her body argued. It wanted food and rest. The battle was decided when Etain went to the door and looked back at her.

Before she got to the door, thunder rolled overhead, and heavy rains began. She was thankful to be inside. The men were already at a table and placing their order when they arrived. The barmaid was a pretty elven maid, who smiled easily at the men. Wearing a low-cut blouse, she attracted and held their attention. Rosalind sensed the making of a good tip.

The food ordered, she sat back and took in the tavern. It felt tame though she couldn't clearly remember other taverns to compare it to. The fire had been stoked and flames licked the stonework around it. An older man in a cloak with the hood pooling around his shoulders sat on the hearth, his hands splayed towards the heat. He looked damp as if he hadn't reached the protection of the inn before the rains came. The ends of his silver-grey hair, parted in the middle with long bangs pulled to the back in a thin ponytail, lay over the hood in drooping strands. His hair concealed his ears, but it was obvious he was elven from the narrow chin and nose and creamy skin tone. His cloak concealed his clothing and weapons, if he carried any. While he seemed intent on warming his bones, his dark eyes surveyed the tavern and its occupants. His expression, more curious than threatening, didn't change regardless of where he looked. When he locked eyes with Rosalind, they remained steadfast and moved on. She didn't feel threatened by him, but she did sense a motive more than warming his body by the fire. Given the lack of attention given to him by the barmaids, he appeared known to them.

Rosalind visually explored the rest of Eldridge Tyde's Tavern, filled with the sound of clinking dishes and quiet mutterings. Sixteen customers were in various stages of dining, and others slowly trickled in, descending the stairs into the warm atmosphere. The server returned with a tray of drinks. Rosalind paid for her apple cider and took a sip. It was sweet on the tongue with just the right fermentation. She took a longer drink. She hadn't realised she was this thirsty. Before the server returned with food, her mug was empty and she ordered another.

The sound of knives and forks on stoneware kept the conversation to a minimum. By the time plates were empty, Rosalind was on her third drink and feeling quite relaxed. She leant against the wooden backrest and watched the many people who now populated the tavern. Many were elven but there were representation from the three other main races: human, dwarf and hauflin. The sun had set, darkening the windows high above. Stragglers who shuffled in dripping of rainwater went directly to the fireplace to warm. The older man who had been there when she arrived still sat on the hearth and talked to each newcomer. Feeling more relaxed each moment, she waited for one of her friends to suggest returning to their rooms to sleep. She was tired, but the atmosphere lulled her into a reluctance to move. Encouragement from them would be needed. She drew a long, slow breath, and her body relaxed further.

When Loggie stood, her senses semi-awakened and she prepared to direct her sluggish body to rise, too, but she spotted his rebec in one hand and an empty ale mug in the other. She resettled into her peaceful respite and awaited the music that would soon fill the air.

"He shouldn't play long," whispered Cormac. "The place is filling up with questionable people."

"Taverns tend to do that," said Jowsey. "Look," he pointed at Cormac, "there's a questionable person right there."

Cormac frowned. "For one who has no money and nowhere else to go on a stormy night like this, you are easy to make jokes."

"It's a habit." He took a drink of ale. "Might even say it's my trademark."

Loggie plucked the strings of the rebec several times while tuning it. Once the sound satisfied his ears, he played a lively tune about a sailor who loved the sea. Rosalind thought it appropriate given the style of the tavern. When the song ended, the crowd clapped. It was a less than zealous applause, but that didn't deter Loggie. He played a sweat love song about a boy losing his girl only to find her again and marry. The women in the crowd loved this, and one stood up and hooted as the final chords were played.

"He has one fan," quipped Jowsey.

"That's one more than you," said Cormac.

"And three more than I have." Rosalind grinned, then seeing their expressions, laughed aloud. "Popularity is a contest I care not to enter."

Cormac considered her and after a long moment, said, "We are long overdue for a good sleep."

Loggie's next song had the crowd clapping. By the end of it, he was tossed his first coin. The night wore on. The music attracted more attention, more applause and more money. More patrons arrived and soon there wasn't an empty chair in the place. While the rain beat on the windows and thunder rolled overhead, the atmosphere inside the tavern was one of pure excitement and good times. Even the older man at the hearth wore a smile and relaxed more than he had all evening.

Rosalind opted for one more drink as did the others to kill time while Loggie earned enough to pay for their rooms and food. When Loggie finally packed up, it was to hearty cheers and many pats on the arm as he wove through the crowd to return to the table. Skin flushed red and eyes wild with exuberance, he plopped onto the bench beside Rosalind. He grabbed her by the shoulders and shook her, awakening her senses. He planted a kiss on the side of her head, then released her.

"Delgrath is a pleasant surprise," he gasped. "We shall stay another night." He secured the rebec in its sack and withdrew a pouch, which he dumped the coins from his mug into. Securing the string around it, he dropped the jingling cloth bag into a leather pouch at his belt. He no sooner had his coins secured when a man appeared at the table.

The stranger was well-seasoned, more like well-mileaged for an elf. His creamy skin bespeckled with faint scars and a dash of brown spots across the bridge of his nose was on the ruddy side. His thick copper-coloured beard and mustache framed thick lips and solid teeth. Thick hair of dark brown reached his shoulders and was swept away from his face with layers. The sparkle in his green eyes implied a full life of curiosity and adventure. He wore a button shirt with the top three buttons unfastened, revealing a hairy chest. It was tucked into brown cotton trousers with hems hovering over the tops of his boots that went mid-way between his knees and ankles. A black leather vest, dagger belted to the hip and a small steel medallion hanging from a chain around his neck finished off the outfit. He carried with him a tray with six drinks.

"Aye, yar one heck of a bardsman," said the stranger in a gruff voice. "Brought the spirit to the tavy tonight, ya did." He placed the tray on the edge of the table. "Ah show my appreciation in drink." He removed the drinks from the tray and set them on the table. "Marigold says these are the drinks yar been drinkin'."

"Thank you." Loggie picked up a mug of ale and took a long drink. "Parched, I am."

Rosalind eyed the apple cider. It was delicious, and while she knew she shouldn't have another, that thought was ignored, and she took a drink of the offered beverage.

"Foreign to Delgrath," said the stranger. "Yar taking advantage of our fine establishment and spending the evening here?"

"Yes," said Loggie. "Our friend recommended the inn." He pointed to Jowsey.

"Aye. A face I've seen in the past." The stranger nodded at the elf. "Let me personally welcome you to me inn and tavern. I be Eldridge Tyde, proprietor and barkeep when I'm not lost elsewhere."

"Happy to meet you." Loggie offered his hand, and Eldridge shook it. "Tharsong Runedelver, the Great Bard of Moore Thyme." He introduced the rest with their made-up names.

Eldridge grinned and shook the hands offered. "Fine names, I hope ya remember when asked again. Another night, you'll stay? Keepin' patrons spirits high is me destiny."

"One more night?" asked Loggie. "I can't see why not. We are tired. Sore, to be exact. We need a good rest before we venture forth."

"Admirable. I'll look for yar rebec evening of morrow." He leant forward, a grin upon his haggard face. "If yar search for a regular place, ah can accommodate. Music fills the spirit, and the songs of the sea touch the heart a woman can't reach."

"I'll keep that in mind." Loggie's grin reached from ear-to-ear.

"Enjoy the rest of yar time." Eldridge straightened. "We'll meet again." He walked away, revealing a limp he hid well but not well enough to fool Rosalind's eyes.

"Looks like this location is excactly the kind you prefer," said Jowsey, smiling mischievously.

Loggie returned the grin. "On the surface, yes."

The drinks consumed, they stumbled from the tavern and dispersed to their rooms. Rosalind didn't feel her head hitting the pillow. Instead, she imaged a soft mound of grass, moonlight dancing on the water and her body sinking into the peaceful dreams of slumber.

19

Formal Introductions

CORMAC STOOD OUTSIDE the gates of Oracle Tower of Enchantment. The others leant against the stone wall, all except Etain. She was permitted inside the gates for an audience with those in charge. When she returned, their plan was to laze around Delgrath, visiting shops to purchase supplies they'd need to travel. They'd stay another night, then leave in the morning. They didn't have a solid plan after that. They talked about defeating Shayde Thornheart as if it was similar to organising a camping trip. Having escaped the wicked woman once, he wanted to avoid her in all future endeavours. Never seeing her again was his solid plan.

The gate swung open, and he jumped. The woman, dressed in a long grey gown with her hair braided to the sides of her head and down her back, poked out her nose. "He will see you now," she said in a solemn voice. "Follow me."

"See us?" asked Jowsey. "What are we to be seen about?"

The woman didn't answer. Instead, she stepped aside to allow them to pass. Once inside, she closed the gate and locked it. "Follow me."

She clasped her hands in the front and walked through the small courtyard. The cobblestone path cutting through the well-tended garden was as straight as an arrow and ended with a thick wooden door made from planks of various widths and held together with large metal hinges. The bottom foot of the door was reenforced with steel.

"Inside," she said, ushering them through the door while she held it open. Once the last one stepped over the threshold, she closed the door behind them.

Inside the small corridor, two men stood guarding the door at the far end. They were well prepared with leather armour, a sword on their hip and daggers at their side. The room was lit with two lanterns, which barely provided enough light to make out details.

"Place your weapons on the table before proceeding." The solemn woman spoke without emotion. "They will be held here for your return."

Cormac hesitated, but the guards watching him weren't impressed. They stared, cold eyes drilling the order into his brain.

Rosalind was the first to place her staff on the table. Her daggers followed. Kneilot placed his spear beside the staff. It was the only weapon he carried. Loggie and Jowsey removed their daggers, which left Cormac with his sword and two daggers. The number of years it had taken him to obtain the sword and the concern he'd relinquish it now without protest didn't sit well in his gut. When he had first strapped it to his waist, it had felt awkward, and he had to adjust his movements for the added weight. Now, it was starting to feel apart of him. The sword fit perfectly. The weight was ideal for his strength, yet...it wasn't worth dying for, and the two men watching him possessed more skill than he could imagine acquiring. He unfastened the belt holding the scabbard. Placing the sword on the table, he touched the hilt and sent a wish to once again hold it. It felt silly, but it wasn't like he said it out loud for others to hear. He removed his daggers and set them next to the sword.

One of the guards opened the door and entered. The other stood watching. The woman led the procession through the doorway and into a long hall. Several closed doors led off the passage lit with only three candles. The flames provided enough light for them to find their way. That was all.

The woman stopped at the last door on the right, opened it and walked inside. Light spilt out and a warm glow illuminated the entrance. When Cormac reached it, he looked before he entered. The room was large, spacious enough to hold 50 people. The walls were constructed of dark wood, and light cascaded in through three large windows that went from floor to ceiling. Bookshelves lined the opposite wall, and they gave him the impression it was a library. A desk rested near the shelves, and several chairs were spread out around the room.

He stepped inside and the woman closed the door.

"This way." She ushered everyone to sit in the chairs provided. "Do not speak unless spoken to."

That sounded like a cruel joke, but Cormac didn't have anything to say. Yet. So, he took a seat and waited.

Near the desk, Etain stood with a man almost as tall as Cormac. When the man turned to address the group, Cormac's thoughts tumbled over his memories. He looked familiar as if...

"That's the man from the tavern last night," whispered Rosalind. She quickly made eye contact. "The man who sat by the fire most of the night."

He took a second look. She was right. He wore finer clothes and his hair was neater, but that was him. He also didn't have a cloak.

"These are my friends," said Etain, gesturing towards them.

"Guardians and escorts," corrected the man.

"No." Her voice was defiant. "They are my friends."

The man wanted to speak but held his tongue. The look on his face revealed his dislike for her words.

Etain introduced them with their real names, then gestured towards the man. "This is Sir Uwen the Noble."

The noble man made no effort to shake their hands or offer a friendship. He simply nodded.

Cormac was unsure why they were brought into the room. When they had arrived an hour earlier, only Etain was permitted with the message that she would return to them outside once her audience with Sir Uwen was completed. He didn't expect nor want to be entertained by this man or any other in this sanctuary.

"Etain has told me of your adventures." The man's face was serious, bordering on angry. "It is a miracle you sit before me. Now your task complete, we assure you, compensation will be given, and you may leave Delgrath at your convenience."

They were being paid to deliver Etain? Skuld had said nothing of this to Cormac. In truth, he had hardly listened to what the shepherd had said. With Clive inside the inn, the leaving was the vital part, not the with who or the why. Since their escorting trip had taken on more of an adventurous spirit and Etain had forged friendships, he assumed she would leave Delgrath with them. Thinking of her remaining at the sanctuary hadn't crossed his mind for so many days, he'd forgotten it had been there.

"And I will leave with you." Etain's voice lacked confidence.

"My dear, we've discussed this," said Uwen. "You are here with the blessing of your family. It is your destiny to become a great magic-user."

"I understand what was told to me," she said, "and I don't wish to disappoint anyone, particularly you, Sir Uwen, but..."

"Your leaving will not only greatly disappoint me but cause great worry in my heart. You are not ready to face the challenges before you. Chasing after this evil woman Thornheart is business better left to others, not you. I am utterly shocked Shepherd Skuld had the audacity to send you into the wilds with this band of..." He moistened his lips. "Travellers."

Cormac's mind had filled in the proper word the man was looking for: misfits. Regardless of what Uwen thought of them, they had delivered Etain safe and sound to Delgrath. That, he couldn't deny.

Uwen turned to the group. "It is vital she remain and complete her apprenticeship. Lachspeur of Yore needs powerful magic-users to keep in check women like Thornheart. It is her destiny to serve the exquisite Oracle Tower of Enchantment.

"Serve?" asked Jowsey. "I thought she was to be a student, not a servant."

"Serving is the path to enlightenment and full powers."

"If you need a servant, hire one." Jowsey crossed his arms. "She's more valuable for defending against devious characters than sweeping your floor."

Uwen was taken aback. "Young man, you would do good to stay out of the business of destinies."

"Sir Uwen," said Etain, gracefully, "I will decide in the morrow. Let me spend one last evening with my dear friends to consider your generous offer. I will return by noon to discuss this with you. Surely, you can grant me 24 hours."

He bowed gently. "Of course, my dear. Arrive in the morn with your possessions. We will take care of the rest."

"Thank you." Before she turned, she spoke again. "Can you send word to Urðr that I have arrived safely and that you see with your own eyes I am well?"

"Certainly. We will dispatch the message within the hour. I'm sure all at Norn Sanctuary will be relieved to hear the news."

"Wonderful. Thank you."

"Hilda will see you out," said Uwen. "And don't forget, by noon, I expect to see you at my door."

"Of course." She followed Hilda, the solemn woman who had escorted them into the tower.

Once outside, Cormac wanted to ask Etain about her real plans. From the short time he'd know her, he knew she didn't lie, but he knew the words she used could be interpreted other ways.

"The cards?" Rosalind whispered to Etain.

Her grave face stared at her. "Yes."

They spent the day leisurely walking around Delgrath. At one point, Cormac, Loggie and Kneilot went off on their own to fish with a group of men they met at the keep while Jowsey tagged along with Etain and Rosalind when they heard about a magic shop in town.

Just before sunset, they met at the tavern for the evening meal. Eldridge Tyde was happy to see Loggie walk through the door and gave him a free drink. This time, they chose a table on the higher level, behind the fireplace. Etain suggested the corner table more in shadow to avoid Sir Uwen if he showed up again tonight to sit by the fireplace. At this angle and distance, he'd not be able to see them.

"You're not staying, are you?" asked Loggie once they got settled.

"I am acutely aware it is expected of me."

"But...?"

"Expectations by others should not rule my fate."

"Then we shall enjoy the atmosphere of this evening and set out early in the morn."

The food arrived, and they ate and drank and enjoyed the evening, sharing their own tales as well as listening to the stories of those who sat near them.

Just before Loggie left the table with his rebec, a man joined a couple at the table beside them. With excitement and anxiousness in his voice, the dwarf spoke about a horrible sight he'd encountered on the road leading into Delgrath.

"Burnt, the wagon was," he said. "Sitting there, in the middle of the road. Nothing left to salvage."

"And the driver?" asked the man originally at the table.

A short silence and a heavy sigh followed. "Not a sight I'd seen in all me dwarfen years, nor will I think to ever see one again. For this will remain in my thoughts till I or the great oak falls. Sitting in his seat, he was. Slouching as to button a fine shirt for labour. Frozen in that black ash like a log engulfed in flame pulled from the hearth."

"What did you do?" asked the man.

"Did you just leave him there?" asked the woman.

"Fearing to leave me mate and the wee ones in Lachspeur without the presence of my spirit, I charged my horse." His voice quivered. "What had done that still lurked. I'd swear into the ancient horn of Goff, it did. What could I do? Unable to reverse the deed as a man sweat and grit, not of magic and sorcery."

"Was the Dredgemen informed?"

"As soon as my horse entered Delgrath."

A rowdy group of humans at a nearby table drowned out the voices. Cormac tried to hear which road the man had travelled, but in his time of listening, that wasn't revealed. Who ever had attacked that poor traveller and his wagon showed no mercy.

"Time to encourage a little happiness." Loggie picked up the rebec and went to the small stage across from the bar. With the first strike of the strings, he had the attention of most people.

Cormac stretched his neck to see if the same old man - Sir Uwen the Noble - sat at the hearth this evening. He baulked when he saw Uwen looking over his shoulder and staring at him. Had he recognised Loggie and knew he'd come from this area of the tavern? Didn't matter. Uwen's gaze took in everyone in the group, then returned to Loggie.

"He's here again tonight," Cormac bent towards the centre of the table and whispered.

"Sir Uwen?" asked Etain, her eyes wide. He nodded, and she stared towards the fireplace but from where she sat, she couldn't see it.

"Are you worried he won't let you leave?" asked Rosalind.

"I feel he may try to remind me vigorously about my destiny and my duty."

"Your duty is to yourself, and your destiny is in your hands, not his or anyone else's."

"While this I know, I feel obligated."

"The power of obligation is both good and evil. It should never dictate our lives nor choose our path." Rosalind leant forward and stared into her eyes. "You have an obligation to yourself to live your truth, not someone else's."

"I fear I will disappoint Urðr. I have lived my whole life seeking her approval."

"Have you thought about seeking your own?"

Her lips froze and her eyes settled on the table. "I have much to consider. I need time to do that. I will find it with my friends."

"Good because I agree with Rosalind," said Jowsey.

Cormac frowned at him. "As a thief, you are one to talk about making wise choices."

"What wrong choice have I made? I am fed, I have shelter and I have good friends. What more can a man ask for?"

"Friends you abandoned while on watch."

"I did not abandon you. I waited at a great distance until I saw you awaken, then I left."

"When did Guthro catch up to you?"

"A mile away." He grimaced. "Apparently, he had been following us, waiting for an opportunity. I gave him that."

"That was extremely kind of you."

"Nobody ever said I was mean."

Cormac was going to respond with, nor bright, but he let it go and turned his attention to Loggie, who was entertaining the crowd. More people than last night enjoyed the tavern, drinks and food. If he had to guess, some had returned and others were told by the owner Tyde that music would be part of the evening.

An hour later, Loggie left the stage to much applause. He arrived at the table, hot and thirsty, and just like the evening before, Eldridge Tyde arrived with a platter of drinks.

"Yar'll stay another night thar, bard?" said Eldridge. "For surely you are Tharsong Runedelver, the Great Bard of Moore Thyme. They miss your company, if I know anything about that town but thar loss be my gain in all sorts of the word."

"I shall return again," said Loggie, taking a long drink, "but I have pressing matters that cannot wait."

"When you enter Delgrath again, be sure I am your first stop. I'll accommodate you and your rebec."

"Thank you. I appreciate that."

"Safe travels, bard, and to yar friends as well."

Eldridge returned to the bar, leaving the band of adventurers to finish their drinks, of which once done, they left the tavern. To reach the stairs, the exit, they had to walk past the fireplace. Sir Uwen was waiting and stood to grasp Etain's hand.

"A healthy sleep, my dear," he said. "I await your arrival at the sanctuary."

"Thank you," said Etain. "May your rest be equally healthy." She withdrew her hand and followed the others up the stairs.

On the balcony overlooking the tavern, Cormac looked down. Sir Uwen was staring up at them, watching every step they took. He knew where they were for the night, possibly even which room they slept in if he had connections with the owner. He'd warn Etain and Rosalind to be extra vigilant while they slept, making sure windows and the door were secured.

He groaned. Those entry ways were often the least to worry about when spending a night at an inn attached to a tavern.

It was late afternoon, and the sun was breaking through the clouds by the time Rosalind reached the bridge across Pebble Creek. The sign indicating the name was secured to the rail mid-span, and she'd almost missed it while admiring the gentle flow of water.

Last night, after she and Etain had settled in their room, she shuffled the Roots of Terra cards and drew three to help Etain decide what she'd do in the coming days. While vague, the cards revealed a journey. They also revealed danger. At first, the energy was calm, then it shot up from the cards and exploded like fireworks near the ceiling. At that point, they put away the cards and went to bed without discussing it further. Rosalind didn't understand the meaning. Were they to celebrate or fear an explosion?

She had awakened before dawn and shook Etain awake. They met the boys at the tavern for a quick meal, bid a final farewell to Eldridge Tyde, then rode out of Delgrath shortly after sunrise. The streets were practically bare with only a few early-risers walking about. Once they left town, Etain voiced her relief.

"I didn't see him anywhere watching me." Etain had thrown a quick glance at her, and there was no need to name the 'him' in question.

Riding off Pebble Creek Bridge, Rosalind prepared for the bend ahead that went around a small mound with shrubs. A dark object protruded from the top of the mound, and she watched it with curiosity. It appeared to be leafless branches of a dead tree. The farther she travelled and saw more of the mysterious object, she decided it couldn't be a tree. Maybe an old building that had been left to decay and rot where...

Her thoughts mumbled in her head. Confused by the image taking shape. It refused to acknowledge what lay before her.

"That's it." Cormac's hushed voice held the uncertainty rattling around in Rosalind's mind.

It. The it they had heard about the night before at the tavern. Overhearing this sight described in words mixed with laughter and boisterous chatter in the safety of a tavern was not the same as seeing it firsthand and smelling the lingering odour of burnt wood and flesh. As described, the driver remained a haunting image in the seat of the wagon, his body slouched forward in a manner to fasten buttons. His hat lay melted to the hind end of one of two horses that lay where they collapsed, still harnessed to the wagon. It was as if one moment this man was singing a lovely tune with the birds, then in a flash, all was silent. Not even the birds continued his song. The forest around her lay still, void of animal life. Not even the flies gathered to bother her or consume the roasted meat of beast and man.

"What in the name of all that is well in Lachspeur could have happened," whispered Kneilot from behind Loggie. He wrapped his arms around his chest, adding an extra layer of protection to his chicken.

"Something evil," said Jowsey. "Never in all my journeys have I seen this upon an innocent traveller."

"But you have on a guilty one?" asked Cormac.

Jowsey stared at him for a moment, then shook his head.

"Everyone went around it," said Rosalind. In the short time it was here, tracks made by other wagons and people on horseback had already created distinct marks that gave the scorched wagon a wide berth. "No one stopped to... It is left for nature to consume?"

"Like we will do," said Jowsey. "I'm not going anywhere near it."

"He's not wrong," said Etain. "A tragedy. We can do nothing for this man nor the horses. I sense negative energy. I will not touch it."

"I'll lead the way," said Cormac. He guided his horse along the same tracks that skirted the road to avoid touching the charred remains.

Rosalind followed, eyes on the horses, then the man and finally the wagon. It was impossible to tell if he was old or young, he was burnt so badly. He would have died not knowing what had struck him. That was a comforting thought, the only one this sight generated. The remains of crates in the rear of the wagon suggested he was delivering goods to Delgrath from... She looked ahead. Which settlement had he come from? Which was the closest? Friesian Ford or Two Elks Collide? One led to Thornheart Fortress, the other to Starlight Ridge.

She thought about asking Coraline, but she hadn't seen the fairy since entering Delgrath. Coraline didn't like the town, not that she liked any town, but Delgrath was different. She sensed strong magic, and she was not ready to face that. Sometimes Rosalind saw her immediately after leaving a populated area. Other times, it took two days for the fairy to lose interest in her activities before joining Rosalind.

Hearing mumbling, she looked towards Loggie, whose face appeared ready to crack. The hushed words came from Kneilot in the saddle behind him. The young cleric was saying words over the remains, perhaps to bring peace to the man whose life had ended abruptly.

Riding abreast of Cormac, she focussed on the terrain ahead. The road was clear, the forest thick. They travelled ten minutes before the sounds of birds touched her ears and other wildlife returned. A red-tailed squirrel darted across the road in front of her and disappeared beneath the undergrowth. Bees buzzed around wildflowers and insects gathered in swarms in the shafts of sunshine pouring through the tree branches.

"Horrible!"

Rosalind jumped at the voice in her ear. Seeing Coraline sitting on her shoulder, hugging the braid that rested there, settled her nerves. "What is it?" she said in whisputter, turning her mouth towards the fairy and trees and away from Cormac.

"The dragon attack."

"Where?"

"The scene that slowed your progress in the forest."

"The wagon scorched on the road?"

"That is it. Sadness. Horrible, terrible sadness."

"Were you there?"

"Nearby. I sensed the approach, then a dark shadow passed overhead. The scream was dreadful and short. The horses barely time to snort before they collapsed, pushed farther by the momentum of the wagon."

Rosalind's first thought went to Kiefwind of Sweetgrass. Would he have done such a thing? Was he truly an evil dragon? "What colour was the dragon?"

"Blue like the pale sky in the morning mist."

Kiefwind was white, so it couldn't have been him. "Did you see where it went?"

"North."

"Are you talking to yourself?" asked Cormac.

Rosalind swung her head to stare at him. Coraline didn't want to reveal herself to him or the others. She was a carefree fairy but lived over-cautiously. "Yes. It's how I work things out."

"What are you trying to work out? The horror we just witnessed?"

"Yes, and which direction I should go."

"I prefer south, away from two people set on destroying each other."

"We are responsible for setting free Kiefwind."

"Not really," he said. "We had no choice if we wanted to live."

"I don't think Kiefwind is a bad dragon."

"You don't know that."

"I know for certain Thornheart is a despicable person, and she will use the dragon to hurt others. If we can prevent that, we not only save Kiefwind but innocent people."

"Is it about that or the quest?"

"Quest?"

"The thrill of the quest regardless of what it is."

She thought about that. Was she going just to go? Did it matter?

"Sweetgrass is an eight-day journey from here...for you," said Coraline. "I can be there in five. I can visit the fairies of the land and enquire about Kiefwind. That should help you decide."

"That would be great."

"What would be great?" asked Cormac.

She raised an eyebrow at Coraline, but the fairy shook her head vigorously, telling her she didn't want to reveal herself. Rosalind turned back to Cormac. "It would be great if we could visit Sweetgrass and ask the dragons if they are good."

Jowsey laughed. "Just waltz in and say, *Well, Mr. Dragon, are you going to eat me or serve ale?*"

Rosalind frowned at him. "We could ask people who live near there."

"None of the four races live near Sweetgrass," said Etain. "Who would we ask?"

"Fairies?"

The smirk on Jowsey's face indicated he didn't believe in fairies. That's what concerned Coraline.

"Or the crows," said Loggie. "We're apt to find one of them."

"It was only a thought," said Rosalind.

"Come now, Loggie," said Jowsey, "if not fairies, we might stumble upon a pixie or a nymph." He giggled.

Coraline gave Rosalind a look that said, I told you so. "I will return as soon as I can. Be well."

"As you. I will look for you in ten days."

With that, Coraline flew away.

"Look for what in ten days?" asked Cormac.

"My messenger to return with news from Sweetgrass." She faked a grin. He prepared to respond, but instead closed his mouth.

20

No Time for Tea

FOUR HOURS LATER, Cormac halted his horse near a small clearing. It was, in the way of many clearings alongside the road, surrounded on three sides by lush forest, possessing the rudimentary requirements of a place to bed-down for the night, its vegetation providing foraging for the horses, its trickling stream offering water to them and the animals. The blackened rocks of a firepit that had seen many travellers linger around its warmed suggested it was a popular overnight location.

"It is seasoned for adventurers," said Loggie. "We'll take it."

Jowsey slipped from the saddle and stretched his back. "I'll love me my own horse again."

"What happened to the one we gave you?" asked Cormac, dismounting.

"I was brought to the cave on its back but in her haste, Thornheart has claimed it mistakenly. I'll ask for its return the next I see her."

Cormac stared, wondering if he was telling the truth or pulling his leg. But Jowsey turned away, robbing him of the answer. Once the horses were settled, the bedrolls laid and the fire lit, he relaxed near the firepit slowly eating a warm meal of fried potatoes, seasoned with thyme and garlic, and toasted bread.

Etain finished her meal, then spread the map on the ground and studied it.

"Has anything new appeared?" asked Rosalind.

New? Cormac was unsure about a map that changed daily. He preferred printed maps that were the same today as they were ten years ago even if in reality places had changed slightly.

"An option." Etain's voice was hushed.

"Where?" Rosalind copied the voice and followed Etain's finger. "That wasn't there this morning."

"No. It is as if the nearer we draw to it, the darker it appears."

"It doesn't matter which road we take, we can change our minds and take the short cut."

"Short cut?" Jowsey bound over and squeeze between them. "From where to where?"

"Here." Etain put her finger on the map. "To here. If we take the road to Friesian Ford and decide after we pass it to travel to Two Elks Collide, we can take this connecting road."

"Makes sense," he said. "The two villages are only a day apart on the shortcut, but four if one travels south to the fork and then north again."

"We should go to Harmon's." Cormac swallowed hard. He didn't want to see the man, but he'd rather see him than Thornheart.

"Why?" asked Loggie, his eyes narrowing.

"I feel less threatened by him."

"A security issue." He mulled this over. "We could split up."

"No! That never works." Cormac remembered the times he and his friends had split up during a game. Someone always died.

"Quite adamant about that, I see. Done it before?"

"Splitting up will divide our strength, not multiply it. Harmon doesn't appear to be a threat. I could be wrong, but Thornheart and her slave dragons are definitely a threat."

"And if Thornheart is on her way to destroy Harmon," said Rosalind, "then we'll find both at one place: Starlight Ridge."

Both? Both. They'd join forces and kill him. Or he'd watch them battle it out and then, they could finish off the survivor. That sounded like a solid plan. No doubt, the survivor would be injured, making it an easy kill... What was he thinking? He'd never killed a human before. The slugs, skeletons and kobolds were one thing, but a human...

"It's settled then," said Loggie. "We trudge to Starlight Ridge."

"Agreed," said Etain. "In the morning, we will reach the fork within four hours. The terrain turns into thicker woods. We shall reach Two Elks Collide on the morn of overmorrow and Starlight Ridge in five days."

Cormac gulped. He'd face his fate in five days. Maybe he could ride slower, give Thornheart a chance to reach Harmon's cabin, then leave...or be defeated. He didn't mind arriving late to the party.

This thought disturbed his evening peace, and he wished he had a mug of ale to wash it down. Instead, he settled for water and two crisp cookies that resembled ginger snaps.

The night passed quietly, and the band rose early the next day. They started riding an hour after sunrise and reached the fork in the road, as predicted by Etain, four hours later. There, they met a wagon drawn by two horses. The man in the seat was elven and said he was on his way from Friesian Ford to Delgrath. When told about the tragedy at Pebble Creek, his face whitened. In all his years of travelling the road, this had never happened. They bid him farewell and safe travels and turned onto the road leading to Two Elks Collide.

Three hours before sunset, they happened upon another well-used campsite and opted to stop for the day. The basic requirements were met: grazing area for the horses, a brook for water and a firepit. With the fire sharing its warmth and the meal consumed, Loggie lay against his pack and played gentle tunes on the rebec, lulling everyone into a serene state.

In spite of drawing nearer to danger, Cormac felt at ease. His injuries were healing, his belly was full and at the moment, he felt safe.

The next morning was a repeat of the day before. Just before noon, they rode into Two Elks Collide, population 1,801, according to the sign. The people were elven, human and mixture of the two. It was a small village with one main street and several shooting off it. For Cormac, it was like many rural places in Nova Scotia. What the traveller saw from the main road was only a small portion of homes in the community. Most were down long driveways or side roads.

They stopped at the keep and picked up food items, including bread, then continued. According to Etain's map, the next settlement, Westdun, was two days away. Or at least she predicted it to be. The terrain appeared uneven on the map, and she was unsure of what to think about it.

"It may be a small mountain," she said.

Either way, they left Two Elks Collide with the sun at their backs. Every few miles along the route, they encountered places where travellers had stopped for the night. They also met others on the road, mostly human or elf. They passed only one dwarf, and he rode alone. The others were in wagons, carrying goods to Delgrath. The short conversations revealed all was well on the road ahead and that it took three days to travel between Two Elks Collide and Westdun because it was near the mountaintop and the road wove to make the climb easier.

This eased Cormac's mind, and as they camped each night, he relaxed in the peaceful setting. The friendliness of those he met along the road added to the relaxation. He drifted off each night, feeling satisfied.

On the night before they'd reach Westdun, they camped on a flat piece of ground overlooking a lovely valley. He sat near the campfire, swatting the odd mosquito that ventured near and listened to Loggie play the rebec.

"On a mountainside before the great battle," sang Loggie, "oh, my heart races and my nerves rattle."

Cormac chuckled. "Rattle?"

"Can you do better?"

"No, I'm no song writer."

"Then hush." He drew the bow across the strings. "In the north, evil has found a home and we must go. In these dire times, it is not me they need but a hero."

Again, Cormac chuckled.

"All great songs start out rough," said Loggie. "I'm working on it. Sing me your song, and I will play the tune."

"Are you holding out for a hero?" asked Rosalind.

Cormac swung his attention towards her. "Do you know that song?"

She thought for a moment, searching the ground for details. When he hummed the melody, her eyes lit up, and she sang the chorus to *Holding out for a Hero*. It was like her mouth knew the song from singing it many times.

She grinned. "I don't know where that came from."

"An inner spirit," said Loggie.

"Or radio," said Cormac.

Loggie raised an eyebrow. "Is that a god in your world?"

"Many worship it." He turned to Rosalind. "Do you remember who sings it?"

Again, she searched her memory. When a smile creased her lips, he knew she'd found the answer. "Bonnie Tyler. I have no source for the name. It leapt into my mind from the shadows."

"Your memory is returning in pieces."

Her eyes rested on him, and the smile he'd grown to appreciate spread across her face. She was unlike any woman he'd known. She possessed the ability to capture a man's attention but unlike many others, she had the power to hold his. Her natural beauty, too weak, or in essence too real, to make her a pin-up model, would easily entice a man to consider spending the rest of his life with her, if he was inclined to settling down and raising a family. Her strong shoulders and fine hips could easily bear many children as well as a staff and daggers. Her voice, once foreign and uncertain, had grown familiar, yearned for in fact. Her skin, with faint freckles dancing across the bridge of her nose to her cheeks, was well tanned in the sun. She resembled many in Nova Scotia, and he wondered... Loggie had said they had the same accent. He hadn't noticed because...well, you don't know things like that when you share an accent.

"Are you from Canada?" he asked, her attention still on him.

"Canada." She said it slowly.

"Is that your land on your world Earth?" asked Loggie.

"It's a country. That's a large section of land ruled by one government."

"Like a city?" offered Etain.

"Larger. Much large. It includes the cities, towns and villages within an area."

"How does a king keep order?" asked Kneilot.

He shrugged. "They just kind of protect the border and make up stuff. Most people do what they want."

"And it works?" asked Jowsey. "Doing what you want?"

"It works here. Why wouldn't it work there?" said Cormac.

"Yes," said Rosalind. "It sounds very familiar."

"Does Nova Scotia sound familiar?"

She thought about it, then quickly said, "Yes. I feel I am from there. Is there an ocean?"

"Almost surrounded entirely by one."

"That sounds amazing."

Cormac was about to speak, but a strange sound reached his ears, stalling his mouth and mixing up his thoughts. It grew louder and he looked down the road towards Westdun. The others followed his line of sight. In the fading twilight, he stared, waiting as the pounding increased. Hand on the hilt of his sword, he prepared for an attack. His pulse beat fast, and his mouth went dry. Whatever it was, it was large.

"A horse," whispered Rosalind, gazing into the distance. "And rider. Fast."

The hooves pounded the hard ground, kicking up dirt and rocks. The rider, a young human in trousers, button shirt and boots, was bent forward, focussed on the road ahead. The moment he saw them, his intense expression changed to fear.

"Danger! Run! Dragons to the north!"

"Wait!" Jowsey stood up and raised his hand. "Dragons, you say? Where exactly?"

The rider slowed but didn't stop. "North of Westdun," he gasped. Dirt and sweat clung to his face. He kicked the horse to go faster and left as quickly as he came in a cloud of dust that settled slowly.

Jowsey whirled around to the others, his face twisted in confusion. "He ran all the way from Weston?" He turned to Etain. "Where is that on the map?"

She plucked it from her pouch and quickly spread it on the ground. "There!"

Cormac stared at the dot indicating Westdun, the village they'd enter tomorrow. "It's four hours away." He grimaced. "He couldn't have ridden like that since Westdun."

"Wish he had time for a kettle of tea and pleasant conversation," said Loggie. "Might have gotten more from the lad than a blustery wind of fear and urgency."

"Thornheart has claimed the will of Kiefwind," said Rosalind in a solemn voice. "And she's using him to..." She looked towards Delgrath. "A dragon killed that man at Pebble Creek."

Etain stared at her, her mouth partially open, her eyes revealing she searched her memories. "How can you be certain?" she whispered.

"I just know. He had no warning."

"No warning?" asked Kneilot cringing from the thought. "Just..." He stared into the distance. "I am unsure how I can help you. Or prevent this from happening. I wanted only to escape Mia the Mystic to save myself and Matilda."

"None of us will survive that," said Cormac. "We cannot fight a beast, no, many beasts with that power. I am not a hero."

"We don't have to fight the dragons," said Rosalind. "Only Thornheart."

"Who is guarded by seven dragons," said Loggie.

The band of adventurers fell silent, and the pounding of hooves faded in the distance. For several long moments, no one spoke and Loggie did not strike the rebec. The only sounds filling the air were those of nature and the crackling of wood on fire.

Then Etain spoke in an even voice. "We shall go to Westdun, assess the problem and then decide. If it is to return to Delgrath, then let it be so. Conceivably this is the danger Sir Uwen spoke about that I am ill-prepared for. Though I do not feel ill-prepared but unprepared."

Cormac returned to his comfortable position, however, comfort did not return to his body though their plans were settled. They'd visit Westdun, then return to Delgrath and venture elsewhere. His nerves began to settle until he caught Rosalind staring at him. The look on her face indicated her plans were different. She was set on saving Kiefwind, which sent his nerves into high gear again.

The final four-hour ride to reach Westdun was tiring. The village was on the side of a mountain, and the road wove back and forth to ease the strain of horses pulling wagons. Upon reaching level ground, Rosalind felt she had travelled the road ten times. It didn't help that Jowsey was on the back of her horse for this stretch of the journey.

"First time in Westdun," he said when the first dwelling appeared. "Always good to visit new places."

She glanced over her shoulder. Sweat on his face mixed with dust gathered on the trail, and his wind-beaten hair looked frizzy. "You've been to many places."

"All over Lachspeur of Yore, but not this area." He grinned. "There are still many places I haven't ventured."

"You're more of a traveller than a thief?"

"Not a thief. A messenger for those who will pay. It is the best way to see the land."

"After we are done at Starlight Ridge, you'll continue on your way?"

He considered the question, shot a quick glance at Etain, then shrugged. "It's a possibility. Where will you go?"

"Not sure. I may look for a way home."

"Leave Lachspeur?"

"This is not my home. I sense another place..."

"But you have friends here."

"I may have family who miss me."

"Will you return?"

She considered it. She'd like to. This was the only home she remembered, the only friends she knew. "I don't know if I can. I don't even know if I can leave." She smiled. "You may be stuck with me."

"You are fine company to be stuck with."

"We'll look for an inn," said Etain.

"It's only mid-afternoon," said Cormac. "We have time to visit the keep and start towards Delgrath. We could get in four hours of riding before sundown."

She stared at him. "We are staying the night."

He fell silent and looked away.

"How he ever passed the last challenge to reach the dragon is baffling," whispered Jowsey.

"Sometimes courage is hidden deep within. It need not be gathered unless absolutely necessary."

"Maybe it was your kiss that gave him the courage." He winked at her.

Shocked from her thoughts, she'd almost forgotten about that. Except at times when Cormac looked at her as if he was remembering the kiss. She had been surprised by the intimate action. It was gentle, warm and stirred dragonflies in her belly. "If that is the case, then I know what to do when we face danger again."

Asking a fellow on the street about an inn, the man directed them to the Three-legged Mare. It was on the main road in the middle of the village.

Rosalind wanted to ask him about the dragon attacks the terrified rider had shouted about as he sped by the campsite the previous night, but she didn't want to needlessly alarm the man unless the claims about dragons were true.

The Three-legged Mare was a small inn of one level. She doubted it had ten rooms. The stable was attached to the building. A stable hand greeted them when they dismounted. He was human, taller and slenderer than dwarf men, thicker than elven men. He held the necessary skill to handle a horse, even the ones less trained. His cherry expression, solid muscles peeking from his rolled sleeves, and his work clothes revealed his dedication to hard work. He appeared to have a kind eye for the horses under his care.

"Fine animals, I see," said the stable hand as he held onto the bridle of Cormac's horse. "Needing a room for overnight?"

"Yes. Two rooms, please. If you have them," said Cormac.

"We can accommodate. The horses, too."

"Sir, may I ask an unusual question?" said Etain.

"Ma'am, it is why I am here," he said, "to answer your questions."

"Last night, we were camped on the road, and a rider came through. He was feverish with fear. Shouting about dragons. Have you heard of such things?"

The stable hand moistened his lips and cautiously glanced down the road one way, then the other. "I am told of such things, but..." His eyes locked with hers. "I've not seen such evil. I know not the man you speak, but two travellers arriving yesterday together reported sights in the sky, north of Westdun, flying east. I've lived here the length of my life, all 47 years, and I've not once heard tell of nor seen such things."

"But there have been reports?"

"Only that one." He chuckled nervously. "Unusual, they were. I believe they may have drunk too much or banged their heads. Maybe under a confusion spell of some sorts. Why else would they tell fantastic stories to...?" His brow bent. "Why do you ask about such things? Because a stranger shouted nonsense or... Do you know more of their claims?"

"We're unsure." She looked to the others. "We believe a woman named Shayde Thornheart has enslaved dragons—"

"That woman!" His face grew red. "She has caused much havoc in Westdun. We have banned her from the village."

Cormac wore an uneasy expression, and his voice trembled when he spoke. "We don't like her," he said. "She's very mean."

Loggie slowly turned his head and gawked at him. "Mean? Is that the extent of your vocabulary?"

"She almost fed me to the water monster," said Jowsey. "I'd call her diabolic, not mean."

"Fiendish even," said Loggie, "but not mean."

"Terrifying is a good word," said Kneilot. "As is horrifying."

"What they're trying to say," said Rosalind, "is we don't like her. She doesn't like us. We're enemies, and we're going to destroy her."

Cormac's mouth dropped open, and he gaped at her. "Hold on a minute. We're to assess the situation, then return to Delgrath."

The stable hand approached Rosalind. "She's dangerous." He looked her up and down. "A pretty little thing as yourself is no match for her wickedness. Now this young man," he pointed to Cormac, "doing all the avoiding, might have a chance."

"We go together," said Etain.

"If we go," added Cormac.

"The more the better. She has reinforcements. Men of dirty deeds, who will steal the alley cat to disturb the peace. But she has a weakness."

"What is that?" asked Rosalind.

"Trust."

"Explain."

"She trusts no one, not even those who serve her. When trust is not had, manipulation is easier. I'm told she killed a horse because she didn't trust it. Killed men, squirrels, even a..." he glanced at Kneilot, "chicken. Once."

Kneilot wrapped his arms around his pet chicken. "She will not harm Matilda."

"Nice name for a hen. Does she still lay?"

"Most mornings." Loggie clicked his tongue on the side of his mouth and grinned.

A wagon pulled up to the stable and stopped.

"Must get busy," said the stable hand. "Boys!" he yelled into the shadows of the stable. Three youngsters, no more than eight rushed out, eager to lead the horses away.

Rosalind relinquished her horse to one of the boys and followed the others inside the Three-legged Mare Inn. She noticed Cormac staring at the ground and dragging his feet. He didn't want to be here. She understood. She didn't want to be here either. Before they entered, he mumbled. It was difficult to understand, but she thought he said, "The last thing I want is to become charcoal for a dragon."

21

Follies of Ancient Magic

VOICES IN CORMAC'S head continued to mumble, and he continued to ignore them. They spoke of doing things he didn't want to do. Going places he didn't want to go. Right now, he wanted only to sleep and forget about what the next day might bring. But the voices persisted. He slammed the pillow over his head to block out the noise and tried to fall into the deep well of sleep.

The strange voices grew louder. Then it turned into only one voice that at first whispered in a language he didn't understand. *Muster thy inner magic to...*

Why would he think that? He held no magic.

Gather thy strength. Summon thy courage.

His courage was protected beneath a thick layer of skin and clothing. It could rest there, and he'd use it another day.

With all the wisdom granted me, turn this creature into a caterial, then let the rising sun transform it into what it once was before nefarious deeds altered her.

His eyes flew open, and a blinding flash forced him to throw the pillow to his face and hold it there.

"What have you done?" asked Loggie.

"Incredible." It was Jowsey's voice. "That's a fascinating improvement."

Cormac removed the pillow and sat up. Looking across the three beds beside him, he saw Loggie and Jowsey sitting up like boys at a Boys Scout camp, grins on their faces, staring at Kneilot on the floor with the chicken. Except... He squinted in the dim lantern light to identify the animal standing before the hauflin. It was not a chicken. Though it had wings.

He crawled to the end of his bed and peered over the edge. "What is it?"

Kneilot, eyes wild, a hesitant smile on his face, took a moment to answer. "It's a..." He gulped breath. "A caterial."

He scanned the floor. "Where's your chicken?"

"Matilda isn't a chicken." His breathing grew regular. "She's a caterial now."

He flopped onto the bed and stared at the creature. It was in every sense of the word a regular cat with hair in shades of gold, like his neighbour's cat back on Earth. The strips of colour on its face were more defined, and its whiskers were blacker and thicker than the cats he'd seen. The ears were pointier with rigid black hairs randomly shooting off them and, if he had to guess from the size of the paws, the claws were sharper. It's tail, well, most of it, was like that of a standard cat except it was three times as long and ended in a puff of feathers.

But what made this cat infinitely different was its wings. Tucked into its sides, they appeared like bat wings. They were divided into arc-segments with elongated bones covered with gold and brown feathers. When it stretched the wings, the span had to be four feet. He slowly retreated towards the head of the bed.

"Is it tame?" he asked. "In the game, we came upon such a creature and it attacked, causing a lot of damage." He recalled another detail. "It's magical. It's said tabby cats are killing machines except they're only seven pounds. But that," he pointed at the caterial, "has the power of flight, and it's stronger than regular cats."

"Tame?" asked Kneilot with a squished up face. "It's Matilda."

Cormac stared at him. The hauflin truly believed it was the woman he adored entrapped within a spell.

"How did you do it?" asked Jowsey. "Where did you get the spell?"

Kneilot faltered and slowly lifted a dirty cloth that looked like it had been used to wash the hind-end of a horse after a long, hot ride. "The spell... I was unsure whether I could perform it or not. If it would work. It's gone." He spread the cloth and looked on both sides. "The writing was there."

"One-time use," said Jowsey. "So, you turned her into a flying cat. That's better than a chicken."

"Speak for yourself," said Loggie. "I'm going to miss the fresh eggs."

"She won't stay a caterial for long." Kneilot patted the cat's head. "The spell said it will turn someone into a caterial only until sunrise, then they'll turn back to their original form." His eyes lit up. "Her original form is hauflin."

"Will she be naked when she turns?" asked Jowsey.

Horror raced across Kneilot's face. "I will wrap her in a blanket when the sun rises."

Still half sleep, Cormac wasn't sure he followed the conversation. It sounded like Kneilot was trying to work through a loophole. "What if it's the original form she was when she was turned into a caterial," he said. "Then she'd just turn back into a chicken."

"But that's not her *original* form." Kneilot lowered his brow. "It has to work."

"And if it doesn't?"

"I'll try another." He guided the cat onto his lap and stroked its back. "We'll fix this, Matilda," he said softly to the cat. "There has to be a way to make you hauflin again."

The cat meowed affectionately and kneaded its front paws against his pants.

"If nothing else," said Cormac, yawning and rolling back onto his pillow, "you keep things interesting." He conjured good thoughts to create a peaceful sleep. At the moment, that's all he could ask for.

Yet, he didn't get it. For the rest of the night, he tossed and turned, saw Thornheart's wicked face in his and had the rear of his pants scorched. By morning, he was only half rested. When he opened his eyes and saw the bright sun shining through the lone window, he shut them halfway until they adjusted. Opening them farther, he saw the caterial sleeping peacefully in the sunshine at Kneilot's feet. The hauflin would be disappointed when he woke and found his woman – if she was a real woman – still a magical creature.

He rolled to his back and stared at the ceiling, dreading the day to come. The way Rosalind and Etain talked, it sounded like they were destined to stop Thornheart and free the dragons. Those darn Roots of Terra cards gave them that idea. They checked them each night and sometimes in the morning. He bet that when they returned to their room last night, they played with them. They were probably trying to read the cards right now before they started their day.

Footsteps in the hall drew his attention. It sounded like two people walked by the door, talking in hushed voices. When they passed, he saw the caterial also staring at the door. It looked at him with its deep green eyes, then settled its chin upon its paws and closed its eyes.

He released a loud, tiring sigh. He didn't want to go back to travelling alone and wandering aimless, but he didn't want this.

Kneilot woke with a start and sat up quickly. His face, when he saw the caterial, was painful. He released his own sigh.

In the next bed, Jowsey woke, rubbed his eyes and looked at the creature. "Maybe it's tomorrow's sunrise that triggers it." He shrugged. "If it was going to fail today, it would be a chicken already."

Kneilot's expression brightened. "Yes. That is clearly what will happen." He scooped up the cat-like creature and hugged it. "Tomorrow, Matilda. You will be you again."

Cormac looked away. He didn't like to see dreams quashed.

A short time later, they waited for Rosalind and Etain at the tavern. The pair were in deep discussion as they approached the table. When Rosalind looked up and saw him, she stopped talking.

Loggie stood and bowed slightly. "Tis a fair morning, my dears. I hope your sleep was as restful and as entertaining as ours." He motioned them into the seat. When they saw the caterial, their mouths dropped open.

"What is that?" asked Rosalind.

"Let me guess," said Etain. "I am an expert on magical creatures, and I say a caterial. The real question is, where did you find it? Is it your familiar? A cleric always seeks a familiar."

"Oh, I suppose so," said Kneilot. "I haven't thought of it that way but for today, it can be."

"Only today?" asked Etain. "Why?"

"You see, this is Matilda and tomorrow at sunrise, she will transform into a hauflin."

"She's no longer a chicken?" asked Rosalind.

Kneilot told the story of the spell, and Jowsey and Loggie filled in parts he missed.

The server arrived and took their order. Other customers arrived and soon, the place was over half full. It was a quiet crowd compared to the evening before when Loggie entertained them with the rebec and a few tunes with the Piccolo flute.

Cormac was on his last slice of toast and mouthfuls of tea when a noise outside the tavern window drew his attention. He took a bite and stretched his neck to learn the cause. What he saw made the toast slide down his throat half chewed, burning as it went and threatening to clog his throat and choke him. Yet the fear generated by this sensation was nothing compared to the sight of many people running for cover and flames shooting from the rooftop of the building across the street. A large shadow passed overhead, then disappeared.

Several people rushed through the door of the tavern, some screaming, some gasping for breath and others collapsing from fright, injury or both. Staff and patrons rushed over to help, including everyone at his table. Except him. He could see perfectly fine from where he sat. Anyways, the commotion near the door only caused chaos, and Kneilot stood back, the caterial perched on his shoulder, watching, it's long tail swinging across the hauflin's back. He couldn't get near anyone who had entered. Not that he could do much. He was only a level one cleric.

Cormac swallowed hard, clearing his throat of mushy toast. He washed it down with tea, then considered the action before him. If this was a game, what would the players do? Watch? Participate? He hmphed. His character would rush out the door, sword in hand, chasing the dragon to see where it went. Then, he and his friends would hunt it. The thought of that sent a shiver down his spine. It was easy to put his life on the line knowing he was going home afterwards to eat pizza and joke about the adventure the next day with friends who also participated. This...this before him was real. There was no pizza in Lachspeur of Yore, and there was no joking the next day if his character – if he died.

The large shadow returned and from his viewpoint, he saw flames shoot across the sky, hit the building that was already burning and send pieces of it flying into the air. It quickly crumbled into a pile of rumble, burning ferociously. Snapping and crackling filled the air, and the glow from the fire illuminated the inside of the tavern. Town folks rushed around with water buckets, throwing it on the flames in a futile attempt to do something.

"Everyone!" shouted a man, who tried to speak over the pandemonium. When the cries drowned him out, he grabbed a chair and stood on it. "Everyone. We are evacuating the inn. Grab your things and exit through the back of the building. Gather your horse there. No one, I repeat, no one exit through the front doors."

Cormac stood and hurried over to the others. Etain was speaking with two young women, who sat in chairs, shaking and gripping each other. When she saw him, she bid the women farewell and good fortune.

"Come," said Etain, and ushered Cormac and the others to follow. "Gather your things," she said, "and we will meet again outside." She grasped Rosalind's arm, and they jogged towards their room.

Fifteen minutes later, they met up, gear in hand and prepared to mount their horses.

"It is the dragon we seek," said Etain. "Thornheart is responsible."

"What are we supposed to do?" Cormac held the reins of his horse.

"What we can to stop it." Etain's horse reared, and she brought it under control. "Let's get away from here. The horses are spooked." She led the horse by the reins away from the inn and the fire. It pranced and jerked its head high, its mane flailing with the motion.

Cormac's horse was doing the same thing. He held tightly and led it down the back alley. They walked for at least ten minutes before the horses settled and they could mount.

"We will head north," said Etain.

"Into danger." Cormac's mouth went dry.

"Or away from it," said Jowsey. "If Thornheart has disputes with this village, she'll keep the dragons attacking."

"I saw only one," said Rosalind. "It didn't look like Kiefwind. It must be one of his yswains."

"We are no strength for seven dragons." Cormac stated the obvious.

"We don't need to fight seven dragons," said Rosalind, "only Thornheart. Defeat her, and we win. So does Kiefwind and his yswains."

"This is a retaliation," said Etain. "Thornheart and this town have come to blows before. Now that she has control of the dragons, she's taking revenge."

Rumbling noise forced Cormac to look towards the inn. There, above the buildings was a dragon, breathing its fiery breath. It was blue, not white.

"Let's go," said Etain. "North. Away from Westdun."

"I shall learn my fate today," said Jowsey, who clung to her waist from the saddle behind her. "Let it be a good one."

She kicked her horse and drove it down the lane. Cormac followed only because everyone else followed. They travelled north, parallel to the main road where the Three-legged Mare was located. Travelling behind the buildings, he lost sight of the dragon, but the sound of its destruction reached him, spurring him on. The people of Westdun were frantic. Those under horsepower, galloped away. Those on foot, ran for cover. Some dove into buildings. Others ran for the forest. That's where he wanted to hide. Not in a building that could be torched, not on the road that offered no cover but into the forest, beneath thick trees to wait until the dragon flew off. But Etain didn't do that. She raced towards the edge of town with Jowsey leaning heavily into her so as not to fly off the rear of the horse. Rosalind was behind her and in front of him with Kneilot clinging to her. The two hauflins and the caterial were faster than he was even though he was a solo rider. Loggie was on his tail, pressuring him to keep up.

In a flash, a large shadow flew overhead, and Rosalind's horse reared, sending her and Kneilot toppling to the ground. They jumped to their feet, but the horse raced after Etain without its riders.

Cormac forced his horse into a quick stop. It pranced and bucked, but he held it in place. "Rosalind!" He held out his hand.

Loggie stopped and reached for Kneilot, who clutched the caterial tightly in his arms.

Rosalind grabbed Cormac's hand, and he thrust her into the saddle behind him. Before she grabbed his waist, the shadow returned and swooped low over them. Its wind brushed back his hair and drove dirt into his face and eyes. Terrified, his horse reared on its hind legs so high, he couldn't hold on. He crashed to the hard ground, the impact knocking air from his lungs. The jarring fall blurred his vision, and he blinked several times before the scene came into focus.

Rosalind was on one knee, gasping for breath and trying to rise. She glanced at him, her face flushed.

He staggered to his feet and leant back in time to avoid the flapping wings of the caterial. A quick glance told him Loggie and Kneilot had also been thrown from their horse. Etain and Jowsey were the only ones still in the saddle. They stopped and tried to halt the stampeding horses, but it was futile.

The shadow returned, and Cormac stared in horror as it flew straight for them. He ran, chasing Rosalind towards the side of a building. Reaching it and racing down the alley, he threw her against the wood siding and held her there in the shadow of the building, hoping and wishing the dragon would not see them and fly by. His heavy breathing mixed with the pounding of his heart and sounded like thunder in his ears. Eyes on the open road, he waited and watched. He couldn't see where Loggie and Kneilot had run. He knew only Rosalind was here with him. Her face, an inch away from his, was strained, her eyes wide with fear. He shared that fear and realised the noises mixing with his pounding pulse and gulps were hers.

"It's gotta pass." She swallowed hard and locked eyes with him. "Right? We can't die here."

"It has to." He held her tighter, wrapping his arms fully around her. "We will not die here."

"No!" Her voice was a low squeal.

He looked to the road and saw the dragon hovering, staring at Loggie and Kneilot tucked into the alleyway on the opposite side of the road. Rosalind fought to leave the wall, but he held her firmly.

"We have to do something," she gasped, latching onto his shirt. "Let me go."

Time froze, and he saw fierce determination in her eyes. Since arriving in Lachspeur, he'd never considered risking his life for another, but... Something in her expression drew feelings that dwelt deep within his spirit. Without further thought, he pulled her from the wall. "We go together."

Acknowledging his pledge, she tugged his sleeve in the direction of the dragon.

"Stop!" she shouted while running towards the dragon. "I come in the name of Kiefwind of Sweetgrass!"

The dragon held its breath and whirled at her. "Who are you?" Its raspy voice was sharp to the ear. Its teeth dripped with clear liquid.

"I am Rosalind." She halted 50 feet from the beast. "I spoke with Kiefwind in Darkmoore Caves."

His thick brow rose. "And you did not rescue him but left him to this curse," he hissed, spraying hot spit.

Cormac wiped the gooey liquid from his face. "We tried!" he shouted. "Thornheart tricked us!"

"She tricked all of us!" said Rosalind. "Then left us there to die!"

The head of the dragon swooped closer. "Yet you are here." Its thin, sharp tongue lashed out to lick the air.

"We escaped through the stream." She took a step forward, and Cormac matched it. "Are you a slave to the same curse?"

"We all are. Forced to do her bidding or suffer an excruciating death." An odd noise erupted from its nose. It sounded like a snicker. "I'm not fond enough of humans or hauflins to endure that."

"We want to help." She took another step forward.

Every bone in Cormac's body wanted to disappear into the shadows, but he slowly took a step. Looking past the dragon, Loggie and Kneilot were waiting, their backs against the wall. Either they were too afraid to run, or they believed Rosalind would talk this dragon into leaving without killing them.

"Don't you want to return to your family?" asked Rosalind.

The dragon swooped closer. "What do you know about them?" he snapped, sending more hot spit through the air to land on Cormac's face.

"Everyone has family. I know Kiefwind has one. I felt it when he visited my dreams to tell me where he was trapped." Her voice wasn't as strong as it had been. "His wish was to see them one more time before he died."

"How do you – an insignificant hauflin – plan to grant that wish?"

"By freeing him from the curse."

His nostrils flared. "You are no match for Thornheart."

"Will you give me a chance or resign to your fate?"

He baulked. "You will die in the attempt."

"Consider it entertainment."

He snickered but considered the offer. "You will not defeat her if I kill you."

Rosalind shook her head. "The best chance you have of returning to Sweetgrass is my friends and me. Let us go and tell us where Thornheart is."

Cormac's nerves were running wild. She talked to him as if she spoke to a bank manager, asking for a loan to buy a car. The worst a manager could do was turn her down; the dragon could eat her.

"She plans an attack on an enemy to the east."

"Harmon in the Woods?"

His neck stretched. "You know much about this vile human."

"Once her wrath is felt, I was determined to spoil her plans. Let us go, and we will race to intercept."

"You'll fail."

"Let fate decide that."

The dragon lurched one way, then other. "I'm ordered to destroy this village."

"The damage you have caused and the lives you've taken have destroyed it. It will never be the same. Now go."

He snorted hot air that sent the hairs in Cormac's nose tingling. "If she's not satisfied, I'll be back."

"What is your name?" He didn't answer Rosalind. "I've given you mine as a gesture of trust. Grant me yours."

"Bendrite," he spat.

"Safe travels, Bendrite. We shall put an end to Thornheart."

"*We* won't do anything. Her fate is in your hands. Or shall I say yours lies in hers." He flapped his great wings, stirring up dust and small pebbles and sending them towards them.

Cormac held up his arm to block the debris. When the dragon turned north, the gigantic lump in his throat shrunk and breathing came easier as it flew over the town and slowly disappeared behind the treeline.

Etain and Jowsey rode up to them and dismounted. "Incredible. That you survived."

"I was thinking the same," said Cormac, wiping sweat and dirt from his forehead.

Jowsey jumped off the horse, picked up Rosalind and swung her around, laughing. "Living on the crenels, walking like you can fly." He set her down.

"You are indeed courageous." Kneilot clutched the caterial and stared up at Cormac. "It is no wonder you were able to pass the final challenge."

"If not for Rosalind, I'd be in the next town by now." He passed it off as a joke, but he wasn't joking. Her quick glance told him she didn't believe him. "How were you able to talk with him like you did? You sounded calm. Like you were talking to Loggie and not screaming with terror inside."

"I trusted he wouldn't kill me," said Rosalind.

"Where did you find that trust?"

"From Kiefwind. His energy was not evil. It was desperate but beneath it was kindness and love for his clan. It did not generate fear. I can't explain it more than that."

"If it gives me another day to breathe, I'll take it," said Loggie. He slung his arm around Rosalind's shoulders and pulled her close. "On the day we met, you promised adventures. You have not failed to deliver." He kissed the side of her head. Although he was dwarf, he was only two inches taller than her. "However, could they be more adventurous and less life threatening?"

Cormac watched her smile that smile he was growing to admire more than sunshine. With the danger passed, his muscles released the tension.

"Let's gather the horses," said Etain. "We've a quest."

The horses were found and brought under control easier than Rosalind thought they would be. Riding from Westdun, she glanced over her shoulder and stared at the plumes of black smoke rising into the clear blue sky. While not completely destroyed, she had told Bendrite the truth: the town would never be the same. Many buildings were burning, some had even collapsed. Many people were injured, some dead. She couldn't have prevented it, and she couldn't change it. All she could do was try to stop other villages from suffering the same destruction.

Etain and Jowsey led the way and set a quick pace. Loggie and Kneilot rode beside them. According to a man they had spoken to before leaving the village, they wouldn't reach Starlight Ridge for at least four days.

She rode abreast of Cormac. He was quiet, but his expression, ever changing, revealed his concern and his want to ride in the opposite direction. When he had pulled her against the wall and held her in his arms to protect her from the dragon, she thought he might kiss her like he had in Darkmoore Caves. His intense stare stirred uncertain emotions, ones she hadn't remembered experiencing before. She believed she'd have to kiss him to trigger his courage, as Jowsey had suggested. But that was unnecessary. He'd gathered it all on his own.

Feeling a smile crease her lips, she glanced at him quickly. He returned the smile. She'd grown to appreciate his rugged good looks, and she wondered if she remembered him from the first time they'd met, would more feelings have grown. Her memories before putting on the necklace were sketchy. They came in flashes of images and feelings she couldn't associate with anything. The more times an image appeared, the more she saw but they were out of order and sometimes they were of people she didn't remember.

The next day, they rode through the high pass between two mountains and continued down the other side. On the second day, they reached a field that stretched for a mile before them and as far as they could see to the right and left. It was the season of growth, and with the sun low in the sky, the fuzzy blue seed heads swaying in the wind gave Rosalind the impression of waves upon the ocean.

"I feel like I'm on a boat," said Jowsey in the saddle behind her.

"Have you been on a boat?"

"Once. It didn't make me feel good. It upset my stomach."

Nearing the end of Fields of Blue, a village came into sight. Accordingly, it was named Blue Sea Village. There were a few hours of daylight remaining for travelling, but dark clouds moved in and just as they reached the first dwelling, rain began. There was only one establishment for travellers: The Three Barrels Tavern and Hostel.

The next day, they travelled six miles to a bridge across a narrow brook. Cormac directed them across the bridge and then onto a trail that ran northeast into the forest. Leaving the main road led them away from villages and towns. From here on, they'd camp in the woods.

Rosalind searched the trees, looking for wildlife and was vigilant for large shadows overhead. With the thick tree growth, there was little chance of a dragon swooping in and frying them without notice. Late in the day, the trees thinned, exposing large sections of the sky. While looking for a spot to camp for the night, Cormac pointed out a large rock sticking out of a blunt hill.

"Dragon's Noggin'," he said. He smiled mischievously at Loggie. "It's on the map."

The look on both their faces made Rosalind chuckle. "Next, The River of Great Turmoil," she said. "With the recent rains, I hope it's not too great a turmoil."

"We'll know soon enough," said Cormac. "It's over that rise."

Nearing the top of the rise, the sound of water reached Rosalind's ears. It sounded fast. Halting on the rise, she looked down the gentle slope to the river below. The watercourse was wide and fast. Cold, wet mountain-top water. It would be a challenge.

"There's a better place to cross up stream," said Cormac. "But the best place to camp for the night is here at the bend."

"It's open to air attack," said Etain.

Jowsey searched the sky. "We've another hour of daylight. Let's move elsewhere."

"Better to take cover in the forest across the water," said Loggie, "than to attract unwanted company from larger insects than my horse."

"You've been where we haven't," Rosalind said to Cormac. "Lead the way."

He brought his horse forward and she followed in single file. At the bottom of the hill, he veered left, following a narrow trail. It wasn't travelled often, but it was certainly used and had been recently with fresh branches broken revealing bright colours within the bark.

They travelled for 20 minutes before coming to a part of the river that widened, creating a gentle flow. Cormac picked his way across this. Water came up to the horse's knees but no farther.

"Looks excellent for a cold shower," said Jowsey over her shoulder. "Refreshing."

"You're welcome to take a dip." She grinned. "But I'll stay dry and warm." The bruises on his face were all but gone, and the cut above his eye was a fading scab that had been picked.

"So, this is The River of Great Turmoil," said Loggie. "Mildly disappointing at this ford." He cleared his throat and sang. "The River of Great Turmoil has a gentle flow like the unfeathered wings of the gargoyle."

"Is that one of those words we shouldn't use or else we call them to our side?" asked Cormac.

Etain laughed. "They're too intelligent to fall for such trickery."

"Good. I'd hate to face a gargoyle tonight while hiding from a dragon."

Flashes of white caught Rosalind's attention, and she gazed into the forest. Squinting in the dim light of the setting sun, she tried to make out what the white spots were. Then she remembered the name of the forest: Forest of Wild Lilies. She followed Cormac along the riverbed and onto a narrow path. Amongst the mixed deciduous and evergreen trees were thousands of blooming white lilies. They were so white, they glowed.

"There's a small clearing up ahead," said Cormac.

"Hopefully not too far," saw Jowsey, "or we'll be floundering around in the dark trying to get a fire going."

Rosalind agreed but kept silent. That was better than sleeping in the open near the river. A few minutes later, they arrived at the site, and she dismounted.

"Quickly," said Etain. "Kneilot, Rosalind and I will take care of the horses. The rest of you, get a fire built."

Within short order, the tasks were done and just as it got pitch black, they settled around the campfire, its flames illuminating the space for a ten-foot radius. The night passed peacefully, and morning dawned with brilliant sunshine.

"You say it's on the edge of the forest?" Rosalind asked Cormac.

"Yeah. The other end. We should be there by morning. I was walking when I came through. I camped twice between Starlight Ridge and the river."

They started out an hour after dawn and as Cormac predicted, they hadn't reached Harmon of the Wood's cabin by sunset. The closer they got, the less chatter the group made. Rosalind understood why. Her thoughts dwelt on what they'd encounter when they arrived. Would they come upon an aged man peacefully drinking tea? Or would they find him scorched to death and his home destroyed by fire?

22

A Secret. Or Two

THREE HOURS AFTER leaving the campsite, Cormac spotted a familiar landmark. It was a great oak. Its branches swooped over the path. They grew high enough a rider on horseback could pass beneath if they leant forward. He recalled the coolness of the shade when he had walked through here many years ago. He had been new to the land, and he was suspicious of everything and everyone, so he constantly scanned the landscape, looking for creatures that might attack and kill him. Remembering those days sent a shiver down his spine. Those were scary times he never wanted to relive.

Besides the coolness, what made this oak stand out and why he remembered it from other mature oak trees was the symbol carved into the trunk four feet above the ground. Two spears, each 12 inches long, crossed at centre to form an X. He had seen several of these markings around Starlight Ridge, and he had asked Harmon about them. The old man said they were protective symbols. When asked what they protected him from, Harmon said evil magic. At the time, he had no idea what sort of evil might hunt Harmon. After meeting Shayde Thornheart, he knew.

This oak marked with the symbol indicated he was ten minutes from the cottage. By foot. By horse, he should arrive within five minutes. Calling up the memories of the last time he had seen Harmon, he wondered how the old man had got on in those four and a half years. Harmon hadn't been a young man then. Now he'd be pushing 60. At the time, Cormac thought of him as a harmless old wizard who had decided to leave behind populated areas to live a peaceful life in the wilderness. He was like Grizzly Adams. A hermit.

That was before he learned Harmon was also from Earth. The old wizard had kept that secret to himself for reasons Cormac could only guess. While breaking the fast this morning, they agreed to not let on they knew Harmon was not from this realm. They'd see what he had to say with regard to Thornheart.

"If he sought protection," said Etain as she rode past the oak tree, "he used the wrong symbol. Here, that's a call to war."

Cormac swung his head around. "Not protection?"

"From discussions with those who visited the Sanctuary, they told stories of seeing such symbols carved in trees, rocks and even in doorways. They'd also seen circles intertwined, sometimes a dozen, all drawn overlapping one another. They said the magic was weak and could not hold back a mischievous chipmunk."

"What symbols are powerful?" asked Rosalind.

"The circle within the triple knot is one most used by magic-users. We call it Tor's Trinity Bound. Another is the Three-pronged Fork. Also known as Warden's Fork."

"Could the spear symbol hold another significance?"

Etain shrugged. "I heard it was a weak symbol rarely used and when it is, it's meant as a challenge. It does not appear to be from this..." Her gaze froze on Rosalind. "His use of such symbols reveals how they have made it to this realm. Those who have come from your world have brought these false beliefs with them. They teach others to use silly images and spread it around like ash from a fire. They do not realise how useless they are." She lowered her brow. "Cormac says there is no magic in your world. I am starting to doubt that. What is not in your world is the knowledge and wisdom of magic."

Cormac stared at her. Was she right? Could he take a spell or a magical weapon from here and use it there?

"Or maybe they lack imagination?" offered Loggie. "Or at least Cormac does. Rosalind just has no ear for music."

She frowned at him. "You never give me a chance."

"I have, my dear. You simply don't remember all the chances."

Cormac grinned. Loggie wasn't wrong. Since Rosalind had bought the Piccolo flute, he'd heard her play many times. It was hard on the nerves and harder on the ears.

"Does this symbol mean we are almost through Forest of Wild Lilies?" asked Jowsey.

"Yes," said Cormac. "We will see the cottage soon. Whether he's there or not, is the mystery. He often went on walks to gather herbs, and he went to villages several days away to gather supplies."

Going around a bend and through a small brook that flowed across the path, they entered an area where trees thinned and grassy patches grew. In the distance, the roof of a small cottage peeked above the wildflowers and tall grass blades. A thin line of grey smoke rose from the chimney. The trees thinned further, and Cormac stretched his neck and looked one way, then the other, searching for the old man. They were almost upon the cottage when he spotted him, leaning against a hoe in the garden, watching them arrive. A crude fence surrounded the growing space, and an elaborate arbour made of thick branches revealed the entrance. Mature vines grew over the arbour and numerous clumps of immature grapes dangled from them.

The old man pushed back the round-rimmed hat he wore. The hat had seen better days, but it still kept the sun from shining on his face. Scraggly grey hair sprouted from beneath the hat, and it matched the grey and faded black outfit he wore. His pants were patched neatly, and his boots were well worn. The button shirt had puffy sleeves that were rolled up to reveal wrinkled hands.

Cormac stopped before the garden and watched the man study his face to place him in his memory. He hoped the man would recognise him. He hadn't changed much since last seeing Harmon. His hair was a little longer, his beard a little thicker. He still wore the same brown pants Harmon had traded a basket of cucumbers for at Blue Sea Village. When Harmon recognised him, the expression on his face eased. Or did it change to curious or knowing something he didn't? Shadow cast by the brimmed hat partially hid his face.

Cormac dismounted and walked to the garden fence. "Harmon. It is me. Cormac. It is good to see you well."

"As it is you, my boy." His aged voice sounded weaker than he remembered. "I see you've plenty of company. I hope you brought food. I dare say I've not the harvest to feed this many mouths."

Cormac smiled, remembering the easy way the old man talked. "We brought food. We'd not expect you to feed us."

"Goodly, goodly." He shuffled towards the gate, a little slower than Cormac remembered. He leant the hoe near the arbour and passed through the entranceway. "Come, come. Introduce me." He lifted his hat and attempted to straighten his hair. Then he brushed dirt from his pants and straightened his shirt. "Few visitors, I have. Being as I'm the only one in the neighbourhood." Harmon hobbled up to him and grasped his hand.

Cormac shook it but not hard. The small hand was feeble. Suddenly realising this man was a senior from his world without any magical power, softened his defenses. Harmon could cause them no harm. "These are the friends I've gathered. Just like you said I would."

The others dismounted and gathered around. Cormac introduced them, and Harmon shook each of their hands. When he came to Etain and Rosalind, he held their hands a moment longer and gazed lovingly at them.

"Goodly, goodly," he said. "A fine day this will be. Ladies at the table. A first for many long years."

Rosalind raised an eyebrow at Cormac, and he wondered what message she was trying to send until she spoke. "Sir, while our company we will share, we are here first on business."

"How so?" Harmon leant forward as if his back was too weak to straighten or he was hard of hearing.

"You see, dragons have been set free."

"Dragons!" He did a quick search of the sky. "No such thing, I'm told."

"I assure you, they are real," said Etain.

"As real as the squash you're tending in the garden," said Loggie.

"Who says?" asked Harmon.

"We've seen them with our own eyes, but that's not the worst of it." Rosalind drew a breath. "A woman you may be familiar with might seek revenge upon you."

Harmon's face twisted. "I've no woman friend." He shook his finger at her. "Only the two of you, which I would like to call so."

"Her name is Shayde Thornheart," said Etain, "and she's enslaved dragons to exact revenge."

Harmon's expression turned from confused, to tense to forced disinterest. But his eyes were set, and they glanced from Cormac to Rosalind.

"Do you know this woman?" asked Etain.

He moistened his lips and pushed his hat from his forehead. "Such silly stories. Where have you gathered them? A knock on the noggin' the works of you. Frightening an old man with such fables. You should be ashamed of yourself."

"She's on her way," said Etain bluntly. "She plans to kill you and burn your cottage to the ground with you in it."

This information tightened the skin in Harmon's jaw.

"Please, Harmon," said Cormac, "pack a bag and come with us. We'll escort you away before she gets here."

"But..." He looked around at his garden and tidy cottage. "This is my home."

"We can't defend you against her and her dragons," said Rosalind.

"She may also bring her henchmen," said Jowsey. "She has a small army to control."

Harmon stared at Jowsey. "A small army." He stumbled to a bench next to the arbour and plopped down. He removed his hat and wiped his brow with the back of his hand. "So, it's come to this, has it?" he mumbled. "An army. Dragons. Dear, Lisa, where is your heart?"

Cormac sat beside him and rested his elbows on his knees. Looking into the old man's face, he said, "Harmon, you do know this woman, don't you?"

Harmon nodded. "Lisa Fraser." He lifted his index finger and dotted the air. "That's her real name. Such a wonderful woman. Sweet lover of my youth."

He swallowed hard. This sounded like a lovers' spat gone horribly wrong. "Can she be reasoned with?"

Harmon released an uneasy chuckle. "If that were the case, the reasoning would have come years ago. No," he shook his head, "completely consumed with jealousy, she is. Always has been."

"Her threat is genuine then?"

"She has threatened in the past, but..." He grasped the hat lovingly in his hands. "It's been years. Decades even since she came with bow and arrow and tried to do me in." He winced. "A horrible shot. Ran out of arrows before one got close to me. I tried to reason with her, but she rode off, vowing she'd finish me." He rubbed the stubble of a beard. "It was so long ago, I thought she'd forgotten about me."

"She's been planning this for a long time," said Cormac.

"Dragons, you say?" When Cormac nodded, he continued. "Over kill. A disgruntled badger would do."

Cormac glanced at Etain, who stood, arms folded in front of the old man. It sounded like he didn't want to leave, and he hoped Etain could talk sense into him. "Will you come with us?" he asked.

"And do what? Hide? Live in a village where she'll hunt me with her beasts?"

"We can find you sanctuary," said Etain. "I know people."

"Do you now, missy. People who can defend against dragons?"

"Yes."

The single word hung in the air, and Harmon stared, as if to evaluate her answer.

"I've no horse," he said. "Only my feet. I travel slow."

"That's okay," said Cormac. "You can ride with me."

Harmon's gaze fell upon him, and the intense stare unsettled him. "I'm an old man. Feeble. I've no fight left in me. My life is not worth yours if she finds me."

"We'll move quickly," said Etain. "She doesn't know we're here. We'll travel under the cover of the forest and when in the open, under darkness. Please, come with us."

After a moment of consideration, Harmon spoke. "Son, will you help me gather a few things?"

"Certainly," said Cormac.

Harmon put his hand out to him. "A lift to ease these old knees." Cormac took his arm and helped him to his feet. "This way." He turned to the others. "The water in the well is sweet. Refresh yourself while you wait."

Cormac walked past Loggie, who gave him a peculiar stare. He shrugged but Loggie's expression didn't change, and he wondered what was on his mind. Once inside the cottage, Harmon picked up a sack, examined it and put it down. He picked up another cloth bag and flipped it around.

"You've gathered many friends," said Harmon. "More than I expected."

"Once I had one, the rest were easy." He looked around the cottage, remembering the time he'd spent here, ate here, slept here. It was the first time he'd felt safe in this realm and where he discovered his memories.

"The hauflin woman," he looked at him sideways while emptying the bag, "she's the one? From your world? What about the rest?"

"Oh, ah, no, I lost her." He swallowed hard, not wanting him to know about Rosalind.

"Lost her? She was the key to you returning home."

"We got separated." He shook his head. "I searched for her but with her losing her memory every night, she forgot about me. That was weeks ago."

"None of them are from your world?" His expression turned dark.

"No."

He picked up a sweater, folded it and stuck it in the sack. "I've not much. Only a few things." Evaluating a mug, he put it down and picked up another and put it in the sack. "Pity you'll never see your home again. I'm getting too old to perform such spells, and if Lisa has her way, I won't be around much longer." He shuffled to a drawer and pulled out a shirt.

"I understand."

"You don't sound disappointed."

"I've made friends. It's changed everything."

"Wonderful." That sounded sarcastic. He shoved a pair of pants and socks into the bag, then reached for trinkets on a shelf and a bottle of blue liquid.

"It is. I never thought I'd make good friends. I was wrong."

"Lucky you don't have an ex-wife trying to kill you at every turn."

"Ex-wife? You and Thornheart – Lisa – were married?"

"Thornheart. She took that name because she said it was like I had driven a thorn into her heart." He scratched his head while he considered other things on the shelf. "Married? Yes."

"Your fight must have been something for her to hate you this much."

"Fight?" He shook his head. "She wanted power. Magic. It's all she ever wanted. I wanted peace." He removed a stick from the shelf and tucked it under his arm. "So, I came here with..." he raised an eyebrow and smiled, "a woman who wanted the same. That didn't sit well with Lisa. She couldn't forget or move on."

"How long ago was that?"

He paused and gazed at the wall. After a moment, he said, "Has to be 35 years now. Surrey has been gone for 18 of them."

"Natural causes?" The question slipped out before he had time to think about it.

"If you call natural dying from an arrow wound to the chest." He frowned, and his dark expression deepened. "I'd hoped to never again see Lisa, but she's causing great turmoil. Great sorrow." He picked up an orb. "There. Got everything I need." He turned. "Lead the way. I've been waiting a long time for this day. Let's equally disappoint Shayde Thornheart as much as she has me."

Cormac stepped towards the door. "I assume she's been here. Knows your location."

"She does." He grimaced. "It won't matter after today."

"I'm sorry you have to leave here. You've created a lovely home. I can't thank you enough for taking me under your wing and helping me when I felt lost."

"Son, you've given me more than I could have asked for. I'm grateful. You've helped me in ways you'll never know."

Cormac walked towards the garden where the others rested. The horses were quietly grazing on the nearby grass. Etain and Rosalind were in deep discussion, and Jowsey was adding comment where he thought it was needed. Kneilot was feeding the caterial a piece of meat, and Loggie was patting it. Since he had left this cottage, he had gathered wonderful friends. They'd changed his life for the better.

When they saw him approach, they stood and prepared to leave.

"Before we go," said Harmon, in a voice that had grown tired since leaving the cottage, "I want you to gather around. In a circle. I want to pay homage to this wonderful land that has given me so much while I lived upon it." He stood with the sack over his shoulder, stick tucked under his arm and the small orb in his hand. It was so small, his fingers almost concealed it.

"Certainly," said Etain. "Leaving a home you've known all this time is heartbreaking."

Harmon stood silent, head down. After a long moment, he spoke. "When I first came upon this land, my wildest dreams were answered. Or so I thought. Living within nature was a great joy. But my body grows weary. The act of carrying water makes me age faster than the years and the winters, well, they chill this body to the core. I am not the young man I was when I arrived. It is why I must return home. I hope you understand. This is not about you but me."

Cormac glanced at him sideways.

"There's only one way for me to go home, to see what is left of my family and friends." He tossed the orb into the centre of the circle they formed. "Ignite!" He held his hand out, palm down facing the orb.

Cormac felt light, and the ground moved away. He looked at the others, and they were also floating.

"What's happening?" asked Kneilot in a shaky voice. The caterial lifted off his shoulder and flew to the nearby bench. "I can't move."

Cormac tried to move his arms, but they were frozen to his sides. He couldn't move his feet or his legs. "Harmon, what are you doing?"

"Going home." His voice rose. "Home. Such a sweet word. And I have you to thank for it."

"You're going to sacrifice me to return?" His heart shuddered.

"You and her." He pointed at Rosalind. "I need the energy of two from our world, not one, to complete the spell."

"Two?" But... This was his plan all along?

"You told him Rosalind's from Earth?" cried Loggie.

"No! I didn't."

"He did!" said Harmon.

"Liar! I said nothing about her."

He pulled a piece of paper from his pocket and unfolded it. "He informed me weeks ago by magic telegram he'd found at Dunvain Downs a young female hauflin by the name of Nimble and that he'd bring her to me." Harmon tucked the paper into his pocket and opened the jar holding blue liquid. "I assume this woman is her regardless of the name."

"Cormac!" Loggie growled at him. "You planned this?"

"No, I didn't. Please, let me explain."

"No, let me," said Harmon. "I lied to him and told him to find another from his world, our world, and bring them to me. I would perform a spell, sacrificing them to send him home." He eyed Rosalind. "My dear, you were his sacrifice."

She stared at him, pain racing across her face. "That's why you rescued me?" Her voice cracked.

The ache in his chest grew. If Harmon was successful, they had only minutes left together. No time to explain. No time to lie. "Yes." His breath caught. "But I couldn't go through with it."

"Yet we're here!" Loggie struggled to break free. "Going through with it."

"Harmon, there is another way." Etain was trying to move her fingers, but they were frozen in place.

"No other way," he said. "I've done my research." He drank the liquid, then tossed the jar. He jerked his head to the side quickly and smacked his lips. "Strong. Nasty. But worth it." He pulled the stick from beneath his arm.

"Please," said Etain, "reconsider. They are our dear friends."

"Remember them fondly." Harmon raised the stick and danced it in the air.

"What about us?" asked Jowsey. "What will happen to us?"

"Nothing," said Harmon. "When I return home, the spell will be broken, and you will be set free."

"And me?" asked Rosalind.

"Turned to dust to be blown away in the wind."

She looked at Cormac with the most horrible expression he had ever seen. She hated him. He didn't blame her. He hated himself for putting her in this situation.

"Sing!" she demanded.

"What?"

"Sing!"

"Sing what?"

"Holding out for a Hero."

He fumbled over the thought. It didn't make sense.

"Let me sing it." Floating beside her, Loggie sang the chorus Rosalind had taught him.

"What wretched song is this?" asked Harmon. "Heroes are archaic. Needless. Dead." He waved the wand and started to recite the spell, but he stumbled over the words. "Shut up! I can't concentrate."

Rosalind joined Loggie in singing the chorus again. Seeing Harmon struggling to complete the spell, Cormac joined in. Then Etain, Jowsey and Kneilot sang, too. Harmon grew frustrated, and he swung the wand with more force.

"Brace yourself!" shouted Rosalind.

Cormac didn't know what she meant until he heard the flap of wings growing louder. He looked up, and his mouth dropped. Flying swiftly towards them were three dragons. Whether sacrificed or roasted, he was going to die today.

Rosalind waited until the last second before she yelled, "Dragons!"

Harmon swung around, looked into the sky and gawked in horror. He stumbled backwards and fell in the dirt. As quickly as an old man could rise, he did, and turned towards the centre of the circle with a determined expression.

"If this is my last challenge, I accept it." He yelled the words to the spell, snapping the end of the wand towards Cormac, then Rosalind. His face flushed red and the veins in his neck swelled. Wind blew his hat from his head and sent his wiry hair flapping. With eyes as wide as the moon, he stared up at the sky and spoke the words that would deliver him home.

Quick movement drew Rosalind's attention away from the approaching dragons. It was the caterial. Matilda. It pounced on the orb and swatted it with its paw, rolling it a few inches. It pounced on it again. Rosalind felt the pressure on her arms weaken. Matilda swatted the orb harder. The orb rolled across the ground. The caterial pounced on it, flopped to its back, clutched it with its front paws and swatted it with its back paws. Rosalind could move her fingers. She called to Kneilot and mouthed, "Make Matilda run with it."

Kneilot was already speaking with the caterial, whispering words of encouragement.

Matilda leapt to her feet and flung the orb outside the circle. Then she chased it, swatting it with both paws and driving it into the garden where it was lost amongst the weeds and vegetables.

Rosalind's arms came free, and she dropped to the ground. The others did the same. Harmon whirled. The expression on his face was pure meanness. The impression of the innocent, helpless old man he had given her when she'd arrive was gone. He thrust the tip of the wand at Cormac and cursed words with such force, spit flew from his mouth.

Rosalind planned to run but waited to see what would happen.

Cormac didn't wait. Once he had found his balance, he darted forward and threw himself at the man, knocking him to the ground. They rolled across the dirt, stirring up dust. For an old man, Harmon was agile and sneaky. Rosalind was going to grab a stick and beat the man with it, but Cormac threw several punches and broke free. He tried to grab the wand, but the man kept it from his reach until he had a chance to drive it into his ribs several times with such force, Cormac groaned and pulled away from him.

"Run!" shouted Etain. She pulled on Rosalind's arm. "Flee."

"You've no spell for this?" Rosalind tried to keep her nerves from running out of control.

"Nothing. Remember the cards?"

She did remember them. They showed a forest engulfed in thick smoke. She had watched it from a bird's eye view. While she watched the scene unfold, Etain pulled her away from Harmon.

Kneilot stood near Cormac. He grabbed the man's shirt and helped him up. "Run," he gasped.

Cormac scrambled to his feet and looked around as if he didn't believe his eyes. The three dragons were charging towards them. The magical creatures would be over them in seconds. Cormac started to run but tripped when his foot got hung up on something. Trying to pull it free, he saw Harmon clutching it.

"If I can't go home, you'll share my fate." The old man sneered.

Cormac hesitated, then kicked the old man in the head, breaking free of his grip. He got up and ran. He stumbled but Kneilot caught him and together they raced towards the forest.

Rosalind followed alongside, more to ensure Kneilot was safe. She looked for the horses, but they had already scattered. A wave of hot air hit her, throwing her, Kneilot and Cormac to the ground. The edge of her pants caught fire, and she beat out the flames with bare hands. Wiping sweat and dirt from her eyes to clear her vision, she saw the dragons circle overhead. She jumped to her feet and helped Kneilot, who had also been scorched, to rise.

She stumbled onward. Cormac tried to help her keep her balance, but she ripped her arm from his grip. "Leave me! You've done enough!" If not for him, she wouldn't be here, running for her life.

"Rosalind, let me explain." He tried to hold her, but she didn't stop. He raced after her. The forest before them burst into flames, and they came to an abrupt halt. She put up her arm to shield against the heat. Cormac grabbed her and spun her around. "I'm sorry about all this!"

"Don't touch me," she growled and pulled away.

She looked for a clear path to enter the forest, but the dragons continued to circle, sending their breath upon the land and every way she turned, she was cut off by a wall of flames. Coughing, sputtering and choking on smoke, she stopped to assess the landscape. She was surrounded by burning forest. The only thing not touched were the four acres within the ring of fire with Harmon's cottage in the middle of it. The heat forced her away from the perimeter and smoke made her stumble on uneven ground. She searched for the others. Cormac, Kneilot and Loggie were near, but Etain and Jowsey were hiding beneath the overhang of the cottage, their backs pressed against the wall.

Harmon stood where they had left him, wand in hand, scowling at the sky. The man looked a pitiful sight against dragons.

The largest of the dragons descended. The shadow on its shoulders took form. It was Thornheart. She slid off the dragon, came to stand in front of it and crossed her arms.

"So, old man, we meet." She chuckled. "For the last time."

Rosalind's mind tumbled over the possibilities. With the two ex-lovers focussed on each other, this left her and the others to find a way to escape.

23

His Last Stand

CORMAC BELIEVED THE dragon standing guard over Shayde Thornheart was the one they'd spoken with in Darkmoore Caves: Kiefwind of Sweetgrass. The last time he'd seen the dragon, it was white. This one was blue. Rosalind took a step towards the dragon, but he held her back. She tried to break free, but he tightened his grip. "If Thornheart wants him, let her have him. We're not involved."

"I'm not out to save a man who'd see me killed." She lowered her brow.

The lump in his throat grew. "I would never harm you." He strengthened his grip around her, fearing she'd run towards Harmon. "I would give my life for you. Don't you understand? I am not that man who found you. But I cannot hate that man." He paused and gazed into her eyes. "He brought you into my life."

Her expression softened. "How am I to know? Actions reveal truths; words camouflage lies."

He gently brushed her cheek with his hand, then sealed his lips to hers, kissing her tenderly and letting the tension of the moment go. When they parted, his eyes were foggy for reasons other than the smoke. "Let us not be fools like those before us. They use love as a weapon." He swallowed hard. Speaking of emotions of the heart was something he'd never done, not even with Clarise. "A chance," he breathed. "It's all I'm asking for. To make this right."

Her gaze swept across his face. "Let's hope we have the opportunity to get that chance, Cormac. If that is your real name."

"Ryan McCormac. My friends from our world shortened it to Cormac." He slowly released her, hoping she'd stay near.

"Time has revealed the true winner." Thornheart took a step towards Harmon. "If life was a game, I'd say you were about to lose the last of your survival points." She cackled that horrible laugh she'd revealed in Darkmoore Caves. "Time to roll a new character, Richard Harmon." She walked around the man, looking him up and down.

"Lisa, you've clearly won the castle," said Harmon. "Now leave."

"Without delivering the final blow? As Adventure Master, you know I can't do that."

"I am Adventure Master!" His face turned red.

"A pathetic one. You barely make a decent mage. No imagination. You wanted only simple, safe adventures. A few skeletons here, a survivable trap there." She flung her hands as she spoke. "But I wanted a real challenge. So did my players. They wanted to face death and taste it if given the chance."

"It was about the adventure! The surviving, not the dying."

"For you." She came to face him. "Your pathetic players avoided all danger, and you let them. Gaining levels with no real experience to back it up. My players earned their levels," she spat.

"They barely saw fifth. Most saw only third. Where is the fun in creating a new character every other game? Not having the time to explore their uniqueness?"

"It was the thrill of killing or be killed. And now, I have brought the ultimate weapon." She gestured towards the blue dragon behind her. "It was what we all dreamt of controlling, and I've done it."

Cormac studied the fire surrounded them, looking for a way to escape. While those two continued their lovers' spat, he'd find a way to the forest and disappear. If he could only find that way and lead the others, maybe they wouldn't look at him like they wanted to murder him. "This way," he whispered to Rosalind. He guided her towards the back of the cottage. Kneilot followed with Matilda perched on his shoulder, and they met up with Etain, Jowsey and Loggie.

"If I could play a sweet love song," said Loggie, "do you think they'd kiss and mend the hurt?"

"There's no love song strong enough," said Jowsey.

"Our only chance is to find a way through the wall of fire," said Cormac.

"Even water would not pass unchanged," said Loggie.

"There must be a hole somewhere." Etain scanned the landscape.

"The stream," said Rosalind. "It's about four feet deep. We could go under the wall of fire."

"Anything," said Kneilot. "We can't stay here."

Jowsey stretched his neck. "It looks possible. It's the best chance we have."

Cormac crouched low. "I'll lead." He looked at Rosalind. "Stay close."

Loggie stepped between the two. "She'll stay close to me."

"Etain." Jowsey pulled her in front of him. "We stick together."

"And me?" Everyone looked at Kneilot.

Cormac waved him forward. "Stay behind me and hold tight to Matilda. She's the reason we have this chance."

Kneilot wrapped his arms around the caterial, smiling. "I told you she was special." Then he frowned. "It took you long enough to notice."

Cormac gulped. The little cleric was not wrong. Mentally mapping a route to where the stream entered the wall of flames, he wondered which would be best: a full dash or sneaking from one point to another that provided cover. With the argument between Harmon and Thornheart heating up, he decided quick dashes between two points with hardly a pause in between.

"Let's go," he whispered over his shoulder. Pushing away from the wall, he darted to a bush, spotted his next target and ran for a tree. As soon as Kneilot joined him, he dashed to another bush. He glanced back to ensure everyone kept up. They did and were anxious to keep moving. He sprinted to a toolshed, then the outhouse. They were almost near the stream where bushes grew along it. Yet, there were still 200 feet from where they'd go underwater.

"Look at them," cried Thornheart. "Bless their young hearts. Thinking they can escape with my treasure."

The memory of Thornheart using that word in Darkmoore Caves caused Cormac to look at Rosalind. Thornheart knew she was from Earth.

"Somehow, somewhere, I knew I'd get another chance to claim her." Thornheart laughed. "Richard, too bad you won't be around to see me reach my full power." She slapped him across the face, and he grabbed her hand. "That's for leaving me." She ripped her hand free and walked towards the dragon. "What's coming is for leaving me for that tramp." She climbed onto the dragon's back. "Let's torch this bad memory from my eyes."

Harmon drew back, his wand limp at his side. Watching Thornheart rise into the air on the dragon may have frightened him, but from the look on his face, Cormac guessed that it also impressed him.

Cormac reached the bushes along the river. Seeing Thornheart's dragon swoop down and breathe fire upon the cottage quickened his steps. The small wooden shack made with much care was soon engulfed in flames, adding more smoke to the already thick air. Using this extra smoke to hide their escape, he openly ran towards the stream where it disappeared into flames. Part of him doubted the plan but the other part saw no other option.

From out of the smoke came one of the other dragons, swooping so close to the ground, it knocked him over and flung him into the water. Breaking the surface and wiping water from his face, he saw Kneilot had also been thrown into the stream. Matilda swam towards shore. When she reached it, she crawled out looking like an extremely disappointed, no angry, cat. She flapped her wings and shook to rid herself of excess water.

Cormac rushed over and grabbed Kneilot's arm, helping him to gain his balance. Assessing the others, they were getting to their feet from being thrown to the ground.

"This way." He supported Kneilot to reach the shore, and they climbed out together. Turning towards their escape route, he saw a dragon swoop across his vision, spraying the land before him with flames. He lifted his arm to block the extreme heat from striking his face. The smell of burning hair filled his senses, and he dove into the water to cool his skin. Hauling himself onto shore, he lay against the ground for a moment to gather his senses. He dragged his palm over his face and discovered his beard and mustache had been burnt off. His eyebrows and eyelashes were also gone. Rubbing his chin, the skin felt sensitive. It was the closest shave he ever had. He sat up and surveyed the area. Thick smoke hid any further routes to escape, and his nerves scattered his thoughts in every direction, giving him no peace to think.

"Watch out!" shouted Jowsey.

At the last second, Cormac turned and saw the dragon fly in, its claws outstretched. It seized him by the shoulder and lifted him off the ground. He grabbed his dagger and drove it into the claw again and again. Blindly, he stabbed it, waiting for it to lose its grip. When it did, he fell and slammed into the hard ground. The wind was knocked out of him, and he lay dazed, unable to see or stand. He heard someone scream, but he couldn't distinguish the voice. He thought it was Jowsey.

In an instant, hands were on him. "Stop fighting! It's me." Rosalind pinned him to the ground and dragged something rough over his face. He blinked and stared up at her.

"Get to your feet." She tugged on his arm.

He got his knees under him but couldn't stop the dizziness that threatened to send him back to the ground.

"Hold on to me." She flung his arm over her shoulder and helped him to stand.

"Keep him steady." It was Kneilot, supporting him on his other side.

Together, they raced for one of the few spots not yet burning. He collapsed in a heap and choked on smoke. Drawing a few deep breaths, his vision cleared. "Where's Jowsey?"

"There." Kneilot pointed to Loggie and Etain helping the elf through the tall grass.

"Any ideas?" Cormac coughed and looked at Rosalind. "Anything?"

She shook her head. "The dragons are fully under her command." Her eyes widened, and he looked to see a dragon soaring low over the grass, heading straight for them. They dove for cover.

Cormac covered his head with his arms, fearing the dragon's plan was to send a wave of flames over them. This was it. He braced himself for the pain. It wasn't supposed to end like this. No one survived dragon breath. A fierce wind pinned him to the ground. In one thorough gush, he was lifted, then dropped as if a great current had swept over him. The pressure gone, he lifted his head. The dragon was flying off with... He jumped to his feet and ran. "Rosalind!" He screamed so hard, his throat burnt. His mouth filled with smoke, and he choked and sputter, but he kept running after her as the dragon lifted her higher. She looked unconscious. Her body limp. "Rosalind!" He reached the wall of flamed and stopped. The dragon flew over the flames and circled the large swath of open grassland.

Screaming behind him forced his body to turn, but he kept looking back at Rosalind every five seconds.

The dragon Thornheart rode lifted Harmon into the air with its claws. The man struggled, but he was no match for the powerful dragon.

"Up, up and onward!" sang Thornheart, ending the words with hideous laughter.

"Lisa, I beseech you!" cried Harmon. "Don't do this! Remember our good times. I can make it up to you!"

"You certain can, Richard." She directed the dragon to hover. "Entertain me."

"How?"

"Die courageously."

The dragon swooped over the burning cottage and dropped the man into the flames. The cry of terror lasted a brief second, then died in the roaring fire.

Cormac shuddered and fell to his knees. Through thick grey smoke, he watched Thornheart fly overhead, waving to the land below as if a queen on her chariot. She flew out of sight, leaving him with his chest burning and his eyes watering. He hung his head, not knowing what to do next. His body wanted to lay in the soft grass and rest, but his mind raced with the possibilities while his heart ached like it had never before.

A quick jerk, and he was on his feet. Loggie's menacing face stared at him. Then he punched him, sending him to the ground.

"You did this!" Loggie picked him up only to hit him again. The dwarf was a few inches shorter, but he was strong and packed a punch. He grabbed him by the shirt and shook him. "She was my best friend!" he screamed in his face. He punched him again. The hard whack echoed in the smoke.

Cormac tried to shove him away. "She's not dead!" He straightened and put up his hands to block the fists.

"Not yet!" Loggie drove his shoulder into his gut, and they wrestled across the ground. "We'll never reach her time!" He swung wildly.

Cormac couldn't hit him only defend his face from the punches. "We'll find her," he cried. "We have to." His voice trailed off, and he considered giving up. But if he did, he'd never see Rosalind again.

"Break it up." Jowsey grabbed hold of Loggie's arm but wasn't strong enough to stop the punch. He tackled him, and they rolled across the ground.

Etain grabbed Cormac by the shoulders. "Stop it! We only fall behind by such actions."

Loggie jumped to his feet and prepared to attack Cormac again, but Kneilot fell to his knees and held tightly to his leg. "Stop," said Kneilot. "In all that is good in you, stop. Let only our enemies treat us with such cruelty."

Loggie wiped his face with his sleeve and scowled. "Do you say he is our enemy?" He pointed at Cormac.

"No. Only a misguided soul."

"You're a fool."

"If being your friend makes me a fool, then so be it."

Loggie stared at him and sucked in a large breath. He choked on the smoke and coughed.

"We need to gather our thoughts," said Etain. "Fighting each other will not save Rosalind."

"As if we have a fighting chance." Loggie's face cracked, and his voice grew hoarse. "I won't see her again, and it's his fault." He lunged at Cormac and threw him to the ground.

Jowsey jumped on him, and the three wrestled across the ground until exhausted, flopping onto their backs, gasping for air.

Etain leant over Loggie and frowned. "A man of such talent but no hope. Would Rosalind give up on you as quickly?" He stared up at her. "While you are set on placing blame and seeking retribution, she'd be catching her horse and riding after you. You have wasted energy better spent on a rescue."

He clamped his lips shut and glanced at Cormac.

"Listen to her," said Kneilot with Matilda on his shoulder. "She is wise. Like those I've heard speak in the square."

Cormac wiped his lip, and his hand came away covered in blood. He dragged his tongue along the inside of his mouth and found his lip cut and swollen. Sitting up, he surveyed the sight before him. They were still trapped in a ring of fire, but the fires were dying. The cottage fire wasn't but that had a lot to burn. He winced, thinking of Harmon. But there was nothing he could do. The old man had chosen his life, made it what it was. All Cormac could do was make a better one for himself.

Loggie pushed himself to his feet. "Let's get out of here." He glared at Cormac. "I will never risk my life for you again," he spat and walked away.

Cormac watched him go. He didn't blame him for feeling that way. He deserved it. The thought of sacrificing an innocent person to return home was wrong. He knew that without a doubt now.

The dragon's breath stole the air from Rosalind's lungs. She gulped but found no oxygen. Smothering in the strong draw, she grew faint. When the dragon seized her, she was too weak to resist. The sensation of rising mixed with dizziness blurred her vision. She heard someone yell her name but couldn't draw a breath, let alone respond. Sounds softened and the crackling of fire and the roar of flames faded in the distance. Below, large plumes of thick grey smoke rose into the air, and the image of fog slipped through her mind like a passing thought that held no interest. Her body went limp, and she lost all use of her senses. Consumed in dark silence, she drifted into nothingness.

When breath finally came, she gagged on it. One-by-one, her senses returned. Sound exploded in her ears, making her only hear static and the echo of her heart pounding. The last to return was her vision. She blinked several times to remove the blur. Her muscles tensed. The land sailed by more than 500 feet below. She flew over a lake, then a forest. She looked back from where they came and saw a huge cloud of smoke distinctly marking the landscape. Even from this distance, she saw flames licking the air.

Beside her a hundred feet away was Shayde Thornheart sitting on Kiefwind. The dragon's colour had changed from white to blue, perhaps due to escaping the dungeon. He glanced at her, gave her no consideration and returned to looking ahead.

Thornheart sat proudly on the dragon, her face into the wind and her hair and short cloak dancing behind her. She appeared pleased with her accomplishments.

They flew for what seemed a long time. The plumes of smoke disappeared over the horizon, and they sailed over grassland, small hills and another thick forest. A village passed below, but the dragons kept flying. Up ahead, a large dark spot took shape. It was beside a lake. The structure was roughly square but long on one side to accommodate a brook that fed into the lake.

Rosalind strained her eyes. It was a fortress of wood. The perimeter was made of upright thick logs. A three-storey gateway blocked unwanted visitors and a taller, three-spiral structure rested in the centre of the grounds. Smaller buildings dotted the area inside the walls. Horses occupied a coral and goats ran freely. Several people, mostly men, watched them approach. The men on the walls were armed with crossbows and swords. The few women, wearing dresses and aprons, stood near the doorway of the three-spiral structure.

This was where Kiefwind hovered above the ground, his great wings flapping to hold him steady, stirring up dust and debris. The pressure around her body released, and she tumbled to the ground. Stiff from the awkward position, her muscles groaned when she tried to stand. She fell forward and landed hard on her knees.

"A weak hauflin," snapped Thornheart. "An inferior race." She bent over her. "Should have chosen human."

"I feel it matters not what I'd chosen," spat Rosalind. "You'd still be an old hag."

A dark shadow passed over Thornheart's face. "I always hated hauflins." She stood upright. "Throw her in the dungeon." She giggled. "I love saying that. I had one built specifically for such occasions."

Two men grabbed her, dragged her to her feet and propelled her through a doorway in a long building. She barely had time to notice the servants waiting in neat uniforms nearby and the room she was ushered through with weapons and tactical gear. She was shoved towards the wall and down a flight of stairs that gently twisted. Lanterns hung from the walls to illuminate the way.

At the bottom of the stairs, they dragged her forward where three cell doors lined each side of the passageway. They opened the first one and threw her in. She landed hard on the stone floor. Attempting to rise quickly, she fell over and rested on her knees.

Thornheart stepped over the threshold. "It will take days to prepare the spell. Until then you'll get the bare necessities to sustain life, but you'll need to fast for two days to make the spell potent. I won't feel your hunger." She left the cell and stood by the door to gaze in at her. "Isn't this exciting. Haven't you always wanted to be imprisoned in a real dungeon? It's part of the game. I assume that is how you ended up here." She smirked. "You played a game you thought was only a game until you experimented with real spells." When Rosalind didn't answer, she huffed. "No matter. Your game is almost at an end." She slammed the door and secured the latch. The only light seeped in through the barred square window from a lantern hung on the wall outside the cell.

Rosalind waited for footsteps to fade in the distance, then went to the door and shook it. It wouldn't budge. She searched for a handle and couldn't find one. She pushed the door again, then threw her weight against it.

Insidious laugher echoed in the hallway. "Cute. But futile." Thornheart walked away.

Rosalind sat on the bed against the wall. With the door secured and no window, she was stuck. She sat for several long minutes, listening to the silence and the distant dripping sound. She thought of Harmon and Thornheart and how they came to end their friendship after all these years. From their argument, it sounded like they had both been Adventure Masters, each with their own philosophy. Harmon played it safe. Thornheart did not. She risked everything for the thrill of adventure.

Thinking about those sorts of campaigns, she stared at the wall opposite the door. If Thornheart had this dungeon built in her style of play, then...

24

The Game Begins

CORMAC WAS THE last to crest the hill and stare at the lake below. Since Jowsey had been to Thornheart Fortress once before, he led the way. On Rosalind's horse, he was guided by Etain, who rode second with Kneilot and Matilda on the back of her saddle, and the ever-changing map that provided the shortest route west to reach the fortress. Loggie rode the third horse, and he never looked back to ensure the last person in line was still there. Since leaving Starlight Ridge, Loggie hadn't spoken to him, had hardly looked at him and when he did, it was a scowl, a look of hate that never cooled even after hours in the saddle.

He tried to put the hateful looks aside and understand what the bard was feeling. He'd known Rosalind the longest, had left his home to follow a dream she had encouraged. He'd not be here, risking his life if not for her. In truth, if not for Cormac, none of them would be here. He had led them to Harmon in the Wood. All of this was his fault.

The setting sun shining on scattered clouds and reflecting on the still lake created a pretty image he couldn't appreciate. At any other time, he'd marvel at the sight and think about the many camping trips he'd taken in his youth. No happy memories or joy came to him today. He lowered his head and stared at his hands on the reins. They were burnt in several places, bruised and cut. They reflected his entire body and the way his spirit felt.

"Enough admiring," said Etain. "Let's go."

Jowsey picked his way down the hill, guiding his horse towards the north end of the lake, the shortest route around it.

Silently, they moved out, and Cormac followed, trying not to think about what they'd find if they took too long to reach Thornheart Fortress. The crazy woman would be admitted to an insane asylum if she lived in the real world. He stumbled over that phrase: real world. Wasn't this world real? It sure felt real when he was punched, when the dragon dropped him on the ground and when the hair was burnt off his face. He touched his swollen lip gingerly, remembering Rosalind's kiss. He had kissed her, and she kissed him back. Her soft lips had frozen time, made him forget he battled dragons. That felt real, more real than any other kiss.

He shoved the thoughts from his head. He didn't want to think of anything. An empty head was a peaceful, painless head.

They travelled until the sun set, made a hasty camp, ate and fell asleep only to rise before the sun and ride again. Early the next day, they came upon a road, checked the map and followed it. A half hour later, they passed Tempered Passage. They didn't bother entering the town. It was half a mile from the crossroads.

The following morning, they entered Haggle's Spring. A great festival was taking place, and the town was alive with decorations, music and dancing. Town folk were dressed in colourful costumes and wished everyone good cheer. A pile of branches and logs was assembled in the centre of town. It looked like a bonfire before the match.

Cormac felt out of place in the celebratory atmosphere. He felt like he was from another world. There was no cheer within him, and he passed through like a ghost at his own birthday party.

They bought supplies at the keep and left. The keeper spoke of the festival and said it was to bring good fortune to the harvest and promote fertility. Etain knew about it. She knew everything. She was like a walking encyclopedia. Spending an entire life dedicated to studying such things would do that to a person. Cormac had done his best to ignore everything about this world, hoping to escape it without need for knowledge. His chest sunk deeper.

The keeper told them Thornheart Fortress was 16 miles away. He advised them to not go, to stay and enjoy the festival, but his warning fell on deaf ears.

Cormac, still in the rear, remained silent as they left the village, the music and merriment behind. It had been three days. Whatever Thornheart had planned for Rosalind, surely she'd done it by now. This rescue mission was more of a recovery mission. Or one of revenge.

Rosalind waited for the morning delivery of water and bread. When the door opened, the guard tossed a flask on the bed and closed the door. She jumped up and peered out the viewing window.

"Where's my bread?"

He smirked. "You're fasting. Water only." He walked away.

Rosalind stepped back from the door. She had hoped to have been rescued by now or something drastic have happened, stalling the evil woman's plans. She had two days left. Matters had fallen into her own hands. Waiting was no longer an option.

She slung the flask over her shoulder and went to the wall opposite the door. Reaching for the stone near the corner, she pushed it one way, then the other. A soft click told her the latch released. She pushed aside the secret door and peered in. It was dark and the cobwebs over the opening had reformed since yesterday. Entering meant travelling by touch. Nothing in her pockets or pouches provided light.

Drawing a deep breath, she opted for the only option offered and crawled inside. She didn't bother sliding the door closed. When Thornheart found her gone, she'd assume she'd found the door and entered the passageway. Leaving it open, provided a glimmer of light in the pitch black. If she had to return, it would guide her.

One decision made, next she had to decide which way: left or right. The other two cells on this side also had hidden doors. She'd already tried them to discover the cell doors had been locked, so she couldn't escape through them.

Knowing Thornheart and her philosophy for the game, she believed one way led to safety. The other led to a lethal encounter. For Thornheart, the thrill of possible death was the reason she played. But which way was which?

She sniffed the air. A fresh breeze came from the right. She crept that way with one hand on the wall to guide her, the other gripping a dagger. The going was smooth. The tunnel twisted in various ways, and she soon lost her sense of direction. She had been heading towards the front of the fortress but now, she could be walking in the opposite direction for all she knew.

The floor felt like it was descending, but the slope was so gentle, she was unsure. One thing was certain, the air was growing cooler and the sound of dripping water was growing louder. Rounding a shallow bend, she saw a light glowing up ahead. She put extra effort into walking silently. Sweat gathered in her palm and wet the handle of the dagger.

Her returning memories provided glimpses of the game Thornheart and Cormac had played. She recalled odd-shaped rolling dice, smiling faces of her companions, who so far had no names, and drawing a dungeon. The game had creatures from fantasy worlds. Whatever the imagination could conjure up, it could appear. Everything from ghosts to goblins, dragons to walking trees. If Coraline was here, she'd guide her, but the fairy hated being underground. She'd die upon the teeth of a great bear before entering a dungeon.

The light up ahead grew, spilling into the passage through an oval opening. It revealed a dead end. She stretched her neck to see more but from this distance, it was impossible to see anything but the solid wall. Slowing her steps, she crept forward. The trickle of water mixed with the dripping. Her eyes grew accustomed to the light the nearer she came to the opening. When she reached it, she stopped, listened, then drew a shallow breath and peeked around the edge.

Inside the room that measured 100 feet square was lush grass, waist-high bushes, a tree and a gentle stream. The light came from a large hole in the ceiling where sunshine beamed in. There were no exits off the room that she could see, but if she could get to the ceiling 50 feet above, she could crawl out. That task looked impossible. The 30-foot tree grew directly below it, but there was no way to get from the flimsy top of that tree to the rim of the hole.

Another thought came to her. While this looked like a peaceful setting, there had to be a threat. Thornheart wouldn't provide a paradise for her to escape to. She studied the room further, scanning the walls and then the floor. Nothing stood out. She stepped into the light and searched for an easy way into it. The floor was ten feet below her. The wall was rough and looked climbable, so she sat down and lifted herself over the side. Halfway down, her foot hit something slimy and slipped from the rock. She clung to the wall and moved her foot to find a secure place to stick it. Not finding one, she opted to jump. She pushed herself away from the wall and landed as softly as she could between the small rocks and mounds of grass.

Taking a closer look at the wall, she found the lower five feet covered in a clear gooey substance. Climbing out of this room would be a challenge.

Turning, she surveyed the room, wondering if another secret door hid somewhere along the wall. She walked the perimeter, checking to see if anything stood out. Nothing did, so she made a more thorough search, occasionally glancing up at the hole in the ceiling, seeing the sun on the lip of it and a puffy cloud drifting by. She could see the outside; she only needed to find a way to reach it.

While searching behind a bush, her ears picked up a low hum. It sounded like two branches rubbing together in the wind. She stopped to listen closer. It was getting louder. Sensing she was no longer alone, she turned. The creature floating ten feet away didn't look menacing, yet she pressed her back against the wall and remained still. It was the size of a dinner plate. Its numerous tentacles dangling from its underside swayed gently as it floated. Two eyes on the end of protruding tentacles on the top of the creature appeared to float aimlessly, sometimes looking at her and sometimes not. She didn't know what it was called, but it reminded her of a jellyfish. If they were similar, those tentacles had the ability to sting.

A memory flashed, and she recalled stepping on a purple jellyfish and getting her foot stung. The pain was excruciating, and she had to soak it in salt water to relieve it.

This thing, whatever it was, was best avoided. It didn't appear threatening, only curious. She looked past it and saw three more, floating aimlessly about in the sunshine. Cautiously, she resumed her search for the passageway, keeping one eye on the creatures and one on the wall.

25

The Unexpected Messenger

CORMAC KNELT AT the stream and dipped the flask into the water. While he waited for it to fill, he glanced at the group up stream. They were talking in hushed voices, probably about him. Jowsey glanced at him quickly, then returned his attention to the others. He didn't blame them for not trusting him. He was the reason they were here.

Turning his attention to the water, he watched a leaf float by and slowly disappear down stream. He wished he could follow it, disappear from here and... And what? He groaned. He wanted them to be his friends. In truth, he needed them. Before meeting them, he'd felt empty and lost. Now he felt like he had purpose.

"Cormac."

He turned and looked to see who had risked coming near him. No one had. He lowered his brow. They were still there, chatting in a close circle.

"Excuse me."

Where did the voice come from? He looked behind him into the bushes. No one was there. He heard a heavy sigh.

"It's me. You don't know me, but I know you."

He froze, the flask filled, and water flowed over it. "Who are you?" he whispered, fearful the others would think him crazy.

"Coraline. I'm a friend of Rosalind."

"Where are you? I can't see you."

"Will you hurt me?" The small voice sounded afraid.

"No. I won't."

"Please, don't be startled. I'm... I'm a fairy, you see. Not everyone can see me. When you don't believe, you see only a shimmer of what we truly are."

He sat back on his feet. "Really? And you know Rosalind?"

"Yes. We are great friends."

He scratched his head. "She's never talked about you. How long have you been gone?"

"Many days. I left her shortly after Pebble Creek. You were riding to Starlight Ridge."

"Wait. You were there?"

"I have always been there."

"But I can't see you?" He thought about the times he'd seen Rosalind talking to herself. "You have travelled with us all this time?"

"No, you can't see me unless I reveal myself, and, yes. I have been with Rosalind longer than you have. Longer than Loggie."

"Incredible."

"But I can't find her. This means she is underground or..." Her voice trailed off.

"Or?"

"No longer with us." The voice trembled.

"Can I see you?" He searched the air where he believed the voice originated. A shimmer of light appeared. It was no taller than seven inches. If he stared and tilted his head to the left, he could barely make out an image of a woman with wings. He squinted, and the vision became clearer. She wore a short, sleeveless green dress with a brown vest, and her red hair was braided over the shoulder. A bonnet with a hole in the top rested on top of her head. "I see you."

"Do you believe?"

"Believe? My eyes tell me you are real. My ears support that hypothesis." The image grew, and he could see her eyes and mouth clearly. She was small, smaller than his sisters' dolls they played with as little girls. Fairies were not supposed to be real, but proof hovered near him. "Your name? Coraline?"

"Yes." She smiled. "Named by my aunt who lives by the sea."

"Were you there when the dragon took her away?"

Coraline's eyes grew wide. "Away? This is why I cannot find her? Did you reach Starlight Ridge?"

"Yes, and we were attacked by dragons. Where were you?"

"On a mission. I travelled to Sweetgrass to seek council with Kiefwind's clan."

"Did you find them?"

"Yes. They were not aware of his entrapment nor the curse. They gave up searching years ago. They do not leave their sanctuary unless trouble finds them. And trouble has found them."

"They left Sweetgrass?"

"A small group is here with me. It is why I travelled so fast."

Cormac half stood and looked around. Fear of dragons was deeply embedded in his mind after battling them.

"Do not worry," said Coraline. "They mean you no harm unless you cause them trouble. They are here to help."

He stared at her. "They're going to fight Thornheart's dragons?"

She shook her head. "They will rescue them by killing the woman."

"They can't do that?"

"Why? It is the way dragons do things."

"Well, if they do. Kiefwind will die."

"That is illogical. Please, explain."

Jowsey yelled, and Cormac looked to see everyone scatter from the clearing. The horses darted into the trees. That's when he saw a large shadow. It darkened, then a dragon sat on the road.

"Is that one of the friendly dragons?" Cormac's voice shook.

"Yes. Let me introduce you." She flew towards the dragon but stopped midway. "Are you coming?"

His brain said no. His feet ordered him to run, but his heart looked for any hope of rescuing Rosalind. He stumbled forward, staring at the fairy, hoping she wasn't an apparition come to lead him to his death.

"Cormac!" shouted Etain. "No! It's a dragon!"

"I'm told its friendly." That sounded so stupid.

"Are you dazed?" asked Jowsey.

"Must have drunk bad water," said Loggie.

Kneilot stood up from the bush he hid behind. "He sees something we don't." Matilda, perched on his shoulder, sniffed the air.

"Rosalind sent us a messenger." Cormac walked before the dragon and gulped hard.

"He's been into the curly mushrooms," said Loggie. "He'll see things we can't imagine."

"Or he has a death wish," said Jowsey.

"Maybe the dragon will get his fill with his large body and leave us alone." Loggie chuckled.

Cormac frowned at him. "Etain, do you believe in fairies?"

"Well, um, I've not heard any stories from travellers that lead me to believe they exist."

"What if I said one has been travelling with us all along?"

"I'd say you've been drinking the wizard's rum without strained milk."

His face twisted. "Strained milk and rum." He shivered. "That sounds horrible."

"Not if you add cocoa and honey."

He shook his head. Still sounded awful. He turned to the dragon. "Coraline says I can trust you."

"Is that a question or an answer?" The dragon lowered its head.

"It's goin' eat him," said Loggie. "I knew it. Can't trust a dragon."

"A statement. If Rosalind trusts Coraline, I do. My fate is in your hands...claws."

"This woman," said the dragon in its deep voice, "Shayde Thornheart. Are you friends?" The last syllable was drawn out.

"Enemies. She has taken our friend, and we go to rescue her."

"And Kiefwind and his yswains? Are they not worthy of your rescue?"

He hesitated, then spoke the truth he knew. "We entered Darkmoore Caves and the dungeon to rescue Kiefwind. Thornheart took him and left us to die."

The dragon considered him. "This can be confirmed by Kiefwind? If it cannot, you will die."

He swallowed hard. "It can. We were all there. He was white when in the dungeon. He is now blue."

"White?" The rise in his voice matched that of his eyebrows. "He was transitioning into the next world. He had lost hope."

"Now, under the control of Thornheart, he and his yswains attacked us and took our friend."

"We will kill this woman and set him free."

"No."

"What?" He lunged forward and stopped two feet from Cormac's chest. "You protect this woman?"

He shook his head. It matched the trembling in his bones with the dragon's mouth this close. "My friend," he gestured towards Etain, "has read the spell book Darkmoore had used to create the curse. If Thornheart is killed before the curse is broken, all those under her control will perish."

"How is the curse broken?"

"Kiefwind must save Thornheart's life."

The dragon pursed its lips. "So, we try to kill her and let him stop us?" One thick eyebrow rose. "But we can't accidentally kill her. That is a difficult matter for a dragon."

"Will the dragons listen to you? The yswains? Is there a way to make them stand down? Long enough so we can rescue our friend."

"And Kiefwind? How are you to help us rescue him and his yswains?"

Cormac opened his mouth but said nothing. He had no way to break the curse. If he tried to kill Thornheart and Kiefwind intervene, the dragon might kill him to protect her.

"I see." The dragon stretched his neck. "You want us to help your friend, but you offer nothing in return. Classic human behaviour."

"Rosalind risked her life, risked all our lives to rescue your dragon friends from the dungeon. It was Thornheart who stopped her." He drew a quick breath. "The reason she went to Starlight Ridge was not to save a human. She wanted to save Kiefwind from the curse. She wanted to rescue him. She could have walked away, but she didn't. Even now, if she's alive, she's probably scheming to find a way to rescue Kiefwind."

"Is she human?"

"Hauflin."

The dragon huffed. "Of course." He looked past Cormac. "You. Hauflin. Step forward."

The colour in Kneilot's face drained, but he didn't back away.

"Come. I'll not eat you."

Kneilot stepped forward. Matilda, who perched on his shoulder, crouched as if she was ready to leap into the air.

"A caterial," said the dragon. "Fitting." When Kneilot was within 15 feet, the dragon stretched his neck past Cormac and came closer to him. "You. Are you an honest soul?"

"Yes," stuttered Kneilot.

"What god do you honour?"

"Eir. I've no other. Yet. I...could possibly follow more with wisdom."

"What is your name?"

"Kneilot. And yours?"

"Flarsprint." He looked to the rest. "Names." They each said their name, then Flarsprint nodded and looked back at Kneilot. "Your friend. Is she worthy of saving?"

"Yes." He didn't hesitate. "Very much so."

"Then we must devise a plan. One that will rescue both, dragon and hauflin. Do you agree?"

"Yes. That is ideal."

"Then let's form an alliance for this quest and see it through." He looked to the others. "Are you willing to join us?"

"Us?" asked Etain. "How many dragons are there?"

Flarsprint smiled. "Nine."

Cormac gulped. Nine. He looked around and only saw the one in front of him. If he was playing a game of cards, he'd bet his nine dragons to Thornheart's seven. The odds were in his favour.

He caught a glimpse of Coraline sitting on his shoulder, arms crossed and a large grin on her face. Her image was clear, crisp, and he wondered if the rest could see her. Since they hadn't mentioned her, he thought not. This fantasy world was starting to look a lot like the game he played, complete with dragons and fairies. He even had a sword. With everyone and everything gathered, it was time to meet the challenge of the quest, defeat the evil sorceress and rescue the princess.

A smile creased his lips. Rosalind was no helpless princess, but he'd do his best to rescue her anyways.

The sun slowly heated the cavern, and the jellyfish-like creatures floated around aimlessly. There were ten that Rosalind could see. They constantly moved, which made them difficult to count. She avoided them, and they avoided her. With the goal of not startling them, she moved slowly around the room, searching for secret levers that opened secret doors. Back to where she'd started from, she stopped and looked around the open-air cavern. If Thornheart was a serious player, she'd keep switching things up. The secret door in her cell was on the wall.

That meant the way to escape this room might be through a trap door on the floor.

She groaned. It was a large area to search. Unlike the walls that were relatively bare with only a few vines growing along them and the slimy goo below the doorway she'd passed through, the floor was covered with dirt, rocks, grass, bushes, a tree and narrow stream that flowed into a pond. Gazing up at the opening, she considered the option of going through there. Even if she climbed the tree to the top, she couldn't get out. The walls were too smooth, and they curved inwards, giving her nowhere to cling.

Not willing to give up, she casually strolled around, looking beneath bushes, kicking aside rocks and avoiding the floating jellyfish. After several laps, she fell to her knees to closer inspect a spot with potential. She pushed dirt aside and lift a rock. Nothing. She crawled to another section and did the same thing and still came up empty handed. Lifting her knee to move again, she found her foot hooked on something. She turned and saw a branch wrapped around it. Pulling her leg forward wouldn't release it. She sat on her bum and used the other foot to force the branch off and another branch wrapped around it.

Staring at the branches, she blinked. The bush had moved. Or at least she thought it had. She reached down and tried to pull off the branch, but it wouldn't budge. Drawing the dagger from the sheath, she stabbed the branch, hoping to cut it. As soon as the blade hit the bark, the branches withdrew only to return with reinforcements and ensnarl both legs.

Rosalind couldn't move. She struck the branches again with the blade. They retracted and before she could move her legs, they lashed out and wrapped around tighter. The bush shook, and its branches stretched into the air blanketing her in shadow. This made the floating jellyfish nervous, and they floated faster, sometimes bumping into each other. When this happened, green dust exploded into the air. She sniffed. It smelt like sulfur.

Searching through her pouches for something, anything to try, she found three sacks from Darkmoore's Lair. They were the ones she had grabbed off the corner of a table when she raced out with her pack. Each contained a different colour powder. There was no writing on the sacks, so she had no idea what they did or if they still did what they were meant to do. They were over 100 years old.

The bush continued to expand and send its branches into the air. They flailed about, slapping other bushes, which triggered the ones slapped to expand. Soon, the room was filled with long branches slapping one another. The floating jellyfish were struck several times. Each time, green dust was ejected and danced in the sunshine, increasing the sulfur smell.

Through all this, the branches wrapped around Rosalind's feet didn't release their grip. She pulled and pushed but her feet wouldn't break free. Choking on sulfur fumes and being slapped about by rambunctious branches, she opened one of the sacks and tucked the others into her pouch. A slap from behind drove her head forward. Sucking in breath, she breathed in some of the powder. It triggered violent sneezes and one after another, the powder resting in her hand got blown over her legs and the plants.

With each sneeze, a bolt of light shot from her nose, striking her legs and the branches around them. She was torn between the unstoppable sneezes and wailing in pain. The bush shook and rumbled. It thrashed about and sent her flying through the air. The sack containing the remaining powder landed hard on the ground and exploded into dozens of bolts that flew in every direction.

She ducked as jellyfish and branches consumed the air, many being struck by the bolts and shattering or bursting into pieces. Material rained down on her, and she fought to reach safe ground. The smell of sulfur filled the air, and she pulled her shirt over her mouth and nose and barged through the branches. She came upon the pond and dove in. Surfacing for a breath, she marvelled at the chaotic scene and wondered how long it would take to calm down. Not seeing it end any time soon, she searched the edges of the pond to see if she could find the escape route.

Her foot struck a rock, and it moved. She dove under and pulled on it. The rock was a lever. Twisting it, it felt like it unlocked a door, but she hesitated to open it. Coming up for a breath, she considered the option. If she opened that door, the water would drain. She'd be sucked down with it. Not feeling she had many choices and seeing the branches continue to swing wildly, the jellyfish explode from being hit and the air growing more and more unbearable, she dove under, yanked on the door and let the current sweep her away.

26

Battle Philosophy

THE PLAN WAS simple. They'd mount the dragons and be flown into the fortress to search for Rosalind. While they kept the humans busy, the dragons would call out Kiefwind and the other dragons and distract them. It was so simple, Cormac knew it would fail. He and the others were no match for henchmen. They didn't fight hand-to-hand combat. They could sneak, they could hide and they could run. Etain had a few spells she'd learned behind her aunt's back, and she had a few things she'd taken from Darkmoore's Lair but otherwise, they were no challenge.

This last thought kept rolling through Cormac's head while he secured his horse beneath the cover of a large clump of evergreen trees with the rest of the horses. They were still a half mile from Thornheart Fortress, but the distance didn't matter if they were flying. They'd be there in a minute.

Jowsey said it was a solid plan. The henchmen who guarded the front gates would think nothing of dragons flying overhead since they belonged there. They were all blue and to a human, they looked so much alike one was as good as the other. He also said Thornheart didn't have as many henchmen as she'd liked to have, a dozen or two at best, and they weren't as loyal as she'd have liked them to be. What she had more of were messengers, like he had been, who searched Lachspeur for weapons and spells. The three women who served her were not fighters. They were maids and tended to her personal needs, of which there were many. She was an old human woman, frail from age and pampering.

What she did have was theatrics. Jowsey had seen her give a great speech and threaten a henchman only to stumble and fall on a strip of crooked carpet. Without her spells, she was as harmless as a doddering child.

Cormac tried to see that. Without the spells, she was just an old woman from Earth. Someone in her 60s who didn't work out at the gym or run ten miles a day. She sat around, letting her muscles waste away with time. Except she did have command of dragons. That alone made her dangerous.

"I will go with you." Coraline's voice shook him from his thoughts.

"Can you protect yourself?"

"They can't see me."

He nodded. "They won't hit what they don't know is there."

"As soon as we touch down, I'll search for Rosalind. Lead her to you or lead you to her."

"That sounds like a good part of the plan."

"What?" Jowsey had been passing by and stopped. "What did you say?"

"Nothing. Just talking to myself."

"A talk to encourage. We're going to need it." He walked on.

"How will you find me?" he asked. "Do you have a sixth sense or something? I mean, how do you find Rosalind though she is far away?"

"We have bonded."

"Magically?"

"I suppose."

"It's time." Etain walked up to him. "I can't say I'm not nervous. I never thought I'd be riding a dragon."

"Me either." He fumbled with his gear, making sure his belts were secure and the leather straps securing the daggers were in place. "But..." He considered her. "You're a good leader."

"I'm no leader. I just know more stuff. Read more books. Talked to people who travelled extensively." She smiled mischievously. "And I have the map."

"That makes you the leader."

"It's better to switch up. Let the one who knows the most in a particular situation lead. And right now, that's you."

"I thought it was Jowsey since he's been here."

She winced. "He's been here as a thief. Thornheart is from your world. You have a better chance of understanding her and that game she plays. The same one you play. Is there anything you can share with us before we leave that may help?"

"Maybe."

"Come stand with us. While Loggie is being unreasonable, we are still in this together."

He followed and joined the circle they made. Loggie wouldn't look at him, but the others did.

"Cormac, tell us," said Etain. "How is this game played? Are there rules she won't break? Where is the weakness?"

"That's tough. She may break every rule of the game. Her weakness will be limited to imagination. And her over-confidence. As for how it's played, there's no real winning moment. Not really. The game is about the adventure. From what she said at Starlight Ridge, she plays dangerously. She likes high stakes. She's pretending to be the ruler of this castle. As such, she's probably locked Rosalind in a dungeon. Castles and dungeons always have secret passageways, secret doors and traps. And roaming monsters, usually skeletons, or hob—those creatures I can't name, or the undead. At every turn, she'll try to injure or kill us."

"Sounds like a fantastic game to teach children you don't like," mumbled Loggie. "Along with ex-lovers and ex-friends."

"Does she always provide a way out?" asked Kneilot.

"Given her philosophy, she probably provides a way deeper into trouble. Carving away at the strength of an individual through injury and exhaustion until they grow weak and succumb to the damage. But she won't be ready for nine dragons." He glanced at the group of large magical creatures standing in the nearby field having their own discussion about the upcoming battle. "That is our ace in the hole."

"What's an ace?" asked Jowsey. "A secret ally who kills her?"

"That's a good way to put it."

"I'm more concerned with the location of the hole," said Loggie. "I think it's in his head."

"We entered Darkmoore Caves with less help and less information," said Etain. "Determination got us through; it will get us through today." She placed her hand in the centre of the circle, palm up.

Recognising the gesture, Cormac was going to tell her the palm was supposed to go down but decided not to. Instead, he put his hand, palm up, on top of hers. Kneilot did the same. So did Jowsey. Loggie hesitated, then slapped his hand down. Etain capped off the hands with her palm down. She closed her eyes and held the hands in place.

"In times of great challenges, it is those who stand together who triumph. May Týr stand with us and let us see this encounter through and rejoice in our success at the drawing of the day. As we believe, let it be done." She squeezed their hands together, then lifted them high and released them.

Cormac drew a deep breath and turned towards the dragons. They were staring in his direction. It was time. While fate and destiny might shape and sway his life, he was the one who determined the ultimate outcome. His actions had brought him here. He would make things right and deliver his friends to safety.

He walked towards the dragons with more determination than he expected. The sounds of his friends following fueled his resolve.

Flarsprint rose before him. His eyes were set, his voice steady. "Mount my back like a warrior or crawl to the fortress. I will not be diminished by a cowardly human."

He stopped a few feet away, stiffened his jaw and stared up at the giant lizard. "Fly like a warrior, or I shall run to the fortress. I will not be flown into battle on a sparrow."

The dragon snorted. "Mount!"

Cormac marched to the side of the dragon and leapt up behind the neck and in front of the wings. Earlier, he and the rest had been instructed by the dragons on the best place to sit and where they'd find a place to hold on securely. Tightening his legs around the dragon, he glanced to the left. Kneilot was settling on the dragon with his spear in one hand and holding on with the other. Matilda was perched on his shoulder. Kneilot wanted her to remain with the horses, but she refused. Apparently, she'd fly there herself if left behind. Cats being cats, Cormac didn't doubt that.

To his right, Etain was adjusting her seat on the dragon. She held Rosalind's staff. It had been left in its holster on the horse when they'd dismounted at Starlight Ridge. Jowsey had wanted to use it, but Etain, sensing it had magic, claimed it. "Only to return it to Rosalind," she'd said.

Over his right shoulder, Jowsey was grinning from ear-to-ear. Poised atop the dragon, he appeared to be ready for anything that came his way. Cormac envied his thirst for adventure regardless of the cost.

Over his left shoulder, Loggie was mumbling something too low for him to hear. No doubt, he was entertaining his dragon with his quick wit while settling into a comfortable and safe position.

Coraline sat on Cormac's shoulder and gripped his shirt collar. Her expression was pleasant as if she was flying to the seaside to gather shells on this sunny day. She winked at him and giggled. "Flying on a dragon is the ultimate way to travel. Fast. Worry free. Eagles will not attack."

The four riderless dragons waited in the rear. They were going to lead the attack. Their goal was to fly over the fortress, then circle back to do another fly over, drawing the attention of the henchmen and the dragons under Thornheart's control.

Flarsprint lurched forward, catching Cormac off guard. The unexpected burst of speed threw him back, and he almost choked on his tongue. Spit flew down his throat, and he coughed to disperse it. Leaning forward and holding on tightly, he mentally prepared to reach heights he'd never been before. Horses were one thing; a dragon ride was something completely out of his comfort zone.

"Relax," said Flarsprint. "Your muscles will appreciate it."

He gulped. No doubt the dragon sensed his tense muscles. Given the creatures magical abilities, it probably sensed his fear. He focussed on his muscles and eased the pressure they applied. Finding a comfortable middle ground of holding tightly enough to not fall off, he tried to relax and enjoy the ride. He inwardly laughed at himself. He was going off to fight dragons and henchmen. This was not going to be enjoyable. It would be if he sat around the table with friends and Willard was at the helm as Adventure Master. They'd be hooting, charging forward with a beer in one hand and the 20-sided die in the other. Seth, Schooner, Jigs, Chris and Gerry would be in their glory. But they weren't here, and he didn't wish them to be.

They climbed to great heights and sored over the treetops, coming in low towards the fortress. He glanced at Kneilot. His face revealed the horror within. Matilda didn't feel the same way. Eyes closed, she lifted her nose into the wind and allowed it to flutter her fur and feathers.

"No dragons in sight," said Flarsprint.

Cormac searched the ground ahead. The fortress was a wooden structure, not stone as he'd expected. It was surrounded by a fence made from logs standing upright. Their tops were pointy. If he fell on them, he'd be impaled. The main structure had three round rooftops. They couldn't land on them. However, they were connected in the rear by a building a hundred feet long and 50 feet wide. It had a flat roof along with merlons made of wood. Several smaller buildings surrounded the main structure. Horses were outside of one. Smaller animals - goats or sheep - ran about freely. There were also a few dozen chickens pecking about.

More importantly, the outer wall didn't have a complete walkway. There were platforms every 100 feet where a guard could stand, watch and fire from. He didn't see anyone manning them, but three men worked near the outbuildings and one woman was in the garden. He saw no dragons. He doubted they'd fit inside the buildings, so that meant...

His heart leapt. Maybe they were harassing a distant settlement or hunting down someone else Thornheart didn't like, leaving the fortress unguarded. This would make the job extremely easy. The henchmen would run from Flarsprint and his clan, and Cormac could find Rosalind and fly her out of there.

The sudden drop and plunge into colder water sent Rosalind into a dark spiral. She swung her arms and kicked, searching for the surface, hoping one was there. When she broke through, she gasped for air. The light from the trapdoor was quickly disappearing as she floated with the current. Spinning around, she peered down the tunnel. It disappeared into darkness. Thoughts of swimming upstream crossed her mind, but the current was too swift. The trapdoor disappeared, and she was consumed in darkness. The sound of rushing water smashing against stone thundered in her ears.

Bobbing along, she crashed into the wall. She tried to cling to the stone, but she was dragged forward. Her arms grew tired and sore. With each slam into the wall, another ache developed. Kicking to stay afloat tired her legs. Not seeing an end to the torment played with her mind. Her heartrate increased, and fear crept into her thoughts.

A loud roar shattered her concentration, and she searched the darkness for the source. The creature roared again, shaking her further. Her hand itched to hold a dagger, but she needed all her strength to fight the water, to keep her afloat and protect her head from slamming into the wall.

The slope of the water dropped quickly, and the fast stream became a raging river, pushing her and shoving her against the wall and dragging her under. She gulped air, taking in water, too. Coughing and sputtering, she fought with aching muscles until the water disappeared beneath her, and she was washed over what could only be a waterfall. She hit the pool below and struggled to reach the surface. Blackness surrounded her, and solid forces swimming by bumped into her. Feeling her lungs were about to burst, her mouth wanted to open, but she held it shut and released small bubbles of the quickly depleting air remaining in her lungs. Just when she thought she couldn't hold it any longer, she broke through the surface and found oxygen. It was stale, but it was air. She gulped and gasped, sinking and rising until her senses felt the calmness of the still water.

Not knowing the size of the pool she'd fallen into or where the edges where, she swam slowly away from the sound of the waterfall and in a direction she hoped to find solid ground or something to hold on to. Weary muscles slowed her progress and dragged her under several times before her feet hit something solid. Feeling relief at finding something, she reached down with one foot to place it on what she believed was bottom only to find the bottom moved.

Her breath caught. She was not alone in this pool.

27

The Dark Pool

THE DESCENT WAS smooth. Cormac prepared to dismount quickly, so Flarsprint could immediately take to the sky. The plan was to make it look like the dragon had simply swooped over the rooftop for a closer view, not to drop off a combatant. To do this, the dragons would arrive in a wave. Cormac was first. Jowsey second.

Flarsprint slowed. Cormac lay against his neck to hide his presence. Upon reaching the building, he quickly swung around to face the rear of the dragon and pointed his feet towards the dip where the wing joined the torso. Flarsprint tilted gently to the side, and Cormac pushed himself onto the dip and slid gracefully down the scales, off the wing and onto the solid roof. That's where the problem arose. At this speed, his feet hit the wood and stuck. He fell backwards and slammed onto the roof. Shaken, but not hurt, he jumped to his feet and ran to the merlon to give the next dragon room to drop its passenger.

He wiped sweat from his brow, straightened the scabbard and watched Jowsey's approach. The man rode that dragon like he was a trick rider. Hair whipping in the wind, his elven eyes wide and his face lit up like fireworks on Natal Day, he waited for the right moment, spun around to face the tail of the dragon, then slid off with such finesse, it looked like he'd done it a thousand times. When his feet hit the roof, he thrust his upper body forward and raised his arms like he'd just finished a gymnastics routine. In Cormac's mind, he heard 'ta-da'.

Jowsey rushed over, grinning. "Incredible. Ride of my life. I want to do it again."

Cormac shook his head in disbelief. "How do stay so calm, so positive before facing danger?"

"Easy. I react in the same manner to fear as I do excitement. I just tell myself this is exciting, and the brain does the rest."

"If it was only that easy."

"It is."

Cormac watched the next dragon approach. Kneilot still wore the look of horror he'd lifted off the ground with. He clutched the dragon tightly and stared straight ahead. Before reaching the roof, the dragon's mouth moved. He could only guess it was telling him to prepare for landing. But Kneilot didn't budge.

The dragon's voice rose. "Prepare to dismount now."

Kneilot turned but too slowly. The dragon flapped its wings to slow its progress, and Kneilot slid down the dip and landed hard on the roof. Cormac cringed. That was going to hurt. The dragon lifted off, leaving Kneilot on his hind end, nursing the pain. Matilda soured around the roof, then landed in front of the young cleric.

Not waiting to see if he'd rise on his own, Cormac tugged at Jowsey. "Let's get him out of the way." The next dragon was already on approach. He grabbed one arm and Jowsey grabbed the other and together, they hurried Kneilot to the side and flopped him down. "Are you okay?" Cormac stared into his face.

"Yes," he gasped. "The most dreadful moments of my life. I shall never experience something that horrifying again."

"Speak to Jowsey." Cormac patted him on the shoulder. "He'll make you love riding dragons." He stood and watched Etain arrive. Like the adventurous elf she was, she slid down the dragon's wing almost as gracefully as Jowsey.

Loggie arrived with little fan fair or trouble. The dwarf leapt off the dragon like he didn't care one way or the other what delivered him. His reason for being here was clear: to rescue Rosalind. Loggie shot him a menacing glare, then searched the roof for the exit. Seeing the door, he walked over to it as if he lived here.

"Quickly," whispered Etain.

Jowsey followed her towards Loggie. Kneilot was next with Matilda on his shoulder. Cormac gave a passing glance to the dragons making long flights over the fortress. They'd fly out of sight, then return from a different angle. This was to keep the actual number of dragons hidden from those who watched.

With dagger in hand, Loggie edged open the thick wooden door and peered in. He nodded to those behind him and stepped inside.

Cormac was the last to enter. He closed the door behind him and descended the stairs to the next level. It was a bunkhouse. Six beds stretched across the wall, and three windows behind them shed light into the room. Various types of footwear and clothing were hung up or set on shelves. Sundry items, such as lanterns, candles, books and mugs rested on small bedside tables. The room smelt of body odour and rotten socks. Doors to the left and right led to other sections of the stronghold, but Loggie continued down the next flight of stairs to the second storey. It was a carbon copy of the third level with six beds, two doors and possessions of men. The lower floor contained a fireplace and three long tables butting up to windows.

Here, Loggie stopped and looked back at the others for a hint of direction. There was a door on each wall. The ones on the front and back led outside. The ones on the end led elsewhere.

Cormac examined the possibilities. If Rosalind was held in the dungeon and the dungeon was below ground, then they had to find that door. From his experience in the game, he often found the dungeon below the guardhouse, not the sleeping quarters. This provided round the clock watch, and prisoners couldn't escape and kill everyone while they slept. The kitchen and bakehouse were usually in the same building as the bunk house.

He peered through the windows, looking one way then the other to see if he could spot the guardhouse. Seeing a building that might be it, he started towards the back door. Before he reached it, he stopped quickly. Etain smashed into him. He caught his balance and turned. "I think I've seen this layout before." He searched his memory. It had been so long ago. "This design. It's in the manual."

"Manual?" asked Loggie. "The attention to detail for killing people like they're puppets in your world is incredible."

He stared at him. "It's not about killing. It's about the adventure. Thornheart is wrong. She'd be a player hated by my friends. We would never have her as an Adventure Master."

"Do you hear what you're saying? Adventure Master? This isn't a game. We are not pawns for you to throw around like sticks. We are flesh and blood. We feel. We hurt. We love. We bleed."

"I know. I see that. If I've learned nothing from being here, I've learned that."

Etain stepped between them. "Rosalind is waiting. Though she won't be surprised to learn we were delayed by you two having a disagreement."

Loggie frowned at her, then turned to Cormac. "If you know the layout of this building, take us to the dungeon."

Cormac pointed at the door. "To the kitchen." He walked over to the door, put his ear to it to listen, heard nothing, then slowly opened it. The two women in dresses and aprons on the other side jumped and held the knives they were using to peel potatoes in a threatening manner.

"We are only passing through," he said. "We mean you no harm." They stepped aside, and he walked towards the door on the opposite side of the room.

"Do you enjoy working for Thornheart?" Kneilot asked the ladies.

The older one huffed. "She's a witch. Horrible manners."

"Why don't you leave?"

"We are not permitted."

"Prepare your things, ladies," said Jowsey. "We're seeking permission for your departure."

The older one lowered her brow. "You're not the first to say that and probably not the last now that she's acquired dragons." She turned to the bowl of potatoes. "Let me know how it goes. The afternoon meal, which her highness calls lunch, will be served at two."

Cormac opened the door and saw the bakehouse. The aroma of baking bread greeted him. He stepped inside and walked to the door on the opposite wall. On the other side of this was supposed to be a room where they stored weapons along with outdoor clothing. He drew a breath and opened it slowly. The man sitting on a stool putting a new handle on an axe head looked up. When he saw it wasn't a fellow henchman, he jumped and ran for the door. Cormac dove for his feet and dragged him to the floor. They exchanged punches before Jowsey and Loggie each grabbed an arm and pinned the human.

Cormac got up, rubbing his jaw. The swelling and bruises from Loggie's punches had started to fade, and now he had more.

Etain picked up a length of rope. "Hold his hands behind his back."

Jowsey and Loggie threw the man on the floor and forced his hands behind his back. When he tried to yell, Jowsey slapped him "Shut up, and we'll let you live. It's better than what you'll get from Thornheart."

The man grunted but stopped struggling.

Etain secured his hands, then wrapped the end of the rope around his legs, pulling his feet to his hands. "That should keep him." She stood and looked at Cormac. "Next?"

He pointed to the stairs against the opposite wall. "If I remember the dungeon map correctly." He grabbed a rag from a nearby hook and shoved it into the man's mouth. Stepping over him, he went for the stairs and stopped to listen. He couldn't see the bottom because they gently curved to the left and disappeared beneath the floor of the guardhouse. This was exactly like the plans in the game book. The dungeon sounded empty, and he rushed down the stairs, lanterns hanging on the wall lighting his way.

At the bottom, he saw a straight passageway. Three cell doors lined each side. That wasn't right. He held back. "This passageway is supposed to be 60 feet long. It's barely 30."

"Maybe she ran out of money," said Loggie. "Or imagination. As humans do."

"It may be due to resources." Etain stepped forward but stopped. "Traps?"

"I don't recall any."

"I'll check. We go slowly." She crept forward, searching the area with every step. Her soft boots were silent on the stone floor.

Two lanterns provided light, but not enough for Cormac to see clearly and detect traps. He followed Etain closely, ready to react if necessary.

She reached the first cell door and pulled. "Locked." She stood on her tippytoes to peer through the barred window. "No one." She moved to the cell across the passageway and peeked in. "The door is locked but no one is inside."

Cormac went to the first door she checked and whispered through the little window. "Rosalind? Are you there?"

"You think she's invisible?" Loggie shook his head.

"She might be hiding against the door."

"Because she doesn't want to be rescued?"

"No, because she doesn't know it's us."

Etain considered this. "Rosalind!" Her hushed voice filled the small space. "If you are here, alert us to which cell you occupy." No one answered. "Rosalind!" she said louder and went to the second cell on that side. "Rosalind?" She shook her head. "Empty."

They checked all six cells. All were empty. Etain grabbed one of the lanterns and held it to the door's window to provide more light. "Nothing." She went to another one. This time, she took longer to answer.

"What is it?" asked Cormac.

She stared at him. "A door on the opposite wall is open."

He took the lantern and held it higher. With his eyes adjusting, the shadow near the head of the bed took shape. "It's a secret door, and she's found it." He turned back to Etain. "That's not good."

"Why? She could have already escaped and be outside the fortress."

He shook his head slowly and his memory of what they encountered when they sneaked through that door took shape. He had barely escaped with his life not only because of the creature's strength but because of its poisonous venom. It even had magic missile and ice storm. Five players had entered; only three left. Seth had lost his arm up to the elbow. It was the game Clarise's character had died a horrible death. She couldn't handle it and left, never to return to the table.

"Does the water naga exist in this realm?" he asked in a hushed voice.

"Water naga?" Jowsey shook his head. "Never heard of it. Etain?"

"No, I haven't. What are they?"

"Magical water snakes. Big ones. Nasty ones with poisonous venom."

"Let's hope lack of money and resources changed the game." Loggie pulled a thin piece of steel from his pouch. "We'll know soon enough." He shoved the steel into the lock and twisted it.

Cormac swung his head towards the stairs. "Hurry. We've got company coming."

Rosalind told herself it was the darkness that brought on the fear. This could simply be a trout brushing against her leg. A big trout. Maybe a salmon. No, bass. Or a seal. A dolphin. They were friendly. But a dolphin couldn't survive in fresh water. Focussing her energy on her legs and arms, she swam slowly, trying to swim in a straight line to find the edge of the pool. All the while, she searched for a light, anything to guide her towards the exit.

The large water creature brushed her hip, throwing off her balance and her concentration. She regrouped and swam forward. Maybe if she didn't bother it, it wouldn't bother her. She had already disturbed it by splashing into its pond, but maybe it would go back to sleep.

The creature bumped her, pushing her back. Still, she continued to swim. It bumped her again, then it dragged its long, slippery body around her midsection. This did catch more of her attention, and she wanted to stop. Freeze. See if the creature would leave her alone and go away. But something deep inside told her to keep swimming. She had to reach the solid ground not only because of the creature, but because her body was preparing to give up.

She heard something break the surface, and she stared into the ink-black space, trying to see what it was. But it was impossible.

"Please," she gasped, "I am not here to harm you." She gulped water. "I want only to escape."

"So do I." The gravelly voice hung in the cool air and surrounded Rosalind.

"You are trapped?"

"And hungry."

Her breathing stilled though her heartbeat raced. "I... I will help you."

"I know you will." The creature dove beneath the water and gently encircled Rosalind's waist. A gentle ripple next to her head told her part of the creature resurfaced. A rough appendage touched her neck. It felt like a cat's tongue. The creature dragged it up her face and played with her hair. It withdrew the appendage and moaned. "Hauflin. Tasty."

"I will help you escape."

"Impossible."

"Nothing is impossible."

"Escaping is." Again, the tongue sought out the skin and licked her face.

"How did you get in here?"

"Trap door."

"That's how I got in." She thought fast. "We can get out the same way."

"Impossible." It dragged its tongue across her throat.

"I can reach it." Her voice shook.

"Not even I can reach it, and I am 40 feet long."

"Surely you can." The pressure around her waist grew.

"It is 60 feet above. Impossible."

"Above?" She stopped kicking her feet and moving her hands. The creature supported her in the water, giving her limbs a much-needed rest. She gazed up into the darkness. "In this room?"

"Of course."

"We came through different trap doors."

"No matter. Impossible to escape." She hissed the S-sounds.

"I will not give up without a fight."

The creature shook with laughter. "Of course."

"Is there a ledge? Can I walk up to the trap door? If I could only see it, I'd have a chance. If you can see in the dark, you could guide me."

The creature hissed and mumbled foreign words. A glowing orb the size of a marble appeared. Before Rosalind's eyes had time to adjust, it exploded into white light, blinding her. Blinking hard several times, her eyes slowly adjusted. Before her, a thousand colourful lights danced in the air. It lit the entire cavern. The oval ceiling was at least 60 feet high. The walls were 200 hundred feet apart, and the waterfall that fed into the pool had a 30-foot drop. She floated five feet away from the narrow ledge that ran along the perimeter and extended over the water outlet by way of a wooden bridge.

The trap door was in the centre of the room. It had two thick handlebars attached to it. They were rusty from the dampness inside the cavern. There was no way she could scale the ceiling and reach it.

She marvelled at the amazing lights illuminating the cavern until her eyes fell upon the creature that had her in its grasp. Her entire body trembled, and spit caught in her throat.

"Welcome to the water world of the naga." A smile erupted on the face that was a cross between human and snake. No hair grew on its head. Instead, it was completely covered with scales. Large gills flared on each side of the elongated head, and its thick tongue shot out, tasting the air, then drew back. The large, round eyes were that of a beast, but she sensed intelligence behind them.

She cleared her throat. "I am Rosalind."

"I do not name my food."

She hesitated, then continued. "What is your name?"

The naga looked up at the trap door, then back at her. "I was once known as Orilla of Malega Lake. Now I am referred to as Moat Monster." The last name was said with disgust.

"Who gave you that name?"

"The woman who trapped me."

"Shayde Thornheart?"

"The Orcus of this world. While she lacks his power, she possesses his evil."

"You serve her?"

Anger struck so fast, Rosalind didn't have time to prepare for the onslaught. The creature threw her into the air. She slammed against the ceiling, then plummeted towards the water, striking it and sinking deep below. Floundering from having the wind knocked out of her from the impact with the ceiling, she struggled to regain her senses. When she did, she sealed her mouth and pain shot through her chest.

The naga wrapped around her waist and drove her quickly to the surface where she slammed her against the wall. She held her there, glaring at her.

Rosalind gulped in air and spit out water. The dancing lights made her dizzy and her body begged her to surrender.

"I am not a servant. A prisoner." Orilla hissed, and her tongue shot out to poke Rosalind's face.

"Then you want to escape." Her voice was just above a whisper.

"Of course. But impossible."

"Never." She drew a deep breath and shook her head. "Only if you surrender."

Orilla bent her neck and increased the angle of her head. "I do not surrender."

"Then escape with me."

"Impo—"

"You've surrendered!"

Orilla shot forward but didn't touch her face. Instead, she curled back and gazed upon Rosalind. Long moments passed, and she eased the pressure around Rosalind's chest and allowed her to draw deeper breaths. "How?"

It was a simple word, a simple question. Rosalind had no answer. She looked towards the water flowing from the pool created by the waterfall. "Where does the stream go?"

"Undergrown for a thousand feet and empties into the river flowing into Malega Lake."

"I can't hold my breath that long. Can you?"

"Yes."

"Then why are you here?"

"Blocked by solid steal rails and encased in a protection spell."

She looked up to the top of the waterfall. "Have you tried reaching the—"

"Too steep."

"And the trap—"

"Too high."

"Are there any secret passageways that—"

"Nope."

"But they might be protected by mag—"

"I detect no magic. Only solid walls." Orilla waited and when no further options were given, her gravelly voice spoke smoothly. "Impossible."

Rosalind considered the only option: the ceiling trap door. The question was: how would she reach it. She looked at the naga. "Can you throw me at the trap door?"

Orilla gazed upward. "Once you escape," she turned to her, "what about me?"

"Can you shimmy up a rope? Can you be out of water for a short time?"

"Yessss." Her eyes widened. "But trust," she hissed.

Rosalind brushed her wet hair from her face. "I promise."

The naga glared at her sideways. "How I got trapped."

She put her hand on the cheek of the creature and stroked it gently. "I am not Shayde Thornheart. With or without your help, I will escape and when I do," she leant forward, "I'm coming back for you."

Orilla recoiled. "Impossible."

"Let me prove you wrong."

Once again, the creature gazed at the trap door, then back at her. "You will grab the bars? Get it open?"

"That's my plan."

The naga shrugged. "If you fail, I eat the dead as willingly as the living. Let us try." She held onto Rosalind and carried her to the centre of the pool, directly below the trap door. The dazzling lights provided the perfect illumination for Rosalind to see the handlebars. She positioned herself on Orilla's neck, then prepared herself for flight. Her body ached but if this was the only way, she'd sacrifice the remaining energy to reach it.

Orilla flung her head and most of her body out of the water, sending Rosalind flying through the air. Rosalind smacked the trap door too hard, knocking the wind from her lungs. As she plunged towards the water, her vision faded. When she went under, she had no strength left to swim. Darkness overtook her, and the last feeling she had was a slimy body wrapping around her.

28

Fresh Air

THREE HENCHMEN RACED down the stairs. Cormac had his sword ready, yet... He'd never killed a human before. Nor anything that resembled a human.

The men rushed forward. One had a spear, one had a sword and the third had a dagger. The distance between them closed, and Etain stepped out and swung Rosalind's staff at the man with the sword. The weapon flew through the air and smashed into the wall. She whipped the staff around and knocked him across the side of the head with it. He stumbled but didn't fall, so she hit him again. This strike sent him to the floor, where he stayed.

Jowsey threw himself at the feet of the man with the dagger. The man fell, and they rolled across the floor, punching each other. The dagger slashed Jowsey's arm, and Jowsey retaliated by driving the dagger into his opponent's chest. The man shook, then collapsed.

Cormac prepared to swing at the man with the spear. When he came within reach and swung, the spear grazed his shoulder, sending a sharp pain up his arm. He lowered his sword and too late realised he needed it higher.

Loggie leapt at the man with the spear and drove him against the wall. He punched him several times and the man fell limp and crashed to the floor. Picking up the spear, he glared at Cormac. "I didn't risk my life for you. I saved Kneilot who would have been killed after you stood there doing nothing and got yourself killed. If you haven't noticed yet, in this world, the henchmen are after the ultimate goal: to brag about killing you. You either kill or be killed." He started for the stairs but stopped when Etain spoke.

"The cell?"

"Couldn't get it open." Loggie looked up the stairs. "We kill Thornheart, we'll have all the time we need to find Rosalind."

"We don't kill her until the curse is broken. Until then, we search for Rosalind." She turned to Cormac. "You say you were through the secret passageway. Where does it lead?"

He sheathed his sword and ran towards the stairs. "Follow me."

Rosalind's senses slowly returned. When she opened her eyes, the first thing she saw were dancing lights. She was lying on the narrow ledge that encircled the pool. Trying to move sent every nerve in search of aching muscles and bruises. She groaned and lay still. The trap door was still closed. In her dream, she has opened it.

A dark green form moved over her, making her tremble.

"You wake." Orilla stared down at her. "Sympathies. Too hard. Next time, softer."

Next time? She didn't think she'd survive a next time. Taking in deep, even breaths, she calmed her nerves. After ten minutes, she stretched her leg muscles, getting them to move again without too much pain. Then she stretched her arms and finally her back. Sitting up, she rubbed her face roughly. She was drenched, dirty, sweaty and slimy. If ever she needed a bath, it was now. A long hot bath, one that would soothe the muscles and send her nerves into deep sleep.

"Ready?"

She stared at Orilla. The water naga was at least willing to give her another chance to rescue her.

"Or is it feast time?"

She gulped and got her knees beneath her. "Almost ready." She braced herself for the pain and stood on shaky legs. If she had a shot of something, she'd take it. Reaching for her flask, she found it gone. She must have lost it in one of the falls.

"Looking for? Something?"

"A drink. Water to refresh me."

"Lots of water." She looked to the pool. "But for refreshment, I have better something."

Rosalind lowered her brow. "What?"

"A spell. Makes you fast. Quick. Forget pain."

"What's it called?"

"Expeditious Retreat. They say it can only be self-casted, but..." she grinned, "they have not spent years alone perfecting their magic without distractions. Except the odd feast visitor. Lost quickly but enough to open the latch."

The lack of energy in her bones told her she'd never reach the trap door without help. Even if she managed to hold on, she still had to brace herself against the opening and force the door open. "Okay."

"Sweet." Orilla positioned her neck close to the ledge. "Hold on."

She climbed on, found no where to hold onto that wasn't slippery and fell into the water. The naga bent her neck for easier travelling, and she climbed back on. Swimming out to the centre of the cavern, she stared up at the door 60 feet above. It was doable, surely. If she failed, she was no match for Orilla.

"Ready?" asked Orilla.

"The spell?"

"Oh, yes. Let me think. It goes like..." She mumbled several foreign words and then hummed a melody.

Energy shot through Rosalind's body like lightning. She'd never felt energized like this, not even after nights of rest and many good meals. Her heart raced with the anticipation of action being taken. She stood and the pain she'd felt disappeared.

"Ready?"

"Yes. Remember. Softer."

"Let's see how well this spell works on hauflins. Maybe too strong for you, but we see."

"What?" She barely got the word out and Orilla flung herself out of the water. At her full height, she snapped her neck upward, sending Rosalind sailing towards the trap door. She grabbed hold and held tightly as Orilla splash into the water. Dangling from the steel, she looked down at her.

The water naga popped her head out of the water and stared up. "Success." Her gravelling voice sounded joyful. "Wait not long. Spell is short lived."

Rosalind swung her legs to the frame of the door. Her strength surprised her. She forced her legs into position and braced her shoulders, leaving the door free to move. Her head felt light, and she giggled. The feeling was amazing. The more the spell grew, the stronger and more energized she felt. Grasping the handlebars, she shoved with all her remaining might and that of the naga spell. The door flew open and bathed her in sunshine. She drew a long, deep breath, sucking in as much fresh air as her lungs could hold. The sight and smells were incredible.

"Orilla, we did it."

"No dawdle. Spell ends soon and you sleep."

"What? I fall asleep?"

"A quick nap. Payment for using reserve."

Finding a secure hold along the frame of the door, she flung herself up and out of the hole. Incredibly, she flew ten feet into the air and came down easily on both legs. Taking in the surroundings, she stood behind the building with three circular roofs. A stone fence six feet tall encased what looked like a garden. Rope. She needed rope to throw down to Orilla, then they'd both be free.

Hideous laughter erupted behind her, and she whirled to find Thornheart standing with six henchmen.

"Wonderful. I knew you could do it, but part of me wished you'd fail." Thornheart smirked. "After all, Moat Monster deserves a feast now and then." She motioned to one of the henchmen, and he went to the trap door and closed it, sealing Orilla inside.

Rosalind didn't know what to do. She could take an old woman, but not six henchmen. And the dragons. She looked around at the stone walls. The dragons weren't here. Her head felt light, and everything went numb. Her body felt like it was swaying with the wind, but there was no breeze blowing. The weight of her legs pulled her towards the ground, and her knees buckled. Falling to all fours, she stared at the grass. This was not a good time to sleep. Not a good time...

29

Down the Garden Path

CORMAC STOOD TO the side of the window in the guardhouse looking out at five men walking by. They carried crossbows casually over their shoulders and chatted in a joking manner. They didn't look in a hurry, so it made sense that they didn't know he was here. The men marched around the end of the building and out of sight. Coraline zipped into view on the other side of the glass. She ushered him forward. He nodded to the rest and went to the door.

Jowsey went to the window and watched as Cormac opened the door. "Nothing moving."

Cormac eased his head out and looked around. The courtyard was empty. While he trusted Coraline, he had to make sure. Jowsey had said there were about two dozen henchmen on the property. They had incapacitated four, and five just walked by, so that left about 13 more to watch for. He slipped out and pressed his back against the wall. Etain followed, then Kneilot with Matilda. Loggie was next, then they were joined by Jowsey.

Cormac sneaked in the opposite direction of the henchmen. If he was right, the secret passageway came out at the well. If Rosalind survived the water naga, that's where she'd be. All that would be left to do was drop the bucket down and haul her up.

"Dragon." Jowsey pointed at the dragon soaring overhead.

"One of ours?" asked Cormac.

"Hard to tell."

"Yes," said Etain.

"I wonder where all Thornheart's are."

"As long as they're not here, we've less of a problem." Cormac crept along the wall. If Thornheart copied the game design, there were two wells on the property. That one to the right, which was only 75 feet away, and the one near the stable, which he couldn't see. "We've got to cross this open ground," he whispered. "The well is behind the building."

"Are you certain?" asked Etain.

"No. I hadn't thought to look when we flew in." He didn't know Thornheart was copying a game plan, or he would have.

"It will leave us completely exposed," said Jowsey. "Let's travel the end of the building first, then cut across."

Cormac nodded. Crouching low, he scurried along the front of the building. As he went, he constantly scanned the landscape, looking for movement. He reached the edge of the building, saw an eight-by-eight structure with four posts as legs to serve as some type of shelter, and dashed to it. This left only 50 feet of open ground before he reached the corner of the stable. Quickly glancing around, he saw two men coming out of the front door of the main building. He squatted low and pointed towards them. A lone woman came out behind them and headed towards the door leading to the kitchen. A minute later, she was out of sight, but the men lingered near the door to the guardhouse, talking. Finally, one went inside, and the other continued towards another building.

"Go." Etain nudged him.

He shot from under the shelter and ran towards the corner of the stable. Covering the ground quickly, he slowed but didn't stop until he came to the rear of the building. He scoured the smaller courtyard. The well was towards the outer wall, 100 feet away. No one was in sight. He stepped forward to get a better view of the stable. The large door was open, but no was near it. A few more feet. Still no one. He hurried to the well, all the while watching for men to appear. No one did.

He threw himself against the stone well and ducked into the shadow the overhead roof created. The water in the well was down only about six feet. It was obvious Rosalind wasn't in there.

Etain looked in. "If she's in there, she's drowned." She stared at Cormac. "Is there another possibility?"

Loggie peered into the well. "We can't see the bottom. I suggest we tie a boulder around his neck," he pointed at Cormac, "and send him down to check."

"Maybe the well near the kitchen." suggested Kneilot.

"This is crazy," said Loggie. "Wells at the start of Apricusal are full from Imber rains. If this is the only way out, she's trapped."

"What about the fountain?" asked Jowsey. "It is large and surrounded by a pool of water." He shrugged. "I saw it when I was here. It might be something to look at."

"Maybe," said Cormac. "There are campaigns with.." He looked past Kneilot and saw six men rush towards them. "Henchmen." He rushed to the other side of the well, sword in hand, ready to fight, yet...

"This is not a game," Loggie growled at him. "Kill or be killed."

Cormac held the sword up. Remembering the many classes he'd taken in fencing, he repositioned his feet and the weapon. This was a competition. One that if he failed would draw real blood. He swung the sword but too soon. Stumbling, he regained his footing and blocked his opponent's sword. Coming back around, he swung again. It was more of a tap on the henchman's weapon, and the offense came quickly. Cormac blocked it, put more strength into the sword and came down hard on the man's wrist, severing the appendage. The sword and hand tumbled to the ground.

Shocked by the damage he'd caused and by the sight of the wound, he stumbled backwards. This gave the henchman time to pick up the sword with the other hand and attack. Cormac blocked it, but the force pushed him against the well. He composed himself and attacked, striking the man in the shoulder.

Remembering more of his lessons, he thought of his classmate Gary and the way he mercilessly attacked him in several competitions. Gary would take this man down without delay. It was like the devil possessed him. That's what Cormac had to do. Drawing on his training, he straightened his shoulders and went on the attack, striking again and again until the man collapsed from his wounds.

He stood, shocked, gasping for breath. This was no game. The ache and wound to his arm that bled through his shirt told him this was a battle for his life.

"It appears you've connected with your character," said Loggie. "Finally." He left the man he had killed and tackled the one harassing Kneilot. Matilda was on the henchman's head attempting to claw out his eyes but seeing Loggie, she leapt into the air and flew in a circle around Kneilot.

Cormac looked to the others, they had either killed or incapacitated their attackers or were dealing the final blows. He locked eyes with Etain, who impressed him even though she had to be 50 pounds lighter than him. Where she lacked muscle, she was ahead of him on experience and method.

Drawing a cooling breath, he turned to Jowsey. "Show us where the fountain is." He caught sight of a dragon flying overhead. They were making their presence known, yet no one was reacting to them. Obviously, the inhabitants thought they were the ones protecting Thornheart Fortress.

"This way," said Jowsey. He jogged towards the stable.

Cormac followed close behind, and the others trailed him. Inside the stable, the soft neighing of horses stilled the air. He breathed in the aroma of fresh hay. Passing by an empty stall, he found a boy about 12 years old with a pitchfork filling a wagon with soiled bedding. He placed a finger over his lips and hushed him. "Keep doing what you're doing," he whispered and kept going.

At the door, Jowsey stopped and looked out. "No one," he whispered. "Stay close." He ducked low and shot out of the stable.

Cormac followed. Kneilot and Matilda were directly behind him. They raced along the front of the building, then the fenced-in yard that held half a dozen horses. After passing under a tree, they raced for another building.

A man stepped out the front door, took one look at them and ran back inside.

Jowsey ignored him and kept running. They passed between two buildings and entered a long narrow courtyard lined by an eight-foot high stone wall. Here, he stopped to check for henchmen. "On the other side of this wall is the garden." He looked at Cormac, then the others. "The entrance is about 200 feet that way. The garden is about five acres. The fountain is on the northwest corner."

Cormac nodded. He doubted henchmen strolled through the garden. The only resistance they'd find would be the gardener or the cook looking for vegetables and herbs.

Jowsey motioned them forward, and he sneaked towards the entrance along the building. Upon reaching the elaborate stone arch and wrought-iron gate, he paused to look at the door leaving the main building. "Let's go." He sprinted to the gate, flung it open and raced inside.

Cormac copied his move, checking to ensure Kneilot was behind him. The smell of roses in bloom filled the air. The garden was like that of old England with defined rows, some only greenery, others filled with colourful flowers. Trees dotted the garden along with benches.

Jowsey stuck to the inside stone wall, running down the pebble path quickly but slow enough as to not lose the others. He travelled several hundred feet before he stopped and crouched low.

Cormac halted behind him. "Did you see someone?"

"Movement. Voices." He pointed towards the centre of the garden.

Cormac stretched his head. Between bushes and trees, he also saw movement. Lots of movement. "Goats?" he whispered. "I saw goats and sheep when we flew over."

"They were over there, beyond the stone wall." Jowsey studied the scene. "It's people. Several." He tilted his ear. "I can't make it out."

"We should keep going. Avoid them."

"What if it's Rosalind?" asked Kneilot.

"And they've captured her?" said Loggie, narrowing his eyes. "I'll go look. Be right back." He sneaked away, staying low.

Cormac didn't know what to do. The group shouldn't separate. Someone always died when that happened.

Etain followed silently behind Loggie. Jowsey shrugged and tailed Etain.

Cormac looked at Kneilot, who looked at him. "After you." Kneilot crept forward, and Cormac stayed close behind him. Ducking behind bushes in full bloom with yellow flowers, daffodils and various types of tulips, they travelled a hundred feet and stopped. Tilting his ear, he heard a distinct voice: Shayde Thornheart's. So, she wasn't away harassing unsuspecting villagers. She was here. That meant the dragons were also here but where? He looked to the sky. A single dragon flew overhead. As far as he knew, this was a dragon that had come with him. What did all this mean?

Loggie crept closer while the others held back. Cormac watched his body language, looking for the signal to move up or continue to the fountain. Loggie took longer than expected to assess the scene on the other side of the shrubs. When he turned and looked back at the group, his expression was questionable as if he was processing what he'd seen. Then, his face changed, and he motioned them to advance.

Cormac waited until everyone else wended their way forward, then took up the rear. They stretched along the shrubs and lay on their bellies to watch.

Cormac found a comfortable spot where twigs weren't digging into his ribs and dipped his head low to see what Loggie had seen.

"Bring the wine." It was Thornheart. From his position, he saw her standing with her back to him. She wore an elaborate silk robe of green and red. Her hair was brought up into a loose bun with strands deliberately left to dangle at the sides to frame her face. A young woman rushed over and set a bottle of wine and a wine glass on a pedestal.

Cormac adjusted his position to see more. Resting before Thornheart were someone's bare feet. The person lay on a table but not a complete table. Their hands and feet were bound to four posts and hung in the air. Their back rested on a platform and their head tilted at an awkward angle.

He blinked several times. The clothes the person wore were similar to what Rosalind wore. Stretching his neck, he gasped. It was Rosalind. He sunk down, fearing he'd been heard. The others frowned at him, but Thornheart never missed a beat, and the henchmen focussed their attention on her. There were at least eight men plus one woman in this section of the garden.

Something poked his ear. Coraline's eyes were wide. "I will go to her. Let her know you are here." Before he could say anything, she was gone.

"Gather around and witness greatness," said Thornheart. "It has taken me years to collect the tools necessary for my triumph and now, they lay before me." She waved her hands over Rosalind.

Cormac slowly removed his sword from the scabbard. The distinct sound of steel sliding against wool as it left the holder made the others turn to him. He locked eyes with Loggie. Rosalind's safety was the one thing they agreed upon. They weren't leaving without her.

Hideous laughter shook Rosalind's peaceful sleep. It was coming from outside her dreams. Squeezing shut her eyelids didn't make the laughter go away. It was replaced with a voice, one she had heard before. Her face muscles relaxed, and she listened.

"It has taken me years to collect the tools necessary for my triumph and now, they lay before me."

The voice was close. Practically over her while she slept. Then she remembered why she slept. A draining spell. But by gosh she'd felt good before exhaustion claimed her. Orilla. The water naga had helped her escape, and it was still trapped. That voice. She knew that voice.

"As we gather here today..." The laughter returned. "I've always wanted to say that. Too bad I heard it many years ago. I might have been a happier woman if I hadn't. But that is neither here nor there now that he's gone off to the great beyond... Wherever the heck that is. It certainly isn't here, and that's all that matters."

A sudden clap of hands made Rosalind jump.

"Wonderful! You're waking up. I need a fully conscious hauflin to increase the energy of the spell."

The smell of wine on hot breath tickled Rosalind's nose, and she slowly opened her eyes. What she saw staring down at her shook her to the bone. The craggy old woman with her grey hair pulled up in a ball of mess with strands dangling by her ears was more hideous than Orilla. The deep wrinkles entrenched in her neck and around her lips and eyes gave the impression particles of dust, sand and ants could hide in them. The bright red and dark green silk robe reminded her of something, but she couldn't place it. She remembered the taste of peppermint. It was somehow connected.

She tried to sit up, but her hands wouldn't move. Tugging on them wouldn't release them from where they were stuck. She looked down the length of her arm and found rope around her wrist. The rope was tied to a thick pole and kept her arm suspended in air. The other arm was secured in the same fashion. Checking her feet, they were also bound. She flopped her head down on the soft pillow. At least something had been provided for her comfort.

"Where am I?" she sputtered. Her throat was dry, and she dragged her tongue around the inside of her mouth.

"In the presence of greatness." Thornheart cackled. "It's time for me to leave, but you will remain here." She reached for the dark bottle sitting on a pedestal and tried to uncork it. Blue veins in her fingers shone through her thin skin as she pulled on the cork. She tossed up her chin and held out the bottle to one of the henchmen standing nearby. "Open it."

He jumped at her command, twisted off the cork and handed both back to her.

She poured the dark red liquid into a tall wine glass, then set the bottle on the pedestal. Taking a sip, she smacked her lips. "It was a good year in spite of the travesties." She took another drink. "First a speech from the guest of honour." She giggled. "That's me."

She gazed over Rosalind to the group gathered around. From Rosalind's position, she could see 12, no 14 henchmen and three women in dresses. The same women who had stood outside to greet her when she'd arrived. According to the expressions on their faces, they were unsure of why they were gathered here.

"My dear servants, after today, you will have no one to serve." Thornheart put up her hand to hush the group though no one made any motion to speak. "I will be missed. You will be lost. But I must go. It is time. This land is not kind to those passing from the prime of their life."

Rosalind wondered who she was talking about.

"Where I come from, there are luxuries beyond the imagination. I plan to take advantage of them. I leave you this fortress. You don't owe me anything more for it. It's yours."

The men looked from one another. A few smiled, but most looked confused.

"Today, I make history." She raised the glass of wine and took a drink. "I will transfer my power from this archaic world to my world, where I will introduce those pathetic losers to the magic of dragons." She swept her hand over seven orbs secured individually in mesh lining and attached to a belt. "I will rule the world from an elaborate castle, taking what I deserve and dealing a swift hand to those who wronged me." She took another drink of wine. Her lips still on the glass, her eyes averted to the sky to watch a blue dragon soar overhead.

Rosalind watched it fly out of sight, then she stared at the glass orbs in the mesh lining. There was movement inside them. These were the same orbs Thornheart had captured Kiefwind in, the same ones his yswains were trapped inside. If these were the dragons from Darkmoore

Dungeon, then where did the dragon that flew overhead come from? And was it under Thornheart's command? It didn't seem to bother her though it did stall her until it passed out of sight.

"Rosalind."

The soft voice tickled her ear. Recognising it, she looked for Coraline. She couldn't see her but could feel her near her head.

"Your friends are near," said Coraline. "They will rescue you." Her voice sounded tense. "I will help. Remain still. You will be free soon."

Rosalind lifted her head to get a better view of her surroundings. She couldn't see her friends. They must have been hiding in the bushes.

"Farewell, dear servants. I will leave you your lives and whatever you can salvage from this decrepit place." She set the wine glass on the pedestal and reached for the belt with orbs. To Rosalind, it looked like a saddle girth. "Marigold, come. Fasten the buckles."

A young woman jumped at the mention of her name. She stood behind Thornheart and fastened the steel buckles to hold the belt in place across her shoulder and down around her hip. It pinched the robe, revealing a middle-age spread. Thornheart adjusted the belt, but it didn't help. She slipped a shoulder bag laden with items over the other shoulder, so the straps crossed at the chest. Wiggling to gain comfort, she staggered to the right. She caught her balance and returned to the pedestal. One more drink, and she refilled her empty glass. Then she came to Rosalind's side, putting Rosalind between her and the henchmen.

"A toast. May all the wonders of the world find me on this day." She took a long drink, then tossed the glass on a stone surface where it smashed into hundreds of pieces. "Nothing can stop me now. I am on my way." She picked up a staff that had been leaning against a statue of a beautiful woman with a butterfly on her index finger. The staff was five feet tall, made of dark wood, had a strip of leather wrapped around the centre and a golden gem affixed to the top.

Holding the staff steady in one hand, she lifted a small white bowl with the other. "Place and places do dance as one." She drank down the liquid in the bowl, shook and made a horrible face. "Nasty." She gagged, leant forward and put her hand over her neck. Her face turned fire red, and she lurched for the bottle of wine. With shaky hands, she held it to her mouth and gulped the liquid. Finally relieved, she dropped the bottle and it smashed on the floor. She staggered back to the spot beside Rosalind and shook herself. "All is good." Her index finger wiped the side of her mouth.

Next, she picked up a second small white bowl and held it over Rosalind.

"I am not drinking that," said Rosalind.

"It's not for you to drink." She held the bowl high. "Place and places dance as one. See my thoughts and..." She bent over Rosalind and squinted in the sun. "What is that?" Shock raced across her face. "Kill them!"

Rosalind lifted her head and looked to where Thornheart was pointing. It was Loggie and Cormac. But where were the others? Were they killed at Starlight Ridge? A cold chill raced down her back. She pulled harder against the rope and stretched her neck to see if the others were there. In doing so, she pushed her hand closest to the henchmen free from the rope. She caught a quick glimpse of Coraline, who zipped towards her feet.

The henchmen drew swords and attacked Loggie and Cormac only to find Jowsey and Etain jumping out of hiding to help. The dragon that had flown over earlier, returned. Seeing the commotion, it flew lower and soared over the wooden fortress. It released its breath and sprayed flames down upon it.

Thornheart gasped. "This can't be happening. Who are those dragons?"

"Not friends of yours," said Rosalind.

Thornheart slapped her across the face. "We'll fight dragon with dragon. I only need six to conquer my pathetic world." She pulled one of the glass orbs from her shoulder girth. Holding it up to the sunshine, she said, "Obey the commands of Kragen Darkmoore. Emerge from your capsule and head my command."

The orb shook and emitted a bright blue light. A stream of smoke poured from the orb and settled on a patch of grass. It filled the area and solidified. When the dragon lifted its head, it roared so loud, it made Rosalind's ears throb. Hot spit flew from its mouth and sprayed everyone within 40 feet.

Rosalind turned away and wiped her face with her free hand.

"I demand you obey me!" shouted Thornheart. "Take to the sky and drive that dragon away!"

At first the dragon hissed and stomped its foot. Then it was stricken with pain in the neck, and its claws encircled its throat.

"Obey me, or you will die!" Thornheart's steel eyes bore down on the magical creature. "Drive that dragon from my home! Now!"

The freed dragon growled as it leapt into the sky. It flew straight for the dragon that had set the large structure on fire and disappeared over the horizon. No sooner had it left when another dragon arrived and breathed fire on another part of the large structure.

"Where are these dragons coming from?" She glared down at Rosalind. "It doesn't matter." She grabbed the staff and held it over Rosalind. Then she took the white bowl and dumped the contents on the hauflin. A cloud of yellow dust floated in the air and slowly settled. "No worries. This won't hurt." She grinned. "For long."

Grunts and groans mixed with clanking of steel. Rosalind shot a glance at her friends, then brought her fist up and drove it into Thornheart's face. The old woman fell back and landed on her rump.

Coraline had freed one leg and was working on the other while Rosalind struggled to free her other hand.

Thornheart hissed and scrambled to her feet. She straightened the belts across her shoulder and her gown, then picked up the staff. "I will not be undone. It is set in motion." She pulled another orb from the belt and released it.

By the time the dragon took shape, Rosalind was free. She leapt from the table, grabbed the coil of rope that lay near it and ran for the trap door. In all the commotion and the smoke billowing in from the burning building, the henchmen didn't notice her, but Thornheart did. Her shouting was drowned out by the bellows and groans of others.

Rosalind flung open the trap door. "Orilla! Get ready!" she shouted into the hole. She quickly secured one end of the rope, then flung the other into the cavern. A solid force struck her and sent her flying to the ground.

"Don't kill her!" cried Thornheart. "I need her alive."

The dragon placed its claw over Rosalind's stomach and held her there while Thornheart stomped over carrying the staff. "Doesn't matter where. Only matters I get the words out." She brushed hair from her face and held the staff over Rosalind. "This is the only thing a hauflin is good for." She shook herself and steadied her hand. "Place and places dance as one!" she shouted. "See my thoughts and grant my wish, send me—"

A brown and green creature flew over Rosalind and into Thornheart, driving her to the ground. She tumbled heels over head, and the staff flew from her hands.

"Promisesssss," hissed Orilla. "Broken."

Thornheart got to her knees. Her hair had come undone and draped over her face. The darkness colouring her expression revealed the evil within. "Kill her!" Veins trembled in her neck and her hand shook as she pointed towards Orilla.

The dragon released Rosalind and pounced towards Orilla, but the water naga was too fast and slithered away. Another blue dragon dropped from the sky and leapt upon the dragon Thornheart had released. Rosalind searched the sky. There were five, six, no seven dragons flying above, some diving to ignite a building, others swooping over the chaotic scene, making everyone duck for fear of their lives.

"This has got to end in my favour!" Thornheart pulled another orb from her belt, held it in her palm and said the magic words. On the last word, Orilla swatted the woman in the back of the head, sending her flying against the ground.

Rosalind jumped up and ran to her. In two quick tugs, she unfastened the girth-like belt and ripped it from the woman's shoulder. It hooked on the shoulder bag, knocking it out of place. Several precious gems tumbled to the grass.

Thornheart turned. Scowling, she scrambled to her feet. "Go ahead, release them. Do my bidding for me."

Rosalind held the belt over her head with both her hands. "Obey the commands of Kragen Darkmoore! Emerge from your capsules and head my command!"

The remaining orbs released their dragons. They took flight, and Rosalind stepped back. With no plan after releasing the dragons and not sure how her friends were faring, she thought about her next move. Run?

30

To Break a Curse

CORMAC HAD SEEN Rosalind tied to the stakes where Thornheart had stood, but in the fight to break through the henchmen, he lost sight of her. Somehow, she had gotten free. He killed two men, then ducked as Thornheart released a dragon. The henchmen were unsure if the dragon would attack them, so they scattered. Once the dragon was in the sky, they regrouped.

"Behind!" yelled Loggie. He flipped sideways to avoid a sword.

Cormac glanced behind him, saw a henchman charge and jumped out of the way. He grounded his feet, positioned the sword and swung, catching the henchman in the gut. Ripping the sword free, he saw Loggie stumble and fall. An opponent charged towards Loggie. Cormac leapt over the body, jumped in front of him and met the man head one. He blocked the sword with his own. Then counter-attacked, driving the man back.

One of the dragons on his side of the battle had ignited the building with the bunkhouse and kitchen. It roared out of control, sending sparks and plumes of smoke high into the sky. The snapping and crackling mixed with shouts and the clanging of weapons.

Another dragon he'd made an alliance with arrived on scene and torched a part of the building not already on fire. The increased flames added smoke to the garden, and he could no longer see the path that led to the exit. Thornheart released another dragon, and one flew out of the sky and tackled it.

Smoke burnt his eyes, and he wiped them quickly. The henchmen were either dead, suffering from severe wounds or had run off. He searched for Rosalind in the chaos. Running to where he thought she'd gone, he stopped abruptly when he saw a monster. His muscles stiffened when he recognised the water naga. Memories from the campaign where he had faced one washed over him. Somehow it had escaped its watery tomb.

Loggie bumped into him and didn't go any farther. "What is that?" he gasped.

"Water naga. Deadly." Thinking of how he'd get past it to reach Rosalind who was dealing with Thornheart, he watched the creature's long tail lash out and knock the old woman to the ground. It appeared to be on Rosalind's side.

Rosalind raced to the fallen Thornheart and ripped a belt from her shoulder.

"Those are the orbs we found in the dungeon," said Cormac. He glanced at Loggie. "Thornheart hadn't released them?"

"From her speech, it sounded like they were packaged for transport."

He stared at him. "Dragons in my world would be very destructive."

"Like they can't be here?"

"You're not wrong."

"Rosalind is releasing all the dragons?" Etain stood beside Loggie, her chest heaving as she caught her breath. Jowsey and Kneilot with Matilda on his shoulder stood next to her.

"I have a bad feeling about this." Jowsey stepped back.

"What if they obey Rosalind because she released them?" Cormac also took a step back.

"That's not what the spell said." Etain pulled Kneilot back with her. "We need to take cover."

"What about Rosalind?" Cormac froze.

"Yes, what about Rosalind?" Coraline hovered near his ear.

"As soon as the dragons are free, I'll grab her." He took a step closer. "Maybe the water naga will protect her."

Loggie stared at him, eyes blinking. "Maybe it will eat her."

"If it was going to do that, it would have done it by now."

The dragons had ignited the wooden fence surrounding the fortress. Wood crackled and sparked, sending up embers that sailed through the sky and littered the garden.

"That's coming for us." Loggie's eyes grew wide as he stared at a dragon flying directly at them. "Scatter!"

Cormac ran, tripped over a garden stone, then picked himself up to run again. The dragon swooped low but didn't breathe its fire breath. Once it passed, Cormac climbed from behind a garden bench. He strained to find Rosalind in the smoke. Figures took on a ghost-like appearance, and he sorted them out by shape and size. Thinking he saw her, he sprinted forward. Hearing feet beside him, he looked and found Loggie. "We get her and get out of here."

"For once, we agree." Loggie grinned quickly, then focussed on the ground ahead.

Cormac spotted Rosalind. She was yelling at Thornheart. No, Thornheart was yelling at her and holding the staff above her head. Rosalind's arm came up, and the glint of a dagger shone through the smoke. She raced forward and thrust the dagger towards Thornheart but before she reached the old woman, a dragon's tail struck Rosalind and sent her flying through the air.

"Rosalind!" He screamed her name so loudly, his throat burnt.

She slammed into a stone statue of a horse, bounced off it at an awkward angle and crashed to the ground. She lay in a crumpled state and did not move.

He raced towards her, his heart screaming in pain as he pounded the ground to reach her. She remained still, arms resting on her legs and head tilted to the side. He fell to his knees and cradled her limp body. "Rosalind? Rosalind? Can you hear me?" Tears stung his eyes. "Please! Wake up!" He shook her gently, but she remained limp.

Loggie dropped in front of him and held Rosalind's head gently. "Rosalind?" He kissed her forehead and pressed his cheek to hers. "You can't go yet. I haven't taught you how to play the flute. I know you can. You just need to try harder." His voice cracked.

Cormac grabbed Kneilot's arm and pulled him near. "Do something. A healing spell?"

"Death cannot be healed." He wiped a tear from his eye and held Rosalind's hand.

"What about a spell to bring her back. A resurrection spell? Anything?"

Kneilot shook his head slowly. "She would be undead if I did that."

Cormac squeezed his eyes shut. This was not supposed to be how the game ended. If anyone died, it was supposed to be him. The one responsible was Thornheart. He lifted his head and glared at the woman.

"Rosalind knew Thornheart couldn't be killed until the curse was lifted." Etain wiped away the tears and stood. "The curse has been broken," she said.

Cormac rested Rosalind in Loggie's arms and stood. There was one final thing to take care of.

"You are free," Etain said to Kiefwind. "So are your yswains."

"Free?" Kiefwind gazed up at the sky at his fellow clan members flying over. "Free to do what I've wanted to do since the day I was rescued from that dungeon." He whirled and flared his nostrils at Thornheart. "Kill you."

Thornheart put up her hands to protest. "You are under my command!" she cried. "You must obey my orders!"

"I obey no one!" he roared and lurched forward.

Before Kiefwind reached her, a dagger flew through the air and dug into her throat. She shook violent and collapsed, convulsing as her body drained of life.

Kiefwind whirled and glared at Cormac. "It was my duty to kill her."

"It was also mine." Cormac stood unafraid of the magical creature. "You are free because my friend sacrificed her life to save you. She knew you'd save Thornheart. It was your curse and when you did, you'd be set free. Your debt has been paid to Thornheart."

Kiefwind gazed upon Rosalind, his face solemn. The fire that raged in his eyes slowly receded, and his brow bent in anguish. "Always the hauflins true to our spirit. Of all creatures upon this land, it is they who have given us more than we could repay." His voice softened further. "We will remember her sacrifice and share it with those in my clan. She will be given a sacred honour in our heroic tales. Return home, I must for my heart aches for its sweetness. We have been prisoners for far too long. Farewell and may peace find you." He spread his wings, gave a great roar and lifted off the ground.

31

Fate

CORMAC WATCHED THE dragons fly off and disappear into great clouds of smoke. Their enormous wings created whirlwinds of grey spirals that spun out of control and dispersed into larger clouds. Their hearts seemed heavy but light. Conversations between them drifted on the air. They were in a language he could not understand.

Staring at the space where they once were, peace flowed over him. His heart was breaking into a million pieces, his body ached and his mind struggled with the logic of all that had happened, yet his nerves settled. It was as if he could close his eyes, open them again and everything would be right in this world. He couldn't explain the calmness that settled the land. It appeared anything but calm. He saw only death and destruction all around him. It should have weighed heavy on his soul, but his spirit was at peace. He was now part of this world permanently.

He lowered his head and turned. The greatest challenge lay ahead: living here without Rosalind. Loggie still cradled her in his arms. His friends knelt around her, watching him. Although they had had their differences, he still considered them friends, and they'd share Rosalind's loss together.

He wiped his eyes to clear away the smoke but knew it wasn't the smoke that made them water. Running his sleeve across his face removed dirt, sweat and blood, but the tears remained.

A ghostly form approached Rosalind and the others, and he rubbed his eyes again to clear the smoky image. Was it Rosalind's spirit looking down upon her? Was it her soul preparing to move on? The figure remained in spite of his dryer eyes, and it grew more defined. It was a woman, and Kneilot stood to greet her. She grasped his hands and spoke softly to him. She was thin and wore a slim dress that reached her knees.

A thick leather belt kept it snug at the waist. Her hair flowed down her back and swayed as if a gentle breeze blew. A band of thick leather with intricate designs carved into it wrapped around her head. She wore no shoes and had delicate elven feet.

In a breath, he knew who it was: Eir, the goddess of healing. He felt her energy more than recognised her. That was what calmed his nerves and brought peace to his soul. She had healed him when he lay dying from the arrow wound. Now she was here to save Rosalind.

He rushed over, then slowed so as not to startle the goddess. Once at her side, he shied away, not knowing what to say. The gods in his world were aloft, above humans. Humans were meant to kneel before them in a beggar's position, not stand with them and converse like old friends at a tavern. In this realm, the gods and goddesses treated them as equals, as friends. It was why she had greeted Kneilot the way she had. When he found his voice, he heard it tremble. "You're here to return Rosalind to us?"

She smiled, and her face brightened. "Cormac." Her voice was as smooth as the best singers who sang love songs. "Fate has chosen otherwise."

The smile had suggested more than her words delivered. "Can't you heal her body?"

"Rosalind has died a hero's death."

"I'd rather she had been a coward and be here with me."

"No, you don't." Her soothing voice and gentle hand upon his shoulder calmed his racing his heart. "In one season you have achieved what many have failed to do in a lifetime. The love between a man and a woman is the perfect love. It is the seed of hope that spawns the future and solidifies one's race on solid ground. There is no greater alliance than a man and a woman for what one lacks the other possesses down to the smallest of intricacies. It is a lesson many fail to learn and while you didn't deny it, I believe now you see it as truth."

"We were just getting to the good part." The lump in Cormac's throat expanded, causing a tear to slip.

"The good part started the moment your eyes filled with her vision."

He couldn't deny that. Still, he wanted more.

She wiped away the tear on his cheek. "I am here to deliver Rosalind to her next adventure." She smiled. "And to grant your wish. The one you've held in your heart for years. Bid farewell to your dear friends."

"Wish? The one to return home?" When she nodded, he panicked. "I change my wish. I wish Rosalind was alive and here with us." His voice cracked, and the ache in his heart exploded. Emotions he'd never felt before overwhelmed him, and his knees buckled.

"Einn árstíð ósk." Eir smiled gracefully. "One."

"Wait. I'm not ready." He fell to his knees and gathered Rosalind in his arms.

"We are never ready, yet we must accept fate for what it is." She waved her hand across her breast, then back again. "We shall see you again, brave warrior. Safe passage and great adventures."

He brushed Rosalind's hair with his fingertips, then kissed her lips one last time. His hand glowed with soft white light, and his arm shimmered. He was disappearing. He gawked up at the others. Their images were sharp against the billowing clouds of smoke.

Loggie's serious expression cracked, and he watched in wonder the magic before him.

Jowsey grinned with excitement, his eyes wide. "The journey of a lifetime." The end of his sentence faded into the distance. Along with it, the sharp crackles and roar of the flames. Cormac's ears were growing numb to sound.

Etain watched as if studying what was happening, recording it in her memory to recite back to others if they asked about what had happened to him and what happened when a goddess returned a human to Earth.

Kneilot clasped his hands in front of him with Matilda on his shoulder. His smile appeared satisfied. His lack of sadness confused Cormac. His faith in his goddess made him strong.

Cormac hugged Rosalind tightly. As seconds quickly ticked by, he felt his grip on her loosen. His body was almost as clear as glass. One last word, he thought. He had to say something.

"I won't forget you. Ever. You will live on in my memories." He looked at Loggie. "I'm sorry. I tried to save her. Please, forgive me."

Kneilot's expression changed, and he shook his head. He spoke, but the words didn't reach Cormac's ears. He spoke again and seemed to repeat what he'd said but still, no sound reached Cormac. From the surprised looks on the faces of the others, what he was saying was important. Loggie reached for him, but his hand went through his arm. Instead, he stared into Cormac's face, smiling and shaking his head. He mouthed something, but darkness closed in, and Cormac couldn't make it out.

Looking upon Rosalind, he thought she was fading, too, but his vision was fading fast. Before he had time to consider what was happening, he was bathed in blackness. He was neither standing, nor kneeling. He felt nothing and was nowhere.

32

Home

A WARM BREATH of wind washed over Cormac's senses. He dreamt he was on a tropical island breathing in warm breezes until the roar of an engine startled him. It sounded like a car.

His body overheated and the ocean disappeared. Darkness swallowed him, and his eyes flew open in a rush. A strong breeze cooled the sweat gathering on his forehead, and he stared at the ceiling of a wooden structure with sunlight beaming in through a glassless window. He was flat on his back in a building that was...

Too small for a real building. He sat up and wiped away sweat. Aches and pains gathered and swept through his body, making him groan. Stretching his back one way then the other, he considered where he sat. He recognised this place. His tree fort? Memories bombarded his mind, and he couldn't keep up with what he saw. The last image of seeing Rosalind laying in his arms made him gasp. The goddess had sent him home.

He jumped up, felt the pain endured by his final days in Lachspeur of Yore and slowed his progress. At the window, he looked out onto the backyard. The old swing set he and his siblings had used was still intact. The small vegetable garden his mother kept was lush and popping with the colours of tomatoes, pumpkins and squash. The lawnmower he was supposed to fix still sat outside the shed, and his dad's canoe was hung to the side of the building. Movement caught his attention. It was the neighbour's yellow cat walking across the backyard. It was exactly like Matilda, but it didn't have wings.

He rubbed his forehead. This couldn't be happening. Had all of what he'd experienced been only a dream? The ache in his heart and his muscles told him no. Remembering the wound he'd taken in the arm from the spear, he pulled up the sleeve of... He still wore the clothes he'd worn in Lachspeur, complete with sword, daggers and pouches. Stretching out his fingers, he examined them. The cuts and bruises were gone, but a few scars lingered. He pulled the shirt off his shoulder. The spear wound was healed but a long scar remained. Eir had healed him and granted his wish. The one he had before Rosalind...

He rubbed he head harder. Having lived that life and returned home to his peaceful neighbourhood, he didn't know how he'd fit in. He was no longer the innocent boy who had left. Reaching for the latch, he noticed his ring finger. It was bare. He felt around his neck. The leather strap with his high school graduation ring was gone. Rosalind still wore it. The ring would be buried with her.

Before opening the latch, he removed the scabbard and wrapped the belt around it. If his parents saw this, they'd really think he'd gone off the deep end and took Mediaeval Dungeon Adventures too seriously. After tucking the sword beneath a bench, he removed the daggers and pouches and laid them on top of it. The weather in Nova Scotia was warm on this September day... September? Was that the month he went away? He removed his outer shirt, leaving only a cotton shirt that resembled a T-shirt. The belt that had secured his memories was worn, tattered. His mother would throw it out if she found it in his room, yet he was attached to it. He'd keep it forever.

Straightening the remainder of his clothes and brushing his hair back, he opened the latch and slid down the rope. To his surprise, he descended easier than he ever had. His body had reshaped itself in Lachspeur, and he was stronger now than he had ever been.

His feet carried him up familiar steps and into the back door. Noise in the kitchen drew him there, and the familiarity ignited a smile. At the doorway, he looked in and saw his mother at the sink. The pan on the stove suggested she was cooking, something she'd done every day of his life. He wanted to tell her about his adventure, the quest he'd gone on but the ache of losing Rosalind was too great. She wouldn't believe him anyways.

He wiped a tear from his eye and silently thanked Eir for returning him home to his family. It was where he had wanted to be until he'd made great friends.

"Mom?" His voice cracked. He stumbled over and hugged her. "Thank you. You're the best." He hadn't realised how much he'd missed her until now.

"Oh, dear. Clarise has you spinning, doesn't she?" She returned the hug and patted his back. "Loss of first loves are difficult, sweetie, but you'll find another. The right one." She pulled away and looked at him one way, then the other. "What on Earth did you do?"

"What?"

"You have no eyebrows." She stroked his cheek. "You shaved your peach fuzz and mustache." She touched his hair. "Did you make a fire in the backyard last night?"

"No." He touched his face. The hair that had been burnt off from the dragon's breath had yet to grow in. "Ah, I think I had one too many beers."

She patted his face. "Drinking won't mend your broken heart." She touched his upper arm and squeezed it. "I swear you boys grow over night. You're as strong as your daddy." She patted him again and went to the stove. "Pancakes will be ready soon. Carlie's already off to work, and Bonnie and Patsy are clogging up the washroom." She turned to him and smiled. "So, use the downstairs washroom to wash the sleep from your eyes. And can you see if Frankie's still alive. He was up late last night."

"What?" His attention focussed on her mouth. "What did you say?"

"Your little brother was up late last night. He's more of a sleepy head than you."

"No, the alive part."

"See if he's still alive?" She raised an eyebrow.

"Alive? Say it again." He watched her lips say the word. That's the word Loggie was mouthing before he disappeared.

www.ingramcontent.com/pod-product-compliance
Lightning Source LLC
Chambersburg PA
CBHW021841010726
47493CB00005B/1504